the
Intermediaries:
BEAT & CASE

TAYLOR DYE

Samanedna

To my family and friends, and their families and friends

To Eric

To Grugra

To Roz, the real Rosalind

And to you, the reader

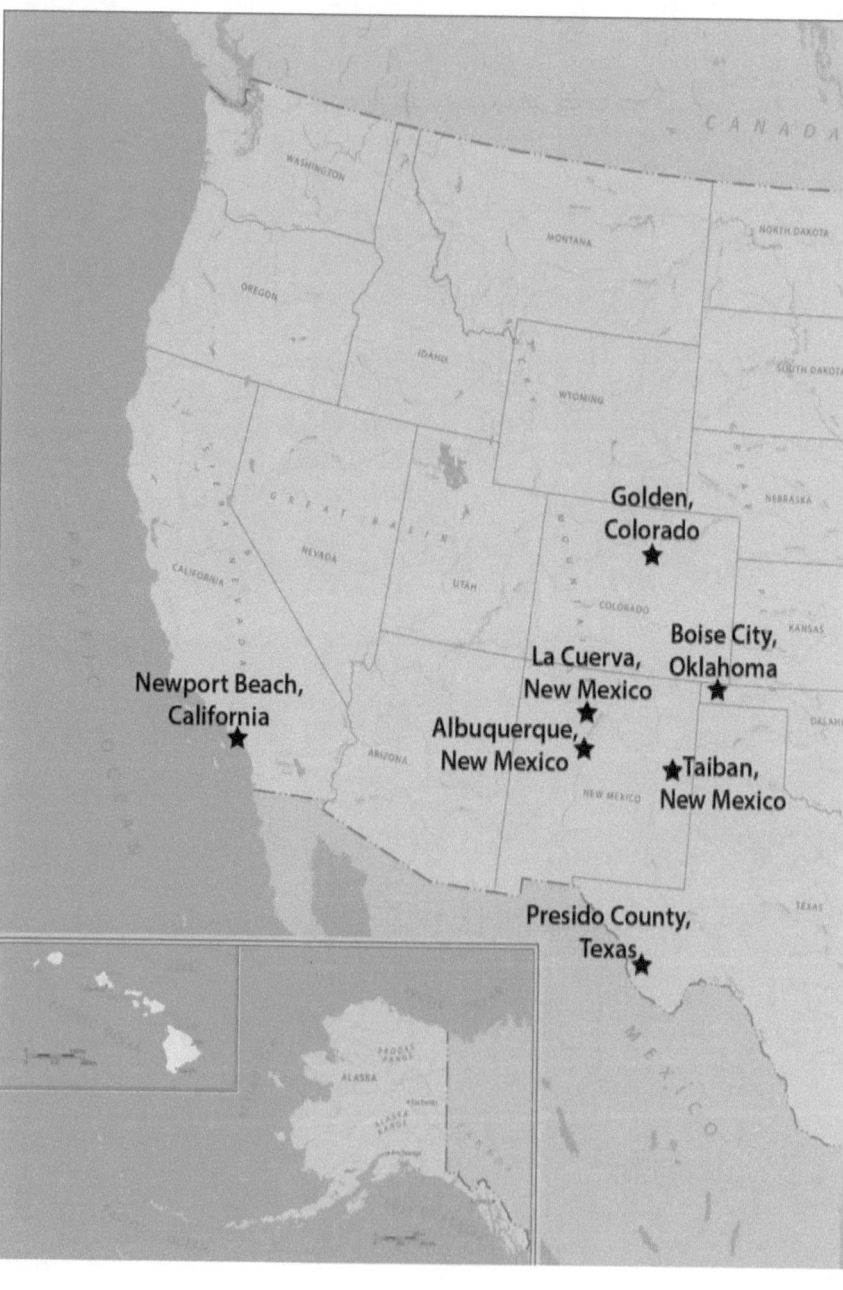

Greenfield, Massachusetts

Cape Cod, Massachusetts

Fort Leonard Wood, Missouri

Johnson City, Tennesee

KEY

State or Provincial Boundry

Major Lakes   Major Rivers

North Office Not Pictured On This Map

Prologue

"THERE'S NO WAY YOU'RE gonna make it outta here, Emily," the man called out through the darkness. "You hear me? There's no way."

Silence fell again.

The woman exhaled softly.

Crack!

A sharp knock echoed incredibly close to her hiding place as a rock slammed against a neighboring tree trunk. Emily started, stumbling, turning her head away from the noise. Her breath caught in her throat.

The crunching of the woodland floor under her feet as she tripped gave her away.

"Emily!"

She started to run again, tearing through the harsh undergrowth, lingering branches snatching, scratching, scraping at her skin and clothes. Sounds of breaking, crunching, ruffling, and snapping resonated all around as she moved through the dark, the frantic chase now even more urgent than before. The glow ahead grew increasingly brilliant, more vivid, although it still appeared to her a fair distance away.

It also made the surrounding darkness much more daunting.

"Emily!"

She slipped again, this time falling completely to the ground, a soft "oomph" forced out of her already sore lungs. The impact caused her to bite her tongue, and blood began to ooze into her mouth. She scrambled forward, recovering hurriedly, but fell again, her foot ensnared in a tangle of roots. Her handcuffed wrist twisted under her as she attempted to catch herself, and she cried out sharply.

"Emily, stop! Stop runnin' from me!"

Stinging, razor-sharp pain corkscrewed up from her wrist into her elbow. She rested much of her weight on her opposite side as she pushed herself off the forest floor, grimacing with the strain. She staggered for a moment, and then carried on, her hobble even more pronounced, searing heat pulsing through her leg with every step. She grasped at another tree, barely making it, and tottered once more.

She knew she had to keep moving.

Still, the fire ahead seemed too far away, and the chance remained that it offered no escape at all.

Doubt began to creep into her mind.

"It's no use, Emily," her attacker called out. "Just stop now. Stop runnin'!"

Judging by his voice, he seemed only a short stretch behind, yet even as she continued to push herself forward, Emily felt slower, her body less cooperative, every stride, every movement becoming more torturous than the last. Every agonized, staggered, aching footstep turning into…

The raging shapes and outlines of the forest fire were slowly becoming clearer, the smoldering stench now unmistakable. In the darkness, Emily lost her footing yet again, falling to her hands and knees. Fresh, nauseating trauma radiated from her leg, her body, her shackled, crippled wrist. She winced but clenched her teeth together to hold back any sounds of distress. Another wave of tears threatened to spill from her eyes as she pulled herself around to the far side of another tree.

Dizzying, sickening pain.

Short, quick breaths.

Intense terror.

The fire … it was too far.

She could not go on. She was not going to make it out.

2

The commotion behind her drew nearer, then lessened, and then stopped altogether. Emily could hear his labored breathing through the shrubbery. She tried to keep her own breathing as hushed as she could.

He was close—alarmingly close. It was only a matter a time, only a matter of moments before he found her.

Emily squeezed her eyes shut. Her heart pounded, sounding to her like persistent, hurried cracks of thunder. Her head—her entire body—throbbed with pain and fear.

Then, ever so slightly, she parted her eyelids, peeking out...

Astonishment gripped her, her eyes snapping open the rest of the way.

A child—a little girl—was staring back at her.

Smiling.

THE INTERMEDIARIES: BEAT & CASE

IN BOISE CITY, OKLAHOMA, THE playground was planted on land composed of hardened dust—a bone-dry, barren space of earth that had no reason to exist other than to exist without complaint. The children who frequented the playground felt no need to object. To them, the rusted slides and swing-sets, the unbalanced seesaws and spring rockers, the fractured and uneven slab of blacktop—they were all home.

Despite rundown appearances, everything functioned properly. Everything was where it was supposed to be; therefore, the children came.

And they had fun.

The unrelenting sun was directly overhead, and with a cloudless sky, the arid, summertime heat offered little hope of a reprieve. The children went on with their games without apology, mocking the weather's petty attempts to make their play uncomfortable. The dusty playground was, for them, a place of solace—a province of undiscovered fun and adventure. It was the reason the children came back again and again.

As always, the swirling slide and the spinning carousel were particularly popular. A constant line formed at the steps to the slide, as both new and repeat riders vibrated with adrenaline, waiting their turn to ascend and then plummet, twisting and turning, back to Earth. At the carousel, children jumped on and off intermittently and with youthful abandon, taking breaks only when the ride's persistent motion became too dizzying. By then, however, it was too late, and they stumbled off in a drunken, woozy stupor, having no ability to walk a straight line.

Case leaned back against a solitary, abandoned portion of wooden fencing—most likely left standing from a past life for this dustbowl land—and watched the children play on the spinning carousel. Even though the weather was insufferably warm and most of the kids had on shorts and T-shirts, Case wore loose jeans and a long-sleeved Henley pullover, over which he wore another shirt, unbuttoned and also long-sleeved. His cropped, icy-blond hair shone brilliantly in the dazzling gleam of the sun. His posture was casual, relaxed, and a contented smile hinted at his lips as he observed yet another kid leap awkwardly off the whirling top, clearly disoriented. Had he been wearing a wide-brimmed hat with a blade of wheat sticking out of his mouth, Case's appearance would have typified that of a teenaged cowboy surveying the land after a hard day's work.

Again and again, his gaze returned to one particular rider on the merry-go-round. Unlike him, she blended in perfectly with the common age of the playgrounders, looking and acting every bit the preadolescent. As she spun on the carousel, her long, dark hair became weightless in the breeze, floating effortlessly all around. Her youthful face was a picture of delight—an emotion shared with her playmates who ran about the park. The younger girl's choice of clothing, like Case's, seemed suited for slightly cooler weather, although its worn, battered look matched the rural Oklahoman landscape. It made no difference, though—none of the children paid her clothes any mind.

Her knitted beanie cap, a familiar accessory, hung on the fencepost beside Case, trusted to his safekeeping.

Presently, the girl relinquished the merry-go-round and gracefully hopped off, completing an artistic twirl in mid-air for good measure. She landed nimbly, as though she had practiced the creative dismount a thousand times before, holding her arms in the air in the finishing stance of a gifted gymnast.

Case shook his head, a chuckle leaving his mouth as the girl received a smattering of applause from a few admiring youngsters. She skipped over to the fence section.

"So, what did you think?" Beat asked excitedly.

"'S all right," Case shrugged, not attempting to hide his smile completely.

"Yeah, right!" she retorted. "Come on, you have to try it. It's so fun!"

"I'm perfectly okay watching from here."

The smaller girl turned to the side and lowered her head, her hair fanning around her face. She then tilted back sharply so the dark strands flew behind. Her ears came into view, lined with glittering jewelry, one of which was a set of small wings, beautifully detailed.

"I could do this all day," she said, grinning back at the boy.

"I know," he responded, "and you often do. But don't forget we're on the clock, as they say."

"And what do you think I'm doing?"

Case arched an eyebrow.

Beat nodded back in the direction of the carousel.

"Do you see him?" she asked.

Looking again, Case spotted him—or rather, the child's green, spiked hairstyle—almost immediately, causing him to wonder how and why he had not picked the boy out earlier. Internally, he blamed it on Beat's frolicking antics.

At that thought, he heard the girl standing in front of him scoff, unconvinced, though he did not bother to glance at her.

Studying the kid on the merry-go-round now, Case saw that he was as expected. He looked the usual height for a seven-year-old, and wore a black, sleeveless athletic shirt with extra-wide armholes, black shorts, and black and white sneakers. The giveaway, of course, was his lime-green hair, gelled into a ridge that ran down the middle of his head—an eye-catching, lime-green fauxhawk.

"You were too busy laughing at the others as they fell off," Beat commented, her eyes twinkling.

"Huh?"

"That's why you didn't notice him before. I heard you. Under that smile, you were laughing your butt off."

"I wasn't laughing."

Beat looked at him skeptically, her hands on her small hips.

"That much," Case amended on the fly. "Anyway, I believe I saw you laughing too."

The girl grinned, shrugging. She then performed a simple pirouette before jogging back toward the ride.

"I hear the snow cones are pretty good," she suggested, turning back briefly, cheerfulness clear on her face, before prancing away again.

IMANI SAT AND WAITED near the front door of the mobile home. She examined the two photos in her handbook again.

Both portraits appeared ordinary, plain, nondescript, with neither person exhibiting any type of emotion. The image depicting Roger Phillips showed moderate stubble along his jaw, his dark brown eyes staring back under a somewhat sloppy ivy-league crew cut. The boy, Connor Phillips, looked similar, save for his youthful appearance and a different hairstyle. There was no escaping the father–son connection.

However, Imani's small handbook offered more than faces and blank stares. She noticed the words, and worlds, behind the portraits, as the people represented within transformed into personalities, thoughts, feelings, and experiences. The very same faces that appeared devoid of expression in fact displayed all expressions, unrestricted and in plain view. She saw it all, their lives—at least those portions most pertinent to her current visit—in her hands.

In Roger Phillips, Imani observed a responsible worker, an admirable father, and a devoted husband gradually and sadly descend into a depressed alcoholic, a troubled drifter, and a heartbroken divorcee. In the child, she noted boundless energy and fervor that was slowly draining away. In both, she saw a situation that was not at all inspiring.

"We've got the child," Imani heard over her earpiece. "Status?"

"Still waiting," she replied coolly, raising her sunglass-covered eyes from the handbook to stare across the patchwork front yard toward the empty, single-lane street. "Until I give the word, keep your eyes open. He may head your way before he comes here."

"Will do," she heard.

Her gaze returned to the pictures.

CASE, A COLORFUL SNOW cone in each hand, sauntered over to the fencepost he had recently vacated. Beat and the boy with the green fauxhawk were sitting against the wooden railing, taking a break from the merry-go-round.

"Hey, Beat, I couldn't remember what flavor you said you wanted, so I just guessed."

Case nodded toward the boy, his eyes still on Beat.

"Who's your friend?"

Beat looked over at the child and stuck out her tongue. The boy giggled in response.

"See," Beat said triumphantly. "I told you that was my real name."

The boy laughed.

"Well, how was I supposed to know you were tellin' the truth with a crazy name like that?"

Beat turned to Case as he handed her one of the cones.

"He said he wasn't going to tell me his name, since I was obviously making mine up."

Case lowered himself to the dusty surface on the other side of the boy and held out the other snow cone.

"Okay, how about this, then. I'll trade you … this cone for your name."

"Really?" The boy's eyes widened.

Beat snickered at the child's eagerness.

"Seems fair," Case said with a shrug.

The boy fell silent, his eyes shifting between Case and Beat. He reached tentatively for the cone. He looked again to the older boy's face.

Case raised his eyebrows slightly, waiting.

Finally, the boy grasped the ice-cold treat.

"Okay," he said, grinning, "I'll tell you what my name is … if you guess it."

Beat and Case groaned. The boy ignored them; already busy slurping his part of the bargain.

"Can't you give us a—" Case started, but Beat cut him off as she started to call out names at random.

"Percy! Bartholomew! Octavius! Persephone!" The boy almost choked.

"Not even close!" he managed to get out around his shaved ice.

Beat took a bite out of her cone.

"Is it Harry Eyeball?" she asked in an innocent tone, her question muffled by her own mouthful.

The child snickered, struggling to keep the ice from spilling through his lips.

"Steven?" Case guessed.

"Gretchen?"

"Tommy?"

"Josephine?" Beat fluttered her eyelashes.

"I'm not a girl!" he exclaimed, appearing thoroughly entertained by Beat's outrageous attempts. He took another large bite out of his snow cone and turned to Case, speaking again.

"Ey, wassyernay?"

The boy's inquiry was garbled around his mouthful of shaved ice.

Case smirked, understanding the muddled question perfectly.

"Now what makes you think I would tell you my name if—"

"His name's Case," Beat interjected. "Isn't that crazy?"

Case exhaled loudly, feigning disgust that Beat had ruined his attempt at negotiation before it had even begun. Over the child's head, Beat stuck out her stained, blood-red tongue at her partner.

"Yeah, it's almost as crazy as yours!" the boy responded, not noticing Beat's gesture.

Imani's voice sounded through Case's earpiece.

"I've got him. Truck's coming up the drive now."

"We're good here," Case mumbled, much too quiet for the distracted boy beside him to hear. Beat, however, heard him clearly.

The pair exchanged fleeting glances before Beat turned back to the boy.

"Hey, my name's not crazy!" she declared, pointing to her chest with her free hand. "Yours is the crazy one ... Timothy Winston Maximillius II!"

The child nearly spat out his shaved ice as he laughed.

VISITORS HAD BECOME UNCOMMON, and unexpected visitors downright rare, so Roger Phillips's curiosity—and his apprehension—heightened as he spotted the brown-skinned woman sitting in one of his lawn chairs. He slowed his late model truck to a stop along the gravel driveway, still peering out of his windshield at the woman as he cut the engine and stepped from the cab.

"I'm sorry, but do I know you, Miss?" he called.

"No," she answered.

The chair, her body, and her gaze were positioned to face the road, as though she were waiting for someone; Roger often found himself in a similar position when he sat outside the trailer. However, other than her response, she hardly acknowledged his presence.

He stepped to the side so he could open the truck's back door. Reaching into the rear portion of the cab to grab the case of beer, he kept his gaze on the mysterious woman. She wore black clothing, complete with dark-tinted sunglasses and intricately braided hair, and sat unmoving, her entire being emitting a tensed stillness that reminded him of a rattlesnake, poised ready to strike.

She seemed dangerous.

Threatening, even.

Roger's mind danced through the possibilities, each slightly more menacing than the last.

But he was getting ahead of himself. He stood up straight again and closed both cab doors.

"You have some business here, Ma'am?" he asked, still partially shielded by the vehicle.

"Yes."

"What?"

"Come have a seat."

"You a cop?"

"No."

The woman's position still had not changed, nor had she turned to look in his direction. Other than moving her lips, Roger would bet she had hardly twitched a muscle.

"What's your business here, Ma'am? Otherwise, I'm goin' to have to ask you to leave. I'm tryin' to be nice."

"So am I," the woman said, her voice smooth and calm. "Come have a seat."

"Look," Roger started, holding the case of beer but not daring to step from behind the hood of the truck, "you just said I don't know you, so why—"

"You don't, but I also said I have business here, and I do know you, so please, come have a seat."

"You know me? What's my name, then?"

"Roger Phillips."

Roger thought for a moment.

"Well ... Ma'am, I'm sorry, but—"

The woman finally moved, slowly standing and turning to face him.

"Roger."

She motioned to the other lawn chair.

"Please."

Roger looked at her, continuing his tense standoff. He glanced toward the door of the mobile home, wondering if there was any way he was going to get in without having to bother with her. He was, he had to admit, a little unnerved. Although their contact had lasted only minutes, there was just something about this woman...

"Ma'am, if you don't—"

"Roger."

Her voice, though still calm, now held a faint edge.

Roger went on stubbornly.

"Ma'am," he declared, with a bit more force, "if you don't state your business, and I mean right now, I'll—"

She gazed at him, not responding, her eyebrow arching slightly.

Roger tried again.

"Ma'am—"

The woman turned her head, glancing toward the street. Roger turned to look as well.

"Roger."

His breath caught. The woman's voice was suddenly very close, and the air around him instantly took on a strange, eerie feel. As he slowly turned back around, he saw that the mysterious woman was now only an arm's length away, and on the same side of the vehicle as he was. That he stood taller than her seemed of no consequence at all.

Roger noticed that the typical, ambient sounds he usually heard outdoors were nonexistent, as though Boise City—if not the entire world—had abruptly fallen silent.

Instinctively, he knew.

It was all because of this woman.

Imani calmly took the case of beer still clutched under Roger's arm.

BEAT AND THE GREEN-FAUXHAWKED boy jumped off the carousel after completing another dizzying cycle, both now

15

walking with exaggerated wobbliness. Case watched with amusement from the fence railing as they staggered over.

"You were so close to throwing up that time, I could almost see it!" Beat said, giggling.

"No way!" the boy retorted. Unknowingly echoing Beat's thoughts from earlier, he added, "I could do this all day!"

Beat smirked.

"Yeah, right," she said.

Case shook his head, his own grin faintly present. He and Beat had finally persuaded the kid to reveal his name—Connor—only after Beat's guesses had become progressively more outrageous. Now, as the other two's laughter died down, he turned to the boy.

"How come I haven't seen you around this playground before?" Case asked. "You seem like an expert on that thing, but I think I would remember seeing that crazy hairdo anywhere."

"Me? What about you? I'm here all the time. I'm always spinnin'!" Connor laughed. "Anyways, I can walk here from my house."

"No wonder you're so good," Case responded.

The boy held up his small arms, flexing his skinny biceps.

"You can't do that! You don't even have any muscles," Beat teased.

Connor then attempted to mirror Case's pose by leaning his back against the wooden fence, his arms resting horizontally along either side of the railing. His shorter stature meant his arms barely reached the second tier. Beat leaned one shoulder against the fence railing, facing Case and the boy.

"So, I guess your mom and dad are okay with you coming up here by yourself?" Case inquired, glancing down at the boy before turning his gaze back to the grassless park. Even with the summer heat, the number of children on the playground increased as the day progressed, their lighthearted shouts and enthusiasm never ending.

Meanwhile, Connor had gone conspicuously quiet. Though the boy attempted to mask it, Case and Beat noticed his posture stiffen.

"You okay, Corny?" Beat asked, using the last name she had guessed for him before Connor had finally caved.

"Yeah. I just don't really wanna talk about it," he muttered. His face then brightened suddenly, the gloominess instantly erased. "So, you ready to ride again, or are ya too scared?"

Case probed another time.

"You're sure you're okay?"

Although fleeting, the boy's expression darkened again before he could hide it. Even without their knowledge of Connor's situation, Case and Beat would have sensed there was more to the green-haired kid than he cared to let on. His habit of concealing his emotions, while not perfected, was certainly practiced.

Just then, Connor abruptly turned, running back to the merry-go-round.

"Race ya!" he shouted over his shoulder.

Beat glanced at Case before taking off after the fauxhawk.

"Hey, that's cheating!"

"**M**iss…"

Sitting in the lawn chair opposite the woman, Roger hesitated, waiting for her to supply her name.

The woman did not answer.

Roger closed his mouth with a snap of annoyance, his jaw tensing at the woman's unwillingness to explain. He then began again.

"Look, I'm not sure what you want me to think here. I find you at my front door, no idea how you got here, no idea how you found me. You know my name. You say you have reason to be here. But you won't tell me that reason, and you won't tell me who you are. I'd appreciate it if you just enlightened me as to what's goin' on."

The woman looked at him a moment before turning her head back to the street. She seemed perfectly at home in the

Oklahoman heat, calm and composed. Roger wiped at his brow again; unlike her, he had long since started to sweat.

"You should understand something," she remarked, still looking away. "I'm not typically given the responsibility of going somewhere just to have a conversation, but I assume your case proves the exception."

She paused, and then continued, turning to look at Roger again, her mirrored shades reflecting his image, her face unreadable.

"It ends now, Roger. Today. Your troubles, your difficulties, your burdens—whatever you wish to call them—as far as you're concerned, those are done with. Your wallowing is over. Your divorce"—Roger quirked an eyebrow in surprise—"was not one-sided. You're not the only one who has suffered here, and you're certainly not the one who suffered the most. You've forgotten that, Roger. Whatever your meaning, whatever your true intent— that is not my primary concern, and it is not why I'm here speaking to you right now. I'm here because you have forgotten someone, and that is very much my concern. Tell me, who am I speaking of?"

Roger did not immediately respond. Shock, confusion, and disbelief rushed through him at her words.

The woman leaned forward, and her gaze, even through her tinted sunglasses, pierced through to his core.

"Say his name, Roger," she murmured, her undertone commanding.

"Connor."

It came out a whisper, so soft that the word was nearly nonexistent.

"Dependent upon your actions from this moment forward," the woman went on, "particularly with respect to your son, this will be the first and last time you see me. But I would like to be clear. This is not who you are, and we both know it. This is not who your son needs you to be. You hold tremendous responsibility. Yes, you have fallen. Yes, you have suffered. But it's time to pick yourself up, and I mean right now. I don't need to tell you how important it is that you don't let Connor down.

"Do not, do not, do not let that happen, Roger Phillips, or I will be back. And then, there will be no need for you to ask me who I am. You will know."

Her face was now only inches from Roger's. He stared back unblinking, frozen. The surrounding air was as tense as it had ever been. His mouth hung open, his throat dry.

The woman leaned away and slowly stood. Roger sat still, his brain overwhelmed. For him, at that moment, the physical world no longer existed—the sun, the summer heat, his trailer, the tattered, collapsible lawn chair he was sitting on. Nothing.

Only her words. Only her warning.

He remained seated as Imani prepared to move past him. Before she did, however, she leaned down and whispered in his ear.

"Always remember who depends on you, Roger."

She rose again and slowly crossed the half-dirt, half-grass path to the gravel driveway. Roger finally stirred from his reverie at the sound of the woman's black boots meeting the crunchy gravel. He stood abruptly and turned to stare at the departing figure.

"Wait! Why did you do this?" he called. "Why did you come to talk to me?"

The woman, all mocha-colored skin and midnight-black clothes, turned to face him, although she continued her slow walk, backwards, toward the road.

"Your son needed me to," she stated evenly, her voice easily carrying back to the front of the trailer where Roger stood. "So did you."

She turned again. When she reached the road, she headed for the playground, the sounds of youthful exuberance distant, but to her, distinctly audible.

Roger Phillips gazed after her, bewildered, until he could see her no more.

"I'M ON MY WAY," came Imani's voice over the ear monitor.

Case continued to look out into the open space near the tall, twisting slide. Beat was in hot pursuit, her face screwed up in feigned irritation, while Connor, playing the role of the rascally kid, laughed hysterically as he ran. As Case watched, Beat made a grab for the boy, but Connor darted sideways, still laughing. Beat embellished the missed capture by flailing dramatically, only to turn and begin the chase again.

Almost time to go, Case thought, knowing his partner would hear.

Across the dusty field, Beat gave a frustrated cry as she grabbed at Connor and missed again.

Case turned his head. From his vantage point at the wooden railing, he could see the dirt road that led down past the Phillips' residence. He recognized a black-clothed figure approaching: Imani, her dark form contrasting sharply with the bright day and dull-colored landscape, her pace casual and unhurried.

He returned his attention to the dustbowl playground. Beat had chased Connor back onto the crowded, rapidly spinning merry-go-round and she made several mistimed attempts at snatching him as he spun. Other kids on the ride had caught on to their game, laughing along with Connor as he evaded Beat's grasp again … and again … and again...

"She's a special one, isn't she?" Imani said, leaning forward from the other side of the railing as Case leaned back against the same lonely portion of fence.

"Yeah, but don't let her hear you say that," Case said, "or I'll never hear the end of it."

Imani's lips upturned a little. She and Case watched the playground antics until, finally, Beat and Connor ambled toward them.

"Is it time to go already?" Beat asked as they approached. "Time flies!"

She turned to the green-fauxhawked boy.

"Guess I'll see you around, Corny."

She held her fist out for Connor to bump, which he did, both of them making an exaggerated exploding sound in the process.

"'Kay," Connor said, his eyes twinkling, "but if I catch you 'round my playground again, there's gonna be trouble!"

"Your playground?" Beat huffed. "That's it!"

She made a grab for Connor's neck, but the boy scooted away and scampered back toward the merry-go-round, laughing uproariously.

Once he was out of earshot, Beat turned back to Imani and Case.

"And thank you, by the way," she said, grinning at Imani. She then reached for the knitted cap Case held out to her.

"Anything to say to me?" Case questioned.

"Umm…"

Beat hummed thoughtfully as she adjusted the hat on her head.

"Nope. Don't think so."

Case rolled his eyes.

"That's why I've always liked her," Imani said, nodding at Beat.

Beat smiled beautifully and batted her eyelashes.

"See?" she said. "I am special."

FOR CHARLIE, IT WAS one of those books.

The title of the novel was *A Flying Penguin*, and yet, three-fourths of the way through, fourteen-year-old Charlize Brown was annoyingly aware that there had been no mention of anything to do with either flying or penguins. Before she had even read the first page, she noticed the blatant lack of a printed description or summary. As it was a paperback, it had not come with a cover jacket, which would have surely included a synopsis. The back of the novel, another typical location for a summary, consisted only of a single, insignificant paragraph taken from early on in the text.

Charlie had stumbled upon these types of books before— books that gave her no clue as to what she was getting in to. Sometimes, the title provided a hint, however vague. Then, after she finished reading, she would find herself pleasantly surprised that the cagey narrative was more than worth the time she had put into reading it.

In other instances, she was not as lucky. *A Flying Penguin* was turning out to be one of those other instances.

If it had not been assigned to her as summer reading, she would have dumped it for another book ages ago.

"Hey, Charlie! Check this out!" her younger brother Colby called.

Lounging beneath a large elm tree in McCormick Park in Norbury, Massachusetts, Charlie glanced to her left, her shoulder-length blonde hair bobbing as she turned. In one of the open expanses of the park, Colby and his identical twin, Caleb, crouched beside a scaled-down, excruciatingly detailed Saturn V space rocket, which sat upon an equally scaled-down and excruciatingly detailed launch platform. Even from some distance away, Charlie recognized the painstaking realism her brothers had afforded their newest project. That realism would soon be put to the ultimate test, since the entire scene, although smaller than an actual launch, was designed to proceed in much the same way.

Both Caleb and Colby anticipated a successful blast-off. Their older sister, however, was not so sure.

Her brothers each took a step back as wisps of smoke emerged from the exhaust bells at the bottom of the rocket.

"Here we go!" Caleb said, glancing over in Charlie's direction before turning his attention back to the rocket.

"Shouldn't you guys move a little further back?" Charlie called out. "You remember what happened last time!"

"Yeah, but last time we forgot to put—"

Caleb stopped abruptly, his face twisting in panic as he turned to his twin. Colby's face showed similar alarm.

"The IU chip!" both boys exclaimed. Caleb gestured frantically to the remote device Colby held.

"Abort! Abort!"

Colby toggled the switches off, nearly fumbling the controller. Both boys stared at the launch pad.

The smoke streaming from the exhaust, which had begun to billow as the moment of takeoff approached, started to subside, turning to lazy tendrils now that the emergency shutdown controls were activated.

The brothers, breathing hard, looked again toward the large tree and their older sister, whose own gaze had moved back to her reading.

"You forgot it again, didn't you?" Charlie asked without looking up, her voice just loud enough for Caleb and Colby to hear.

The boys hesitated.

"No!" they answered back, clearly ruffled.

Charlie laughed quietly.

Out on the field, Colby looked to Caleb.

"Please tell me we didn't leave the Instrument Unit chip at home," Colby said.

"Maybe it's mixed in with the auxiliary equipment," Caleb replied, beginning to jog over to the tree where Charlie sat. "Hold on a sec."

Caleb's curly brown hair bounced in rhythm with his footfalls as he hurried over to the belongings resting beside his lounging sister. Charlie, meanwhile, turned another page in her book.

"What's up?" she asked in an innocent tone, still not glancing up.

Caleb mumbled something unintelligible as he rummaged about in the bag resting alongside her.

"Check the front pocket," Charlie offered.

After looking at her a moment, Caleb did as she suggested. All too quickly, his hand brushed across what he had been searching for and he pulled it from the pocket. He examined it briefly, turning it over in his hand, before looking to his sister again.

"I was going to look there next."

"Okay," Charlie replied, shrugging.

"But you don't even know what it does!" Caleb said, exasperated.

"And yet…" Charlie rested the book on her folded knees while tapping her finger to her chin. "I knew where to find it. Isn't that funny?"

Caleb was silent, fuming.

"Aww," Charlie said in a mock maternal coo. "You're so cute when you're angry. Yes you are."

She reached out and pinched the flesh of his cheek. Caleb exhaled loudly and rolled his eyes, giving a final huff of irritation as he turned and trotted away.

"Got it!" he yelled to his brother, who was busy tinkering with the top portion of the rocket.

Before Charlie could return her attention to *A Flying Penguin*, however…

"Heads up!"

Instinctively, she raised the sturdy paperback to protect her head. A moment later, she heard a *whoosh*, and a split-second after that—*slap!* The impact jolted the book toward her face, but her speedy reaction meant it only grazed her cheek. Had she not heeded the warning, whatever had hit her book would have slammed into her head full-force.

Charlie lowered the novel and looked around her, taking note of the football near her feet. Then she turned her book over. *A Flying Penguin* looked unscathed, even after taking the brunt of the hit. She smirked.

At least it's good for something, she thought.

As hurried footsteps approached, she looked up.

"Wow! I'm so sorry. Are you okay?"

The boy standing over her looked only a few years older than she was and wore a sleeveless T-shirt and black athletic shorts with *PROPERTY OF NORBURY HIGH* artistically stenciled on them in block lettering. He was fit without being overly muscular, and his visibly damp hair and glistening skin alluded to recent physical activity. Charlie could not help staring, but she quickly snapped herself out of it, hoping the boy had not noticed.

"Wha—? Oh, yeah, I'm fine." She gestured to the football. "I guess that's yours?"

The boy reached down for the ball.

"Yeah," he said sheepishly. "I kinda told my friend to throw it deep, but I—"

"Hey, Charlie!"

Both Charlie and the boy turned in the direction of Colby's shout.

"Yeah?" Charlie called back.

"You okay?"

"Yeah!"

Charlie looked back up at the older boy and shrugged.

"Hey, Charlie!"

She glanced in Colby's direction again.

"Yeah?"

"Who's that boy you're talking to?"

The boy was still gazing out at the field.

"Jace!" he called out.

"Jade?" Colby questioned, cupping his ear.

"No, Jace!"

"Jason?"

"Jace!"

"Jed?"

"You heard him the first time, pipsqueak!" Charlie interjected.

Caleb laughed at the exchange, and Colby grinned and gave the thumbs-up sign.

"Good one!" Jace shouted, and gave his own thumbs-up.

"Don't encourage him," Charlie warned. "He'll think he's actually being funny."

Jace grinned as he looked back down at Charlie, who was opening her book once more.

"Hey, those were some nice reflexes earlier," he commented, clutching the football with both hands, the muscles along his arms tensing slightly. "I thought for sure you were a goner."

"Eh, just lucky, I guess," Charlie replied. "Thanks for the heads-up."

She then shrugged again, adding, "Anyway, a little concussion here or there never really hurt anyone."

Jace chuckled.

"I'll have to remember to tell the football team that one when we start practicing. I always thought it would be more interesting to play without helmets."

"Yo, Jace!" a voice called out from Charlie's right. "What's taking so long, man? You askin' for directions or something?"

Charlie followed Jace's gaze to the figure some distance away, a boy comparable in both age and athletic attire to Jace.

"I'll be there in a minute!" Jace yelled. "Consider this your break, Mike! I know you need it!"

The other boy's boisterous laughter carried across the open space.

"Well, I think there was more to those reflexes than just luck," Jace said, resuming the dialogue as he softly tossed the football to himself. "If I didn't know any better—and I don't—I would say the move was almost, umm, sporty?"

Charlie slowly tilted her head, her blue eyes shifting from the book to Jace's smirking face.

"I dabble," she stated, a smile tugging at her lips.

"Okay, 'I dabble,'" he said, his tone not hiding that he was unconvinced.

Out on the grass, his friend was busy performing an odd-looking calisthenics routine. Jace's gaze returned to Charlie, and he grinned.

"Well, from what little I've seen, I would definitely say you have potential. Perhaps you should look into playing organized sports, maybe with your school or in some type of recreational league."

Jace pointed the football at Charlie melodramatically—like a former star athlete might in a television commercial.

"What are you, twelve? Thirteen?"

Charlie whipped her blonde hair away from her face as she looked up at him abruptly.

"I'll be fifteen in December."

Jace laughed, though his amusement trailed off quickly as he noticed Charlie's expression.

"What? I was close!" he reasoned, arms outstretched in a gesture of admission. "So that would put you in the"—head angled upwards, he nodded slightly as he counted to himself—"what, seventh grade?"

"I'll start high school in the fall."

"Wow. Okay, okay," Jace conceded, obviously detecting her tone. "You should definitely go out for something, then. What school are you going to?"

Charlie took an extended glance at the boy's chest. Jace looked down, and then back at her.

"What, Norbury?"

Charlie clicked her tongue in acknowledgement.

"Looks that way," she said. She held up her copy of *A Flying Penguin*. "Mrs. Ethridge."

The older boy, grinning, shook his head.

"Oooh, now that's unfortunate. She's crazy. And I don't mean crazy like, 'Oh, she's so hilarious and fun to be around'... although she is that, too, now that I think about it. But she's also crazy as in she should really be institutionalized, for all of our sakes."

Jace pointed to the book.

"That book is the first piece of evidence. I hate to break it to you, but it has absolutely nothing to do with a flying penguin, yet it's one of her favorites."

"Yeah, I've kind of gathered the no penguin thing," Charlie replied, smirking.

"And do you have any idea what it is about?"

Charlie hesitated.

"Exactly," Jace said. "It's about everything else you could ever find in a book, except anything to do with flying or anything to do with penguins. And Mrs. E is going to have a really corny joke when you guys start talking about it in class."

"What? Don't judge a book by its cover?"

Jace gazed at her with a deadpan expression before his face suddenly broke into a wide smile.

"Oh, you're good. But when she tells it, just remember to laugh like it's the funniest thing you've ever heard. Otherwise…"

He grimaced through his grin, resulting in a look that was an amusing combination of the two expressions. Charlie laughed.

"Your face went totally weird just then!"

Jace waved her off, smiling. "Whatever. So I guess I'll see you around the hallowed halls of Norbury High when school starts again in the fall, eh?"

"Oh, I doubt it. Isn't that school pretty big? And by 'pretty big,' I mean, isn't that school humongous?"

"What? Norbury?" Jace looked confused. "No, it's not that big. I mean, not really. I don't know … maybe … whatever. Anyways, I'm sure I'll see you there—I see everyone else without much of a problem. So, I'll say it again, I guess I'll see you around … Charles, is it?"

Charlie shot him a smirk.

"It's Charlize, actually," she corrected him. "My family and friends call me Charlie."

"Charlize it is, then. So, I'll see you around, Char—"

"Charlie's fine," she said, her voice slightly lowered.

Jace smiled faintly.

"Okay, Charlie" he said, chuckling. "See you in the—"

"Hey, Charlie, we got it! Here it goes!"

Both Charlie and Jace turned and watched her brothers scurry away from the miniature rocket as white smoke puffed from its bell-shaped vents. Once they were a safe distance away, Colby manipulated switches on the control device as his twin looked on expectantly. The deep, rumbling sounds coming from the rocket became louder, and louder still, drowning out the natural noises of the park and drawing more than a few onlookers. As Colby toggled the controls, the billowing smoke spewed out in increasing amounts and the sounds of the model spacecraft altered slightly, though its intensity remained just as powerful.

The three arms of the launch tower, attached to the side of the rocket, began to rotate out of the way, scraping small shavings of ice off the rocket's surface as they let go. Another arm at the top of the rocket rose up and away, removing the last obstacle in the vehicle's path for liftoff. A moment later, even greater clouds of smoke shot out from underneath the spacecraft, and the rocket slowly, forcefully, lifted off, the deafening noise like a long, thundering explosion. It cleared the launch pad, instantly enveloping the structure in smoke, fumes, and fire, completely obscuring it from view. Blue, orange and yellow pyramids of flame crackled and flashed through the discharged smoke, their noise soon drowned out by the powerful reverberations of the rocket as it propelled itself higher and higher still, cresting the surrounding treetops and leaving a rising swirl of white and gray smoke in its wake.

On the ground, Colby monitored the rocket's flight path while Caleb turned to the large tree that sheltered Charlie and Jace. He let out an exhilarated whoop as the small audience witnessing the spectacle cheered.

"Did you see that?" he yelled, the noise from the rocket still audible. "Charlie, did you just see that?"

"That is ridiculously cool," Charlie heard Jace utter, his wonder obvious in his breathy tone.

"They're not out of the woods yet," Charlie said, turning her attention back to *A Flying Penguin*. Strands of hair curtained her face as she looked downward, obscuring her features from Jace's view.

"What do you mean?" Jace asked.

Suddenly, an explosion—somewhat faint yet all too distinguishable—followed almost immediately by another, this one louder and much more obvious.

Some of the onlookers gasped.

"No!" the twins cried.

"That's what I mean," Charlie offered, looking up to the older boy again before shifting to her brothers.

"I guess it wasn't the Instrument Unit after all!" she shouted to Colby and Caleb, both of whom were gazing up toward the remnants of the exploded rocket, shielding their eyes from the sun.

"Not helping!" came their irritated reply.

WHITNEY RAINIER HEARD THE knock at the door as she bent down to pick up one of Skylar's toys that had been haphazardly discarded in the hallway.

"Sky, what did I tell you about leaving your toys where someone could fall over them?"

She straightened to her full height, clutching the gray stuffed elephant, and walked toward the door.

"He was sleeping!" Skylar yelled, running out of his room to retrieve the stuffed animal.

Whitney looked down at the little boy as he came to a stop beside her.

"Well, from now on, he sleeps in your room, okay?"

She handed him the elephant.

"Okely-dokely!"

Skylar grabbed the toy with both hands and sprinted back to the bedroom he shared with his sister, his tan legs racing as he turned the corner and vanished out of sight.

"And what did I say about running in the house?" Whitney called after him, smirking just slightly. She was ready to wipe it away in an instant should the boy poke his head out of the doorway.

"Okely-dokely!" came the response.

Technically, "okely-dokely" did not answer her question, but Whitney decided to let it go. She turned back to the entranceway.

"Coming!" she called, alerting whomever was outside that she had not forgotten about their earlier knock. It was most likely one of the kids' friends, wanting them to come outside to play.

Fat chance of that happening, Whitney thought, reaching for the doorknob. *Not while* Jake's Crazy Big World *was on.*

Upon opening the front door, Whitney was met with the familiar faces of Brigadier General Jackson Hawes and Lieutenant Colonel Savannah Hawes, husband and wife and both close friends of Whitney and her husband, Warrant Officer Jack Rainier. Officially, Jackson Hawes was Fort Leonard Wood's commanding general and superior officer, and Savannah Hawes was one of the base chaplains. Both wore their formal service uniforms, but neither displayed the warm smiles that typically accompanied them at the Rainier doorstep. Noticing their somber faces, Whitney tried to will away the instinctive dark thought that follows all military families with loved ones involved in active combat.

Don't you dare even think about jumping to a conclusion like that, she chided herself silently. *You don't know why they're here. They're probably just getting off duty, or they have some official business nonsense that needs straightening out, and they just decided to drop by.*

Her mind raced, one stream of thought smoothly and unconsciously transitioning into another.

They're probably not even here for the same thing. Just a coincidence. Or maybe it's some type of joke—

"Whitney," Savannah said, finally breaking Whitney's frantic inner mutterings.

Whitney's gaze came into focus, and she realized she had been staring at a box Jackson clutched delicately in front of him. Being a military wife, she knew of its significance, but the reason he held it now was because...

No, she thought again. *It's just another one of "My Two Jacks" completely tasteless, utterly ridiculous, borderline repulsive pranks—a prank only the "Two Jacks", Jackson "Jack" Hawes and Jack Rainier, would think was even remotely funny. Getting Savannah to go along with the scheme must have taken some real work, since she hates their pranks as much as I do. And they've got some type of nerve bringing that box out here like this, as if they were actually—*

"Whitney, please."

This time, Jackson Hawes drew her out of her ruminations. Whitney forced her attention away from the box and up to Jackson's eyes. The general's six-foot-four frame cut an imposing image, and while he seemed to be trying to keep his dark face expressionless, the stoic message hadn't reached his eyes, which strongly hinted at an emotion Whitney had no intention of naming.

She arched her eyebrow cynically.

Laying it on a bit thick, aren't we, Jack?

Whitney then shifted her gaze to Savannah. Excluding Jack Rainier, Savannah happened to be Whitney's best friend, with the chaplain's occasionally annoying husband alongside her running a close second. Next to the general, Savannah Hawes was short, although still distinctly taller than Whitney. The chaplain's pale blue eyes, usually so amiable and warm, now seemed on the verge of...

Whitney turned back to Jackson.

"Well, General," she voiced, exaggerating his title as she was prone to do in unofficial circumstances, "I don't—"

Her words snared in her throat as her eyes drifted back to the box gripped in Jackson's hands. This time, Whitney was able to halt her dark musings.

"I don't care to know what terrible practical joke you've cooked up this time, Jack, so I'll just stop it right here before you can start. I would, however, like to know"—she turned toward Savannah—"how you managed to rope our fair chaplain into this, since we all know she is well above the infantile wallowing of you and my husband."

"Mrs. Rainier—" Jackson started.

Whitney's eyes cut swiftly to the general again.

"Don't you dare," she broke in with whispered menace.

She was aware of the possibilities that stemmed from his use of a formal greeting, and she was not about to let him get away with it.

"Whitney, please," Savannah spoke up softly, her voice wavering. "This isn't..."

Whitney noticed that the lieutenant colonel's expression was slowly crumbling, her face a window into discouraging thoughts. The two women stared at each other for a moment—Whitney's eyes narrowed, her mind still unconvinced; Savannah's gaze timid, a depiction of regret—both waiting for the other to crack, for the truth to finally be realized.

"Mrs.—"

Jackson attempted to speak again, only to be cut off once more by a piercing glare from Whitney. The general closed his eyes briefly and exhaled. His voice slightly softer than before, he went on.

"Whitney, it is with a heartfelt—"

No, Whitney thought. *This is not happening. Stop. Stop!*

"—and tremendously deep sense of regret that I am here to inform you—"

"Mommy?"

Whitney jumped and spun around.

Maria Nightingale Rainier, Whitney's daughter and Skylar's younger sister, had her hands clasped together dramatically.

"Mommy, can I please get a Box O' Juice out of the refrigator?"

Whitney hesitated briefly before switching back into mommy mode.

"I don't know, can you?" she asked. "And what is a Box O' Juice? You mean a juice box?"

"Box O' Juice is what Jake drinks in *Jake's Crazy Big World,*" Maria said, as if the fact of what the title character drank on her favorite television show should have been common knowledge.

"Maria, you know you don't have to ask me for something to drink," Whitney replied.

"I know, but Jake always asks for a Box O' Juice."

"Okay, but get one for your brother, too."

"Woo-hoo!" the little girl cheered in the endearing way only a small child can. She turned and power walked to the kitchen, careful not to run.

Whitney still had a slight smile on her face as she turned back to the door, though it vanished immediately as she caught sight of her two visitors again. Neither one was presently looking at her, however. Lt. Col. Hawes's head was bowed, her gaze toward the ground. The commanding general was looking off to the side, grimacing. Whitney shifted as she heard her daughter approach again.

Maria held one juice box in each small hand. She had already opened one, and she took it away from her mouth, displaying it to her mother in triumphant fashion.

"Yeah! Box O' Juice!" she exclaimed, imitating the television character. The little girl then noticed the familiar company in the doorway.

"Aunt S'vannah, Uncle Jack, wanna Box O' Juice?"

Savannah gave a small smile, while Jackson responded softly, "No thanks, Night," in reference to the girl's middle name.

Maria, slurping on the straw of her "Box O' Juice," did a short bow before abruptly spinning and returning to the bedroom, the arm holding the unopened juice box swinging purposefully.

Whitney stared at the spot where her daughter had stood, and then turned back to the two at her door. Both soldiers now met her gaze, and it seemed as though Maria's brief interruption had allowed them time to compose themselves.

Jackson, hiding the small box behind his back during the interlude, brought it around to the front of his body. Whitney's eyes were drawn to it again momentarily before her gaze swung back to Jackson's face. Then, she looked to Savannah.

"Aunt S'vannah," Maria had called her, not yet capable of fully constructing the name verbally. Still, the mispronunciation held a sentimental charm, a charm perfectly embodied by the chaplain even on her worst days, and it gradually dawned on Whitney that she had been correct from the beginning.

Savannah Hawes, her best friend, would never—could never—take part in such an irresponsible "My Two Jacks" hoax. Whitney knew her friend's demeanor, and her daughter had unknowingly reminded her of it. She shook her head in denial, realization finally sinking in.

"Mrs. Rainier," Jackson began, "it would probably be better if we came inside—"

"No."

Whitney shook her head from side to side, as if in a daze.

"No."

"Mrs.—" Savannah's voice broke as she spoke the word. She tried again, dropping the formality. "Whitney, we asked—"

"Don't do this to me," Whitney whispered, pleading with her eyes. Begging.

"We asked to be the ones to tell you," Savannah said quietly. "It is not customary—as you know—but when we were notified, we ... we thought it would maybe be just a little ... a little easier, coming from us. I am so, so, so sorry."

Whitney was on the edge of the cliff now, the precipice where any sense of poise and security ended. The dark, infinite abyss of the unknown waited to envelop her in nonexistent arms. The darkness, the nothingness, the unforgiving, bottomless pit—it was all only inches, seconds, away. All she needed was a little push, a faint tap, to send her falling.

A confirmation.

Her head turned slowly, almost numbly, to General Jackson Hawes, Jack's best friend aside from Whitney herself.

She knew that Jackson would be the one to finish her.

He would be the one to push her over the edge.

And Jackson Hawes knew it, too.

He could see it in her eyes when comprehension finally seized her, and he could see it now as she was nearly gone—or in fact already gone—like a prisoner being led in shackles to the execution chamber.

The imposing Brigadier General of the United States Army looked down and away from Whitney's already haunted gaze, away from the eyes that would greet him in his nightmares for many nights to come. He looked to the box he held carefully in front of him, in the center of his chest. It was, by a twist of morbid fate, very close to Whitney's eye level. He held it with one hand and tenderly stroked it with the other, his trembling fingers barely making contact with the polished wood.

"I'm so sorry, Whitney," he whispered, still not looking up, his usually booming, baritone voice barely audible.

"No."

It came out as an anguished whisper, and as the cliff gave way, Whitney collapsed, Jackson and Savannah reaching for her before she hit the floor.

MEANWHILE, NEARLY ONE THOUSAND miles away, Lexion—Lex, as he was more commonly known—leaned gently against the pool stick he clutched in his large hands, careful not to rest his full weight on the delicate staff of wood.

"Yo," he muttered.

In Presidio County, Texas, the light scattering of customers in the roadside bar scarcely gave him any notice. His ear monitor, however, captured his low tones perfectly.

"One minute," Lex heard over his monitor.

"Just wanted to make sure you hadn't forgotten about me, sweetie," Lex replied, his heavily bearded face hinting at a smirk. He glanced up at one of several television screens situated throughout the bar.

"Couldn't even if I wanted to," came the response over his earpiece.

FORTY-SEVEN SECONDS LATER, IMANI pushed open the doors of Joe's Roadhouse Tavern and stepped inside.

She wore her usual black, which blended flawlessly with the biker-style environment the tavern presented. Her gait suggested a calm readiness as she moved toward the counter, and through her peripheral vision, she recognized the overly bulky and aggressively tattooed frame of her partner folded over a pool table, positioning his pool cue for a shot.

In Presidio County, the tavern seemed purposely located miles from anywhere in particular so as to be a welcoming—and singular—rest stop for an otherwise road-weary traveler. Fashioned in the style of the Wild West, gun-slinging drinking holes of the 1800s, the bar's interior furnishings and usual clientele did nothing to discourage the scene. Joe, the owner and head barkeep, dressed the part, wearing a vintage, Western-style waistcoat, a showy pocket watch attached to a long chain, and keeping a worn cowboy hat always within arm's reach.

Imani, her sharp, dark outfit attracting a few prolonged glances but little else, saddled up to a barstool and ordered a locally brewed bourbon. The drink, particularly the alcohol, was unnecessary since it had no effect on her, but she had gotten into the habit of ordering such a beverage to help her blend in. She knew Lex would have a drink close at hand as well, most likely some local beer.

Her drink was soon placed in front of her on a fancy embroidered napkin—*Joe's Roadhouse Tavern: A Taste of the Wild West*. Imani pulled out her handbook, the usual early evening barroom sounds reverberating all around her. Her eyes flashed to the portrait of one-half of her objective for the evening, Dexter Toohey. She had looked at the page earlier, but now she examined it again, keeping her face blank as she took in the details.

"Oh, hell yeah!"

Imani heard Lex's exclamation clearly over the din, and turned to the pool table. Lex had his hand out, a wily smirk showing through his beard as another patron slapped a few bills into his open palm. Lex glanced toward her at the bar, not attempting to hide his grin, his eyes twinkling. Imani shook her head just barely, knowing Lex would catch the gesture, before returning her attention to the handbook—this time to examine the second portrait, that of a young Latin American male.

Soon enough, she looked up again to catch Joe, the owner, attempting to steal a glance at her book while unconvincingly wiping an already clean beer mug. Joe's eyes shifted to her face, and then did a double take when he realized he had been discovered.

"So, uh…"

He gestured vaguely to Imani's hands and cleared his throat as he continued to clean the spotless mug.

"Whatcha got there?"

"A book," Imani responded cryptically, taking a sip of her beverage.

"Anything interestin'?"

"Very," she said in a dry tone.

Joe paused, clearly trying to decide whether she was being truthful or sarcastic.

"Really? Who's it by? I always like watchin' out for ah good read."

Imani felt her mouth twitch.

"I don't know if you'd believe me if I told you."

"Oh? How 'bout tryin' me then, lil' lady?"

"He goes by a few names."

"Lay one on me."

"Do you have a pen?" Imani asked.

Joe looked puzzled before he caught on.

"Oh, right. A pen."

The barkeep retrieved one, sliding it across to her along with an additional napkin. Imani wrote quickly and slid both across the counter again.

Joe took the napkin and shrugged.

"What, he goes by initials? Never heard of 'em."

Now, Imani smiled.

"Sure you have."

"Give me another name."

Imani motioned for the napkin again and wrote another name.

"Looks foreign. I can't even pronounce that," Joe said, looking at it.

"More or less, it translates to 'I will be who I will be,'" Imani answered, staring at him intently.

"So it's some kinda riddle, then?" Joe asked. "I say there's somethin' fishy when a man can't even go by his real name."

"Hey, Joe, can I get another one down here?" requested a patron from the other end of the counter.

Joe placed the thoroughly cleaned mug down on a ledge underneath the bar.

"I'll be right back," he commented. "Let me go get this guy."

A loud guffaw arose from the pool tables. Imani did not bother to turn around, though a smile ghosted along the edges of her lips. She took another sip of her drink and focused on her handbook again.

WHITNEY BOYD RAINIER, THE very recent widow of Warrant Officer Jack Reuben Rainier, sat in silence on the couch, staring, unblinking, toward nothing. Skylar Hightower Rainier and Maria Nightingale Rainier—both now fatherless—lay against her on either side, sound asleep.

The house was quiet, and, besides its regular residents, empty. For Whitney, the emptiness was significant—the so-called "final nail in the coffin." Typically, after she put the children to bed—and it was well past their bedtime already—she would embrace the soothing quiet while she performed the necessary chores before turning in. After a day full of childish summertime antics, the concluding calm was always welcoming.

Yet even with Jack on deployment, the house never felt this empty.

Because this is how it feels to be truly alone, she thought.

Jack always seemed to be around, even when he was on the other side of the world. The other army wives gently brushed her off whenever the subject was brought up, assuming it was the young couple's continued "puppy love" phase, or the vibrant residual of Jack's characteristically riotous presence. Whitney did not dismiss the reasoning behind the latter, although it never wholly accounted for the feelings, the atmosphere, which forever lingered within their home. It was comforting. It was relaxing. It was reassuring, as though the Rainier family was always together, even when Jack was more than twenty hours away by military airlift.

But now, tonight, it seemed empty. Something was definitely missing.

Jack was gone—this time for real. He was gone, and there would be no coming back.

The house had held numerous guests since Savannah and Jackson Hawes had notified Whitney of her husband's death. Neighbors, acquaintances, friends, well-wishers, military wives— they all stopped by for a moment, a minute, a few minutes, an hour, a few hours, once the word had traveled through the Leonard Wood circuit that Whitney and her two young kids were alone now.

They felt it was their duty. They felt it was their obligation. Their responsibility.

It was protocol.

"You are not alone, Whitney," they all had said, in one form or another, some even reciting the line outright. "You are not alone, Whitney. You are not alone."

She was appreciative of their vainly comforting lies.

Jackson and Savannah had returned to the Rainier household, minus their dress uniforms, and stayed for dinner. With the multitude of dishes visitors had brought, food preparation was minimal. Not that Whitney was acutely aware of any of it; Savannah had effortlessly taken over the domestic duties. Whitney was too out of it to notice. She did not eat anything, but, through her fogginess, she received reassurance that Maria and Skylar were being fed.

You are not alone, Whitney.

Savannah had had the presence of mind to serve ample helpings of the kids' favorite dishes. Where and when she had the opportunity to fix those meals, or whether another visitor had brought them, Whitney had not a clue. It was still unclear to her just how much Skylar and Maria were able to grasp the situation, or the permanence of it all. They had lost their beloved father, a man they enjoyed climbing all over whenever he was in any reclined position. "Mt. Rainier," Jack would call himself, both children clinging to his shoulders. Whitney would roll her eyes every time. When Jack was around, Skylar and Maria never stopped giggling in innocent delight.

But did they realize just how real their loss was? At their age, could they be expected to? A part of Whitney almost wished they would not understand, that they would continue to believe Daddy was still "out of town, looking for bad guys."

Only this time, he wouldn't be coming back to tell them how many "bad guys" he had found, or calling them to say how many "munchkins" he had seen in the market streets that reminded him of "Sky-High" and "Night." He wouldn't be coming back—at least, not in a way that would satisfy them.

You are not alone.

Whitney was grateful that Jackson and Savannah had stayed around for a while after everyone else had left. It was almost like old times ... almost. Whitney was nearly able to get her mind off the reason they felt a need to remain. But then, one look at ... anything ... and the walls would come tumbling down again. Jackson and Savannah, along with a few of the others from earlier, said they would return tomorrow. Savannah said she would stop by in the morning before she went in to work on base.

They were all gone now, though. The house was quiet, and empty. Savannah and a few of the other wives had offered to stay the night multiple times, but with a small, sad, pathetic shake of her head, Whitney had let them go home, back to their happy circles, back to their unbroken familial lives. For even if they had stayed, they could not have stayed forever, and even if they could have somehow stayed forever, they would not have been able to fill the hole Jack left behind. Friends and neighbors could do a lot, but even they could not manage that. It was not their fault, it just was.

Lt. Col. Savannah Hawes, ever the capable chaplain, had suggested she stay behind and pray with Whitney that night, just the two of them, alone, together. Whitney had asked for a postponement, which the chaplain had accepted with an accommodating smile.

Jack Rainier had once described Whitney as "religious ... kinda. More spiritual, just right." Jack himself was less committed than she was, although she couldn't immediately recall them getting into an in-depth discussion about the topic. They lived good, they did right—although Jack would occasionally toe the line when he and Jackson were up to something, which was a not-uncommon occurrence. Still, it seemed to always turn out fine in the end, and Whitney had never heard of anyone getting hurt as a consequence of their pranks.

At least, that was what was told to her.

Perhaps the permanence had not quite settled in for her either, much less for her two young children. When it did, would that make the loss easier, or harder? Would she and the kids feel less alone, or would that feeling remain? Would it get worse before it got better? Would it get better? What about on Jack's birthday, or the kids'? What about Whitney and Jack's anniversary? What about Thanksgiving? Christmas?

What about tomorrow?

Whitney continued to stare straight ahead, not flinching as a solitary tear wet a path down her face. She had not cried all day, her emotions somehow beyond that, like an injury so painful, so agonizing, that it smoothly and thoroughly eclipsed the threshold of pain to produce no feeling at all, only numbness. And yet, the absence of feeling weighed just as heavily, as if the hurt had been there all along.

Emptiness.

It was incredibly strange what emptiness actually felt like. The sheer weight of it—impossible. Whoever said hate was the opposite of love had never felt the sensation of emptiness.

"You are not alone, Whitney," they had said. "You are not alone."

Whitney jumped slightly. Maria shifted beside her on the living room couch, seeking a more comfortable position in her sleep. The faint push was enough to bring Whitney out of her trance and back to reality. She looked down at her two slumbering children.

Unexpectedly, a new chapter in their lives was soon to begin.

SHE HAD JUST PUT Maria and Skylar to bed. Had this day not been during their summer vacation, Whitney would not have thought twice about holding them out of school the following day. The school would not have thought twice about pronouncing the absence "excused." The local high school at which Whitney taught would have been equally understanding.

Whitney returned to the living area, taking up her position on the couch. She reflexively looked over at the clock, though she did not bother trying to comprehend the time. Time was of no concern to her at the moment. She had all the time in the world—or absolutely none at all.

Whitney brushed a hand over her face, a gesture she had adopted from Jack when they were first dating. Of course, his version was more for comedic effect, but Whitney had started to use it whenever she felt a little ... off. Now was definitely one of those times. The familiar action eased her stiffness. She leaned forward and rested her head in her hands.

After a few minutes, she started to cry.

Her Jack was gone.

At THE SAME MOMENT, along a vacant road on a piece of the desert landscape in Texas's Presidio County, the Rebel Fist Motorcycle Club rumbled toward Joe's Roadhouse Tavern.

Their arrival produced a prominent, dull roar over the typical chatter and unremitting din inside the bar. Lex and Imani heard the motorcycles first, but soon enough the other patrons recognized the rumblings as well. From the moment the sounds were heard, the atmosphere in the saloon took on a different tone. Tension ratcheted up slightly. The regulars within the tavern, anticipating the change in mood, shifted themselves accordingly as the motorcycles began to pull in.

Behind the bar, Joe exhaled loudly in resignation. He then ambled back to where Imani sat at the counter.

"Ma'am," he began, his voice more cautious, more earnest, "you're, of course, welcome to stay if you choose, but this crowd that's about to come in can get pretty ugly. I don't know if you wanna be privy to that."

Imani, who had been studying her pocket-sized handbook, looked up at the barkeep blankly.

"They can, or they will?"

Joe glanced at the front door.

"They may."

Imani looked back down to her notebook.

"And you allow it?" she asked calmly.

"I always get th' sheriff or th' state troopers if they start tah get outta hand," Joe responded. "But they don't care tah deal wit' 'em too much. Not to mention tha troopers always take ah little while tah get out here anyway."

Imani did not immediately reply.

Joe looked toward the saloon entrance again. He cleared his throat, obviously unsettled.

"Ma'am, I'm only thinkin' of your own safe—"

He hesitated, and then swore under his breath as the tavern door opened.

"I'll be fine," Imani assured him.

"Sure hope so," Joe muttered, as the first of the Rebel Fist riders stepped through the doorway. Joe moved toward the other end of the bar.

"I sure hope so," he said again.

MEMBERS OF THE REBEL Fist Motorcycle Club acted in characteristic style upon their arrival at the Western-styled tavern—invasive, though not overbearing. Each member intentionally toed the delicate line between presence and heavy-handed dominance, wanting patrons to feel their company without having to overtly proclaim the fact. It was a restrained and practiced form of intimidation, and it was effective.

Rebel Fist members did not mingle; more so, they performed a sensitively forced infiltration. As they entered the barroom, they did not move as a large group—they broke apart. Various riders staked out various areas—pool tables, barstools, sit-down tables, televisions, or the modernized jukebox. Rarely were there more than four or five in any one cluster.

They were not overly loud. They were not rambunctious. They socialized among themselves, only occasionally entering a dialogue with another patron when circumstance called for it. They were not blatantly rude, but they were by no means blatantly polite. They were not blatant at all.

Nevertheless, they were definitely there. It had become their usual practice.

The Club was well known—to those looking for them—throughout the southwestern United States; however, their present methods were still relatively new. The Club had transformed itself from a brash, rudimentary bike gang to a minimized, though quickly growing, syndicate. They were shadowy, a blossoming criminal enterprise.

The Rebel Fist still hit hard on occasion, illustrating the dispassion and viciousness for which gangs—motorcycle gangs in particular—were notorious. Yet, after such instances, they had become harder to pin down, more difficult to convict in court, and impossible to eradicate. They could no longer be dismissed as a simple irritant or nuisance. To those who were aware, they were now a concern, an increasingly important entity.

For law enforcement, the main cause for unease was the uncertainty of the Club's power. The justice system was only beginning to decipher the gang's reach, and how much farther the Rebel Fist's reach was capable of extending. The public, while familiar with the Rebel Fist moniker and able to recall their more obvious transgressions, was, for the most part, oblivious to the Club's current criminal capabilities. As far as Rebel Fist was concerned, ignorance was indeed bliss.

Also an issue for those concerned was the questionable existence of any official ringleader. The gang never appeared to follow a singular, consistent voice. Individual members did not trumpet a person in charge to anyone outside the Club, or if they did, it soon became obvious that the name, or the person, was bogus. Law enforcement had its suspicions, and some were vaguely accurate; however, evidence to any contrary opinion was credible enough to cloud and muddy even their more reasonable estimates.

In fact, there were only three individuals wholly knowledgeable of the complex inner and outer workings of the Rebel Fist Motorcycle Club, and all three were in attendance at Joe's Roadhouse Tavern that evening.

The first was Lex.

The second was Imani.

And the third was the Rebel Fist rider in Imani and Lex's handbook—the rider named Dexter Toohey.

WHITNEY HAD NO CLUE how long she had spent quietly sobbing. It felt continuous, never-ending, though for now, surprisingly, it had stopped.

"Why?" she whispered to no one, her voice barely audible. "What? Is this ... is this some sort of punishment? Is this what you leave me—leave us—with? Is this what you think we deserve?"

Click.

Whitney heard the lock on the front door unbolt. She looked up, her face illustrating not surprise but a weary resignation. She watched, unmoving, as the knob turned, and the door swung slowly open.

A stunning woman walked through the doorway, followed by an equally captivating man. After they were both inside, the man closed the door softly. He stayed near the door, while the woman, slowly and calmly, moved to where Whitney remained seated on the couch.

The woman, dressed in a gown of pure elegance that looked as if it had been made with only her in mind, gracefully folded her legs under her body and kneeled. She reached out and captured Whitney's hands. The woman's skin held the same tanned shade as Skylar's and Maria's.

The woman looked up from their joined hands to stare into Whitney's eyes. Her lips curled into a small, comforting smile. After a moment, she spoke.

"Is this okay?" she asked softly, her voice soothing and melodic.

Whitney looked at her hands, clasped in the woman's reassuring hold, and then back up into the woman's eyes. They were caramel-colored, warm brown flecked with gold, matching her flowing hair. She was a vision of beautiful tranquility.

Whitney, her voice quiet, trembling with astonishment and uncertainty, finally spoke.

"Are—are you what…"

Her attention shifted from the woman kneeling before her to the man at the front door.

"Are you…"

The woman watched Whitney. The man, holding his position near the door, nodded and gave a small smile. His dark brown skin was nearly black, and his clothes, like the woman's, matched his form flawlessly, lending him a distinctive, divine elegance.

Whitney's attention returned to the woman.

"You're … you're an …"

The woman tilted her head to the side and smiled.

"You're not alone, Whitney. I promise."

Whitney's hands gripped the woman's fingers tightly, her eyes becoming watery once more.

The woman gave a tighter, reassuring squeeze of her own.

"May we sit with you?" she asked, her voice still calm and soft.

"Please," Whitney replied.

LEX NEVER HAD MUCH problem blending into a rough-and-tumble barroom setting. What was slightly surprising, however, was Dexter Toohey's lack of concern for Imani's presence. Imani, while not expecting a full-on altercation, was also not expecting only the few, quick glances Toohey sent in her direction. To earn only a few looks—and seemingly innocent ones at that—was a welcoming, though overall insignificant, turn of events.

"It's because you're pretty," Lex had said earlier in a faint murmur from his station at the pool tables.

Those nearby did not hear his mumblings, but he had no doubt his partner across the room heard him clearly, even without her earpiece in place.

Imani, however, had chosen not to dignify the comment with a response.

Like Toohey, most of the other Rebel Fist members stole quick glances at Imani, too; others stared, although they did not approach. A few looks were openly hostile, but most ranged between inquisitive suspicion and pure curiosity.

After a time, one member finally took exception, although, again, it was surprisingly not Toohey. The rider was set apart from the rest of Rebel Fist by being noticeably shorter than his fellow members, along with the fact that his bald head was the canvas for a detailed tattoo depicting the targeting crosshairs of a gun. He came up to stand beside Imani's barstool and signaled down the bar for Joe.

"Think ya might be in tha wrong place, lil' lady," he said, staring straight ahead, leaning against the counter.

His voice was reedy, and even with the well-placed Texan inflections, Imani could tell he had not been raised in the area.

"Is that so?" Imani also faced forward, scanning the labels of the domestic beers and liquors that lined the display cases behind the bar.

Joe appeared on the other side of the countertop, his face wrinkled with a dim wariness. The barkeep glanced toward Imani again in forewarning.

"Get me what's on tap," the short Rebel Fist rider requested.

"Buried Rose Dark good?" Joe asked, looking at the rider.

"Yeah."

Joe threw Imani another look before retrieving the beer.

"Think ya might wanna get outta here before it gets ugly," the shorter man continued, unknowingly sharing Joe's sentiments of caution to Imani from earlier. "I'd wager this ain't really your type ah place."

"Really?"

"Yeah, 'cause ya see, ol' Joe there don't really run this place when we're here—we do. And we can refuse service—"

"Excuse me," Joe announced somewhat forcibly, positioning himself across from the rider again. "You want this or not?"

"Yeah, Joe," the diminutive rider said, with an obviously feigned grin, "course I want it."

He took the mug from Joe's outstretched hand.

"I was jus' tellin' Miss Foxy Brown here that we can refuse serv—"

"We?" Joe chuckled darkly. "We can't do nothin'. I can refuse service, and since I don't refuse service to you, I sure ain't refusin' to serve a perfectly law-abiding visitor such as this young lady sittin' right here."

"Who says I ain't law-abidin', Joe?" the man's mocking grin turned malicious. "I ain't done nothin' wrong. I just thought you knew tha deal here."

The short rider gazed around the saloon. When he spoke again, his voice projected louder than before, so others could hear. In response, other sounds fell quiet.

"Think ya mighta forgotten who runs this, Joe, 'cause when we say, for instance, that we don't want no Black Barbie, ghetto—"

"Sims."

The voice was deep and rasping. Both Joe and the short club member turned to one of the men sitting near the end of the bar.

It was Toohey.

"Lay off, man."

Sims scoffed. "You know how this goes, Dex. Think she might feel a bit more comfortable in some hippity-hop strip bar in the city somewhere with the other nig—"

"Sims," Toohey said again, a little louder this time, his tone a little more persuasive. "Think ya might wanna chill out and take a seat somewhere."

Sims looked at Toohey in disbelief, as if waiting for the punch line. None came.

"Just move away, man."

Sims looked at Imani.

"Looks like today's your lucky day, Foxy," he muttered, sneering, before turning and walking back to a table near one of the overhead televisions.

The cavernous barroom was quiet for a beat.

Then, Lex's gruff laugh was unmistakable.

"Ha ha! That's classic! You guys are hilarious! I'mma have to stop by this place more often."

The barroom clatter resumed. Toohey turned in his seat to look at Lex, his face expressionless as Lex lined up a shot. Lex, catching Toohey's stare, grinned, winking, before sending one of the balls smashing into the corner pocket. He moved to arrange for his next shot as Toohey turned back around to continue his conversation with another one of the Rebel Fist members beside him.

Imani looked on silently.

Toohey's behavior thus far was not what she was anticipating.

She lifted her nearly empty glass and mumbled, her lips hidden, "Any idea what's going on here?"

"I got no freakin' clue!" Lex responded eloquently, and loudly, most likely startling those next to him, who might wonder to whom he was speaking.

As TIME PROGRESSED, SO did the intoxication of the Rebel Fist riders. Most of the regular, non-gang-related patrons of the tavern had since trickled out, leaving only a resilient handful. The club members gradually grew louder and more animated, though still they remained in check.

Lex—playing a role yet simultaneously acting completely himself—seemed to intuitively mirror the vanishing reserve of the Rebel Fist riders around him. However, his behavior could not be blamed on alcohol, no matter how much he consumed. With his burly frame and defiant motorcycle style, Lex fit in perfectly with the Rebel Fist crowd, winning one pool game after another and talking brashly, his deep voice carrying easily and distinctly throughout the saloon.

At the bar, Toohey appeared unaffected, too occupied with talking to those around him to concentrate fully on drinking himself into a stupor.

Imani hardly received any attention after the earlier encounter with Sims, and she was given a wide berth whenever the riders strode to the bar. She kept her gaze on her handbook, and sporadically sipped her drink, which she had finally allowed Joe to replenish.

Joe's Roadhouse Tavern was under control, for now. Then again, the second half of Lex and Imani's reason for being there had not yet arrived. After that, control could very well be up for grabs—at least briefly.

THE DESOLATE, DARK ROAD they traveled cut through the moonless desert, and Hugo Jimenez had little trouble spotting the artificial lighting in the distance. He glanced across to his wife.

"*Her-mo-sa*," Hugo whispered in a singsong tone, gently nudging Kim's side. "*Her-mo-sa*."

"Hmm?" Kim responded semi-consciously, caught between dreaming and wakefulness.

After another soft nudge from Hugo, she wearily came to life.

"What?" She bent her head down and rubbed her eyes. "Are we here?"

Hugo smiled.

"Not quite, *Hermosa*, but I'm going to stop at this place up ahead—whatever it is—to see if they can point me toward some gas."

Kim was still gathering herself. She blinked and looked ahead, attempting to focus.

"Is that even a gas station?"

"*No está seguro*," Hugo said, as much to himself as to his wife. "But since it is out here in the middle of nowhere, I'm sure they at least have some gas cans—pricey gas cans, if nothing else. That should be enough to make it to the next town."

Kim shook her head from side to side and raked her fingers through her strawberry blonde hair, leaving it more disheveled than it had been moments before.

Hugo looked in her direction, noticing her tousled display and the vacant, weary expression on her face.

"*Perfecto*," he said with a smirk.

Kim rolled her eyes but did not hide her smile. She hit him on the shoulder playfully, not disturbing his grip on the steering wheel.

They were drawing steadily closer to the solitary building in the wasteland, and while it did not look like any gas station she was familiar with, the number of vehicles outside gave her some encouragement. At last, they pulled into the parking lot, and Hugo maneuvered into a space with a clear view to the entrance.

He glanced toward the neon-lit sign arranged over the edifice.

"Joe's Roadhouse Tavern," Hugo read aloud in an exaggerated country accent. "Well, that explains all the Harleys."

"Not every motorcycle is a Harley, Hugo," Kim commented, amusement apparent in her tone.

"Nope, only the respectable ones."

Hugo, still studying the building, pointed to one side of the tavern.

"There they are."

Two outdated, though seemingly functional, gas pumps stood stoically under a flickering overhead light. He unbuckled his seatbelt.

"I'll just pop in to see what I have to do to get those pumps operating," Hugo said, "and then we'll be on our way."

He turned back to Kim.

"There may be a rowdy crowd in there at this time of night, so it may be best for your virgin ears if you stay out here."

"Oh, please."

Kim dismissed him with a wave of her hand.

"With you gone, at least I'll finally have some peace and quiet. No more of your singing."

"But, *Hermosa*," Hugo retorted, opening the driver's side door, "with me gone, you'll have nothing pretty to look at. Nothing but a bunch of Harleys and—"

"Oh, just go," Kim said, practically shoving a chuckling Hugo out of the car. He closed the door behind him, looking back to see Kim still waving him off. Hugo smiled and shook his head before moving around the car and toward the door of the saloon.

STRETCHED OUT ON HIS stomach in a flower-filled meadow, six-year-old Skylar Hightower Rainier tentatively reached his small fingers toward Beat's smirking face. His actions were measured, delicate, cautious—as though he fully expected Beat to vanish at any moment. Beat, also stretched out on the grass, grinned as the boy's fingers inched closer.

At last, he touched her, timidly tracing her smooth features, grazing the light tendrils of the bangs on her forehead, down the side of her face, and then starting at the top again, slowly navigating the delicate bridge of her nose. As his hand neared her mouth, Beat startled him by blowing lightly, causing Skylar to jerk back in surprise. Beside him, Maria Nightingale Rainier also started, and then giggled. Case, lying alongside Beat but facing Maria, smiled.

"So, what do you think?" Beat asked. "Am I a ghost?"

Skylar only grinned in response.

Before long, Beat and Case looked up, someone's approach having caught their attention.

"Well, well, well," a familiar voice remarked behind the two Rainier children. "I can't believe I caught the munchkins just bummin' around out here, doing absolutely nothing."

Skylar and Maria quickly turned their heads, looking over their shoulders.

"Daddy!"

They rose and spun simultaneously to jump into their father's waiting arms. He picked them both up without much effort, though he feigned struggle by groaning mightily.

"Jeez Louise, how much weight have you two put on?" Jack said. "That's it. I'm telling your mother to limit you both to only one gallon of Box O' Juice a day."

All three Rainiers laughed. Their humor soon quieted, however, as Skylar and Maria stared at their father—a father they had been told would no longer be smiling and laughing and talking. Maria snuggled her head against his shoulder as she absently fiddled with the dog tags around his neck.

"Daddy," she spoke up, her voice soft, "are you dead now?"

Jack glanced down at his daughter, and then to Skylar, who was listening intently for his father's response. Both children tightened their hold on him slightly.

Jack's smile was warm and reassuring.

"Hmm..."

He was silent a moment, thinking.

"Can I ask you a question?"

"I don't know. Can you?" Skylar replied automatically.

His father's chest rumbled lightly as he chuckled.

"Okay, munchkin. May I ask you a question?"

Receiving no objection, he went on.

"Let's say I am dead. Do you think you will remember me? Even if maybe we don't get to talk to each other like we used to? Even if I can't hold you or pick you up like I used to? Even if I can't kiss you goodnight like I used to, or play and have fun with you like I used to? Even if I can't do all that, do you think you will still remember me?"

"I will always remember you, Daddy," Maria said quietly.

"Me too," Skylar declared.

"Then I can't really be dead," Jack explained, smiling gently as both of his kids looked at him. "Not in the way you think. I'll always be around. As long as you remember all the bunches of things we did together, then I'll never really be gone, will I? I'll always be with you, for as long and as often as you need me. And anyway, I'm talking to you munchkins right now, so what's that tell you? What am I, a ghost or something?"

At the mention of ghosts, Skylar, his head still on his father's shoulder, shifted his glance toward the two older kids from earlier. It took him just seconds to realize that they had both disappeared.

UPON ENTERING THE BAR, Hugo was hit with a wall of noise. While not completely debilitating, it was enough to disorient him for a moment. He squinted, adjusting to the sights and sounds.

Though he was not a frequent visitor to any sort of biker bar—or even an occasional visitor, for that matter—Joe's Roadhouse Tavern lived up to Hugo's Hollywood-influenced expectations. He moved toward the back of the saloon, to the long mahogany counter that seemed to stretch on forever. All around him, patrons were busy drinking, talking, laughing, drinking, playing, watching, and drinking some more. The pool tables seemed a particularly popular draw, and televisions overhead screened various sports and races; some turned up loud enough to hear the commentators' excitement.

Because the noise level was so high at his entrance, Hugo did not notice the subtle lessening as more and more eyes turned to him. He came to a stop behind one of the numerous chairs that lined the bar, leaning forward to rest his hands on the countertop.

To his right sat a striking woman with flawless skin darker than his own, her hair fashioned in an exquisite pattern of braids that ended near her shoulder blades. She had a similar frame to Kim—average height for a woman, Hugo supposed, and she was toned, perhaps even more so than his wife, who exercised religiously.

Well, no need to figure out if anyone in here could kick my butt, Hugo thought. In a tavern full of bikers, the statement sounded sarcastic, but based on the woman's appearance alone, it was also completely honest.

His gaze shifted from the woman to the barkeep, who was topping off a drink for a long-haired gentleman wearing a black vest. As the customer turned, Hugo noticed the intricate fist emblem on the back of the man's vest, with *Rebel Fist Motorcycle Club* embroidered around the symbol. He glanced around the tavern again, observing that quite a few of the men—a majority even—donned comparable wardrobes.

Interesante. A real-life motorcycle club. And it only took me until now to notice.

He turned back around just as the bartender behind the counter met him.

"So, what's—"

The bartender halted in mid-speech as he looked at Hugo. A movement to Hugo's right told him the woman beside him had also noticed the sudden pause.

Hugo clenched his jaw slightly.

Mierda. Here we go. I haven't been called Mexican in a while. I guess I'm due.

The barkeep noticed Hugo's tension.

"Look, chief, I—"

"'Chief?'" Hugo interrupted, keeping his voice low but allowing his irritation to seep through. "That's a new one."

The bartender looked confused for a moment before realization dawned. He held his hands up in apology.

"S-sorry. Poor choice of words. It's jus' somethin' I call people. I was jus' gonna say—"

"Hey, Joe! We got a problem or somethin'?"

"**S**O," JOE THE BARKEEP began, "what's—"

As he paused, Imani threw a swift glance to Dexter Toohey at the end of the bar. He, like her, had not moved from his seat at the countertop the entire night. Imani had noticed him complete an obvious double take when Hugo Jimenez had first approached the counter, but the gesture seemed to signify the height of Toohey's interest. He had then proceeded to take a long drink from his frosted mug and shift his attention back to the Club members beside him.

"S-sorry. Poor choice of words," Joe was apologizing as Imani returned to the conversation. "It's jus' somethin' I call people. I was jus' gonna say—"

"Hey, Joe!" Sims called louder than necessary, suddenly appearing at the bar once more. "We got a problem or somethin'?"

As Hugo turned to identify the voice, Imani heard Joe mutter under his breath, "Or somethin', you short son of a—"

"No, we're fine, Sims," the barkeep interrupted his own mumbling, displaying a forced grin. "Jus' gettin' this gentleman's drink order."

Joe turned away from the disruptive rider and toward Hugo.

"Sorry," he apologized again. "Now, what was that you said you wanted, Mr....?"

He let the inquiry hang.

"It's just Hugo, but—"

"Now, jus' hold your horses, hombre," Sims cut in. "Think ya might owe an apology to me and Joe here."

Hugo was quiet for a beat.

"An apology?" he repeated.

"Yeah," Sims answered, taking a swig from the mug he held. "That's what I said. An apology."

Without looking around, Imani could tell that the tavern was now filled almost exclusively with Rebel Fist riders, all turning their attention to the young Latino at the counter. At the other end of the room, Lex kept his billiard game going despite the lack of small talk as other players made an effort to eavesdrop on the conversation at the bar. Imani, seated directly in the midst of the escalating confrontation, did not look up from her drink.

Hugo stared at Sims for a period, his expression showing faint disbelief, before turning back to the bartender.

"Hey," he started, although Joe was already waving him off, "I apologize for almost jumping down your throat—"

"It's not ah problem," Joe interrupted. "My fault. Let's jus' us all forget it. So, what can I do you for, Mr. Hugo?"

"Actually, I just wanted to know—"

"Hey, hey, hey, hey, hey," Sims interjected, drawing a few quiet laughs from his compatriots. "Aren't ya forgettin' somebody, compadre?"

Hugo turned to Sims, keeping his face blank.

"No."

He looked back at Joe.

"I just came in to ask—"

"Hey, uh, hombre," Sims said, louder. "I'm talkin' to ya. Think ya might owe me an apology, too."

"I think you're mistaken, '*hombre*.'"

Hugo's derisive tone was unmistakable as he spat out the final word.

Sims offered a condescending smirk in response. Imani tilted her head lower still, almost willing herself to become invisible, but stopping just short.

Sims spoke again, his tone considerably less humorous than before.

"Look here, Julio Iglesias," he started. "This ain't no Taco Bell or Burrito Hut or wherever y'all usually go to, an' ol' Joe here ain't about to whip up no flippin' margaritas, so why don't you just apologize and—"

"Joe."

Every head in the tavern turned toward the seated biker at the end of the bar. Dexter Toohey motioned toward his empty mug.

"How about hittin' me up again, eh?"

The bar was silent. Behind the counter, Joe started to move toward him.

"Wait a minute," Hugo spoke up, obviously failing to notice Toohey's raised eyebrows in response to his objection. "All I wanted was to ask about the gas pump—"

"You don't get tah ask nothin', kid," Sims cut in again, "'til you apologize to me."

"Now jus' calm down, Sims," Joe said, before Hugo could respond. "Nobody's lookin' for any trouble in here this evenin', 'cept you. You know I'm not afraid to call the troopers."

Sims set his mug on the bar, and then pinched his nose, his expression similar to that of an overburdened parent.

"Jesus H. Christ, Joe," he said under his breath before moving his hand away from his face and vaguely pointing it in Joe's direction. "Look, the next time I want you openin' your mouth about somethin', I'll tell ya, all right?"

"What is your problem, man?" Hugo leveled his attention at Sims once more.

Sims snickered with disdain.

"I'll tell ya what my problem is, *man*. We gotta flippin' Ricky Sanchez in here at our bar, and I seem to be—"

"Sims," Toohey's smoky voice carried from his end of the counter. "Shut up."

He then gestured to the old barkeep.

"Hey, Joe, hit me up. I'm on dregs over here."

Sims' jaw tightened.

"What the hell, Dex!" he retorted forcefully. "What is this, a welfare office? First we let Serena Williams here sit down without..."

Imani heard the sound of splintering wood coming from the pool tables, followed swiftly by a low curse, as Sims continued his boisterous tirade. She pretended to take a sip from her glass.

"Calm down," she muttered, directing her comment to Lex.

"Huh?" Sims asked, turning to her, his reedy voice pitched high. "Oh, you talkin' to me now, huh, Soul Sistah?"

Imani's mouth twitched as she lowered the glass from her lips. She did not reply, staring down into the watery depths of her drink.

"Hey!" Sims leaned closer to her. "What, you suddenly can't hear me now or somethin'?"

The alcohol on Sims's breath became even more apparent as he leaned in, although Imani still ignored the short biker.

Hugo interceded.

"Look, I don't know your name," he said, "and I don't know anything about you. I'm not looking for a fight. But if you call either of us"—Hugo gestured to himself and Imani—"a name other than the names we go by, I swear to God I will beat your face in, in front of all your 'hombres.' You understand me, or do I need to start speaking in redneck?"

Other than the sounds coming from the televisions, the tavern was dead quiet.

Finally, Toohey spoke.

"Joe," he said, his voice still resonating a cool control as he gestured to his mug for the third time. "Come on."

Hugo, not breaking eye contact with a frowning Sims, waved absently in the barkeep's direction.

"I just wanted to know if the gas pumps outside are operational, and if I needed to pay upfront."

Joe opened his mouth to answer, but Sims beat him to it.

"Who ya think ya talkin' to, huh? Who ya think ya talkin' to? Think ya might wanna stop worryin' 'bout the damn gas, Speedy Gonzalez, and start—"

"*Eso es todo, comemierda*," Hugo said menacingly, his muscles tightening. "I told you—"

"Hugo?"

All heads turned to the feminine voice at the tavern's entrance.

KIMBERLY ANNE JIMENEZ PRESSED the illumination button on the cheap, cartoonish watch she wore on her wrist. Reading the time, she leaned against the armrest and rested her head on her hand.

Three minutes, she thought. *He gets three minutes, or he's going to be super embarrassed when I walk in there.*

The notion made her recall her and Hugo's first meeting, their initial encounter.

In fact, the "meeting" was not the first time they had seen each other. At the time, they were both sophomores at the

University of South Florida, and it was possible they had occasioned across one another in brief, anonymous passing. Hugo would later insist that was the case, vowing that he remembered every time he sighted her. Kim remained doubtful, since she now knew him to have what could be kindly described as a "selective" short-term memory.

Nevertheless, they did eventually learn each other's name when they shared the same sophomore seminar class. Honors Seminar in Practical Ethics.

The class was intriguing, and quite untraditional, striving to "free conventionally educated students and encourage them to educate themselves by otherwise unconventional means"—or so their professor always told them. Kim had learned Hugo's name, and Hugo hers, as their freewheeling professor called on students in a random, haphazard, and absurdly humorous fashion. They never directly spoke or responded to one another in class, a feat usually impossible in a seminar setting. Yet no one, including Hugo and Kim, noticed.

Their true encounter came just before their first group meeting to discuss a mid-term class project. Kim, as was her personality, arrived at their meeting place in the Marshall Student Center a few minutes before the agreed upon time, yet she would soon realize that she was the second among her group to show up.

"Hey, man—!"

Kim heard someone curse and stopped short of the doorway.

"Just get out of here, *pendejo*, before you regret it."

Kim recognized the barely controlled comeback as her classmate's. She brazenly turned the corner and stood at the entrance to the room.

"Hugo?"

Nineteen-year-old Hugo Jimenez, his back toward the door, turned abruptly at hearing his name.

"Kimberly?"

She stared past Hugo to the gangly boy standing behind him.

"What's going on?"

"Nothing I can't handle, *Hermosa*," Hugo remarked, smirking as he turned back to the other boy in the room.

Neither Kim nor the other boy spoke Spanish.

"You think you can handle me now, huh?" the gangly youth said, glaring daggers at Hugo.

"You make a move, and I'll show you how much I can handle," Hugo answered before cursing again.

The two boys edged closer.

"You're nothing," the other boy sneered. "I've got no idea how you were even allowed to come to this school, much less—"

"Hey!"

Both boys looked to Kim, who, unobserved, had moved to stand right beside them. She stared at both of them before her gaze settled on the boy opposite Hugo.

"What's your deal?" she asked, her tone level.

The stranger glared at Hugo as he answered.

"I was just asking *him*"—the gangly boy emphasized the pronoun—"if I could use the room—"

Kim cut him off.

"We've already reserved this room for a class project. You can check with the help desk downstairs if you don't believe me."

"I told you," Hugo spat, issuing another swear word.

"Stop cursing," Kim directed, glancing at him, to which Hugo fell silent.

The other boy's jaw clenched as he looked from Kim to Hugo and back again. After a moment, he readjusted the book bag on his back and made to walk out of the room, mumbling a curse in Hugo's direction as he passed. Hugo made obnoxious kissing sounds toward the boy's retreating form. Kim crossed her arms and rolled her eyes at the adolescent display—a gesture she would rely on frequently in later years in response to some of Hugo's actions.

Once the other boy was out of sight, she circled around to Hugo, who continued to stare toward the empty doorway.

Realizing he was not going to explain himself, she decided to prompt him.

"Well?"

Hugo stayed silent.

She arched her eyebrow in inquiry.

Finally, he relented.

"He was being an as—"

"Yeah, I got that. Stop cursing."

She paused, then added, "What was that word you called me earlier?"

Hugo's face tensed briefly, but then he smirked as he replied, "'*Pendejo*' means as—"

"Stop it," she said sternly, hitting him on the shoulder. "I'm serious. That's what you called him. The other word—you were looking at me when you said it. 'It's nothing I can't handle, hemosa, hemosan'—something. What does that mean?"

Hugo's lips curved upward.

"You seem like a bright USF student," he offered snidely. "Why don't you just look it up when you get back to your room? And, by the way, it's pronounced '*herm-o-sa*.'"

"Fine," Kim said. "In that case…"

Literally turning up her nose, she walked to the front of the meeting room and set her book bag on the tabletop.

Pulling out a power cable, she said, "I'm so glad I remembered to bring my laptop with me."

The boy was now visibly grimacing, but Kim grinned at him cheekily, her eyebrows arched—the same provocative grin that would be directed toward him again and again in months and years to come. She turned back to her laptop and pressed the power button.

"'*Hermosa*,' you said?" she asked rhetorically, not looking back at him. She did not see Hugo bring a hand to his face and drag it slowly downward, briefly stretching his facial features in the process.

She did hear him curse yet again under his breath.

"I heard that."

Kim swung to look at him as she waited for her computer to boot.

"Of course you did," Hugo acknowledged, softer still, his hand still rubbing his jaw. "You hear everything."

She soon discovered that *hermosa* meant "beautiful," and now, close to seven years later, he still called her that. She glanced at her illuminated cartoon watch again and then brought her arm back down, unbuckling her seat belt.

After closing the car door, Kim started for the tavern entrance, glancing up at the nighttime desert sky. In the clear, cloudless night, infinite twinkling stars were visible. At the tavern door, she tilted her ear to the entryway.

Must be naptime, she thought, not hearing any commotion from inside. She cautiously pulled one of the oaken doors open and stepped in, using some of her weight to keep the door ajar. Everyone's attention was directed to the bar at the back of the saloon.

"—gas pumps outside are operational, and if I needed to pay upfront," she heard her husband say.

A short man with some type of tattoo on his forehead answered him back in insults.

Even from where she was standing, Kim noticed Hugo tense. She watched his jawline sharpen and clench, knowing from experience that he was about to explode.

"*Eso es todo, comemierda.* I told you—"

"Hugo?"

She said it even before she was completely aware of her decision to announce herself. Everyone in the barroom turned abruptly in her direction, but she kept her focus on her husband. Hugo's eyes were wide as he spun toward the doorway.

"Kimberly?"

HIS SUBSTANTIALLY LARGE FRAME in a tavern full of relatively large motorcycle gang members notwithstanding, Lex's movements were unnoticed as he headed for the saloon entrance. Barring some utterly random motorist—an incredibly unfortunate traveler arriving at Joe's Roadhouse Tavern at that instant—he knew exactly who would be coming in next, and he wanted to be at, or very near, the door when that particular visitor entered. Like his partner, Imani, at the counter, he had taken a few glances at his handbook concerning this assignment.

As if on cue, a car door closed outside.

Kimberly Jimenez would soon be making an appearance, as she most likely sensed her husband was in some sort of trouble.

Lex moved along the barroom wall, behind the turned backs of the patrons. Ornamental chains attached to his clothing swayed with his movements but failed to alert anyone with the dissonant noise of metal clinking on metal. The earrings that crowded each of his ears did not make a sound either.

He was but a few feet away from his objective—*close enough*, he thought—when the door opened almost silently. Kim's entrance was stealthy enough not to divert attention away from the argument at the counter. Lex paused, leaning back against the wall, only a couple of arm lengths away.

He kept his attention on Kim as the scene at the bar intensified, watching her relax just slightly when she spotted her husband.

"Who ya think ya talkin' to, huh? Who ya think ya talkin' to? Think ya might wanna stop worryin' 'bout the damn gas, Speedy Gonzalez, and start—"

He saw Kim's eyes widen—perhaps in reaction to the insult, or perhaps in reaction to Hugo.

"*Eso es todo, comemierda ...*"

Kim's eyes grew wider still, her mouth forming a word.

Here it comes. The thought breezed through Lex's mind.

"I told you—"

"Hugo?" Kim said.

Lex felt the focus of the room shift suddenly to the tavern doors where the young woman stood.

"Kimberly?" Hugo's tone echoed his disbelief.

And—

There.

Lex saw it immediately.

At the front of the bar.

Hostile movement.

TIME SEEMED CONDENSED, HOURS worth of conversation elapsing in mere minutes. Sitting between the two mysterious visitors, Whitney Rainier did most of the talking. There, on the couch, in the quiet of the house, she was shrouded in a blanket of calm. As the three conversed, Whitney could feel her despair begin to ease, replaced by something else.

Compassion. And relief.

She felt no need to address the pair by name, and neither volunteered any such information. It was not needed. Whitney understood why they were there, and that was enough. She found the man's voice and demeanor just as calm and soothing as the woman's; so easy was it for her to talk to them that her thoughts, feelings, and emotions seemed to flow out of her mouth unconstrained. The abyss she had floundered in since Jackson and Savannah Hawes arrived at her modest doorstep with their earth-shattering news was no longer one she had to navigate alone.

The man and the woman now sitting with her on the couch lightened her burden, pulling her out of the darkness and into the light once more.

"I just don't know about Maria and Skylar, though," Whitney said quietly. "I don't know if I can be ... I'm not sure I'm strong enough by myself, strong enough for both of them."

"Being strong enough for yourself," the strikingly handsome man offered, as he held one of Whitney's hands, "means you are strong enough for them. I don't have a doubt that you are strong enough, but it's all right if you do. That's why we're here."

As he finished speaking, he and the beautiful woman that had accompanied him turned to the hallway that led to the bedrooms. Whitney, with her face tilted downward, did not notice. An instant later, a small head appeared from around the corner.

"Mommy?" Maria called sleepily.

Whitney turned at the voice of her daughter, watching the child attempt to rub the grogginess from her eyes.

"I looked in your room, and I didn't see you," Maria continued.

"I'm sorry, Night. Is everything okay?"

"What are you doing?"

"I was just"—Whitney shot a quick glance in the woman's direction, who smiled and shook her head gently—"I was just thinking, sweetie. Are you all right? Is anything wrong?"

"No," the little girl responded, her face beginning to contort humorously. "I just wanted to see if"—she yawned—"you were … still here."

Whitney smiled, though she herself could feel it was somewhat saddened. Her eyes watered again.

"I'm here, Maria," she said, only just keeping her voice from breaking. "I'm here."

She rose from the couch and moved to the hallway where her daughter stood, her two visitors following closely.

"Are you ready to go back to bed, now?" Whitney asked, offering her hand.

The little girl nodded and took it. Together, the two walked back to the children's bedroom, with the man and woman trailing silently.

Maria's bed hugged the wall next to the door. Skylar, still asleep, lay on his bed on the far side of the room. He faced away from the door, his body curled into a ball under his covers.

Maria slid between the bedsheets as her mother held them open. Whitney tucked the sheets in tightly, the way Maria liked, and kneeled down beside the bed as she always did, bringing her face close to the reclining child. Both visitors kneeled as well— the woman lowering herself beside Whitney, facing Maria's bedside, the man on his knees closer to Skylar's slumbering form.

Maria, tucked in once more, looked at her mother with drooping eyelids.

"Are you okay?" she whispered, turning the inquiry back on her mother.

Whitney smiled and stroked her daughter's dark hair.

"I'm okay if you're okay."

Maria smiled faintly, already beginning to drift.

"What if I'm not okay?" she asked, her voice fading.

Whitney leaned in closer.

"Then I'll be okay for both of us until I can make sure you're okay again."

She placed a faithful kiss on the child's forehead. When she pulled back, her daughter's breathing was already even with sleep.

Whitney turned to Skylar's bed. Both her son and the man who had come to console her met her gaze, though Skylar was unaware of the man's presence. Whitney scooted over to Skylar's bedside, and the scene was reversed—the man now beside Whitney and his partner remaining beside Maria. The woman maintained her watch over the little girl with her elbows resting on the bed and her hands placed under her chin, mirroring the man's posture from moments before.

Whitney leaned in close to her son and looked into his eyes, waiting to see if he would speak. The boy gazed back, sleepy yet inquisitive, silently asking a question that both his mother and the man beside her easily translated. Whitney answered with a heartening smile, stroking the boy's head as she had with Maria. Skylar's lips upturned as well, his eyelids fluttering closed, and the routine was completed with another light, maternal kiss on the forehead.

Whitney, still on her knees, her hands clasped loosely in her lap, leaned back and positioned herself to observe both children. Muted lighting from the moon and streetlamps outdoors penetrated the half-drawn blinds, illuminating the bedroom with a soft orange glow. Both outside and inside, drifting sounds and stray noises were absent. A gentle, calming hush remained.

Help me, Whitney said silently to herself.

At that moment, she heard a familiar chuckle behind her. "Okay."

At her husband's whisper, Whitney spun, her heart instantly pumping at a hurried pace.

In the shadows of the children's bedroom stood a man: her husband, the love of her life and the father of her children, Jack Rainier. His clothing, his posture, his expression—it was all there, all that she remembered and would never forget, standing a few feet away and watching her kneeling form with a mischievous smirk, as though all was perfectly fine and he had never left.

As though the entire horrible episode had been exactly that, a staged experience she had just awakened from, and now she would be thrust back into her happy, normal world, her family intact and together again.

As though it were the most twisted, sickening prank "My Two Jacks" had ever come up with, and only now was the joke revealed, once she had suffered enough.

If only that were the truth.

Whitney gave a strangled cry as she struggled to her feet and lunged at him. He caught her, as he always did, and, enveloped in his arms once more, she began to weep uncontrollably. In that moment, she did not care how loud her cries were, nor that her slumbering children—her and Jack's slumbering children—lay peacefully behind her. In that moment, it did not matter. Jack wrapped his arms around her tightly, firmly, lovingly, and she clung to him, her face buried in the hollow below his collarbone.

In that moment, his voice, his face, did for her what no one else's ever could—it gave her reason to believe that everything truly would be all right.

"Help you?" he asked playfully, chuckling still. "I think you're confused, Mrs. Rainier. You were always the strong one. I believe in you. Maria and Skylar believe in you. You're going to do just fine; I know it. I'll always love you, and I'll always be proud of you."

WHITNEY JUMPED SLIGHTLY. MARIA shifted beside her on the living room couch, seeking a more comfortable position in her sleep. The faint push was enough to bring Whitney out of her trance and back to reality.

She looked down at her two sleeping children, and a sense of déjà vu overtook her. Strangely, she also felt a sense of comfort.

Unexpectedly, a new chapter in their lives was soon to begin.

But now, Whitney Rainier felt they would be ready to face it.

WHILE LEX SAW THE movement, Imani felt it.

Like a silent predator, able to detect even the slightest disturbance in her vicinity, the first twitch of muscle behind her was all the warning Imani needed.

Anyone watching the scene play out would call it a lucky guess.

She and Lex knew better.

Imani had not turned at Kim Jimenez's interruption, instead continuing to stare into the cloudy drink in front of her. A subtle change in Hugo's inflection, however, brought her eyes away from the glass.

The difference was his orientation. While speaking to Sims, Hugo's voice had been directed to Imani's ear. When Hugo spotted Kim, his voice modulated slightly, concentrated away from Imani toward the saloon entrance. In all, it amounted to a quarter-turn of his head. The difference was minor, almost insignificant, but more than enough for Imani to note.

It was also enough for Sims to take a chance.

That was when Imani felt the shift—the same initial, discordant twitch that Lex had immediately noted across the cavernous, crowded tavern. It was almost a flinch, and most likely instinctual on Sims's part, so abruptly quick that his body hardly distinguished its occurrence.

Imani was already responding, already reacting; the rest of Sims's effort was already a foregone conclusion. If the twitch amounted to a ripple of disturbance for Imani, Sims's fist clench was a tidal wave.

Imani twisted in her seat, readying to meet Sims's sucker punch with a surprise of her own. Her revolution was effortless, lithe, swift, nearly instantaneous—or it would have been for anyone observing her. To Imani, however, her response was choreographed, measured, practiced, and progressing in slow motion. As she moved, she caught a fleeting, split-second glimpse of Dexter Toohey at the end of the bar.

He was looking directly at her.

Imani brought her hand up as she spun, her palm open, maneuvering past Hugo, who stood directly behind her. Hugo was facing away from the punch Sims aimed at him, his attention focused on his wife. Sims had not noticed Imani's lightning-fast reaction either, as he was focused on making solid, bone-crunching contact with Hugo's jaw.

Her palm caught the biker's fist in mid-flight, still about a foot from its intended target. The stop was brick-wall immediate—terminal, abrupt, like an object in complete freefall speeding through the air only to be met with the concrete surface below.

There was a sharp, cracking sound.

Across the room, Lex grinned.

"Aaahh!" Sims yelled at the instant pain of snapping bone. He swore loudly as Imani closed her hand around his fist, securing it in place without applying additional pressure.

Yet.

Everyone else in the saloon frozen in shock, Hugo spun quickly, instinctively dodging before he noticed that the hands close to his face were not moving. Also instinctive was his attempted counterpunch.

"Stop," Imani ordered calmly, sensing the punch without bothering to glance in Hugo's direction.

Hugo's fist paused in mid-air as he restrained his strike.

"Hugo!" came Kim's worried call from the entrance.

"Aaahh!" Sims continued to yell and curse his agony, his fist held in Imani's grip.

Imani turned to Hugo, whose clenched fist was still raised in the air, his pupils dilated.

"Put your hand down," she issued softly.

Hugo's hand slowly lowered.

"Joe," Imani said, switching her gaze to the barkeep. His eyes, usually narrowed slits that gave him a wizened appearance to match his vintage clothing and his Wild West tavern, were now completely circular. Like the rest of the crowd inside the bar, his stupefied gaze was on Sims's fist, still seized in Imani's hand, and his mouth hung open slightly.

"Joe."

More moments passed without response.

"Joe," Imani said yet again, more forcefully.

This brought about the appropriate reaction.

"Huh? Ah, uh, what?"

Imani nodded at Hugo.

"Ask your question again, Mr. Jimenez," she said in her usual unruffled monotone, her gaze returning to a cringing Sims.

"I ... I just came in here to ask," Hugo began again, taking another look at Imani, "how to work your gas pumps outside."

Joe, clearly still flustered, replied, "Uh, ye—uh..."

Toohey's raspy voice interrupted the bartender's stammering.

"Key. There's a key. Hand 'em one of the keys, Joe."

"Key, yeah."

Joe finally snapped out of it. He cleared his throat.

"Yeah, the key. Yeah."

After locating it on a panel underneath the bar, he handed it over to Hugo.

"Yeah, uh, just use the key there, an', uh, yeah, that'll get 'er goin'."

Hugo glanced down at the key, then to Imani, and then back to the bartender.

"Do I pay now, or—"

"No, no, no," Joe said, waving his hands and shaking his head. "No charge. It's on th'—"

His gaze moved back to Imani's hand.

"It's on th' house."

"Please, please, okay, okay, please, please…"

With Imani looking at him, Sims attempted to curtail his curses, but he could not stop the whimpers. The pain was too intense. Despite his earlier rough-and-tumble posturing, Imani wondered how many altercations the man had been involved in by himself, if any.

Still studying the Rebel Fist rider, she directed her question to Hugo.

"Are you ready to go now?"

Hugo hesitated, but only briefly.

"Yeah."

Imani nodded at the door.

"Your wife is waiting."

Hugo, still clutching the key, started moving.

"W-wife?" Sims sputtered in disbelief.

Hugo froze mid-stride.

"Oh, no," said Kim, at the entrance.

Beside her, Lex grinned again.

"How does a fu—ahhhh!"

Sims's screams filled the tavern as Imani tightened her grip on his hand ever so slightly to send white-hot, searing pain coursing though his knuckles, wrist, and forearm. The Rebel Fist rider squeezed his eyes shut, but did not dare move away from the eerily composed woman who crippled him. No one else in the bar dared try to assist.

Imani kept her expression unreadable.

"Keep walking, Hugo," she said louder through a break in Sims's agonized screaming.

Hugo resumed his pace.

"Ahh! Please!" Sims cried. "Please! Please! Ahh!"

Throughout, he continued to curse.

As the young Latino approached his equally young, strawberry blond wife, his head turned toward Lex, noticing the man's nearness. Guarded, he stared into the large man's eyes.

"It's okay," Kim said quietly, reassuring him. "He's with her." She gestured to Imani at the bar.

Hugo gazed at Lex a moment longer, and Lex nodded. Hugo, his shoulders easing again, relented. He turned to his wife, clutching her lightly.

"Are you okay?" His voice was a rough whisper. "Kim?"

Kim nodded. "I'm fine. I'm fine. I was worried. You were taking a long time."

Lex maneuvered behind them and opened the door.

"Your gas pump awaits," he said in a gruffly courteous tone.

Hugo nodded his thanks, and then hurried his wife through the door, not looking back. Lex followed, his considerable frame shielding any view of Hugo and Kim from those inside.

At the bar, Imani was the image of detached ruthlessness as she held Sims's fractured fist in her grasp, studying him. Sims had managed to bring his agonized sniveling down to a low moan.

"Why did you do that?" Imani questioned.

Sims turned his head only slightly in her direction, avoiding direct eye contact.

"Please ... aaah ... aah ... please..."

"You tried to instigate a fight. Twice."

She leaned in closer.

"Why is that?"

"I ... ahh ... uh, I—aaahhhhh!"

Imani lightly intensified her hold. Sims's hand seemed on the verge of actually crumbling, and he swore loudly.

"Aaahhh! I don't do ... we don't ... I ..."

Imani tilted her braided head to the side, curious.

"No, no, no, no! Wait! Wait! We don't ... ahh ... we don't really ... 'sociate with ..."

His eyes darted around nervously.

"Look, you gotta ... you gotta understand, lady. We don't usually..."

Sims closed his eyes again and moaned.

"Yeah," Imani muttered. She suddenly released his broken hand, the hasty release nearly as agonizing as an increase in pressure.

"Ahhhhh!" Sims yelled.

He bent forward, collapsing to the floor, cradling his mangled hand to his chest.

Imani's eyes found Toohey's.

This isn't right, she thought as she looked at him, his face just as unreadable as her own. *Sims wasn't the assignment. He wasn't the reason we came.*

You were.

Everyone in the tavern—excluding Sims, sniveling and kneeling on the ground—stood motionless, still stunned, watching Imani's every move as she turned to the proprietor behind the countertop.

"You okay, Joe?"

The bartender jumped.

"Yeah, yeah. I'm okay. I'm okay."

Imani indicated Toohey.

"I think he was asking for a refill earlier."

"Yeah, you got it—I mean, yeah. Comin' right up."

The tense air in the barroom lessened, but only a little. Imani knew the tavern would not return to normal until she and Lex were long gone.

Joe was finishing with Toohey's drink when the sound of the tavern door opening again turned everyone around.

Lex's hulking figure filled the doorway. Eyes followed his lumbering passage to the bar, where he presented the barkeep with the gas key before turning to his partner, smirking.

"What's up?" he asked, his amusement apparent.

Before Imani could verbally respond, the wounded Rebel Fist member on the ground interjected.

"And you're, ahh … you're with her?"

Pain was evident in the man's shaky voice, but so was a lingering trace of malice.

A soft curse issued from someone else in the barroom, the first response since Imani had stopped Sims's punch.

"Would you shut up, Sims?" another rider muttered.

Sims grimaced and readjusted his wrist.

Lex looked down at him, his expression as inquisitive as Imani's had been earlier.

"I think you're goin' to need that checked out."

"Think so?" another rider mumbled sarcastically. Further evidence that tension was still unmistakably present.

Lex chuckled heartily, holding up his hands in mock surrender. Imani rolled her eyes and strode to the center of the saloon.

"Okay," she started. "I am only going to say this once. None of you will remember what you saw here tonight. That is not a veiled threat; it is simply a fact. No one will remember him"— she gestured to Lex—"and no one will remember me. None of you will remember the couple who just left. The only reason I am telling you any of this is because of what I say next."

She made sure she locked eyes with each person in the barroom.

"All of you will remember this warning. All of you will remember this lesson. But, of course, it is up to you whether you choose to follow it. The next time any of you see either of us, you will remember this moment. You will remember exactly what I am telling you right now. If that encounter were to take place, I assure you the experience would be gravely unpleasant."

Her eyes lingered on one burly biker in particular before she looked back to her partner, who still leaned on the bar.

"You ready?"

"Yo," Lex replied.

Reaching into his pockets, he pulled out wads of money he had collected from his earlier billiard wins. He put them in a crumpled pile on the countertop and nudged them in Joe's direction.

"Thanks for the beer. Put my friend's watered-down"—he leaned over to inspect Imani's glass and frowned—"whatever, on that, too."

He pushed himself away from the counter.

"But that's—that's way too much," Joe told Lex's retreating back.

"Gratuity!" Lex called back, waving his hand.

"But still, it's—"

"Have a good 'un!"

When they reached the door, Lex held it open for Imani to pass. She paused, looking back into the bar. Her partner followed her gaze.

Dexter Toohey was the only person not watching them. Taking a deep swig from his frosted mug, he stared down at the countertop in front of him, tracing his finger over the polished wood. He seemed to have dismissed their presence before they had even left the tavern. Imani considered the rider's lounging figure a moment longer before she exited.

Now outside, Lex stopped to stand beside her as the door closed behind them.

"Where are they headed?" Imani asked, quickly shifting her focus.

"Still going to visit her parents in Arizona, crazy kids. But they're going to stop at one of the hotels in the next town. Speakin' of which...you know how far that drive is from southern Florida? Why they didn't choose to just fly is beyond me, but they had to have taken a wrong turn. If they had stayed on the interstate coming out of—"

He stopped as he noticed Imani's expression.

"I say we go with them," she said. "Make sure they get to the hotel okay."

A grin appeared through Lex's beard. He stared down the road in the direction Kim and Hugo Jimenez had taken.

"Nothing else is happenin', you know. They've got a full tank, which is the only reason they stopped in the first place, so—"

Imani did not try to conceal the slight upturn of her own lips.

"So we go with them," she said again.

Lex gave a deep chuckle.

"So we go with them," he repeated.

They stepped off the porch and onto the gravel of the parking lot. Lex snapped his fingers.

Somewhere in the lot, a motorcycle roared to life.

INSIDE JOE'S ROADHOUSE TAVERN, the mood was pure Texas-bred saloon—casual without being too disorderly, lively without getting too disruptive. The scene was typical, with a scattering of groups congregated around busy pool tables, some lounging and laughing near television sets, and several lined along the length of the mahogany counter. There was laughing and talking, jokes along with conversations dealing with content more serious. Joe, the namesake and proprietor, presided behind the bar.

The Rebel Fist Motorcycle Club was in attendance tonight, a telling indicator being the large contingent of Rebel Fist motorcycles parked outside, and the equally large number of Club members found within the tavern. One of the Rebel Fist cadre had a shattered hand—visibly disfigured—most likely the consequence of some dim-witted, god-awful display of macho recklessness. Others—in fact, most—of his fellow bikers had been in a similar condition at one time or another, so the injury came as no big surprise. As the night progressed, the numbing effects of alcohol took the place of any immediate medical treatment. The hand could wait until morning to be checked out properly.

Another of the Rebel Fist ridership took only occasional sips of whatever drink was in front of him, only half-listening to the discussions he appeared to be a part of. He responded at the appropriate breaks, but his mind was elsewhere.

Dexter Toohey took the time to draw another small swallow from his mug and then set his drink down again. He resumed tracing imaginary, incoherent lines and figures on the countertop.

On the eighteenth floor of the sleek office building, Emily Hendricks straightened the disarray of documents on her desk as her lunch break loomed closer. She placed a small packet of papers into an artfully decorated, hand-woven tray set to one corner of her desk, and kept the rest near the center, in front of her computer, to look over when she returned. Then she turned the monitor off, knowing the machine would automatically fall into sleep mode in five minutes anyway.

She had been with the company only four years, straight out of college, but the office—spacious, although not expansively so—was part of an extraordinarily quick promotion for her high-quality, expedient work and was now decorated with her own keepsakes and personal touches. It also included a near wall-to-wall view of the downtown Albuquerque cityscape.

Not bad.

That was what her father had told her a month or so before, when he had visited her workplace to treat her to lunch. He had driven more than ninety miles to get there, and as he gazed around her office and out at the panoramic Burque skyline, Emily noticed her father's stern, disciplined façade crack with obvious appreciation and pride.

"Not bad," he said. "Not too bad at all."

She had floated on air for the rest of the day—actually, the rest of the week. It was the greatest compliment her father could have given.

Now, she glanced over to the clock affixed to the opposite wall.

12:59.

She grabbed her handbag right as someone knocked on her already open door and stepped in.

"Hey, girl," Cassandra greeted, glancing down into her own purse briefly. "Are we still on for Plácido's?"

"Oh, yeah," Emily replied, rising from her comfortable office chair. "I've been waiting for one o' clock all day."

"I know, right?" Cassandra agreed. "I can already taste the quesadillas melting in my mouth."

"Stop it," Emily said, chuckling. "It's like you're in my head."

The two left Emily's office, making their way out into the sizable outer office area, filled with open desks and cubicles. Cassandra, though a few years younger, had been working for the firm nearly as long as Emily. The younger woman could easily pass for a high school student, and sometimes did, to her annoyance. Emily joked that seeing her friend in a professional setting served to make her resemble a sophisticated high school senior instead of an inexperienced sophomore or freshman. Typically, Cassandra did not find Emily's jokes all that funny.

Cassandra reached the bank of elevators first and pressed the call button.

"So," she said, running her hands through her hair, "was that part of the Delaney script I saw in your outbox?"

"One and the same," Emily replied, "and if you wouldn't mind handing it off to Mr. Edwards, that would probably save me a lot of—"

"Well, hello ladies."

Another coworker approached the elevators. Cassandra looked back at her friend and rolled her eyes.

"Karlton," Emily addressed him, clearly unenthused.

"Oh, no need to be so formal, Emily."

The man's smirk was lecherous as his gaze shifted between the two women.

"You can both call me Karl."

The elevators slid open.

"If I wanted to be formal, Karlton," Emily said, as all three stepped into the compartment, "I would have referred to you as Mr. Atkins, now wouldn't I?"

Karl pressed the button for the lobby and the doors slid closed.

"Mr. Atkins actually doesn't sound so bad when you say it. Okay, you can use Karl or Mr. Atkins. I don't mind."

His eyes moved to Cassandra.

"You too, Cassie."

Cassandra kept her eyes straight ahead, on the gold-toned elevator doors.

"I think I'll stick with Karlton."

The descending elevator car slowed, and then stopped on the fourteenth floor. The doors opened to reveal one of the heads of the company, Aemetri Edwards.

"Ah, three of my favorite associates," he declared warmly as he entered. He immediately turned to Emily, the elevator doors closing promptly once more.

"Miss Hendricks, do I accurately recall you saying you would have the manuscript from that Delaney character to me sometime later today?"

"Yes, sir. Actually, I heard you would be out of the office until later, but I can have it in your hands as soon as I return from—"

"That's just great, then! By chance, is it in your masterfully woven outbox? Beautiful craftsmanship, Miss Hendricks, if I may say so. I may stop by and pick it up when I go back upstairs. Would that be all right?"

Before Emily could respond in the affirmative, Mr. Edwards turned his attention to Cassandra.

"Ah, Mrs. Hope! An absolutely splendid suggestion on that canary note."

He leaned in closer, grinning and whispering conspiratorially, "Don't look now, but I believe that office a few doors down from Miss Hendricks has your name on it! And I have heard that particular office comes with a nice bounce in the checkbook as well."

"Gosh, thank you so much, Mr. Edwards," Cassandra replied, half startled by the older man's quick tongue. "But you—"

"Hendricks and Hope, Hope and Hendricks," Mr. Edwards went on merrily. "What a pleasant ring that has, hmm?"

"And, Mr. Atkins," he went on, as the elevator reached the lobby level with a soft *ding*, "do you have a moment? Some colleagues recently inquired as to your admirable work on the Phillip Wilson project last week, and I would be just delighted to show you off in their snotty little faces."

The group stepped out of the elevator, Emily and Cassandra snickering softly.

Karl glanced at them briefly before returning to Mr. Edwards.

"Actually, sir, I was just off to lunch with Emily and—"

Emily's breath caught in her throat. Both she and Cassandra looked at Karl with stricken expressions, though Mr. Edwards did not seem to notice.

"Oh, this will only take a few moments, Mr. Atkins," Mr. Edwards promised, waving him off. "Then you'll be on your way. I'm sure these lovely ladies will save you a seat at..."

He turned to the two women expectantly. Karl's eyes shifted eagerly to the pair as well.

Emily froze. Karl knowing where she and Cassandra would be eating—and then incessantly bothering them—was too much to cope with. Fortunately, her friend was quick to provide an answer.

"The usual place," Cassandra said, flashing a pretty smile at the men.

Mr. Edwards slapped the Karl on the back, beaming.

"See, Mr. Atkins?" he assured Karl. "The usual place. Now, her office is right this way..."

The senior man ushered Karl away from the elevators, still talking excitedly and taking no notice of Karl's reluctance and fleeting backward glances.

Cassandra and Emily grinned and waved.

"Bye, Karlton!" they teased, both grateful their high-spirited boss had saved them from Karl's bothersome presence, even if he had also nearly doomed them too, and all in a matter of seconds.

"We should probably get Mr. Edwards a gift for that," Emily said as they walked to the exit, all smiles again.

"And then take it from him, and then immediately give it back to him again," Cassandra laughed. "It's only fair."

CHARLIE LOOKED UP FROM *A Flying Penguin* to watch Sandy Ellsbury—"Miss Sandy," as the Brown siblings and their friends called her—cross the threshold into the sunroom and place a plate of sliced apples on the table. The pleasantly gregarious older woman, whose name stemmed from her seemingly eternal sandy-blonde hair, settled into the couch, reclining next to the teenager.

"So," Charlie, Caleb, and Colby's loving caretaker of nearly six years began, "do you want to go to Bahia Bay tomorrow after dinner? I was thinking of asking the boys. We could all make a night of it—you know, cause a little public disorder, maybe get arrested, whatever comes to mind."

The large, curving windows of the sunroom offered ample lighting, which highlighted the blonde tresses of both Charlie and Miss Sandy and provided a picturesque view of the landscape behind the Ellsbury residence—a well-manicured yard with bordering foliage and the blue waters of the bay beyond. The vantage point was rivaled only by a similar room directly above, on the second floor. Either space made for a relaxing sitting area and was also ideal for study sessions during the school year.

The teenager raised her eyebrows at Miss Sandy's offer.

"You had me at arrested," Charlie replied.

Miss Sandy chuckled. She then nodded at the book Charlie was holding.

"You've already gotten that far?" she asked incredulously. "I thought you just started that the other day?"

"Actually, I probably should have finished it by now, but I haven't opened it since I went to McCormick Park with Caleb and Colby a few days ago. You know those books you can't seem to put down because they are just so fascinating?"

Miss Sandy's eyes widened.

"Really, it's that good? And here I was getting the impression you didn't like it very much, since you never talk about it. What is it about? I'm guessing a penguin of some sort, probably of the aerial variety?"

Charlie grinned.

"That would be a very good guess, Miss Sandy, but ... you didn't let me finish. It's why I'm not done reading it yet. Anyways, those stories I was talking about, the ones you read from cover to cover in, like, a few hours or something? *A Flying Penguin* is absolutely, definitely, completely not one of those stories, even though I'm sure Raven probably read it all on the trip up to Tanglewood because she's weird like that—"

"That's right," Miss Sandy cut in at the mention of Charlie's friend. "The music camp in Tanglewood. When is she getting back again?"

Charlie shrugged. "I think she's up there for another week, but I always lose track. Anyway, I'm just—"

Miss Sandy interrupted again.

"You know, I've heard The Berkshires are just lovely this time of year."

Charlie looked at her pointedly.

"Anyway," she started again, stressing the word and noticing Miss Sandy's grin, "I put it off for a few days, but I'm thinking now it would just be better to get through it as quickly as possible, like taking off a Band-Aid. It's much more painful if you draw it out slowly."

Miss Sandy laughed aloud.

"Oh, way to overdramatize. My poor Charlie."

"And no," Charlie went on, "it's not about a flying penguin, a walking penguin, or any kind of penguin. There is no penguin. No penguin, you hear me? Besides the title, I don't remember even seeing the word 'penguin.'"

She paused, taking in Miss Sandy's amusement.

"It's not funny, Miss Sandy! I think this teacher is playing some sort of sick joke. It's that terrible. But this boy at the park, who I guess had Mrs. Ethridge when he was a freshman, said he wouldn't be surprised if she were committed to an insane asylum in the near future, so I'm assuming this summer assignment is one, big, crazy, awful prank."

Tirade over, Charlie looked back down at the page, shaking her head. A moment passed, the only audible sound the steady *tick-tock* of the ageless grandfather clock that stood sentinel near the door.

"'Boy at the park'?" Miss Sandy repeated.

Charlie, slowly, carefully, lifted her gaze to the woman seated on the cushion next to her. She was met with a knowing smile.

"Hmm?" Missy Sandy intoned, as though the teenager had said something.

"I didn't say anything," Charlie responded, arching her eyebrow again.

"Oh." Miss Sandy shrugged, a playful smile on her lips. "Okay."

After another silent moment, Charlie exhaled loudly, shifting her gaze back to her book.

More silence.

"You can look at me all you want," Charlie muttered. "I don't care. Doesn't bother me at all."

Soon, after her third attempt at rereading the same paragraph proved just as unsuccessful as the previous two, she looked up again. Miss Sandy met her gaze once more.

Charlie rolled her eyes and sighed.

"You're not really going to do this to me, are you?"

Sandy Ellsbury grinned.

"I guess it's like you said. 'It's much more painful if you draw it out slowly.'"

"Who's drawing it out?" Charlie burst out, exasperated. "I was talking about Mrs. Ethridge!"

"Oh. So the 'boy in the park' was just some random, strange stalker-guy who all of a sudden came up to you and started talking about a book you say is terrible? Whew, I'm so glad you cleared it all up, because that makes me feel much better."

Charlie sighed once more.

"It was just a boy who goes to Norbury," she explained, "or, at least, he acted like he did. I thought I mentioned him before."

Miss Sandy tapped the side of her face with her finger.

"Hmm, nope. No mention of boys at all, although I did receive a rousing play-by-play on a Saturn V rocket explosion from your brothers, which, frankly, I'm amazed I didn't hear about on the local news. But I digress. Did this 'boy in the park' offer an actual name, or did he specifically request that you refer to him as 'boy in the park?'"

Charlie moaned again. She flipped *A Flying Penguin* over, saving her place, and twisted herself so that her head thumped back against the corner of the sofa.

"This isn't happening," she murmured to herself. "This is just some weird dream—or nightmare."

She was swiftly impacted with something soft as Miss Sandy flung a throw pillow at her head.

"This is not a nightmare, young lady!" the woman announced loudly, causing Charlie to laugh despite herself.

Miss Sandy's voice returned to a more reasonable volume.

"In any case, I don't believe I was the one who brought up the 'boy in the park.'"

Charlie crushed the cushion against her face to muffle her maddened scream.

"Argh! I wasn't even talking about him!" she said, once she had removed the pillow. "I was talking about the crazy teacher! Crazy—like you!"

She glanced over at Miss Sandy.

"And why does it sound as though you're putting 'boy in the park' in air quotes?"

"Probably because I am," Miss Sandy replied. "But I didn't force you to mention any boys in any parks. You included that little tidbit yourself. You could have said—I don't know—'I heard ...' or, 'Rumor is ...' but no. You thought I needed to know that the 'boy in the park' said it. In the medical world, my dear Charlize Brown, that's called 'a slip of the tongue.'"

Charlie rolled her eyes again with great exaggeration.

"Okay, Dr. Ellsbury," she chided. "First off, I think the non-medical world calls it a 'slip of the tongue,' too. Second, I think you may need to take a break from all of those courtroom dramas."

"Your Honor, the witness is obstructing!" Miss Sandy said with dramatic flair. "Please instruct her to answer the question before the court!"

"Overruled!" Charlie declared, playing along. "The witness has already answered your question by giving the aforementioned 'boy in the park' as the original source behind the issue of Mrs. Ethridge's sanity. I think it would behoove the court that you move on, Dr. Ellsbury."

Miss Sandy smirked.

"Who's watching all of those courtroom dramas, you say?" she asked, eyes twinkling.

"More like listening to you and Raven's dad," Charlie returned, grinning as she referenced her friend's father, a lawyer. "And, anyways, where do you think my interest comes from? You! And Raven's dad!"

"You know," Miss Sandy replied, "your mother actually pulled me into watching those things. She was always slipping them into the conversation, gossiping about them as though they actually happened in real life. It's not to say your interest in rousing courtroom antics is genetic, mind you, but ... you know."

Charlie lapsed into silence briefly. Before long, Miss Sandy nudged her thigh, ending her contemplation.

"I guess I can let the 'boy in the park' thing go for now," Miss Sandy offered. "But, in all seriousness, you know it's absolutely no issue if you want to talk to me about those kinds of things, right? I know it may not be hip or cool or rad to talk to poor ol' Miss Sandy about it—that is, Miss Sandy, MD, PhD, I remind you—but really—"

"I think I've got it, Miss Sandy," Charlie assured her, smiling softly. "But really, he's just some random boy I ran into—or who ran into me—at the park, and no, not random as in strange stalker-guy. I seriously doubt I'll ever see him again, unless it's at school, and if I do, it probably means I'll have dodged another football hurtling directly at my face."

"Hmm?" Miss Sandy's eyebrows raised in question. "Football? What football?"

Charlie shook her head, her blonde hair swaying.

"Nothing."

"Okay then."

Miss Sandy reached across and nudged Charlie's thigh again, and then rose to her feet, grabbing a slice of apple from the plate on the table. "I should probably go down to check on the boys again. They said they were working on spacecraft propulsion. I'm no rocket scientist, but I think that probably involves things exploding—explosions that could perhaps blow up the entire house."

She set off for the entryway.

Charlie's quiet voice stopped her.

"When you said it was all right if I wanted to talk to you about 'those things,' were you just talking about boys, or..."

She left the question unfinished.

Miss Sandy turned to look at her.

"Either, Charlie," she said, smiling. "Anything. Anytime. Always."

Charlie's nod was barely noticeable before she flipped open her book to resume her reading.

Miss Sandy turned away again.

"He said his name was Jace, if you must know."

Miss Sandy paused under the archway for a moment, and then continued on, her smile remaining hidden from Charlie's view.

IN JOHNSON CITY, TENNESSEE, the weather could not have been better. On this occasion, for Whitney Rainier and her children, for the supporters, hand-holders, and well-wishers, and for Jack Rainier—the weather was just right.

It seemed as if the entire city had shown up at the gravesite to give condolences and pay respects. The area around the cemetery was packed, well-wishers even spilling over to keep vigil on surrounding pathways and neighboring gravestones. The usually quiet streets bordering the cemetery were crowded with double-parked cars, trucks, vans, buses, bikes, and motorcycles. Some of the vehicles were occupied or closely attended by townspeople who were unable to get any nearer to the hometown hero and his family.

It had hardly been a week since Whitney had heard that her husband had been killed in combat, yet Johnson City, miles away from where the Rainier family lived at Fort Leonard Wood in Missouri, had somehow made the effort to arrive in their Sunday best. All because they had received the same message:

Jack's home.

"Allow their words to not go unheard," Lt. Col. Savannah Hawes continued, her usually soft voice now resonating with prophetic conviction. "Allow their actions to not go unappreciated. They are the symbols that represent the best in all of us. They are our guiding lights. They are our virtuous principles. We will certainly not forget them, so allow history to follow in their hallowed footsteps."

Whitney Rainer, Skylar, Maria, Whitney's parents, Jack's parents, and Brig. Gen. Jackson Hawes wearing his service uniform, with ribbons and medals proudly displayed, were seated in front. Good friends and extended family were close at hand, acquaintances slightly further away, and the public encircling them all. The military honor guard detail held their customary positions. Savannah Hawes, also in uniform, presided.

"Jack Rainier was not Superman, he was not a mythical deity, he was not a legendary or ubiquitous entity, one that walked on water or healed the sick with his touch—he was not any of those. But Jack Rainier was just as good. Jack Rainier was a worthy son, an honorable husband, an admirable father. He was a charitable friend and a praised colleague. He was a fearless soldier. He was—and is—a hero to each and every one of us. Jack Rainier was that. Warrant Officer Jack Wilson Rainier, United States Army, was that."

Even now, as she sat in her chair, her eyes focused on the chaplain, Whitney could vividly recall the traumatic, life-changing series of events from days prior.

The seemingly harmless knock at the front door.

The momentary confusion, the heavy-handed denial, the unspecified anger coming from and directed at no one person in particular.

The ominous, sinister clouds collecting on the horizon.

The heart-wrenching, life-taking, life-breaking, words of death at the tip of a remorseful tongue...

And then the walls came tumbling down.

Darkness.

Blurry ... Skylar and Maria ... Jackson and Savannah ...

The stillness, and the quiet.

The emptiness.

The permanence.

You are not alone, Whitney.

Compassionate support ... divine mediation ...

Removed from the swirling darkness, away from the menacing cliff.

A reserve of strength, a labor of love.

Calm.

Peace.

Resolve...

Jack.

"Let the word ring out," Savannah urged, "in the hills and valleys, from this place and time—we are not afraid. We are not afraid to do what we can, we are not afraid to do what we must. We will do good and be good. We will do more and be more. We will do better and be better, come what may. We are not afraid. Jack was not afraid to do good for us, to do more for us, to do better for us. Let us not be afraid to do more for him, to do good for him, to do better for him. We can, and we will, because we are. We will do better for each other, because that is what Jack Rainier would have wanted. We are not afraid."

Everyone within range of the chaplain's voice listened with bated breath, her words captivating the minds of the audience. Even Skylar and Maria listened to "Aunt S'vannah" without fidgeting.

The chaplain closed.

"Over the years, I've gotten to know Mr. Jack Rainier pretty well, along with—as Jack would say—his infinitely more beautiful and intelligent wife, Mrs. Whitney Rainier"—a host of chuckles from the listeners—"and his exponentially more talented and amusing children, Skylar Hightower and Maria Nightingale Rainier."

More laughter, and giggles from the front row.

"It has been an absolute honor and privilege to know them all. I hope and pray to continue to be in their good graces for years and decades to come. Like others here, I consider them to be dear friends of myself and my family, friends that I would not—could not—ever forget or let slip away.

"I've always kind of favored Jack as a sort of rock star. You know—lively, animated, full of life, overflowing with energy, forever memorable. Mind you, this is not counting the numerous times Jack proclaimed himself an actual rock star. I would dismiss him when he said that, but in the back of my mind, I always knew he was speaking some version of the truth. There was no way I would tell him that to his face, though. I wouldn't want to put Whitney through that torture."

Savannah smiled at Whitney, who flashed an acknowledging grin in return.

"Nevertheless, thinking of Jack, I also remember perhaps the only lines I recall from my Shakespearian studies in high school, when Juliet says of Romeo: 'When he shall die/ Take him and cut him out in little stars/ And he will make the face of heaven so fine/ That all the world will be in love with night/ And pay no worship to the garish sun.'

"I thank you all. Thank you, Mrs. Whitney Rainier. Thank you, young Skylar and Maria. And, of course, thank you, Jack Wilson Rainier. We will always miss you, and we will always remember."

WELL-WISHERS STREAMED PAST JACK Rainier's family, congregating to pay their compliments. They all gave Whitney a comforting hug and kiss on the cheek. They all folded themselves down—some slightly awkwardly—to shake hands with Maria and Skylar. They all verbally acknowledged Savannah Hawes's stirring eulogy, which Savannah accepted in her usual self-effacing manner. They all praised the precision and demeanor of the honor guard, who performed, as always, superbly. They all filed past, and eventually, they all made their way home.

"Please tell me you have time to stop by my parents' house before you leave," Whitney said as she hugged her best friend again.

"Of course," Savannah whispered. "Actually, I was just telling your mother that Jackson and I didn't need to report back until Tuesday, so if it was all right with you, you could have us for another two days."

Whitney smiled gratefully.

"Yes, I think I can take it, although two more days with Jackson Hawes in Johnson City is bound to stir up some sort of trouble."

"Hey, hey, hey," Jackson admonished, straightening himself back up after bending to give Maria and Skylar a military salute at their eye level—for him, a mighty feat. "I will have you know, Mrs. Rainier, that I am a general in the United States Army, and I am offended by that sort of profiling."

Jackson then hugged Whitney, steadily tightening the squeeze. Savannah had to thump his back from behind to get him to release his hold. He was grinning as he pulled back.

"Let's see what the chillins have to say about it," he declared.

He gazed down at Skylar and Maria.

"Hey, chillins, is it okay if Aunt Savannah and I stay over for a few more days?"

He pouted, making a saddened puppy-dog expression.

Both of the "chillins" darted their eyes to their mother. Maria clasped her hands together.

"Can Uncle Jack and Aunt S'vannah come back with us, pa-lease?" she asked with pleading determination.

Whitney rolled her eyes at Jackson and smiled at her children while Savannah tried to cover her laugh with her hand.

"Okay," Whitney said, feigning caution. "But you have to remember to take Uncle Jack out for a walk if he starts getting too hyper."

"Woo-hoo!" Maria and Skylar exclaimed in tandem, mimicking the celebratory cry from *Jake's Crazy Big World*. Brig. Gen. Jackson Hawes attempted to mimic them, but failed clumsily.

"It looks like you have a few more well-wishers," Savannah commented, nodding back to a family that stood near the elevated casket, "so we'll get going. Did you want to ride back with us?"

"If you don't mind."

Whitney then took a quick glance at the solitary group, recognizing none of them, since their backs were turned.

"We're at the truck," Savannah said as she and Jackson made to leave. "Take your time."

Whitney watched them walk along the path leading away from the gravesite. With Jack Rainier's service concluded, the cemetery's usual air of quaint barrenness had returned, save for a sporadic visitor here and there. As testament to the beautiful weather, the grounds crew had adorned each grave with simple yet elegant fresh flower arrangements. The scene was peaceful at the moment, even if it was a setting that normally conveyed sadder emotions.

Movement and murmuring nearby drew Whitney's attention away from the landscape. She turned to greet the final well-wishers.

An adult couple stood before her, and a pair of children before Skylar and Maria, who were conversing in quiet tones.

The adult couple were the picture of beauty and grace. The man was remarkably handsome, smiling kindly. His companion—her appearance suggesting an ethereal magnificence—also smiled, her head tilted in such a manner as to convey compassion rather than pity.

The youthful pair kneeling in front of Skylar and Maria exuded the same illuminating presence. The boy, a teenager, was the older of the two, his distinctive silver-blond hair glinting softly in the sunlight. His clothing was less formal than that worn by the older couple, but just as neat. The girl who stood beside him, perhaps only a few years older than Skylar and Maria, was dressed similarly, and possessed the same fluidity and charm.

All four visitors were clothed in white. Whitney was immediately captivated.

None of the Rainiers recognized the final well-wishers.

The beautiful woman took Whitney's hands in her own.

"My name is Elianna, and this is Elias. My condolences, Mrs. Rainier," she said graciously.

"It is nice to meet you, and thank you for coming," Whitney replied, her eyes shifting between the woman and the man—Elias—standing alongside. "Please, call me Whitney. Did you two know Jack?"

"We had met," Elias spoke up. "A delightful man, a real character, if I may say so. I thought the chaplain's words were spot on."

"Yes, she did an outstanding job," Whitney agreed. "She is actually a close family friend, and I've heard her speak many times before. She always seems to know just what to say, and just how to say it. I think Jack would have had a few observations, though."

"He wasn't much for speeches?" Elianna asked, her tone lightly amused.

"Either that," Whitney said, "or all of that praise would have gone right to his head. He would have been insufferable for months."

Whitney and the couple laughed softly. All three glanced down to where the blond boy was whispering quietly to a giggling Maria and Skylar.

"SO, WHAT DO YOU think about that?" Case whispered.

Skylar and Maria, still laughing, nodded.

A breeze wafted through the group, delicately tracing their clothing.

"You know a lot," Skylar said.

"So do you," Case returned.

"May I ask a question?"

Case, his eyebrows lifted slightly, replied, "You may."

"You're not gonna laugh?"

"Only if you would like us to."

Skylar shook his head, his dark curls bouncing.

"Then we won't," Case said, glancing to Beat, who nodded.

The small boy looked to his sister briefly, and then at the ground.

"Do you ... do you know where my daddy is?"

Case smiled.

"Can I answer your question with a question in return?"

"I don't know. Can you?"

Maria giggled. Beat laughed quietly as well.

"Okay," Case said, smiling. "May I answer your question with a question?"

Both Rainier children nodded.

"Where do you think he is?"

The children's eyes darted to the polished casket nearby, and then back to Case's face. Case turned his head smoothly, sending a calculated gaze to the casket. The Rainier children, following his gaze, looked at the gravesite once more with increased interest.

"Do you think he is in there?" Case asked tenderly, still gazing at the grave. "Do you think he is in there, sleeping?"

He turned back to the young Rainiers, who stared at the grave as if expecting something to happen, and motioned for them to lean in closer.

"I know where he is," Case whispered, softer than before. He leaned back, staring into the wide, youthful eyes that stared back at him. He glanced up to Whitney, who was still speaking to Elias and Elianna.

"I think your mom knows where he is, too."

The two children looked up at their mother, their expressions hopeful. Whitney, as though sensing eyes on her, glanced down and smiled reassuringly. The children turned their attention back to Case.

"Yeah, I think your mom knows where he is, and, if you think really hard, even you know where he is. It's the same place he has always been. Your mom knows where to look, and"—he gestured to the gravesite again—"it's not in there."

Case paused, his gaze intent.

"I'm looking at him right now."

He pointed to Maria's widening eyes, and a triumphant grin played across his lips.

"I can see him in there," he said. "I can hear him"—he tapped Skylar's chest lightly with his finger—"in here."

He paused a moment.

"Do you feel that?"

On cue, a gentle gust of wind blew through the nearly empty cemetery, ruffling the children's hair and clothing.

"Who do you think that was? Do you honestly think he isn't here watching you, right now?"

Case looked to Beat, who grinned.

"That casket," he went on, gesturing over to the site once more, "all of these graves, they're kind of like markers. They're here to remind us. And they're here for those who may have forgotten where to look."

He nodded to Skylar and Maria.

"But, you two will remember."

WHITNEY AND SAVANNAH ENSURED Skylar and Maria were securely buckled into the rear of the rented SUV before they climbed into their seats in front.

"I know I'm not supposed to swear," the chaplain said, watching in the rear-view mirror as her husband buckled himself into a seat in the very back of the car, "but sometimes I swear I married a hormonally-mutated nine-year-old child."

Whitney chuckled as she strapped herself in.

"You're preachin' to the choir, Reverend."

They both laughed. Savannah's laugh settled first, and she looked over at her friend with sweet concern. As Whitney's chuckling faded, Savannah spoke up.

"So, how do you feel now? Do you think you're going to be okay?"

Whitney thought for a moment.

"I think so," she replied at last. "I think so. I don't know, I just have this feeling, I guess, that everything's going to be all right. I can't really explain it. But with you, and all of my family and Jack's family, and all of our friends, and even"—Whitney gulped dramatically—"Jackson back there, I think we are all going to be okay in the end."

She paused again before concluding, "Jack's always going to be around in one way or another."

Savannah nodded.

"Definitely," she agreed. "And you know Jackson will keep up those ridiculous pranks, and I'll need your help slowing him down. 'My Two Jacks' is forever."

"Oh, please, don't remind me," Whitney said, giving her friend a playful grin.

"Isn't that right, Jackson?" Savannah called to her preoccupied husband, who was talking to Skylar and Maria in the back.

"Huh?" Jackson looked up at his wife.

"See?" Savannah directed to Whitney as she turned the wheel. "Doesn't even listen to me."

Whitney laughed again.

"Uncle Jack! Uncle Jack!"

"Huh? What?" Jackson Hawes turned his attention back to the children.

"I forgot to tell you about the dream I had the other night," Maria said.

"Yeah, me too!" Skylar added.

"Dream? What dream?"

"It had ghosts in it!" Skylar said.

"Yeah, yeah," Maria agreed enthusiastically. "Mine too!"

"Ghosts, eh?" Jackson said. "Did they scare you?"

"No!" Skylar scoffed, as if the thought was ridiculous.

"They were the good kind," Maria said seriously.

"Huh? How do you know? You told each other about this dream or something?"

A small smile lit up Skylar's tanned face, while Maria's was more somber.

"Daddy was there, too," Maria said, quieter now and with youthful sincerity.

Jackson leaned forward, resting his arms on the top of the children's back supports.

"Really?" he asked, mirroring Maria's tone. "Did he talk to you?"

The children nodded.

"He said as long as we remember him and all the things we did, then he can't really be dead because he'll always be here," Skylar answered, to which Maria nodded again.

Jackson was quiet, looking between the two children. After a moment, he spoke again.

"You know what, I think he's right."

He paused.

"That's a really good dream you guys had. Maybe you'll have more."

"He also said we were heavy when he picked us up," Maria remarked.

"Now, that definitely sounds right," Jackson said, grinning. "Both of you are getting fat. It's all that darn Box O' Juice. Loaded with sugar. I'll have to suggest to Whitney to limit you two while I whip you munchkins into shape."

"That's what Daddy said!" Skylar exclaimed excitedly.

"Skylar, Maria, turn to the front, please," Whitney said from the front of the SUV.

Jackson leaned back in his seat and exhaled loudly.

"I was trying to tell them to turn around, but no…"

He let the sentence hang and winked at the kids.

Skylar rolled his eyes and Maria stuck out her tongue before they both turned around. Jackson reached forward and ruffled their hair.

THE FIGURES STANDING NEAR the gravesite watched the Rainier family leave the cemetery before they turned back to the casket adorned with wreaths and sentimental tokens. The scene had acquired a particular tranquility in the absence of onlookers, a solace now without spectacle or contrived expectation.

A young man stood at attention beside the casket, his posture one of relaxed vigilance, his bearing collected and serious. As was the practice among those like him, his brilliant, illuminating gold wings were tucked neatly and comfortably behind his back, visible but not brazenly displayed. His serene stare was aimed straight ahead, as it had been throughout the funeral service, although his attention was focused all around, ever aware of his surroundings. Presently, his focus shifted to the four others who remained behind.

"It was a nice service," he offered, his posture unaltered as he spoke.

Elias, Elianna, Beat, and Case all agreed.

"All done?" the man then asked.

Elias and Elianna looked to their young cohorts.

"We're clear," Case affirmed.

"As are we," Elias said. "Beautifully done, by the way."

Case inclined his head in acknowledgement, and Beat grinned.

"Where to from here?" Case asked no one in particular, the question somewhat rhetorical.

"Wherever is next," answered Elianna with a small smile.

"That sounds about right," the young man with the gold wings assented.

Now that Warrant Officer Jack Rainier's plot was finally devoid of family and visitors, a group of cemetery caretakers moved to the site to begin the closing burial preparations. The five invisible figures near the casket watched their approach.

"This must be our cue," Elias murmured, although the workers would not have been able to hear him even if he had spoken normally.

As the workers approached the grave, Elias and Elianna soundlessly accelerated into the sky, immediately becoming specks in the cloudless cover, and immediately after that becoming indistinguishable in the blue. They were quickly followed by Beat and Case.

The remaining man stood a few moments longer, letting the grave workers come within arm's length of his invisible—and intangible—body. At the same time as the first caretaker laid his gloved hands on the pristine casket, he turned to them.

"Until next time," he uttered.

Then, he too shot effortlessly into the skies.

The cemetery workers—without ceremony, without spectators, without demonstration—went about their duties, their movements unhurried, their actions practiced, professional, and precise.

N<small>ICK</small> <small>STROLLED ALONG THE</small> boardwalk parallel to the California shoreline, easily avoiding passersby while staring at the open packet he held in front of him. His pace was casual, as was his outfit, and he fit in nicely with his fellow beachgoers and the lighthearted ambiance of a summer day on the coast.

He wore a multi-colored hooded sweatshirt, unzipped and with no shirt underneath, which now and again provided a glimpse of his lean chest. His board shorts were of the multipurpose variety, perfect for nearly any warm-weather activity, as were his low-top sneakers, worn untied and without socks. A plain-white fitted baseball cap, trendily turned sideways, completed the ensemble.

It was late morning, and the sun had not yet reached its zenith. The sweltering heat would hold off for a few more hours. Neither the beach nor the boardwalk had yet attracted their usual seasonal masses, although both were populating steadily as lunchtime approached. Nick would soon be looking for somewhere to eat as well—he hardly ever turned down an opportunity for food—but, for the moment at least, he focused on the neatly bound sheaf of paper in his hands.

The portfolio contained the most up-to-date sections of the ever-evolving primary list, eloquently termed The List, sent to him multiple times a week by staff at the North Office. Though typically hand-delivered, more often than not by someone Nick was well acquainted with, it was also true that The List could present itself nearly anywhere, sometimes in the most unlikely of places.

The current elegantly trussed bundle had been waiting for him on the beach, propped alongside his shoes and discarded jacket and cap while he bodysurfed the morning waves of the

Pacific Ocean. Given his fondness for sports in and on top of the water, it was not the first time he had received The List in that manner.

On occasion, the Office felt the urge to get inventive, devising more imaginative, and more uncertain, means of transport. The North Office personnel constructing The List thought of it as some sort of joke, and Nick was well versed in their brand of humor. Yet, through all of their ingenious methods, they had never once failed to deliver, and as long as the newest portion of The List ended up in his hands, Nick had little reason to complain.

Even if he did complain, nothing would change; they thought their methods hilarious.

For his part, Nick could admit they were clever.

Not to mention utterly ridiculous.

As Nick strolled the boardwalk of Newport Beach, Case gazed up at an abandoned structure in Greenfield, Massachusetts, while Beat studied her handbook again. She thumbed through a few pages, and then closed it and smoothly tucked it away. Mimicking Case's pose, she looked up at the building as well.

In a dreary, rundown area of Greenfield, the shop appeared uninhabited and had been for a while. A faded section above the obstructed entrance bore the only hint of previous business:

Ferri's Sh—

The last part of the title had deteriorated, lost to oblivion.

Between a narrow, trashed lot and a ramshackle fence, the brick walls of the shop were undergoing a tremendously slow yet steady crumble. The rundown appearance of the structure suggested an urgent need for major renovation—or merciful annihilation. For now, it stood as another eyesore in a forgotten part of town that was already lacking in charm.

Beat and Case glanced away from the ruined building and took in the surrounding area.

The building was situated at the extremity of a dead-end road. Beyond it, a wide, debris-littered hollow formed a tolerable boundary between the building and a busy interstate on the other side. A scraggly fence was stationed at the close of the street, in case a lost driver failed to realize the potholed road was suddenly about to end.

There was little foot traffic on the deserted road, and the few passersby hardly paid Beat and Case any mind, so accustomed were they in gazing down to the end of the lonely street and to seeing nothing of consequence. Any sounds of life and activity were muted, as if a prevailing, invisible barricade shielded the blighted street from the rest of the world.

Beat and Case stood alone; hidden, as always, in plain sight. Case shifted his focus away from the scene and back to the building.

"Over there," he said, pointing. "The right side, top floor."

Beat followed his indication.

"Are you suggesting the window?" she asked, allowing her amusement to show as she looked sidelong at her companion.

Case grinned.

"Seems reasonable enough," he offered.

Adjusting the knitted cap on her head, Beat walked to the corner of the building, looking up to the floor Case had motioned to. Case followed close behind. All of the windows were undressed and lacking glass, just bare holes in the brick walls. The top floor was elevated five stories above where Beat and Case stood.

Beat noiselessly launched herself off the ground, ascending to the window opening on the fifth floor and peering inside. She floated in the air for a moment before directing a glance down to where her partner stood watching her. Then she entered, propelling her legs up and over the sill and disappearing from view.

Case circled back around to the front of the building. He stood before the blockaded entrance, where weathered wooden boarding was nailed over the doorframe. For anyone wanting to get inside, entering through the front door would be a difficult and time-consuming option. However, the wide-open portals of the first floor—where windowpanes used to be—provided readily available routes for gaining entry.

For Case, the choice was easy.

He reached for the nails and pulled each miniature spike out easily, laying them in a neat pile on the ground beside the entryway, his actions making only the slightest whisperings of sound. As he reached the final nail, he stepped aside. The boarded obstruction eased away from the doorframe, slowly at first, before gaining momentum and crashing solidly to the ground, producing a small cloud of dust that lifted into the air. His gaze followed the fall, and then he stepped onto the board and kneeled to place the final nails on top of the pile.

Rising back to his full height, Case entered the building through the now wide-open front door.

NICK MADE A QUICK sidestep without looking up from what he was reading, narrowly avoiding two kids zipping past him on skateboards. He turned and watched their reckless retreat as they wove between pedestrians, whooping and shouting.

"Timothy Simmons and ... Mario Delgado," he mumbled to himself. "Timothy: brash but sincere. Mario: considerate, trustworthy."

He turned again and continued walking, glancing down at The List, only to diverge from his path moments later to duck into a 1950s-style ice cream parlor facing the boardwalk. For Nick, it was an unscheduled, although thoroughly predictable, detour.

He soon found himself second—technically third—in line behind a pair of young women. At first, he took in the older of the two.

Jessica David, Nick reflected, *caring, strong-willed.*

Classic, high-topped canvas sneakers. Always a respectable choice.

Toned legs, tanned. If she lives around here, she must run on the beach.

Jean shorts, fashionably frayed, and a black T-shirt, probably with some band on the front that only a handful of people have heard of.

Bracelet, handmade—some type of craft project? Simple. Intimate. Telling.

Long hair, brown—nice.

Hmm, interesting smell … like ….

As he thought, Nick noticed the second young woman—a girl, really, all of eight years old—staring at him with a slight smile. Apparently, she had already received her order; Nick was quick to identify the bag of oversized chocolate-chip cookies clutched in her delicate hand. He watched as she held out a cookie in his direction. Nick performed a short yet elegant bow, causing the little girl's smile to widen, and accepted her gift graciously.

"Rebecca David, very nice," he said softly.

Rebecca beamed, revealing a few missing teeth.

Nick straightened just as the older girl, Jessica, turned away from the counter. Nick knew her to be twenty-four years old, twenty-five in a few weeks. She issued a low "Excuse me" as she moved past him, one hand holding a small cone—*butter pecan on waffle,* Nick observed—and her other hand holding little Rebecca's. Nick stepped out of their way, biting into the cookie Rebecca had given him, watching as they passed.

That is a very interesting smell, he mused again, a smile pulling at his lips as he chewed.

Lost in thought, he only registered the *swoosh* of the door closing, the two girls already moving on to their next destination.

"Jessica David, very, very nice," he said to himself, almost inaudibly. He continued to stare at the exit.

"Hey, bro! You gonna get something or what? I ain't got all day, geez."

Nick turned to see another young skateboarder, reminding him of Timothy and Mario from only minutes before. This one—*Jonnie Alvarado*, his name springing instantly to Nick's mind—wore his hair in intricate cornrows under a white visor that was flipped upside down and turned sideways. He leaned on his board pretentiously, like an aristocrat leaning on an expensive cane, a pose more for style than necessity.

Nick smirked.

"Whatever, dude," he said, returning to the counter.

Jonnie laughed, the pitch and frequency high enough to be considered a giggle.

"Ha, ha! Man, that was so weak!"

Nick ignored him and started to order, noticing the old man behind the counter attempting to hide a grin.

"Okay, let's see. I'd like one extra-large cup with chocolate, vanilla, and strawberry ice cream. Just keep alternating the scoops and get as many as you can fit in there. Then add, um, those Reese's Pieces, M&Ms, pecans, walnuts, chocolate sprinkles, those Oreo crumbles, and chocolate chips, with whipped cream and chocolate, and some of that caramel sauce on top. And I'd also like some of these chocolate-chip cookies in a bag, please."

He held up the nearly finished cookie in his hand.

"Sorry, but was there any topping you didn't want?" the old man fixing his order chuckled. "What about these gummy worms? You didn't mention them."

Nick turned his attention to the display again.

"Oh, yeah. How did I miss those? Thanks, yeah, you can put some of those on there, too."

"I don't know if this is all going to fit."

Nick shrugged, smiling.

"Surprise me, then. You're the ice cream expert. I trust your judgment."

"Wow, Mr. McButterpants," Jonnie accused from behind him. "Why don't you just get all the ice cream while you're at it? You won't even be able to fit through the door once you're through eating all that!"

Nick spun again, arching his eyebrow.

"Mr. McButterpants? Who you callin' Mr. McButterpants?"

Before the smaller kid could react, Nick reached for Jonnie's visor, turning it right side up, facing forwards. He then jerked the bill down, completely covering Jonnie's eyes.

"That's more like it," Nick said, turning to the counter once more.

For a few moments, Jonnie seemed too stunned to move. He stood motionless, leaning against his skateboard, blinded.

"Dude," the boy uttered at last, reaching up to adjust his visor. "That was so completely uncool."

The old man behind the counter laughed out loud.

MEANWHILE, BEAT SAT ON the dust- and grime-covered floor, slowly tracing her fingers through the dirty layers that highlighted the abandonment and neglect of the empty building.

The small corner room on the top floor was, as expected, replete with harsh nothingness. A lingering, dimly musky smell indicated past use and present lack of care. The walls were exposed, soiled, and shabby, as was the floor, as though the extended inactivity had done more to pollute the place than the bustle of goings-on ever could. It was rejection personified.

A small boy sat in the corner furthest from the door, near the window through which Beat had entered the room. His knees were tucked into his chest and his arms curled around, his small head down, concealed beneath tousled black hair. His jeans were frayed and worn out, more from continuous use, Beat knew, than any type of fashion statement. They held the patterns of fresh dirt on the shin and kneecaps, most likely from the boy's entrance through a first-floor window.

Quiet sobbing echoed in the empty room. The child had not moved from his position when Beat entered the room, nor when she sat opposite him. The boy, a repeat runaway, seemed unaware of her company, and yet there Beat sat, steps away.

A muffled crash sounded downstairs. The boy raised his head, and then he jumped, doing a swift double-take when he realized Beat's presence. Inhaling sharply, he wiped at his eyes with his arm.

"Go away!" he said, his voice clearly betraying his anguish.

Beat carefully moved her attention away from the ground to the boy in the corner, remaining silent.

"I said go away!" the boy cried again, his tone even more agonized. "Go away, or I'll hurt you!"

The child's hand left his knee to ghost over his pants pocket.

Moving slowly, Beat mirrored the boy's fetal pose, drawing her knees up and reaching her arms around to clasp them in front. She rested her head on the top of her knees, never breaking from the child's tormented gaze.

Still, she said nothing.

The boy's attention darted to the doorway, surprise evident on his face. He seemed to recoil even more into the corner, his already clinched body stiffening at the room's newest arrival.

"I said go away! Please! Leave me alone!"

Case's stride never wavered, as if the boy's cry had gone unheard. The troubled runaway watched as the older boy entered the room, his steps soundless where the younger boy's movements had creaked and groaned on the floor with the slightest pressure. Case moved to a spot just behind Beat, directly against the wall. Once there, he slowly slid to the ground, a low scuffing sound finally announcing his arrival as his back rubbed against the worn surface. He came to rest in a similar position to Beat and the boy, although his knees were angled more casually. Then he rested his arms on his knees, his head tilted back against the wall behind him. Eyes partway opened, his attitude seemed completely relaxed. However, his attention was focused on the boy in much the same way as Beat's was—quietly, respectfully, and with careful consideration.

The boy wiped at his eyes and sniffled again. His gaze whipped from Case to Beat and back again. Both were dressed in a similar manner to the boy—inexpensively, not in total rags, but certainly not in high-priced or trendy fashion.

Worn, weary, almost resembling runaways themselves.

Beat took in the boy's flittering glances and disquieted sniffles. Both she and Case remained silent from their positions on the other side of the room.

Still.

Quiet.

"Please go away," the boy said again, his voice less harsh than before but equally as pained.

He rested his head against his legs for a moment, and then sniveled again, although he tried to mask the sound behind his knees.

Slowly, the minutes ebbed past. The grim, empty room was hushed, save for the boy's sniffling. On the other side of the empty window, the natural sounds of outdoors were barely audible. The sporadic creaks and shudders of the building only illustrated the stillness.

The child slowly lifted his head, and cringed into the wall, sucking his breath in softly.

Without a sound, Beat had moved across the room. She was now sitting directly in front of the boy in her former, cross-legged position, her arms folded across her knees. The barest hint of a smile graced her lips as she looked at the runaway, her earrings dancing in the glimmering shafts of light that pierced the empty room.

"Why won't you leave me alone?" the boy whispered, sniffling once more.

Beat tilted her head, indicating the question intrigued her, but said nothing.

The boy looked past her to Case, who lounged against the other wall and regarded the runaway carefully. Case's slight grin echoed Beat's as he deftly fingered the thin necklace that hung down to his chest. A small pair of wings, identical to Beat's earrings, fell loosely between his fingertips.

The child lowered his head to his knees.

Another sniffle.

Seconds, and then minutes, passed, without a word. The two visitors regarded the boy's every action, every fretful tic and utterance, every hint of awful worry that raced through his consciousness, in consoling silence. Neither attempted to rush the process—although they could have. Instead, Beat and Case waited, allowing the child to act at his own pace, his anguished emotions gradually fading.

When the boy looked at them again, questions raised themselves in his frown, although he did not immediately give them voice.

Finally, however, he spoke.

"Why didn't you leave when I said I wanted to be alone?"

Case spoke up from across the room.

"We'd rather wait for you."

The boy's eyes widened. He returned Case's stare for a moment, and then quickly glanced down again. He wiped at his face, bringing his small palms to his eyes and rubbing forcefully, as if to prevent tears spilling out. Beat rested her elbows on her knees and cradled her head in her hands. She continued to smile reassuringly.

The child met her gaze.

"What?" he asked. "Why are you smiling?"

Beat just shrugged.

There, in the corner of the empty room on the top floor of the deserted building, with dust and filth and the mildewed smell of the past on the floorboards, and on the ceiling, and in the stilled, stale air, the sun easing through the glassless opening to brighten the abandoned space in a soft, ambient light, the sounds from outside muted and the sounds inside otherwise nonexistent, Dylan again put his face down closer to his knees—

—hiding a small, faint, grateful smile.

THE SIGHTS AND ATTRACTIONS along Bahia Bay Boardwalk, located on the southern edge of Norbury, were a long-standing favorite in Cape Cod. Even now, several decades into the boardwalk's existence, it continued to draw both local residents and out of town vacationers with its quaint, unassuming atmosphere and attention to detail. At Bahia Bay, the food was somehow more delicious, the fun more fulfilling, the breezy air coming off the neighboring body of water more refreshing. It captured a childish magic and a mature, patient enjoyment all at once. Bahia Bay was a carnival from another era, and summer seemed only to enhance the festive environment further.

Charlie and Miss Sandy looked on as Caleb and Colby scurried to the next gaming attraction, this one promoting a prize in exchange for a successful basketball shot. The illuminated, twinkling displays of Bahia Bay threw a glow into the evening sky, and Miss Sandy chuckled as the twins handed over a small stretch of pink tickets to the young man supervising the attraction.

"This should be interesting," she commented to the teenager alongside her.

The attendant handed the boys a slightly worn orange basketball, and the pair watched with amusement as Caleb and Colby both pointed to another one.

"You mean interesting like the last time they played this game?" Charlie asked, glancing to the older woman.

"Actually," Miss Sandy replied, "I was thinking about the time before that, but yes, last time, too. Oh, who are we kidding? They're all interesting."

The two laughed.

At the counter, Colby and Caleb finally agreed upon a basketball, one banded colorfully in red, white, and blue. Colby spun the ball a few times on his fingertips, and then dribbled on the wooden-planked boardwalk. As he readied his attempt, Caleb whispered something into his ear, gesturing vaguely at the hoop situated ten feet high and a fair distance away. Then, Caleb backed off, giving his brother room.

Colby shot the basketball into the empty space between him and the hoop, the orb lifting, gaining a perfect arc, spinning tightly until its colors seemed to blend together. The shot would have been right on target—if the hoop had been moved to the left and brought in slightly closer. The ball plummeted back down, not quite reaching the rim, thumping against the supportive layer underneath, which rolled the ball toward the counter once more.

The twins quickly switched positions. Had they been wearing the same clothing, the change could have easily gone unnoticed. The attendant handed over the basketball again, this time to Caleb.

As Caleb fiddled with it, twirling it casually, Colby leaned in closer and the two conversed once more, occasionally motioning to the basketball or the hoop in the distance. The youthful attendant observed their antics, seemingly entertained.

"I think the idea is to get the ball to go through the hoop," Charlie announced, causing the pair to turn to her in annoyance. "I'm sure this guy has better things to do than watch you two ninnies come up with some complicated blueprint on how to shoot a basketball."

Miss Sandy elbowed her in admonishment, doing her best to hide her chuckle. Caleb turned back to the basket, still rolling his eyes, while Colby directed an ill-amused expression Charlie's way.

"It's cool," the attendant remarked, laughing under his breath. "This is the funniest thing I've seen so far tonight."

"We'll see who's laughing after I nail this," Caleb declared.

Charlie covered her mouth to hold back her snicker. Miss Sandy elbowed her again, and Charlie elbowed her back, both chuckling quietly.

As Colby backed away, Caleb dribbled the basketball on the planks a few more times and then prepared to shoot. He crouched, before launching the colorful basketball into the air.

It was immediately clear that the shot was aimed at the left side at an extreme angle, straight for the netting designed to keep wayward balls from flying away from the area of play. The ball ricocheted off the left side support, propelling toward the right side while still hurtling for the rear of the attraction. It then bounced away from the right-side netting, bringing it into a direct line with the basket.

The small group in front of the attraction watched, captivated, as the ball banked softly off the backboard and rolled slowly around the hoop—to the left, to the right, around to the left again —

—before spilling off the front of the rim. It dropped to the curtain underneath with a *plop* before rolling back down to rest against the other basketballs stationed near the counter.

Charlie stood unmoving, astonished. Miss Sandy, meanwhile, gave an encouraged cheer.

"Good try, boys! That was so close!"

Caleb and Colby fell into a huddle once more, occasionally glancing at the basketball hoop.

"I have to admit, that was an amazing shot," the attendant agreed, "but I don't think I could have given you a prize even if it had gone in."

The twins jerked their heads toward the attendant in unison, each boy's curly brown hair bouncing lightly.

"What?" Colby demanded, his brow furrowed. "What do you mean?"

"I'm pretty sure you're not supposed to use the netting on the side as a prop," the attendant explained. "It's unfair, and unrealistic. You're supposed to imagine that it's not even there, like in a real basketball game."

"What?" Caleb all but cried. "Where's that rule?"

"You mean it's unfair like the shape of that hoop?" Colby challenged. "That shot would have gone in easily if the basketball were the shape of a watermelon!"

"I promise it's all regulation," the attendant said, holding his hands up in surrender. "But I thought that the rule went without saying. I mean, you don't get side supports in a real game, do you?"

"Pretty sure you don't get an egg-shaped rim in a real game, either," Colby muttered.

The attendant could only shake his head and smile.

"Okay, you two," Miss Sandy called. "On to the next—"

"What'd you say?" Caleb asked abruptly, shooting a glance in the attendant's direction.

The attendant met his gaze, his eyebrows raised in surprise. Meanwhile, Colby turned back to Charlie and Miss Sandy.

"Uh," the attendant started, "I didn't—"

"Charlie, this guy just said he bet you couldn't make that shot," Colby declared.

Almost immediately, Miss Sandy burst with laughter.

The employee's eyes widened.

"No! No, I didn't!" he implored, his voice becoming frantic. "I didn't say that! I didn't say anything!"

Miss Sandy shook her head as she continued to laugh.

"No ... it's okay," she tried to say, struggling to control her amusement. "It's ... it's just ..."

Charlie stared intently at her brothers, her eyebrow arched, her lips upturned faintly.

"You want to say that again?" she asked.

"I think you heard me," Colby replied, the barest trace of a smile making its way across his impish features.

"Miss, I absolutely did not say that," said the attendant. "I don't really know what these two are talking about, but—"

Still chuckling to herself, Miss Sandy waved him off.

"It's okay," she managed to get out. "It's no trouble. She knows it wasn't you..."

"Give him the tickets," Charlie said in an eerily calm tone, not breaking eye contact with Colby, still grinning softly.

Both brothers backed away as Charlie stepped up to the counter. The attendant's eyes flicked nervously from the twins to

Charlie, before returning to the boys again. Caleb slid the tickets across the stall.

"This is only enough for one shot," the attendant noted, turning to Charlie, whose focus had shifted to the hoop.

"All she needs is one," Colby offered. He leaned on the counter in anticipation.

The attendant glanced fleetingly at Charlie again.

"Um, any ball in particular that you want to shoot with?" he asked, indicating the basketballs that lined the edge.

"It doesn't matter," the three Brown siblings answered simultaneously. Charlie broke her focus to look over at Caleb and Colby; both were trying to conceal their grins behind a mask of indifference.

The attendant plucked a basketball out of the bunch at random, coming up with a red, white, and blue ball similar to the one the twins had used. He handed it over to Charlie.

"Good lu—"

Before he could get the word out, Charlie lofted the ball toward the rim. An instant later...

Swish. Nothing but net.

The attendant turned back to the girl, his mouth open in astonishment.

"Whoo! Nice shot, Charlie!" Miss Sandy applauded from behind.

"Whoop, whoop!" Caleb and Colby exclaimed. They started to dance in place.

"Wow," the attendant breathed. "I don't know if I've ever seen anyone shoot it that quickly and make it on the first attempt."

He then indicated the various stuffed animals and trinkets hanging along the edges of the booth.

"Your choice," he declared.

"We want that big purple one over there," Colby cut in before Charlie could reply. He pointed to a plum-toned, bear-like creature with an oversized head and goofy smile.

"Well, guys, since you weren't the ones who actually made the shot, I don't think—" the booth worker started to object.

"It's okay," Charlie said. "I'll let them choose."

The attendant trained a glance in her direction before returning to the twins.

"You said the purple one?" he asked, to which Colby and Caleb both said, "Yeah."

He unhooked the purple creature and placed it on the counter. Almost as soon as he set it down, Charlie neatly snatched it away.

"Hey!" both boys exclaimed.

"What's your deal?" Caleb added.

"What?" Charlie replied innocently as she inspected the prize. "I said you could choose, but I made the shot, so it's my prize."

Colby and Caleb stared at her in disbelief.

"What are you talking about, 'your prize?'" Colby questioned. "You wouldn't have even had the chance to shoot if it wasn't for our tickets, so you have to give it to us!"

"Really?" Charlie asked, looking around the booth. "Where's that rule?"

The boys huffed, petitioning the booth attendant. Only a few years older than Charlie, he shrugged, although he did not appear to try very hard to hide his grin.

"Sorry, guys," he said, adding, "Anyway, you just tried to get me in trouble a few minutes ago, so I'm not sure why you want me to save you now."

The boys huffed again.

"But that's an obvious rule!" Caleb cried, glowering at his sister.

"Obviously it's only obvious to you two," Charlie remarked. "Otherwise, I'm sure you would have more support. See how your nefarious schemes can backfire?"

Colby threw his sister a skeptical expression.

"Nefarious schemes, Charlie? Really?"

"Miss Sandy," Caleb implored their guardian for help, his childish voice suddenly ringing with purity, "don't you feel the need to punish Charlie pretty severely after just witnessing her cheat us out of a prize that is rightfully ours?"

Miss Sandy appeared to be looking in every conceivable direction except at the twins.

"Oh, hello, Ellen!" she pretended to greet a friend, waving enthusiastically to someone—no one—in the distance.

Caleb slumped his shoulders, pouting.

All of the siblings were familiar with Miss Sandy's "cold shoulder" routine; it was often used against them when they tried to wiggle out of a situation. To witness it as an innocent onlooker was amusing, but to be on the receiving end was particularly bothersome. Nevertheless, the lesson was usually learned in short order.

In this instance, Charlie and the booth attendant were the ones amused.

Caleb and Colby, on the other hand, clearly were not.

Lesson learned.

"SANDY?"

Miss Sandy flitted around to identify the speaker.

"Rosalind! Hey!" she greeted, spotting the tall, black-haired woman heading in her direction. The woman was accompanied by a younger, slightly shorter version of herself.

"And Raven! Back from Tanglewood, I see. I thought we wouldn't be expecting you until sometime next week."

"Hi, Mrs. Ellsbury," Raven replied, winking at Charlie. "Yes, Charlie always seems to get the dates mixed up—even when I tell her a thousand times."

There was no mistaking Raven Cristiana Summerset Dos Anjos for anyone but Rosalind's daughter. With their silken jet-black hair, flawless beige complexions, expressive eyes, exquisitely sculpted bone structure, and long, lithe bodies, they perfectly embodied Wampanoag tribal beauty. Raven, bearing the influence of her equally handsome Portuguese father, possessed a distinctive appeal that would only flourish as she grew older. To virtually anyone who encountered them, their beauty was all but unfair. Yet it seemed as if Rosalind and Raven Dos Anjos were unaware of the allure that everyone else noticed immediately.

"Now, there you go, Raven," Miss Sandy said in mock indignation at the girl's remark. "Forcing me to punish you already. I believe I have asked you repeatedly to please call me Sandy, but here I am, talking to you for two seconds, and you deliberately disobey me. "

Raven shrugged sheepishly and offered her mother's close friend a reserved smile.

"But," Mrs. Dos Anjos explained, "if you recall, Sandy, I told her to continue to address you as Mrs. Ellsbury, and if I ever heard her calling you—her elder—anything different, I would be the one forced to punish her."

Raven and Charlie rolled their eyes at one another, smiling at the typical banter.

Miss Sandy scoffed.

"Well, Raven," she remarked. "I guess the important question becomes, who are you going to listen to? Me, your wise and knowledgeable elder, or your mother—who, I'm afraid—simply doesn't know any better?"

"Sandy!" Rosalind Dos Anjos scolded through a smile.

"I think it would be better for me to listen to my mother, Mrs. Ellsbury," answered Raven.

"Mmmm hmmm," Miss Sandy intoned disapprovingly, crossing her arms and arching her brow.

Mrs. Dos Anjos chuckled.

"I have to say that I'm disappointed in your choice, young lady," Miss Sandy continued, "and for that, you just earned yourself two weeks punishment that I have absolutely no authority in enforcing."

In the meantime, Raven's mother turned her attention to Charlie.

"And, with all of that fluff out of the way, how are you, Charlie?"

"Just fine, Mrs. Dos Anjos. And you?"

"Charlie, please, Rosalind is fine."

At that, she and Miss Sandy shared a laugh.

"Is it okay if we walk around?" Charlie asked, addressing both women.

"So long as you stay in the pattern," Miss Sandy cautioned, referring to the walking route she and the Brown children usually took through the Bahia Bay attractions. "Meet me by closing time, if not sooner. I'll be right behind you. And remind the boys if you happen to run across them."

"And don't do anything you would be embarrassed to tell me about, Miss Raven Cristiana," Mrs. Dos Anjos added, looking at her daughter.

"Yes, and that, too," Miss Sandy agreed, smiling at Charlie.

Charlie smiled and nodded before turning away and walking with Raven further down the aisle.

"Okay," Raven started in as soon as the pair had moved out of earshot of the two women, "are you actually going to force me to ask about the purple bear you're holding, or am I supposed to act like I don't see it?"

Charlie glanced at the bear she clutched and sighed.

"The Tweebs," she said simply.

Raven nodded, understanding the situation immediately.

"I had to save him," Charlie went on as the two continued down the aisle. "There's no telling what they were planning on doing, but I had the feeling it would result in a severed head, or a fluffy explosion of some kind."

"No need to explain. I don't even want to think about it."

Raven grimaced at the notion.

"Like that stuffed snake they won at their school carnival last year," Charlie said, shuddering.

"Or that cute little electronic dog they built," Raven added. "I still have nightmares about that."

"Or that teddy bear Miss Sandy gave them. I really had no clue that the inside of a stuffed toy could turn gooey like that…"

"I said I didn't want to think about it!" Raven cried, covering her ears. "For the love of everything good, please change the subject!"

"So, um…"

Charlie hesitated.

"So ... I guess ... gosh, I can't get that poor teddy bear out of my head now ..."

"Oh my—Charlize Brown!" Raven moaned, drawing a few curious glances.

"Okay, okay! Um ... so ... you're back early. Why did I think you would be at Tanglewood for another week?"

Raven settled down, laughing as she finally uncovered her ears. The ringing, tinkling, clanging, and buzzing sounds of Bahia Bay carried on all around them as they strolled the length of one aisle before beginning down another.

"See? I knew you would forget. The camp was only two weeks this year instead of three, and let me tell you, we were super busy. It was action-packed, Charlie."

Charlie laughed aloud.

"Really?" she responded. "Wall-to-wall excitement at the summer camp for the musically gifted? I can only imagine."

"I'm serious," Raven assured her. "It's not even close to what you're thinking. In fact, it's pretty fantastic. There is so much to do, and really, you pick-and-choose—you don't have, like, a mandatory schedule that you have to follow with everyone else. There's so much freedom. And, of course, the music is always amazing, no matter what type you like. They know it all."

She paused for a moment before adding, "I'm telling you, you would have so much fun. If you went, not only am I certain that you would fit in perfectly, but everyone would be lining up to work with you, including the instructors. Everyone is so nice, and the boys ..."

Raven wiggled her eyebrows suggestively, causing Charlie to laugh again.

"Presley thinks you would like it too, you know," Raven added, mentioning the girls' mutual best friend who had also attended the music camp for the past two summers.

"And how would Presley even know I would fit in?" Charlie questioned. "Did a certain someone tell him a certain something that the certain someone promised they would keep secret?"

"Oh, okay," Raven admitted. "I may have, accidentally, a little, just slightly mentioned your singing to a few people at camp, but really—"

"A few?" Charlie abruptly stopped strolling, horrified. "Raven!"

"No reason to get mad at me because you're such a good singer," Raven stated.

"But—"

"Charlie, calm down. When I accidentally—and I do mean accidentally—let it slip to Presley, a couple of the instructors might have overheard, but trust me, it's absolutely not a big deal if you don't want it to be. I promise they won't come knocking at your door begging you to come to Tanglewood next year. But that doesn't mean I won't..."

"What?"

"Nothing," Raven declared sweetly, grinning at Charlie.

Charlie shook her head, unable to hide the smile that eclipsed her face.

"What am I going to do with you?" Charlie declared.

Raven continued to smile prettily, and the two girls laughed.

"But," Raven said once their laughter eased, "coming back a week earlier means more time on the field before soccer tryouts in the fall."

"True, and I need all the practice I can get."

"Aren't you excited, though?" Raven asked, her eyes widening as she looked over at her friend. "We're going to be freshman in high school! You know how much I love summer break, but at the same time, I can't wait to see what it's like, to see how it all feels. I've never even been inside Norbury High, especially the new campus. It looks so cool from the outside."

"You sound like Colby and Caleb," Charlie remarked, laughing, as the pair continued their stroll, "but I think they just want to see the science labs."

They turned another corner, leaving one brightly lit row of sights and scenes at the pavilion and arriving at a different one, which they immediately recognized as the row dedicated to locally made arts and crafts. Decorative exhibitions, most with a summertime theme, filled the many stalls. Suspended multi-colored lights streamed across the tops of the booths, bringing a further festive air to the carnival.

"Aren't you a little, I don't know … nervous, though?" Charlie asked as they sauntered past a painting depicting a pleasant Cape Cod waterfront scene.

"Sure. Maybe a little," Raven replied, "but that's probably normal for, like, every freshman in the history of civilization, so when you think about it like that, it's not really so bad. Anyway, it's probably not even nerves so much as—"

She halted, her words paused in mid-thought.

Charlie glanced over to her, and then followed Raven's gaze.

"What?" she asked, searching around. "What is it?"

"Who are they?" Raven inquired, her tone laced with amazement. She inclined her head in the direction of a trio of boys huddled in front of a booth further down the aisle.

Charlie followed her friend's gesture. She recognized one of the boys immediately—the one in the middle—even though she and Raven were some distance away and she could only see him from the side.

Jace, the so-called "boy at the park." He and the two other boys were examining something inside the booth.

"Oh, man!" one said loudly. "If that seashell was, like, ten times bigger, it would look exactly like you, J."

"Wow, you're full of jokes today, aren't you?" Jace replied. "Did you get them all out of the same book, or are you just making them up as you go along?"

The other two boys laughed. Without warning, Jace turned in the girls' direction, and his face registered slight surprise. Capturing the attention of his two companions, he then motioned over to Charlie and Raven and said something too low for Charlie to make out. She could feel Raven's inquiring glance as the three boys began to approach.

"Are you kidding me? You actually know them?" Raven asked. "Charlie, this should really be the first thing out of your mouth after two weeks of me being gone. Not just, 'Um, hey, Raven, gee, you're back early,' but, 'Hey, Raven, shut up. Before you say anything about camp, I feel it is my obligation as your best friend to tell you that I met this amazingly cute guy the other day, along with his amazingly cute—"

"Hey, Charlie!" Jace called as his small troupe drew near. "What, barely a week after meeting you for the first time ever, I see you again? And summer's not even halfway through."

His smile was casual, and his eyes seemed to twinkle playfully.

"Yeah," Charlie acknowledged, feeling slightly bashful as she ran a hand through her hair. "I guess that's the way it goes sometimes."

Jace chuckled before turning his attention to Raven. He offered his hand.

"Hi, I'm Jace. I don't believe we've met."

Raven's tanned skin took on a rosy tinge as she shook his hand.

"Raven," she replied, her voice, as always, pleasantly harmonious, but now with a sudden coyness too. "I've been friends with Charlie since ... almost forever, I guess."

Jace grinned.

"Almost forever, eh? You both must be pretty old, then. Here I thought I was meeting another soon-to-be high schooler."

Raven laughed quietly while Jace indicated to the two young men who stood on either side of him.

"Before I forget, these two knuckleheads are Michael and Gabriel. I guess I've known them for almost forever, too, although sometimes it seems like saying 'a lot longer than forever' would be more accurate."

The boy Jace called Michael waved him off dismissively. He was a dark-skinned teenager every bit as athletically built as Jace. His head was nearly clean-shaven and his short-sleeved shirt and shorts concealed less of his form than Jace's long sleeves and loose, tattered jeans. As he extended his hand, Charlie realized she had seen him before as well.

His grip was deceptively gentle.

"Ah, the infamous Charlie," Michael said. "We finally meet. Jace wouldn't shut up about you after you two ran into each other, so I naturally thought he had made you up completely."

"Actually, I've seen you before," Charlie revealed, to which Michael's expression registered surprise. "Weren't you playing football in the park with Jace the other day?"

"That depends," Michael responded, shifting slightly so he could grasp Raven's hand in his silky-smooth grip. The two exchanged pleasantries before he added, "Was I winning?"

"I'm not sure how wise it would be to ask her that," Jace remarked, "seeing as you were the one who almost decapitated her with your throw."

Jace gestured to Charlie melodramatically.

"Meet your almost-victim."

Michael's smirk vanished.

"Wait, that was you? Geez, I am so sorry. Jace was talking a lot of trash, egging me on, and I guess the throw just got away from me a little bit."

Charlie waved his concern aside.

"That's why you should stick to catching the football," Jace advised, earning him an antagonizing glare from his friend. "Leave the throwing to the grown-ups."

Michael rolled his eyes.

The boy named Gabriel had been shifting his attention between Charlie and Raven, his expression a mixture of skepticism and anticipation.

"Um, I hope I am not out of line asking this," he started, his eyes on Raven.

"Uh-oh," said Jace ominously. He and Michael shared a fleeting, wary look.

"Are you," Gabriel went on, "by any chance, Wampanoag?"

Jace and Michael exhaled audibly.

"Actually, my mom is," Raven replied. "I'm half."

The curly-haired boy nodded. Gabriel was shorter than the two other boys, although he appeared just as fit. He was certainly just as handsome. He grinned, one side of his smile rising higher than the other.

"I can tell because of your eyes. They're very deep. Very expressive."

Raven smiled shyly, shrugging.

"And she doesn't have a boyfriend, if you can believe it," Charlie interjected.

Raven turned on her abruptly, mouth agape. Michael and Jace chuckled, but before Raven could issue a defense, Gabriel spoke again.

"So, are you two, like, models or something?"

The laughter from the other boys swiftly diminished to a groan.

"And, there it is," Jace said in a lowered tone, glancing pointedly in Gabriel's direction before turning to Charlie and Raven. "I have to apologize for my friend here. His mouth has never been properly potty-trained, so sometimes stuff just comes out without him giving it any thought."

"What? No, I didn't mean it like that," Gabriel attempted to explain, "although, I mean, really, come on."

He looked to Jace and Michael, and then gestured to the girls. "I could mean it like that."

Both Raven and Charlie looked down at the boardwalk, sheepishly.

"I meant that they looked familiar," Gabriel continued, "like maybe I had seen them somewhere before."

Michael raised his eyebrows.

"So, since you thought you remembered them from somewhere, you automatically jumped to the conclusion they were models?"

He shook his head, grinning.

Gabriel combed a hand through his unkempt hair, a nervous grimace apparent on his face.

"No, wait," Jace said, "I want to hear you explain your way out of this one. What publication do you seem to recall these two nice young ladies modeling for? And, even if that were true, I'm really interested in why you feel familiar enough with their work to be able to identify them walking down the street—or, say, hanging out here at Bahia Bay Boardwalk, of all places."

Gabriel shifted anxious eyes from Jace to Charlie and Raven, and then back to Jace again. He shrugged limply.

"Does never forgetting a face sound good?" he offered.

Michael unleashed a guffaw.

"Hey, I said, 'or something!'" Gabriel declared. "I just meant they looked familiar, that's all."

He turned to the girls once more.

"I'm sorry if I offended you. I didn't mean that the way it came out. But you understand what I mean, right? About you looking familiar?"

"Actually, I'm not so sure," Charlie said as she glanced to Raven teasingly, suddenly gaining confidence at seeing Gabriel's distress. "What modeling jobs did you say you recognized us from, again?"

Gabriel groaned, his hands moving to his hair again.

"Hey, Charlie!"

The circle of teenagers turned at the sound of a youthful voice calling for Charlie's attention. Colby and Caleb ran to them, skirting past amused strollers populating the arts and crafts aisle.

"Charlie," Colby began, panting slightly, though his words emerged at a normal volume, "do you think we could borrow—"

Both boys suddenly noticed who stood alongside their sister.

"Oh ... ah, hey, um, hey, Rave—ahem," Colby attempted to clear his throat. "Um ... yeah. Hey."

Beside him, Caleb was speechless.

Raven smiled.

"Hey, you two. What's up?"

A moment of silence passed before a response came.

"Hey, um ... I mean, uh."

Colby cleared his throat again.

"Ahem, nothing, ah, you know, nothing much. How was, um, sorry, how was your music camp?"

"Did you two want to ask me something," Charlie interrupted with an arched eyebrow, "or were you going to spend the next thirty minutes drooling over Raven ... again?"

In her peripheral vision, Charlie noticed Gabriel elbow Jace in the side, although she kept her eyes on the twins.

Colby cleared his throat a third time. He blinked, as though coming out of a daze.

"Um, what? Oh, yeah, right. Charlie, can we borrow your bear?"

Charlie held up the purple bear.

"You mean, this bear?"

"I was going to ask about that, by the way," Jace said from behind them.

Caleb and Colby leaned around Charlie to look at the older boy, as though just realizing they had a larger audience.

"Hey, look, it's Jade!" Caleb said.

"You mean Jake," Colby corrected.

"It's actually Jace," Jace declared. Beside him, Michael and Gabriel tried to stifle their laughter.

"John?" Caleb questioned.

"Chase?" Colby asked.

"Okay," Charlie cut in, reclaiming the twins' attention. "Why do you think there is even the slightest chance of me handing this defenseless bear over to you, even for a second?"

"We promise we aren't going to do anything to it," Caleb implored. "You'll get it back just the way it is now—no scratches or scuffs or anything."

"Not unless we accidently drop it on the ground or something," Colby added.

"But that won't happen," Caleb finished.

"And even if it did," Colby sweetened the deal, "we would wash it for you."

"We'll wash it for you anyway, if you want," Caleb said.

"But," Charlie stated, "you promise you won't return it to me missing a head, or an arm, or a leg, or an eye, or—"

"Scout's Honor," Caleb declared.

He made the sign of the cross on his chest.

"Pretty sure crossing yourself isn't the symbol for Scout's Honor," Charlie said.

Jace laughed.

"And besides," he added, "you're doing that in the wrong order."

Caleb looked confused for a moment, turning to his brother. They each attempted to make the sign of the cross before abandoning the gesture altogether. Caleb turned back to his sister.

"Charlie, we promise!"

"Okay, okay," Charlie relented, passing the purple bear over. The twins beamed.

"Remember, no scratches, no scuffs, no eyes popped out," she warned again. She then nodded her head toward Raven.

"I don't think Raven would like you very much, then."

Raven gave an embellished pout, on cue.

"You got it," Caleb acknowledged, grinning broadly. "We won't let you down, sis."

"I don't care what they say," Colby said. "You're the greatest, Charlie Brown!"

"Ha, ha," Charlie muttered sarcastically as the boys rushed off with the stuffed animal in tow, soon disappearing down another aisle.

"You sure know how to make those little guys happy," Jace observed, grinning, at which Raven giggled softly.

"Simple gifts," Charlie said, shrugging.

"Hey, what's up with you, man?" Michael questioned, looking at Gabriel.

Gabriel's expression was furrowed again as he studied Charlie.

"So, I hope I'm not out of line by asking this," he began.

"You probably are," Jace commented.

"Is your last name really Brown?"

"Yeah," Charlie replied, nodding. She exhaled softly, awaiting the obvious question.

"So you actually go by the name Charlie Brown?"

"Well, Charlie's kind of a nickname, so ... yeah, I guess."

"That's cool," Michael said. "I think it'd be fun to have a name like that."

Gabriel's features danced with genuine excitement.

"That's it!" he all but shouted. "That's where I know you from!"

Fortunately, his cry drew little attention.

"You play soccer! You both play soccer!"

He turned to Michael and Jace.

"It's them! I knew it! Charlie Brown and Raven Summerset! Hah! I told you I recognized them!"

He pointed to a bewildered Michael.

"In your face, man!"

He pointed to Jace.

"And in your face!"

He then returned to Charlie.

"And kind of in your face, too," he said, his voice returning to a more regular pitch, "because you doubted me."

The smile that appeared on his face was both confident and reassuring at the same time.

"Don't ever doubt me."

Charlie and Raven shared a puzzled glance.

"You two must play some pretty good soccer, if Gabe's getting this excited," Michael suggested.

"No. What? 'Play?' No way," Gabriel retorted, almost vibrating with energy. "They don't just *play* soccer, Mike. They own it! They destroy it! Listen, the only reason you guys haven't heard of them—yet—is because they're girls just coming out of middle school."

He shot a glance in Charlie and Raven's direction.

"And I say that with all possible respect," he added before turning back to his high school buddies.

"All of that is going to change soon, though," he went on, "because they won't be in middle school anymore, and they won't be going up against middle school talent. And the whole girl thing won't matter once people see them play. I'm telling you, once they get to high school, the coach of the boy's squad will probably be on his knees begging them to play on his team."

He looked at Charlie and Raven again.

"You're both going to Norbury High, right?" he went on. "Please tell me you're going to Norbury."

Charlie and Raven, thoroughly dumbfounded, could only nod in response. Gabriel exhaled audibly as he patted his chest.

"Oh, man," he said breathlessly. "That's a relief. I think I almost had, like, a mini heart attack or something."

"Dude, seriously?" Michael inquired, looking at his friend. He then drew an imaginary line in the air at about eye-level.

"Look, Gabe, I need you somewhere around here, and right now, you're, like, way, way out there somewhere."

He gestured dramatically to the night sky.

"Well," Jace said, grinning at Charlie, "it sounds like my finely-honed athletic instincts were right. You are—dare I say it again—sporty."

"*Sporty!*" Gabriel declared in disbelief. "Are you kidding? Jace, I'm serious. You just wait and—"

"Hey, calm down, guy," Michael said.

"Like I said," Charlie replied, "I dabble."

She and Raven exchanged a glance.

"Yeah," Jace said, "I do remember you saying something like that before. We'll probably have to challenge you two to a little soccer match to see what you've got."

"J," Michael spoke up before either Charlie or Raven could respond, "think about what you're saying. I know you probably don't hear this very often, but when it comes to soccer, you ... you kind of stink, man."

Jace looked over with raised eyebrows.

"Stink?" Gabriel parroted, chuckling. He then shrugged. "That's one word for it, I guess. I would just say you're downright rank, man. You're kinda terrible."

"Oh, you're too nice," Jace said, feigning a tight smile. He then shifted back to Charlie and Raven.

"I don't know if I said this earlier," he told the girls, "but these are two of my very bestest friends in the whole wide world."

"Dude," Gabriel started, "you know we don't mean anything by it. It's just that, you know, you're actually, really not good at it. I mean, really not good. Quite frankly, you're awful. Terrible. When you step onto a soccer field, I don't know what comes over you, but it's, like, all of a sudden, every athletic bone in your body suddenly becomes very un-athletic, and—"

"Okay, then," Jace said loudly, clapping his hands to interrupt his friend's unique brand of support. "I guess it's about time for us to move along. We wouldn't want to bore Charlie and Raven with all of those details."

He smiled again as he looked at the girls, his grin captivating enough to entrance a stadium full of onlookers.

"If everything goes according to plan, I would say we are scheduled to unexpectedly run into each other again sometime early next week?"

Charlie laughed. "I guess so, and I look forward to being surprised to see you in the very near future."

"Great."

Jace turned to Raven.

"And it was a pleasure accidently meeting you. I'm sure we will do it again when we least expect it."

Raven smiled, almost—but not completely—suppressing her musical laugh.

"Yeah," she agreed. "I'm sure we will all unpredictably find ourselves in the same place at the same time again. Stranger things have happened."

Michael and Gabriel exchanged departing remarks with their eventual schoolmates at Norbury High, with Gabriel again expressing his desire to see both girls on the soccer fields in the fall. In time, the three boys departed, leaving Raven and Charlie to stroll the boardwalk attractions once more. The crowds were beginning to dwindle, Bahia Bay's closing time looming.

"I don't know if I should hit you, shake you, or just break down and beg you to tell me everything," Raven said after a little while.

Charlie acted indifferent.

"What do you mean?"

"What do you mean *what do I mean*?" Raven turned to her as they walked. "I'm sorry, but were you not talking to the same guys I was talking to a few minutes ago?"

"How could I not?" Charlie mumbled under her breath.

"And you seriously didn't think it was important enough to tell your most loyal, honorable, closest friend that you met a group of through-the-roof-hot high school guys while I was at

Tanglewood? You know, I think that kind of selfishness is grounds for the termination of our friendship."

"Okay," Charlie said. "Then I guess I don't have to tell you how I first met Jace if you're not going to be my friend anymore."

"And, scene," Raven said, her face brightening with a smile. "That was great. I totally had you. You know you'll always be my friend forever, Charlize Brown, which means now you have to tell me everything."

Charlie rolled her eyes, grinning.

"Anyway," she said. "I think you made a beautiful first impression, as you always do. I told you, you should do some type of modeling during the summer."

"And now you're talking crazy just like that cute, wild-haired one—Gabriel," Raven replied, snickering. "Don't forget, he thought both of us were models, so if I have to go, you're going to be right there beside me."

The pair turned a corner, their route taking them back to the boardwalk's only entrance and exit. Charlie turned to her attractive, delusional friend.

"But, Raven, he—"

And then, impossibly, for only an instant, out of the corner of her eye, she noticed something.

Someone.

A fleeting image whispered through her thoughts.

Icy-blond hair. Gray eyes.

Gray eyes.

Gray eyes staring back at her.

Hours after their encounter with the runaway in Greenfield, the vendor inside the food stand waited for Case's order.

"May I have one small—"

"Large, please," Beat interrupted as she stuck her head closer to the food stand window.

"Excuse me, one *medium* frozen lemonade, please."

Case emphasized the size, glancing toward Beat, daring her to argue.

Beat grinned back impishly.

"That will be one dollar," the man said, while a woman busied herself preparing the drink.

Case reached into his pants pocket, but before he could pull out the correct amount, Beat laid a bill on the counter. An instant later, the vendor slid over the drink. Case retrieved it and passed it along to Beat.

"And no change, please," Beat requested, moving closer to the window. Case looked from her to the vendor.

"But this is a ten dollar bill," the man said, sounding almost amused.

"Yeah," Beat said, grinning. "But I know this is going to taste amazing!"

The man looked to Case, his expression disbelieving.

"I did say that a medium frozen lemonade only cost a dollar, right?"

Case shrugged as he started to back away from the window.

"She kind of likes these shaved ice things," he explained. "A lot."

"Well, in that case," the man replied, smiling, "thank you very much. We appreciate it."

"No, thank you!" Beat called in a jubilant shout, already moving away from the stand and guzzling the flavorful concoction.

"This is great!" she added, holding the cup high in the air.

She then glanced around at the amused bystanders observing her display.

"This is terrific!" she said to everyone. "You have to try this!"

Case walked up to her, smiling, his hands tucked loosely into his jean pockets.

"You sure know how to draw an audience, don't you?" he asked with typical coolness.

The two began to saunter past the animated exhibits again.

"This is so good," Beat gushed. "Really, you have to try it. I feel like I'm buzzing."

"You're always buzzing," Case commented with a chuckle as he accepted Beat's offer of a taste. "I'm surprised you're just noticing it now."

"I love this," Beat continued. "Don't you love this?"

She turned a pirouette as they walked, her arms gliding into space effortlessly, her long hair floating from beneath her knitted cap as she twirled. Beat's face was dazzling, giving off a similar joyous energy to the blinking, glimmering, sparkling attractions they walked past. As she finished the twirl, she grabbed the lemonade out of Case's hand in one motion, smoothly taking another sip.

"That's pretty good," Case responded, "and yes, I love all of this—the sights and the sounds and the smells. But I mostly love it because you love it, and because I know why you love it so much."

Beat's lips curled into a cheerful grin.

"And you think I love it because everybody else loves it?"

"Exactly," Case replied.

"You know what?" Beat remarked as the pair turned a corner and moved down another aisle. "I think, after all this time, you are finally beginning to learn me."

She turned to look at him, smirking. Case rolled his eyes, slightly smile hinting faintly on his features.

"Whatever," he allowed simply.

They passed assorted displays and attractions—games to win prizes, food and drink counters, exhibits that promised the amazing, the beautiful, the horrifying, or the downright unusual. Visitors to the pavilion were clearly enjoying themselves, wrapped in the cozy, carefree pleasure of cheerful enchantment while not bombarded with lights too flashy, or spectacles too over-the-top. Cheerful enchantment was thick in the air, and Beat and Case absorbed it all.

Beat danced ahead nimbly, turning to walk in reverse. Case watched her, content.

"Do you want to go on the Vortex again?" Beat asked, speaking around the straw of her drink.

Case's eyebrows rose.

"And, before you say no," she continued, "let me give you a few reasons why I think you should."

"Humor me," Case responded, grinning, moving forward as Beat continued to move in reverse.

"Well," Beat began earnestly, "first off, it's so fun."

Her light tone dripped with elation, an emotion Case knew to be typical Beat.

"That's a good start," he admitted. "What else?"

"What else what?"

Case chuckled, his white-blond hair and snow grey eyes seeming to glimmer, reflecting the flashing displays along the boardwalk.

"You said you had a few reasons. I think a few means you should have a little more than one."

Still comfortably strolling backwards, and somehow able to avoid bumping into passersby, Beat just snickered around her straw.

"Anyway," Case said, "I think this place is about to close soon."

Beat returned to her forward-facing stride alongside Case.

"You think?" she asked. "It still seems early."

"What time do you think it is?"

"Um … 8:37."

Case snorted at her wild guess.

"Not even close. Try again."

Wait.

There.

He saw something. It was fleeting, very nearly imperceptible.

"Um …9:44. No, wait. 10—"

"Beat."

There it was.

That look.

Case's eyes swiftly shifted to the approaching girl. There were two of them, but one girl had sighted them and was now sneakily looking at him and Beat with more intent.

"What is it?"

Seriousness was immediately apparent in Beat's tone. Without needing to ask, she delved into Case's racing stream of thought.

Case's brow furrowed. He tilted his head down, attempting to avoid the girl's stare. Beat followed suit.

"Get ready," he whispered, so quiet he was certain only Beat would hear.

They passed the girl and her friend, casually trying to avoid her inquisitive glance. And then, a split-second later, Beat and Case immediately shot into the night sky at breakneck speed and in complete silence. So swift was their departure, anyone who had seen it would have thought the duo had vanished into thin air.

A nearby trashcan thumped lightly as an empty frozen lemonade cup dropped inside.

High in the darkened sky, stars twinkling above and the Bahia Bay Boardwalk miles below, Case stared back down to the ground. It was impossible—even for them—to make out the girl from that distance, but Case searched for her all the same. He then looked to Beat, his eyebrow arching curiously before he returned his focused gaze to the ground far below. He knew Beat understood.

This was a problem.

"*A*ND NOW YOU'RE TALKING *crazy just like that cute, wild-haired one—Gabriel,*" *Raven was saying.* "*Don't forget, he thought both of us were models, so if I have to go, you're going to be right there beside me.*"

The *cozy, warm, carnival-like atmosphere of Bahia Bay Boardwalk enveloped them as they strolled, the lights and simple, pleasing attractions comforting to the senses. The pleasant summer air washing across Nantucket Sound floated through the night in a leisurely manner. Charlie's gaze shifted to a child receiving a stuffed prize from a booth attendant. The kid showed off his reward to his parents, his cries of delight humming across the walkway before mixing into the general, vibrant din of the boardwalk.*

She began to turn back to her friend to respond.

"But, Raven, he—"

And then, the boy.

Icy-blond, almost silver, hair. Pale, snow-gray eyes.

His image was quick, almost like a dream or a flashback. As though she had seen him before.

And the smaller girl beside him—

"Pancakes are up!"

Miss Sandy's cheery call jerked Charlie out of her daydream. Fortunately, neither Miss Sandy nor the twins seemed to notice her jumpiness.

"Pancakes?" Colby questioned, setting his orange juice back on the table after taking a sip. "I thought we were having flapjacks?"

"Pancakes, flapjacks, griddle cakes, hot cakes, drop scones, johnnycakes—they're all pretty much the same thing," Miss Sandy explained as she placed a platter of food in the center of the table. "It just depends on what ingredients you use, what part of the world you're in when you're eating them, and whether or not you're in the late-1800s when you're eating them."

Colby reached for a pancake as soon as the serving dish was set. Caleb began scooping scrambled eggs onto his plate.

"I think flapjacks sounds better," he commented. "Or griddle cakes. Or hot cakes. Anything with 'cake' in it, really. It makes it sound like you can make them out of almost anything, and they still turn out awesome."

"Yeah," Colby agreed, "I like flapjacks better than pancakes."

"Should I make more, then?" Miss Sandy asked. She set her steaming cup of coffee down next to her plate as she settled into her place at the dining table. "That way, you can take some out to yer horses when ya mosey on down to tha corral."

Charlie snickered lightly as Caleb tipped an imaginary cowboy hat in Miss Sandy's direction.

"That'd be mighty fine ah ya, Mizz Sandy," he drawled.

Miss Sandy shook her head, smiling, as she reached for one of the breakfast dishes.

Sparkling rays of sunlight spilled through the French doors that separated the dining area from the veranda and the impressive landscape that bordered the beachfront. Through a stand of trees, Charlie could make out a wide swath of sandy shoreline that gradually dipped down to the cerulean waters of the Cape. Wispy clouds temporarily interrupted the otherwise blue sky, hinting at another clear New England day in Norbury.

"You guys never told me whether you had fun at Bahia Bay yesterday," Miss Sandy said after a moment of silence as everyone dug in to the food.

"Has there ever been a time when we didn't have fun there?" Charlie asked before taking a swallow of juice.

"I just like to hear the validation of yet another great idea I had," Miss Sandy replied, grinning.

"It was g—" Caleb started before he began coughing, having forked too much food into his mouth. Soon recovering, he readied himself for another large serving of pancake. The others at the table laughed as he bit into the food again.

"We saw Raven there yesterday," Colby remarked. "She's back from music camp."

Miss Sandy chuckled as Charlie rolled her eyes behind a piece of toast.

"I think she was asking about the boardwalk, not the nature and condition of my friends," Charlie stated.

"But she was at the boardwalk," Colby argued, "so that counts."

"He is right," Miss Sandy said. "I think it does count."

Charlie shook her head but said nothing.

"And what about you, Charlie?" Miss Sandy went on. "I didn't mention it last night, but when you came back with Raven, you had a … look on your face."

Charlie's thoughts flashed to icy-blond hair before just as quickly returning to the conversation at hand.

"Oh, I see it, too!" Caleb voiced, pointing at Charlie, who flinched back. "There it is! Oh, wait. No, that's just your usual face."

He and Colby laughed.

"Touché, Tweeb."

Charlie flicked a stray crumb in Caleb's direction.

"I'll have to remember to tell Raven you said hi."

She fluttered her eyelashes and made kissing sounds.

Caleb broke off a piece of crispy bacon, preparing to fire it at his sister.

"Don't you even think about it, Caleb Brown," Miss Sandy cautioned. "I would hate to accidently lock the basement door today just when you started working on that new rocket."

Icy-blond hair. Snow-gray eyes.

Caleb gobbled up the bacon, and Charlie returned to Miss Sandy, who was now sipping her coffee.

"It's probably nothing," Charlie said, attempting to dismiss the older woman's earlier inquiry. "At the boardwalk, I thought I saw someone…"

She let the thought taper, turning instead to Caleb and Colby, both of whom had resumed eating. Caleb flinched, as if expecting Charlie to throw more food at him.

"Did you two happen to notice—"

"That guy with one giant eye in the Unusual Hut?" Colby guessed, around a mouthful of pancake. "I know, it looked totally fake, but when we asked Mr. Sharpshire if we could see it up close, he—"

"Did you say one eye?" Charlie asked, glancing at Miss Sandy again.

Sandy Ellsbury, MD, PhD, who had probably seen a lot of strange things in her years actively practicing medicine, did not seem in the least bothered by the abrupt turn of the discussion.

"Yeah, and it was huge and bulging, like a Cyclops," Colby went on. "Believe me, we didn't think it was real, either. But when he poked at it, he—"

Charlie interrupted again.

"Okay, I would like to add Cyclops and all Cyclops-related creatures to the list of unmentionables while I am eating," she stated, looking at a chuckling Miss Sandy again before shifting back to the twins. "How can you two even stand going in there, anyway?"

Both boys grinned.

"It's inspiring," Colby offered.

Charlie grimaced, before calming herself.

"In any case, that was so far from what I was going to ask you, it's not even funny. I was wondering if you two noticed a boy and a girl at the boardwalk. The boy—"

"Wait, wait," Caleb said. "A boy and a girl?"

He turned to look at his brother.

"Did we see a boy and a girl there?"

He struggled to suppress his laughter.

"A boy and a girl?" Colby tapped his chin thoughtfully. "I don't know. Does seeing a girl, and then a boy, count as seeing a boy and a girl, or does—"

"The boy," Charlie interrupted, ignoring the boys' snickering, "had blond hair, lighter than mine, I think, closer to white— almost silver. I would guess he was a little older than me."

Charlie furrowed her brow as she tried to recall.

"The girl was younger than you guys. She had long dark hair, and I think she was wearing some type of knit cap or something, I'm not sure. But her hair still hung down underneath. It's weird … something about them … I don't know if…"

Her words faded again.

"Ah … nope," Colby answered after a moment's thought, while his twin simply shook his head. "I mean, maybe. I don't know. I don't remember seeing anyone like that, but that doesn't mean I didn't. It just means I don't remember."

Miss Sandy took another sip of coffee.

"Maybe they—the boy, at least—went to Walker last year and you just can't place him," the woman offered, alluding to the middle school Charlie had graduated from a month or so earlier, the same one Caleb and Colby would start in the fall.

"Or perhaps," Miss Sandy went on, "you've seen them around town and just not consciously realized it until you saw them again at Bahia Bay last night."

Charlie shrugged.

"Maybe. It's just that, I don't know, something …"

"Hey," Caleb said, after he had finished a bite of his eggs, "is that kid Jeff going to be a freshman with you next year?"

"Huh? Jeff?"

"Not Jeff. Jake," Colby corrected, shifting his focus from Caleb to his older sister. "He means Jake. You know, that kid from the park that you were talking to last night with Raven."

Miss Sandy perked up. "You mean Jace? The random-stalker boy from the park Jace? You saw him last night?"

Her eyes took on a certain sparkle.

Charlie attempted to melt into her chair, feeling her cheeks flush pink.

"Jace," Caleb echoed, looking to his brother slyly. "You're way off, Miss Sandy. I think you mean Jason."

Colby laughed and glanced at Charlie, who wanted to be anywhere else in the world besides sitting at the table discussing the "boy from the park."

"Hey, about that boy and girl you asked about."

Charlie straightened.

"When you say 'a boy and a girl,'", Colby began, "does it still count if it's a girl, and then another girl that kind of looks like a boy, and then…"

Charlie reached for her orange juice and slumped down in her chair again.

"**U**GH, YOU SOUND JUST like Brad," Cassandra complained as she and Emily drew closer to the bank of glass doors leading out of the office building. "Like him, you didn't even let me finish what I was going to say. So, after the guy was gone, I—"

Emily, barely listening to her friend's story, hesitated as they stepped into the downtown Albuquerque sunlight. Her pause was a faint waver, nearly unnoticed, as she glanced around quickly, attempting to take note of everything in an instant, scanning, searching for something—or someone—out of place. Her walk faltered as well, allowing Cassandra to get a few steps ahead.

Cassandra turned back to her briefly, and then glanced around, too, although with no inkling of what she should be looking for. Her gaze soon returned to her friend.

"Emily?"

At hearing her name, Emily snapped to attention, instinctively putting on what she hoped was an assured smile.

"Yeah," she said. "Sorry. I was just thinking about something. Let's go get some food."

It was an eerie, spine-tingling feeling that had returned as Emily stepped outdoors—a peculiar feeling of being watched. She had first become aware of the tantalizing sensation only days ago. So strange, so unusual, so unfamiliar, it was barely there, below the surface; yet, at the same time, it felt almost tangible to her, as though the feeling could somehow reach out and touch her whenever it chose to, like a hand lightly coming to rest on the small of her back, or the faintest whisper of wind fluttering over the nape of her neck.

However, unlike those other sensations, the feeling of being observed was neither comforting nor relieving.

The two coworkers passed others on the busy sidewalk, most wearing similar business attire, and Cassandra continued to carry the bulk of the conversation. However, Emily's preoccupation soon caused Cassie to once more abruptly interrupt her own words midstream.

"Emily, stop."

Cassandra drew to a halt in the middle of the bustling lunchtime sidewalk, making Emily pause as well. Cassandra ignored the irritated huffs the pair received for so unexpectedly holding up foot traffic and focused on her friend.

"You're starting to scare me. It's that stalker thing you were talking about, right? Don't you think you should go to the police? Or what about the security firm in the office? I'm sure they could look into it."

"No, no."

Emily shook her hand.

"Really. It's just ... some stupid thing, I don't know. I probably watched something scary and it's just carried over. Don't worry about it."

The two started to walk again.

"Or, maybe I'm developing my very own spidey sense," Emily said, smiling mischievously.

Cassandra rolled her eyes.

"Joke all you want, but don't even get me started on that," she said. "I told you Brad and I were going to see that new movie last night, right? Well, let me tell you ..."

Her voice faded away as Emily's ponderings began once more.

Unknown, unseen, unwanted eyes focused on her. Simply paranoia, or was it real?

Both?

Neither?

The feeling only emerged occasionally, and only outside her workplace—when she arrived in the morning, when she departed at night, or, as was the case now, when she headed off to lunch at midday. For some reason, it did not follow her home. Still, it was more than enough to put her on edge. The feeling of being watched—without knowing by whom or from where, and definitely without permission—made her pale skin break into goosebumps, her breath catch and accelerate, and her heart rate quicken. It was, quite frankly, a crawling, creeping, encroaching feeling of dread.

The feeling lingered as she passed the storefronts and businesses in the commercial district, a multitude of faces approaching and leaving, all with no unique focus on her.

But, perhaps, there was one, somewhere, whose eyes remained on her, unwavering, noting her every step, even right now...

"Emily!"

Emily looked up at Cassandra, who wore a pleading expression, like that of a child who is not being adequately listened to. Cassandra held a door open, signaling for Emily to enter before her.

Emily's eyes shifted to the archway above; *Plácido's* was written in funky, cursive script.

"Did I mention you're really starting to make me feel weird?" Cassandra asked, only half-jokingly, as Emily passed through. "Be honest. What are the chances your feeling is more than just a feeling? I mean, is it possible that—"

Emily waved her off, shaking her head.

"I don't even—I don't know. It's just a thing. Really, Cassandra, don't worry about it. I think I'm just obsessing over it or something, so now it's starting to eat into my brain. I don't even know why I'm thinking about it so much anyway. We both know that if anyone should be worried about a stalker, it should be you."

"Oh my God!" Cassandra said, shoving her friend gently. "That is, like, the worst—"

Emily grinned.

"And it would probably end up being some lovesick high school boy who saw you, and—"

"Emily!"

"Ah, *Emilia! Cassandra!* My two *favoritos, más bellos,* customers!"

The owner of Plácido's strode over to them, his burly arms wide in familial greeting.

"Come in! *¡Entra, entra!* You know I always have a place ready for my *hijas preciosas.*"

THE CHARMING BELL ABOVE the entrance to the soda parlor jingled delicately as Beat and Case entered, the old-world, cobblestone walkways amidst the island of Nantucket giving way to the store's interior. The parlor, complete with a counter and barstools at front, possessed a laid-back, old-fashioned air perhaps not far removed from those of the earlier half of the 20th century. The tables and chairs scattered about the shop looked both decades old and sparkling new at the same time, although an obvious renovation was the arcade room at the back of the shop. It was no wonder the parlor consistently enjoyed numerous customers, particularly those with children. Today was no exception.

Case and Beat seated themselves across from a well-groomed, casually dressed man, his forearms folded over the metal tabletop as he sipped at his drink through a straw. His eyes followed their movements as they sat. Two beverages rested before them, awaiting their arrival.

Beat immediately grasped for her straw, taking a long gulp, her posture on the tabletop mirroring the man's. The man on the other side of the table continued to sip his drink, too, both he and Case watching with amusement the way Beat attacked her soda.

At last, Beat released the bendy straw from her mouth.

"Ahh," she breathed.

Then she burped softly.

The man looked surprised; Beat's grin was her only response. The man, who had been steadily drinking since the pair sat down, finally pulled away from his own cup and gave a satisfied sigh.

And then he belched, slightly louder than Beat's.

Beat and Case stared at the man, Beat's face displaying a mischievous appreciation. The man returned Beat's gaze, eyebrows raised in challenge, a nearly nonexistent smile curling his mouth. Case took a slow, careful drag from his drink and slyly surveyed the rest of the soda shop.

Beat belched again, louder than the man's or her own previous effort. She grinned, leaning forward to catch her straw in her mouth again before turning to glance at her partner. Case quickly shook his head in response to her silent question. Beat turned back to the man.

The man looked at her, his eyes narrowed. A moment later, he let loose a second burp, loud enough to draw the attention of nearby customers. He barely had time to gloat before Beat responded, her burp louder still and attracting even more notice.

The man's jawline clenched. He ground his teeth in mock offense, preparing himself for his next attempt, when, suddenly, another burp sounded from a few tables away. Beat, Case, and the man turned in the direction of a young boy, who giggled and covered his mouth. His mother, in the process of reprimanding him, tried to mask her own laughter.

Another belch issued from one of the tables near the back, and then another from the front. Beat burped again, and the man followed, adding to the chorus of burps echoing through the store.

"Hey, hey!" the heavyset shopkeeper called from behind the counter. "Knock it off! Knock it off! I'm trying to run a respectable business here, not some kind of flimflam burping shop."

He flapped a small dishtowel at the table Beat and Case occupied.

"And I know you two started it," he said, gesturing to Beat and the man seated opposite her. "So pipe down."

The man put up his hand in submission.

"Sorry about that, sir. I guess we got carried away."

The shopkeeper *hmmphed* before edging down the bar to take another customer's order. At the table, the man turned to the pair sitting across from him. He was met with Beat's grin of delight.

"I win," she said simply, grinning, before taking another taste of her drink.

The man attempted to imitate the storekeeper's *hmmph*, but it turned into a chuckle. He shook his head.

"Does that happen often?" Case asked.

The man looked at him, smiling.

"It happens a lot," the man replied.

"Which one? Burping, or getting scolded?"

The man seemed about to respond, but then thought better of it. He shook his finger at Case in concession.

"Ah, good one. I'll have to think about that."

He reached for his drink, took a long sip, and placed it on the table again. For a moment, no one spoke.

"So," said Case at last, "I think we may have an … issue."

"Well, I doubt that."

The man took another swig of his soda, which, inexplicably, was still completely full.

Case looked across to the man, not speaking.

"You doubt that?" Beat asked. Her voice held a trace of surprise.

"What's the problem?" asked the man, shrugging. His lips curled into a playful smile around his straw.

"'What's the problem?'" Beat repeated

She looked over at Case.

"Don't fall for the bait," he warned, keeping his eyes on the man, though his lips also upturned slightly.

"Did you hear him, though?" Beat declared, incredulous. "He just asked what the problem was."

She leaned forward in her seat.

"Look here, buddy…" she started in.

"You're falling for the bait," Case told her in a singsong tone.

"Let her fall for the bait," the man remarked, smirking.

"Oh, you better believe I'm falling for the bait," Beat said. "What's the problem, you say?"

"Yes, what's the problem?" the man asked again. "So someone maybe, possibly, kind of, perhaps recognized you. You act like that could turn into some sort of thing."

Beat's mouth dropped open in astonishment.

"You like seeing her like this, don't you?" Case asked the man.

"Oh, I love it," the man answered.

Beat stood up in her chair and leaned across the table in as intimidating a manner as her petite frame could manage, her finger directed at the man's face. Her normally cheery eyes seemed to glint. Opposite her, the man's grin only widened.

"Look here, buddy," Beat said again. "If that girl recognized us last night, and—oh, don't give me those Basset Hound eyes. You know what I'm talking about. If she recognized us, and if she remembers where she recognizes us from, then yes, this could turn into 'some sort of thing.' I'm sure I don't need to remind you of that, though. I'm sure I don't need to remind you of what happened last time. I don't even need to remind you of what happens when people even so much as think that something even remotely extraordinary is involved. A thing? Mister, you better believe it could turn into a thing! Try the Participant Reformation!"

"Protestant Reformation, you mean," Case corrected softly.

"The Protestant Reformation!" Beat attempted again.

She looked down at Case.

"What did I say?" she muttered.

"Participant," Case replied.

"That was kinda close," Beat assured him.

Smiling, the man across from them held up his thumb and index finger a tiny distance apart, showing that she was, indeed, quite close. Beat finally glanced around the parlor, becoming aware of the eyes focused in her direction, including the shop owner's. Suddenly, she raised her hands in the air, grinning.

"Free drinks and ice cream for everyone!" she exclaimed.

"Yea—" the children in the shop began to answer, but the shopkeeper quickly cut them short.

"No!"

He shot another aggravated look at Beat's table.

The man with Beat and Case motioned his apologies once more, while Beat lowered herself back into her seat. She reached for her soda again and took a long gulp.

"I'm hoping this question is unnecessary," the man started, "but I just want to make sure by hearing you answer it out loud. You know that none of those events you were referencing were caused because of the actions of any of you, correct? That is, you understand those things were going to happen anyway, including the"—he grinned—"Protestant Reformation?"

Beat gazed back at him in response, still drinking.

"Beat, what was the Protestant Reformation?" the man asked.

Beat shrugged innocently.

"I actually have no idea. It sounded pretty good, though, didn't it?"

The man caught Case's eye and chuckled again. Meanwhile, Beat's attention shifted to the rear of the store, toward the arcade.

"Oooh," she voiced. "I'll be right back."

She hopped up from the chair, but then turned back around, glancing at her partner.

"Now, are you going to be all right if I leave you alone for a little while?" she asked Case in a patient tone.

"I think I'll be—" Case started, but Beat was already skipping away, sending an "Okay, see ya!" over her shoulder.

"Fine," Case finished to the spot Beat had occupied a second before.

The other man laughed, shaking his head, and Case returned his attention to him.

"So, there is really nothing to be worried about?" Case asked, going back to the original topic.

"You're worried?"

Case arched his eyebrow in response.

"Tell me about the girl, then," the man suggested. "What do you remember about her from the first time?"

"Her name is Charlize Brown, though she commonly goes by Charlie. She was in a car crash about six years ago, along with her parents, her two brothers, and the driver of the other vehicle. Beat and I took the children."

He paused, his brow furrowing further.

"When she first looked at me, once we were away from the accident," he continued, "she ... she looked ... her eyes were ... I don't know, different somehow. I can't really describe it. I'm not sure I've ever seen that look before, not from a human being. It's as though she were able to see ... into me, as though she could see ... the truth."

The man, listening intently, nodded.

"But, it was just a moment," Case said, "a flicker. Very faint. Barely there."

The man leaned back in his chair, gazing at Case, the illusion of a smile on his face.

"Interesting," he commented softly.

Case lowered his gaze to the tabletop, and then brought his head up to meet the other man's eyes.

"Have you been, um, you know..."

Case scratched at his pale-blond hair uneasily.

"...watching..."

He indicated that the man should finish the thought and respond.

The man studied Case for a moment.

"I find your feelings very curious right now."

"It almost feels as though it's not my place to ask," Case said.

The man waved him off.

"Your place is much more inclusive than you think," he replied. "It's always all right to ask the question. You're wondering if I have been paying particular attention to her in light of this ... issue, as you called it? My answer is that I pay particular attention to everyone in light of anything. You're wondering if I have talked to her? My answer is, again, yes. I talk to everyone, all the time.

"Of course it's always all right to ask," he repeated, "but I'm pretty sure you already knew the answers to those questions, so they might as well have been rhetorical. Next?"

Case smiled.

"But if she, in fact, does remember," the teenage-looking boy proposed, "if she remembers the entire event, what happens then?"

"Is that another rhetorical?" the man asked. "Because from how you just described this girl, it sounds as though you know that answer as well."

He then smiled at Case's thoughtful expression.

"Nothing's changed," the man declared, shrugging. "You go where you're needed. You're really not that different from me, at least—"

His words halted as he realized the cup he was reaching for was empty. He glanced at Case again.

"That's it?" he asked, chuckling. "You're cutting me off?"

Case put his hands up and shook his head in denial.

"Well, okay, then."

The man rose.

"I'm sure the guy behind the counter will at least be a little happy to see us leave."

Time to go, Beat, Case voiced in his mind, also rising from his chair and following the man to the parlor counter.

Almost immediately, Beat was back at his side.

"I was done, anyway," she announced. "I was getting so tired of beating all those kids in there, you wouldn't believe it."

She straightened the cap on top of her head, allowing long stands of dark hair to fall down underneath. Her earrings sparkled in the light of the soda shop.

"Really? You were losing that badly, eh?" Case returned, grinning.

Beat responded by casting a cheeky smile in her partner's direction. As the group approached the cash register, Case reached into his pocket for money.

"You're kidding," the man commented, not even bothering to glance in Case's direction.

Case removed his hand from his pocket. He and Beat began to head for the exit.

"You'll know when it's time," the man said.

Beat and Case suspended their progress to look back at him.

"Maybe not today," he continued, turning and meeting their eyes, "maybe not tomorrow, maybe not next week. But eventually. Should she realize something, you will know what to do. You will be ready. I trust you."

The pair near the door nodded at the man's parting words.

"On the other hand, you may want to think about why you decided to go to that boardwalk yesterday," the man observed casually. "Coincidence?"

He then laughed, as if he had just made a joke, before facing the approaching shopkeeper once more.

Case's gaze was frozen on the man's back.

Beat stood on her tiptoes, reaching up to rub his pale-blond hair.

"You're falling for the bait, you know," she said, grinning.

"Yeah," Case said quietly, as he continued to stare at the man. "Yeah, I know. I'm supposed to."

"**I** DON'T THINK THAT'S a very good idea, honey. He looks like he's sleeping."

"But it'll only be for a second, and then he can go right back to sleep."

With his sunglasses perched over his eyes and the sun beating down on his head, Nick did indeed appear to be snoozing on one of the benches positioned along the southern Californian boardwalk. In any event, even through his haze, he could still comprehend the mother and daughter's conversation.

"Okay," the mother consented, still reluctant. "But do it lightly, honey. Lightly."

Nick felt a sharp, insistent poke on his thigh, followed quickly by another. In spite of it, he remained unmoving.

"Not so hard, sweetie," the child's mother admonished. "You don't have to stab him."

"Sorry, Mommy."

However, the child's next poke was just as adamant as the ones before, if not a little more so.

Glasses still hiding his eyes, Nick slowly rotated his head toward the source of the prodding. In his mind, he imagined the movement was slow enough to look intimidating, or at least a little creepy.

Meeting his gaze was a seven-year-old girl. Her smile was small and cute, almost mischievous. Closely behind the girl stood her mother, who was smiling at him in apology.

"I'm so sorry if we woke you up," she began to explain, "but, for some reason, my daughter was very insistent about speaking with you."

Nick slipped off his shades.

"So, was that turn I did with my head just now a little scary?" he asked.

"Not really," the girl replied, still smiling. "I've seen that in a movie. You're not really scary."

Nick looked back up to her mother, who shrugged.

"It really wasn't a very scary head turn," she agreed. "I think your face is too friendly for that to work."

Nick grinned.

"All right," he said, returning to the girl, "what's up?"

"Can I sit on your lap?" the child asked, twisting nimbly from her left to right foot and back, speaking in the way little girls do when using 'adorable' to their advantage.

Her mother gasped.

"If I had known you were going to ask that, we would have kept right on walking and not disturbed this nice young man."

She began to apologize to Nick again.

"But, Mommy," the girl looked up at her mother with doe-like eyes. "I have to sit on his lap to ask him my question."

"What, like Santa Claus?" the woman chuckled as her daughter's face lit up at the mention. "Honey, Christmastime is almost half a year away. Anyway, don't you think this boy is a little too young to be Santa?"

"It's no problem," Nick offered. He widened his stance on the bench so the little girl would be able to sit on one of his legs. "I think I've seen how they do it in the malls and stuff. It doesn't look to be too hard."

Both Nick and the girl turned to the mother.

"Oh, all right then," she relented. "Just so long as you know what you're getting into."

The girl hopped on Nick's knee with little difficulty, although Nick feigned a grimace.

"A little heavier than I would have imagined," he commented, grinning. "I guess I need to work out more. But, I'm hangin', though, I'm hangin'. So, let's see if I can ..."

He cleared his throat.

"Ho, ho, ho!" he pronounced, his voice taking on a magnificent, deep-throated quality that the little girl on his lap instantly recognized. "So, what does little Marena just have to tell me, hmm?"

The child seemed tickled at Nick's marvelous change of voice, not to mention that he somehow knew her name without asking.

Her mother, however, was decidedly less than thrilled.

"How do you know her name? Have we met before?"

"Ho, ho, ho!" Nick chortled. "Isn't Santa supposed to know the names of all the good little children? Ho, ho, ho!"

"Okay, ha ha. Very funny."

Humor was not at all evident in the mother's tone.

"Seriously, how do you know her name? I certainly don't remember ever meeting you, and you're much too old to be a classmate of hers."

Nick chuckled again.

"You can't tell me that you just guessed that name out of thin air," the girl's mother added.

"It's okay, Meredith," Nick assured her, still speaking with the deep-throated, wizened voice of someone much older. "I actually know your name, too. It's ... well, it's Meredith. I just said it. Ho, ho!"

The woman stood speechless. Nick winked, smiling, before shifting his attention to the girl.

"So, back to Marena. Go ahead with what you wanted to ask me, although I think I may already know what you're going to say. Ho, ho—ha!"

He broke out of his Santa voice and laughed normally, glancing from Marena to her mother, and back again.

"I feel like I may be laying it on a little too thick," he said as his laughter subsided. "Is it too thick? I think it's too thick."

Marena shook her head, still grinning from ear to ear.

"No," she said. "You sound just like I thought you would. It's perfect."

Meredith regained her ability to speak.

"How—how did—wha—how...?"

Nick leaned in closer so Marena could whisper into his ear. After she finished, he looked at her.

"I'm not sure I even know what that is," he replied, keeping his expression blank.

The little girl gazed back at him, thoroughly unconvinced.

"Okay," Nick amended, his face breaking into a smile once more. "I may have a teeny, tiny idea of what it is. But, as far as I know, they won't be in any toy stores for a long time. Not until Thanksgiving, at least."

Marena whispered into his ear again.

"Even when it comes out," Nick explained, "it may be hard to find. I'm sure a lot of people are going to be trying to get it, especially so close to Christmas."

Marena fell silent, her eyes losing some of their sparkle. Nick looked up to Meredith, who was watching their exchange with skepticism. When their eyes met, Meredith's brow arched in unspoken question.

Nick returned his attention to Marena.

"Tell you what, I'll talk to some people," he offered.

Marena's face brightened.

"We'll put our heads together, and I'll see what we can come up with. But, you have to do something for me in return."

The little girl looked at him with rapt attention.

"You know what I'm going to say," Nick hinted, grinning.

"Be good, and listen to Mommy and Daddy, and listen to Mrs. Morgan at school," Marena replied.

Nick slipped back into his Santa Claus voice.

"So, do we have a deal, little Marena?"

She nodded earnestly.

Nick grinned.

"Excellent! Ho, ho, ho!"

Nick offered his hand, and Marena shook it, her hand enveloped.

"Ho! Geez, your grip is strong."

Marena giggled.

"Okay, Marena," her mother announced. "I've been crazy enough to let you talk to this young man, who, for some reason unbeknownst to me, actually knows both of our names"—she shot Nick another curious look—"and I wouldn't be surprised if I have to call the nice policemen later, because he somehow knows where we live."

Nick shook his head, grinning, as Marena hopped down from his lap.

"Although I've been to your home plenty of times, I'm not really that good with addresses," Nick said, his normal voice returning. "The reindeer handle that part."

Marena laughed again. Meredith continued to stare at him with an incredulous expression as she took her daughter's hand in her own. They began to turn away.

"And you don't have anything to ask me, Miss Meredith Anthony?" Nick called out.

The mother–daughter pair paused. Meredith looked back at Nick.

"It's Mrs. Meredith Joyner, if you must know," Meredith returned.

"Of course," Nick said. "Now, it is."

He gestured to the little girl.

"And Miss Marena Joyner," he affirmed, inclining his head in salute. "But before that, I seem to remember a Meredith Anthony. You used to live in…"

He closed his eyes, concentrating, before opening them once more.

"Grove Gardens, correct?"

Meredith laughed, shaking her head.

"Wow. Not even close."

"Well, hey, like I said, I'm not so good with addresses. But you are from California, right?"

"Way to go out on a limb!" Meredith exclaimed. "You just assumed I was from California, so you picked a city at random!"

Nick shrugged, enjoying the exchange.

"Do you still like to roller skate?" he asked.

Meredith froze, stunned into silence once more.

"You remember that Christmas, don't you?" he added. "The year you got those brand-new skates with the strings all different colors?"

Meredith glanced down at her daughter at the same moment that Marena looked up.

"We personally designed a lot of those that year, including yours," Nick noted. "They were pretty popular. I remember that was the only thing on your list."

"I told you," the little girl whispered, smiling up at her mother.

"It's okay if you don't recognize that feeling that you have right now," Nick observed, causing Meredith's eyes to find his again. "You used to understand it, but now you don't because you've forgotten. But that feeling, that excitement, it's still there. You know how I know?"

He grinned as Meredith remained speechless.

"Because you stopped to talk to me. You let Marena talk to me. You are aware of the feeling, even though you can't quite identify it. You know who I am; you're just afraid of what it could mean if you admit it. But don't worry. It'll be our little secret."

Meredith stood unmoving, while little Marena seemed to vibrate with energy, her gaze swinging between her mother and Nick.

After a few moments, the woman broke from her trance.

"O-Okay, Marena," she said, her voice softer, weaker than before. "I think it's time to go. We still have a lot of stops to make before Daddy gets home."

She tugged on her daughter's hand, keeping her eyes fixed on the young man sitting so casually on the bench. Slowly they turned away again, but only managed a few steps before looking back at the boy.

"And no more hogging the playhouse at school," Nick said, pointing and smiling at Marena. "That's not very nice."

The little girl's face shone with pure delight. She waved happily, while her mother exhibited utter disbelief. Nick waved when they glanced back a final time; then he reached for his sunglasses.

The summer foot traffic in Newport Beach, California, didn't pay him much notice. Sighing, he relaxed back onto the bench. He closed his eyes. The sun beamed down warmly.

As though on cue, his stomach rumbled.

He opened his eyes again.

EMILY HENDRICKS PULLED OPEN the door to her apartment building and stepped into the ornate foyer, her pocketbook on her shoulder and a shopping bag clutched in one hand.

Having joined Cassandra on an impulsive shopping detour right after work, Emily had, at last, purchased a pair of designer heels she had been eyeing for weeks. On the very same outing, her friend and coworker had amassed a few bagfuls of not-inexpensive articles, seemingly on sight.

Emily smiled as she recalled teasing Cassandra for her apparent addiction to spending.

"Don't judge me," Cassandra had said, feigning stubbornness. "Geez, you sound just like Brad. And my mom."

Emily could only shake her head and laugh at the time, and now, she did the same. Her happy mood was a welcome distraction from the ominous feelings that had cropped up in her life over the last week or so.

"Good evening, Miss Hendricks."

It was Walt, the apartment building's security officer.

"Walt," Emily replied as she approached his desk on the way to the grid of mailbox slots on the far side of the lobby, "if you want me to keep calling you by your first name, you have to call me Emily. It's only fair."

"My apologies, ma'am. Miss Hendricks it is, then."

"Okay, Mr. Flannery, but two can play that game."

Emily grinned at the portly guard before turning to her mailbox.

"Someone seems to be in a jokey mood today," Walt remarked.

"Spending time with Cassandra outside of the office can do that. Anything interesting go on today? Have to beat up any vandals?"

"Well, Miss Hendricks, of course I can't discuss my covert activities for security purposes, but this did come for you by means of being slipped under the side entrance doorway. I would tell you what it was, but"—Walt held the envelope up to the overhead lights—"nope, my X-ray vision seems to be on the blink today."

Emily walked to the guard's desk once more, a handful of mail firmly in her grasp. Walt's station was positioned in front of the small bank of elevators and the main stairwell, giving him a perfect view of any movement in the lobby area. Television displays along the walls of his table captured live shots of the building's entrances, exits, and corridors.

"I'm pretty sure reading someone else's mail is illegal," Emily declared.

She dropped the shopping bag momentarily and took the envelope Walt offered. *Emily* was scrawled on the front in cramped lettering.

"And don't think I didn't hear that 'ma'am' you tried to slip in there earlier," she added.

The guard shrugged, his attention returning to the displays at his desk, while Emily flipped the envelope over and then quickly back to the front again.

"How do you know I'm the Emily this is addressed to?"

"Believe it or not, Denise said you're the only Emily who lives in the building," Walt replied without glancing up, referring to the building's property manager. "She's actually the one who found it slipped under the door."

"Emily," she muttered the name under her breath before tearing open the envelope. "That's a little weird."

Walt shrugged again, still studying one of the monitors.

After a few moments of silence, the guard glanced up, then looked down, and then instantly looked up again.

"Miss Hendricks, are you all right? You're as white as a sheet."

Walt's eyes dropped to Emily's hands, which trembled slightly.

"Miss Hendricks?"

The young woman appeared frozen in place, too shocked to move, too shocked to even breathe. Walt leaned over the desk's partition and gently removed the paper she clutched in her hands.

Emily's hands stayed in the same position, her eyes now staring down at nothing.

Walt turned the letter so he could read it, but before he began, something attached to the bottom of the page caught his eye.

It was a photo of Emily, captured from some distance away. From the clothes she wore, it looked as if it had been taken during a workday. The Emily in the photo was obviously not posing, nor did she even seem aware someone was taking her picture. It was a swift, hurried snapshot, thoroughly unprofessional, and thoroughly terrifying in its invasiveness.

Walt glanced up again.

Emily had not moved.

The security officer reached for the phone on his desk. His movement broke Emily's daze somewhat, and her eyes turned to him, unblinking and unfocused.

"Miss Hendricks, I'm calling the—"

Just as his gaze shifted to the keypad on the telephone, a subtle, worrying shift caught his eye.

"Emily!"

Letter and phone forgotten, the tubby security guard rushed around the desk with surprising quickness. He caught Emily's slumping body just before she collapsed onto the polished marble floor.

RAVEN AND CHARLIE STROLLED down the beach, the sun-bleached sand shifting under their bare feet as they walked. A cool, gentle breeze swirled off the water and ruffled the beach grass, creating yet another picturesque, tranquil day in Norbury. The two teenagers were a fair distance down the sand from Miss Sandy's home, where they had ditched their shoes. On this stretch of seashore, however, everyone knew everyone else, and leisurely wanderings were not only permitted, they were encouraged.

The ambling pair soon came to a woman standing off the wood-planked balcony of another beachfront manor lining the coast. She waved as the girls approached.

"Charlie. Raven," the woman greeted as the teenagers acknowledged her wave. "How are my girls today?"

"We're fine, Mrs. Kennedy," Charlie answered. "Just enjoying the beautiful weather."

"Isn't it fantastic? This must be your favorite part of summer so far, Charlie. Sandy told me last night that the boys were off to space camp in Florida."

"Yeah, they left yesterday. They've been working on another space rocket, so actually, this camp is right on time for them. I just hope they don't find a way to blow up the real thing."

"Yes, Sandy told me about that, too," Mrs. Kennedy said, laughing.

She gestured in the direction Raven and Charlie were heading.

"I think Presley started up a volleyball game further along down the beach. I'm sure he would be forever grateful to have you both on his team."

"But then we wouldn't be able to experience the joy of beating him," Raven responded, grinning.

"That's exactly what I told him!" Mrs. Kennedy laughed again, waving goodbye as the girls continued walking.

They were hardly out of earshot before Raven spoke up.

"And now, since you won't bother to bring up more important matters," she said, turning her alluring brown eyes to her friend, "I will have to. Any word from Jace or his friends?"

Charlie rolled her eyes.

"It's barely been a week, Raven. Anyway, it's not like I have their numbers or any other way to contact them."

"Yeah," Raven said, sighing. "I thought about that after they left. I didn't even think to ask while we were talking to them. Too—"

"Distracted," the girls said in unison, causing them both to fall into a fit of laughter.

"It's times like these when a Facebook account would come in handy," Raven noted.

"So get one," Charlie challenged, poking at her friend. "Who's stopping you? That'll keep you from badgering me about them.'"

"No, you get one," Raven returned, poking Charlie back. "And then I can keep badgering you."

"No, you!"

They laughed again.

As they calmed down once more, the teenagers paused along the sand. A red-tailed hawk, a common sight along the beachfront, swooped in from the air, plunging down as though on an invisible spiral staircase. It flattened itself before diving headfirst, tucking its wings into its body, its head forming a perfectly straight line with its plummeting form as it readied itself for a catch. In mid-dive, the hawk aborted the attempt, extending its wings out and slowing its speed to a soft glide just beyond the water's reach.

Shaking out its feathers, the hawk then glanced around casually, hardly seeming to acknowledge its audience of two, who stood watching silently. The bird's head swiveled back and forth, as if wondering how its potential meal managed to skirt away at the last moment. It then began walking in the direction Charlie and Raven had just approached from, on to other interests.

Raven easily picked up the conversation where it had left off.

"How are you going to find them to play soccer if you don't have their numbers?"

"Who said anything about finding them?" Charlie replied.

Loose tendrils of her blond hair danced lightly in the breeze before she pushed them down again.

"Anyway," she went on, "if we're at McCormick a lot, chances are we will run into them there. I don't remember seeing them there before, but Jace and Michael seemed pretty familiar with it, like they went often."

"Yeah, well, you've seen them twice so far without planning it," Raven acknowledged. "Knowing you—as I do so well, I might add—you'll probably see them again before you know it."

"You're just hoping I do, because you'll most likely be with me, and then you will see them again, too."

"Oh, don't act so innocent with me," Raven offered, grinning. "I saw how you were looking at him—all of them, really."

Charlie shook her head, and they both laughed again. Down the beach, they could see the volleyball game Mrs. Kennedy had mentioned; sounds from the match were dampened by distance and the surf, but grew steadily louder as they wandered toward it.

"Do you remember those two people we saw at Bahia Bay after we talked to Jace and his friends?" said Charlie unexpectedly, glancing over to her friend for a moment before returning her gaze ahead to the approaching volleyball game.

Icy-blond hair. Snow-gray eyes.

"The two people we saw at Bahia Bay?" Raven parroted. "I think you'll need to describe them a little more than that."

"You remember," Charlie began, turning to her. "It was a boy and a girl. The boy was older—around our age—and the girl would be in, like, elementary school—younger than my brothers, but not by much. He had whitish-blonde hair, and the girl had long dark hair like yours, and she was wearing a beanie."

Raven looked at her blankly.

"Remember, you caught me looking and asked me if I knew them?" Charlie pressed further.

"Um…" Raven shook her head slightly. "You're sure I said that? I don't remember."

Charlie sighed.

"Why?" Raven asked. "Did you know them?"

She grinned cheekily.

"Was the boy cute?"

Charlie scoffed.

"You're obsessed," she scolded her laughing friend. "But seriously. When I saw them, it was kind of weird, like I should know them from somewhere. I don't think I even got a good look at them, it was too quick, and with people around and everything. We were on one side of the aisle, and they were on the other, so we never got that close. Still, I can see that boy's face in my mind, and his eyes—like a picture, as though he were standing right in front of me.

"Maybe he went to our middle school or something," Charlie went on, "and I just vaguely remember him. Or maybe I'm getting them both mixed up with someone else. On the other hand, maybe I don't even know what I'm talking about. Maybe I'm just going crazy."

As she lapsed into thought, a glimpse of the boy swept through her mind again.

Raven smirked.

"I won't disagree with you on the crazy part," she remarked, "but maybe, after seeing three amazingly hot guys, you were so delusional you only thought you saw that other boy and the girl—like a hallucination."

Charlie looked at her skeptically.

"If I'm crazy, I think I can assume I got it from you," she said. "It transferred to me by osmosis."

"I don't know," Raven argued in a singsong voice. "It doesn't sound that unbelievable to me. I can see how you could become delusional just after meeting three amazingly hot and adorable high school guys, who you will probably see plenty more of once school starts in the—"

"Raven, Charlie! Yes! Finally!"

Presley Kennedy, Mrs. Kennedy's youngest son and a close friend to both Raven and Charlie, was the first of the volleyball players to spot the girls' approach. Having turned away from the match, however, he was instantly belted in the back of the head, the volleyball then rocketing into the air before dropping to the sand. Presley spun around in annoyance.

"Really, man?" he exclaimed, raising his arms. "That was such a cheap shot!"

"The match was still going, dude," another boy, Trevor, remarked, grinning widely. "Point for us!"

Presley ran to Raven and Charlie at the edge of the playing area.

"Fine," he called back, his arms over the shoulders of both girls. "Just for that, Raven and Charlie are on our team."

Loud groans issued from Trevor and his teammates on the other side of the volleyball net.

"That's not even close to fair," Trevor retorted. "Anyway, that gives you two extra—"

"Sorry. I can't hear you over the sounds of your crying," Presley teased. "Game on!"

He smiled at Charlie and Raven, his expression bright with anticipation.

"He's just scared because he knows he has no chance now," he said.

The girls looked at him, and then at each other, shaking their heads and smirking.

"Well, don't get used to it," Charlie advised, poking Presley in the chest. "After we beat up on Trevor, we're coming for you."

Presley let his arms drop.

"You talked to my mom, didn't you?"

"**L**ex."

"Why, hello."

Lex's gravelly voice sounded clearly through Imani's ear monitor as she streaked across the amber-tinged sky, many miles above the ground.

"To what do I owe the honor?" Lex continued.

"I'm headed to New Mexico."

"Yo."

"Checking in on our motorcycle friends again."

She could hear his rumbling chuckle.

"You expectin' something to go down?"

"I'm hoping to stay in the background," she responded.

"And I remember what good that did you last time. Just watchin', eh? That's boring. Something pop on that Toohey guy? I know you said there was something weird there."

"No, but I still think we're missing something. The handbook was off."

She was referring the handbook that, weeks earlier, had detailed Dexter Toohey as a prime concern in a barroom scuffle in which he, in fact, barely played a part.

There was a brief pause over the connection.

"The handbook's never off," came Lex's response.

"Yeah," Imani said, her sunglasses firmly over her eyes, the sun just beginning to descend to her right. "Exactly."

"You hear about that other thing?" Lex asked. "With Beat and Case and the girl?"

"Yeah."

Imani soared through the atmosphere, completely invisible from below, her speed swift and effortless.

THE FINAL THUNDERING MOTORCYCLE engine quieted as the Rebel Fist Motorcycle Club pulled into the lonely gas station in sparsely populated Taiban, New Mexico, along US Route 60 and 84. The first bikes to have exited the highway were already in front of the fuel pumps, while the others waited their turn in a loose queue. Riders disembarked, falling into conversation in relaxed groups or venturing into the gas station for food and drink.

Dexter Toohey stood near the front, his heavy bike being pumped with gas. He glanced at the numbers twirling by on the price ticker, and then back at his fellow riders. His jaw tensed as he picked out the man who had been called to his attention.

"Hey, roll me off when I'm done," he remarked to one of the Rebel Fist contingent standing alongside him. "I'll be back in a minute."

Toohey moved around the formation of motorcycles and bikers, soon reaching the member in question.

"Cole, let me talk to you for a sec."

Cole shifted his attention away from the biker he had been speaking to and looked at Toohey, his eyebrows raised in inquiry.

"What, you mean now?"

"Yeah. It'll just be a second."

Both men stepped away from the group, walking to a small section of grass near the open interstate. Above, the orange-hued sky signaled the earliest phase of sunset.

Toohey stood a few inches taller than Cole, but Cole would never be classified as a small man. In his late thirties, with a curious mane of wheat-blond, black, and silver hair falling from under his black leather bandana, and a goatee to match, Cole's dark clothing outlined his broad-shoulders and complemented his moody demeanor, making him very much an archetypal Rebel Fist member.

"What's up, Dex?" Cole asked, hands on hips.

Dexter Toohey eyed him coldly, his expression deliberately blank.

"Stop it."

Cole's expression turned quizzical. He scoffed lightly.

"Stop wh—"

Toohey's fist slammed against Cole's mouth before he could finish the question, the sudden impact taking him completely by surprise and jolting him back a step. Steadying himself, Cole reached up to his mouth. He shot Toohey a heated look.

Toohey's expression remained ice-cold.

Cole wiped his mouth to check for blood, chuckling darkly. Suddenly, he lunged. Before he could reach Toohey, however, strong hands reached out, holding him back. Fellow riders, who had rushed over as Toohey's punch connected, restrained Cole, and a few more stood between the two men, separating them.

"Hey!" Cole yelled as he struggled against his restrainers. "What was that for?"

"You know what it was for," Toohey answered, a menacing edge to his usual flinty tone. "You've had the first warning. This is the second. Stop it."

"What?" Cole asked loudly, clearly exasperated. "What are you talking about?"

He switched his attention to the men holding him.

"Get off me! Get off me!"

The other riders did not relinquish control, still struggling to keep him from jumping Toohey.

"Cole, Cole! Chill, man. Calm down."

"Get off! I said, get off me!"

Toohey advanced a footstep closer. The members between him and Cole, while not physically holding him back, barred him from coming any closer.

"Don't play dumb, Cole," Toohey warned. "Listen to what I'm sayin'. Listen! Second warning. You know what I'm talkin' about, and now you know that I know. So, either"—Toohey attempted another step forward, his way still barred—"either make your move, whatever it is, or back off. But stop what you're doin', or else you'll bring everyone down, and that's not gonna happen. You understandin' me?"

"I don't even know what you're talkin' about," Cole said vehemently. "But if you ever try to sucker punch me like that again, I'll make sure you wish you hadn't. I don't care who you are."

"You heard what I said, Cole," Toohey replied. "Don't bring your issues into the Club—that's the first rule. You need help dealin' with it, you freakin' ask and we got you. But this way, what you're doin'—it's not gonna work. Use your head."

Toohey nodded to the riders separating him and Cole, and they stepped back, giving him room to return to the gas pumps. Those holding Cole released him as well.

The two men exchanged an intense glare.

Toohey started to move. Just before brushing past Cole, however, he stopped.

The other members edged closer once more, but Toohey gave them a reassuring glance. He turned his face again, looking just over Cole's shoulder, not bothering to meet the other rider's eyes.

"You're angry," he said in a low tone, so the other members were only able to hear murmurs. "You probably want to deck me right now, and I understand. I probably should've gone about that better."

He met Cole's gaze.

"But, you ever make a threat on me like that again, I swear to God I'll put you in the dirt."

Finished, Toohey resumed walking, grazing Cole's shoulder as he headed back to the mass of motorcycles near the fuel pumps. Riders who had remained at the pumps watched his return silently, knowing not to ask questions—for the moment, at least.

Cole glared at nothing in particular, looking out across the highway, his jaw tensed tightly, fuming. Finally, he too turned away, walking back to the gas station.

LEANING AGAINST A DECREPIT storefront, Imani silently watched the Rebel Fist rider glower—seemingly right at her—before he stoically turned away. The other members allowed him a wide berth as he moved to the gas station's entrance. She then shifted her sunglass-shielded gaze to the other biker who had caught her eye.

Dexter Toohey was looking directly at her.

Though she was standing across the street, the wide tarmac of the interstate separating them, she knew the Rebel Fist leader could still see her relatively clearly. However, to him, she was a perfect stranger. She remained motionless, returning Toohey's gaze with a calculated one of her own, thoughts and theories instantly streaming through her mind, evaluated, analyzed, and cataloged.

Toohey's gaze, just as it had at Joe's Roadhouse Tavern, gave away nothing.

However, his heated discussion with the other rider had given something away. Exactly what that was, Imani remained uncertain.

Toohey's attention was at last diverted, drawn by a conversation with another club member.

Imani continued to watch until the gang departed.

AS SOON AS SHE pushed open one of the tinted glass doors, Emily's eyes instinctively flitted around, taking in the midday happenings of downtown.

Everything appeared the same—a typical, on-the-go workday, with people dressed for long hours at the office, like she was, and none of them issuing her a second glance. The bustling sounds of a metropolis filled the air, and the New Mexico sun shone brightly between towering buildings.

She noted the police car parked on the far side of the street; the young officer, about the same age as she, already becoming a familiar face. He stood on the sidewalk beside the car, somehow seeming to sense her presence, so that he peeked in her direction even as he listened to the pedestrian who had engaged him in conversation. The exchange between Emily and the officer was momentary, and to a casual observer, nonexistent. The cop looked away again, responding to whatever the person alongside him had said, but his attention remained on Emily as well.

The informal police presence near her office building was a recent occurrence, although Emily had grown used to it and had been told to expect it, even if she would not always be able to spot it. More times than not, she noticed the same young officer, sometimes a block or two ahead of or behind her building.

A few days earlier, he and another officer had turned up at Plácido's. Plácido himself had graciously attended to them while still finding time to cater to his "precious daughters." Sitting with Cassandra, Emily had a hunch his appearance at the restaurant was not entirely by chance.

Around her apartment building in the evening hours, he and other officers Emily happened to spot maintained a lurking, indistinct existence: watching her but not really, driving by slowly but not stopping, and typically not acknowledging or greeting her unless in casual passing. It was all founded on the impossibly small chance that one of them might chance upon something … someone … that did not belong.

When the Albuquerque Police Department first began their investigation, Emily had requested that she not be notified of what they discovered about her stalker until the offender was caught. They did, however, reluctantly answer the one question she had.

No, they told her. She was not the only one being followed. The police were reasonably sure the same person was stalking other women as well, thus the police presence near her work and home. The other women were under a similar off-the-record watch by law enforcement.

Today, Cassandra had been summoned into a so-called "working lunch" in one of the firm's grand conference rooms, where she had to give a presentation alongside Karl, and so Emily walked to the bistro on the corner, alone in a sea of passing identities.

As always, she had no idea if one of those passing people was the one for whom the police now searched.

No idea if that face, that person, that stalker, lurked barely out of sight behind a blind corner or in the shadows of a nondescript awning or tree. In any case, the frightening sensation of being watched—stalked, hunted, unknowingly—remained, the stalker still watching, still waiting. She could feel it.

Emily reached the café and slipped inside, at last out of range for prying eyes.

For the moment.

WITH EACH PASSING DAY'S persistent, if sometimes unnoticed, police attention, Emily's anxieties were eased.

But not erased.

She pushed open the door of her apartment building and stepped onto the sidewalk, her German Shepherd, Duke, trailing her closely before trotting slightly ahead. The Albuquerque air at dusk was calm and warm, a refreshing break from the dry heat of the day. Shades of blue, pink, and purple colored the sky, signaling the onset of twilight and the looming nightfall.

Though leading, Duke remained near Emily as they made their way to a section of grass that served—among other things—as a rest area for the canine tenants of the building. Emily removed a bag from the proclaimed "Take the Waste" station that bordered the patch of lawn as Duke stepped onto the green, sniffing, searching, and critiquing past visitors.

"I wish Dad had thought to train you to take your own waste," Emily remarked with a grin as she observed the dog's antics.

Duke, who had heard, and perhaps remembered, the very same statement uttered from his owner's mouth many times before, glanced over and sniffed loudly, seeming to turn his snout up in almost indignant fashion. He then returned to his activities.

Just beyond the reaches of downtown, and little more than a ten-minute walk from her office, Emily glanced around, taking in the subdued shadows cast over surrounding buildings and storefronts. As she stood watching, the lamps lining the street flickered and blinked on.

Behind her, Duke emitted a low, rumbling growl.

"Oh, stop it," Emily said, turning to look at him with some amusement. "I didn't ask for any of your sass."

Duke's growling grew louder and more insistent. The tips of his menacing fangs peeked from around his mouth, and his head moved left and then swiftly right, as if seeking out an unseen threat.

"What's going on with you?" Emily asked. "You know it's not very nice to—"

The familiar, unnerving feeling of being watched swiftly gripped her. Goosebumps pricked her skin despite the mild temperature. She scanned the area again, seeing nothing unusual, and glanced at Duke once more, following his threatening gaze to the street corner ahead...

Suddenly, someone appeared.

Emily's senses immediately spiked, but then shrank.

A laughing couple strolled across the street, not once looking down the sidewalk in her direction. She turned again, further surveying the lamp-lit evening. She had no clue, no realistic idea, who she was looking for, but her frantic eyes focused on anything that seemed at all suspect.

This was a change.

It seemed her stalker was no longer satisfied with simply watching her leave and enter her office building. Receiving the sinister letter at her apartment was threatening enough, yet Emily had never considered the perpetrator actually being there— perhaps standing and looking through the glass doors to where Walt sat in the lobby, perhaps watching other residents leave and enter the building, or perhaps noticing the same area of grass on which Emily and Duke now stood.

The eerie, prickly sensation rapidly spread across her pale skin and sent a marked and conspicuous signal.

Even at her home, her unwelcome shadow observed her. At any moment—*any* moment—her stalker could be only an arm's length away.

And what could she do if that someone suddenly decided to come even closer?

She searched the darkness, seeing nothing, as Duke maintained his cautionary growl.

"OOOH!**"**

Eric's friends cringed as they watched him smash into the acrylic boards encircling the ice rink. Distress for their buddy's condition was quickly forgotten, however, as each attempted to gain possession of the now loose hockey puck. Sammy, Eric's best friend and the player who had delivered the crushing hit, backed away slightly as Eric theatrically slumped to the ice.

"Got you good that time, didn't I?" Sammy laughed, his fallen friend looking up from his back as he lay on the rink. "You didn't even see me coming."

"You're just lucky you're getting your shots in now," Eric retorted. "Because once league play starts in the fall, I won't go so easy on you, and you won't be able to catch me again."

Sammy reached out a gloved hand, pulling his friend to his skates.

"Yeah, right," Sammy said, laughing again. "You just keep telling yourself that story. Looks to me like maybe you've lost a step."

"Yeah, and you keep telling *yourself* that," Eric grinned. "We're fourteen. You're, like, two months older than me anyway, so if I lose a step, it'll be two months after you've lost a step."

"Whatever, dude. You know you can't—"

"Hey, you two gonna kiss or something?" another boy called as he skated past. "In case you forgot, we've got a game going on here."

"Watch your mouth, Ricky," Sammy charged, slipping back into the action with Eric following close behind. "Or you'll get what your buddy just got—a faceful of glass."

Though the boys all lived in Golden, it was drop-in period at the indoor ice-skating rink in nearby Arvada, Colorado. At midday, the arena was mostly empty. The boys playing the impromptu game, all friends, were allowed to take up one-half of the rink, leaving the rest for regular skaters. Their play was aggressive, yet unstructured, as no teams had actually been designated, the sport turning into a classic "one versus everyone else."

Just as Sammy managed to lay his stick on the hockey puck, it was just as swiftly snatched away by Eric. The young teenager smoothly glided away from the others, circling around the back of the net and skating toward center ice before turning again. Sammy was the only player to chase after him, but Ricky and T.J. hovered a short distance behind.

"That's my puck, you know," Sammy said, crouching into a defensive posture in front of Eric. "It literally has my name on it."

Eric grinned mischievously.

"Well, it seems to like me a lot more than you," he answered, "seeing as how I always end up with it."

"Ah, very clever, young apprentice," Sammy replied. "But we'll see who it likes better when—"

Sammy stopped in mid-sentence, glancing behind Eric.

"Huh," he declared, "I didn't know Shelley came to skate here."

"What?"

Eric spun around to look.

"Ha!"

At Sammy's shout, Eric returned his gaze forward, attempting to protect the puck with his stick, but he was too late. Sammy skated away, the puck safely in his possession.

"Works every time!" he called, not turning to look back at his friend as he slid past another player en route to the net.

Eric glanced to the far end of the rink again, just to make sure. A laugh brought him back to the game.

"Dude, she's not here!" Ricky exclaimed from close to the net as Sammy hooted. "Stop looking!"

"Good," Eric said, as he started to skate over to them, "so when I promise to kill you both, I won't have to tell her I was only joking!"

"Eric Johnson, I heard that!" a motherly voice called from outside the rink.

"Sorry, Mom! I was just joking!"

The other boys laughed.

"HEY! SOMEBODY GET THOSE birds away from my nuts!"

Nick watched, amused, as the sloppily obese man attempted to hurry, gathering up his recently purchased greasy food as fast as he could. The man tossed a few bills indiscriminately at the worker occupying the hot dog cart, not bothering to wait for change. He then began to waddle erratically towards the sandy beach, juggling hot dogs, side orders, and a sugary drink in a large plastic cup.

A small flock of ocean birds had assembled on one towel along the golden sand, munching away at something obscured from Nick's field of view. Presumably, it was the large man's aforementioned "nuts"—a snack the man did not seem to have a desire to share, at least at that moment, with a flock of birds. As though sensing that their free feast would soon be ending, the flock only increased their frenetic pecking, the large man bumbling closer.

"Stop it! Shoo! Get outta here, idiot birds!"

The flock scattered at the very last moment, most not even bothering to fly away but rather taking a broad, floating leap out of immediate reach, in case the opportunity for a free meal presented itself again.

"Bunch o' thieves," the big man said, loud enough for nearby beachgoers to hear. "That's what you all are, just a bunch o' stinkin' thieves."

The birds did not appear to mind the scolding.

Nick's gaze leaped from the man to the hot dog stand he had just vacated. His stomach grumbled.

Soon, he approached the short queue directly in front of the stand. His sunglasses, perched on top of his spiked, black hair, were the only article covering the upper half of his body from the sun. As usual, board shorts and fashionably unlaced sneakers completed his ensemble.

The line moved quickly, and before Nick realized, he was standing before the uniformed vendor. He studied the menu stationed beside the stand for a moment before beginning his order.

"Okay. I'd like two Heart-Attack Dogs, one medium fry the same way, and one—"

"Hold on."

The vendor looked about high school age, perhaps only slightly younger than Nick appeared.

"Did you say you wanted the fries the same way as the hot dogs?"

"Yeah, they taste really good," Nick said. "I order them like that sometimes. Actually, it can get kinda hard to eat on account of all the stuff piled on top, but I find that if you—"

"Hey, come on, man! I ain't got all day!"

The childish voice was familiar. Nick turned around.

It was Jonnie, the same boy from the ice cream shop some weeks previous.

"You again!" both Jonnie and Nick exclaimed simultaneously. Nick's tone expressed humorous delight, while Jonnie's hinted at annoyance.

"Hurry up, dude!" Jonnie said. "If you want to have a whole conversation with him, just get his phone number or something. Geez!"

As the boy was speaking, Nick noticed Jonnie's hand unconsciously moving to grip his upside-down visor. Nick grinned and turned back to the vendor.

"Where was I again? Oh, yeah—one large fry, fully loaded, and one—"

"You said you wanted a medium fry before," the vendor interrupted.

"Oh. Well, change it to a large. And one large ... lemonade. Yeah, that sounds about right."

"Dude," Nick heard Jonnie giggle behind him. "You are so Mr. McButterpants."

Nick started to turn again.

"All right, little dude, you—"

Even before he could face the kid, Nick caught sight of an unexpected visitor. His approach had been so subtle that Nick had not even been aware of his presence until just then.

Lucifer.

Lucifer appeared all of ten years old, and his clothing choice seemed out of place—both for the casual atmosphere of Newport Beach and for the summertime heat. He wore baggy attire in varying shades of black—an oversized, short-sleeved shirt faded to the point of almost being gray, and dark cargo pants, slack and dragging, that looked more suited to someone ten years older and fifty pounds heavier. His sneakers, somewhat concealed by the overriding length of his pants, were also black, frayed and battered. His jet-black hair—a color hair dyes desired to imitate—was long enough that he had to brush it out of his eyes, and it curled languidly below the neckline of his oversized shirt.

Nick knew that Lucifer was most likely unaware of his fashion faux pas. He also knew that even if he had been conscious of it, the boy would most likely not know—or care— how to correct it.

To Nick, it was one of the many qualities that made Lucifer so exceedingly interesting … and so extraordinarily powerful.

Nick glanced at the notebook the smaller boy clutched in one of his hands, and then rose to meet Lucifer's mesmerizing hazel eyes. Forgetting about the annoying youth behind him, Nick looked to the vendor, and then to Lucifer again.

"You want something to eat, dude?"

Lucifer shot a glance at the menu and then at Nick, his intention clear.

"Can you add two more—"

A nudge at his hip interrupted Nick's request. He glanced down at the boy. Lucifer gazed back, his face emotionless.

"More?" Nick asked, surprised.

Lucifer's brow furrowed, barely.

"Don't worry. I'll eat the one you don't," Nick assured him with a sly smirk.

The younger boy's frown faded.

"You want those loaded up, too?" the vendor asked.

"Oh yeah," Nick replied automatically, grinning. "And another large lemonade for my buddy."

The teenage vendor made quick work of the additions.

"That's, uh ... thirteen dollars. Even."

As Nick reached inside one of the pockets of his shorts, he detected movement out of the corner of his eye.

"No way, dude," he declared, as Lucifer mirrored his actions. "Your money's no good here. It's not every day I get the privilege of picking up the bill for my hero."

Nick grinned as Lucifer brushed the bangs out of his eyes again, clearly unmindful of Nick's halfway sarcastic remark. Nick handed over the money and gathered up the large paper bag full of food.

"Keep the change."

He turned to Lucifer once more.

"How much money do you have, anyway?"

Lucifer reached into his pants again and turned the empty pocket inside out.

"That's not even funny, dude," Nick said, although he could not stifle his chuckle.

Of course, he received no reply.

NICK WITHDREW A PAPER-WRAPPED hot dog before setting the bag on the sand. With Lucifer watching, he brought it up to his nose, inhaling the greasy aroma.

"Hmm, smells like ... heaven."

He held it out to Lucifer, who still clutched the bound papers under one arm. Lucifer, his expression giving no sign of either contentment or unhappiness, held out a hand in acceptance. Just as Nick placed the hot dog in his hand, a sound, very faint, turned their heads toward the water.

"Sounds like someone's having fun," Nick said, scanning the surf.

The ocean along the Balboa Peninsula was only moderately crowded, with swimmers and surfers and boarders gliding and carving and tumbling through the waves.

Another prod jabbed Nick in his side.

"Oww, dude! That's really starting to—"

Lucifer offered the still-wrapped hot dog back to him, unopened.

Nick gave a quiet laugh.

"What? Trust me, it's delicious. Just because it—"

The sound came again. Even through the surrounding din along the beachfront, Nick and Lucifer honed in on the faint noise. Meanwhile, the other beachgoers failed to notice anything amiss. Even if the volume along the waterfront had been muted, the crashing waves would have done well to conceal the misplaced sound.

Nick accepted the hot dog from Lucifer, followed by the bound papers.

"And here I thought you'd just come to deliver my List," Nick said as Lucifer started to move to the water.

Lucifer glanced over his shoulder, but said nothing.

"Don't you at least want to take your shoes off?"

Nick's teasing remark yielded no reaction from Lucifer, which was as crystal-clear as any verbalized answer could have been.

It was rhetorical anyways, Nick mused before hearing the sound again.

LUCIFER STROLLED CALMLY TO the water's edge, unhurried, stepping into the encroaching and receding waves, his shoes sinking into the sand. His relaxed movements were his cover, and he attracted only a few inquisitive glances, mostly because of his peculiar dress sense, although Lucifer would never connect the two.

In any case, a few moments would render his appearance trivial.

As he waded in, the water level quickly became chest-deep, enough for him to submerge himself completely, his act undetected by onlookers even if they had a vague idea of where he was...or where he should have been. He deftly lowered his body, crouching as a wave began to break above him, expelling unneeded air in the process. As soon as the ocean had completely enveloped him, he shot forward with considerable force, rocketing just below the surface like an accelerating torpedo, low enough that no one would be able to distinguish his speeding body but not so low to prevent a significant wake forming behind him—waves originating and spreading from an unknown source counter to the tide and current.

Fortunately, Newport Beach provided plenty of distractions. No one appeared to have spotted him.

Nᴉᴄᴋ ᴛᴏᴏᴋ ᴀ ʟᴀʀɢᴇ bite out of his hot dog as he stared at the place he had last seen Lucifer. He was surprised—but only a little—to notice just how few glances Lucifer had attracted as the small boy stepped to the waterline, and how many fewer when the boy submerged completely.

They probably see weird stuff out here all of the time, Nick thought as he chewed. *It is California.*

He realized, belatedly, that his bite had been too large; the hot dog's mushy contents began to seep from one side of his mouth.

"So good," he moaned softly to himself.

Chewing and swallowing, he wiped his mouth as a child would, on his bare arm, still clutching his large lemonade. His sloppy habits were untraceable, his arm just as spotless as it had been moments before. He switched hands, bringing the dripping, overloaded hot dog to his widening mouth again, closing his eyes in delicious anticipation.

The bustle of rising panic distracted him as he bit down into the fatty mess affectionately termed a Heart-Attack Dog. His eyes blinked open and swiveled in the direction of the hubbub, only a soft throw's distance from where he sat. There, a frizzy-haired woman was becoming increasingly frantic, her antics drawing the attention of onlookers despite attempts by others to soothe her.

Nick glanced down the beach to a lifeguard post erected a short distance away. Another beachgoer was already speaking to the young woman on duty, gesturing occasionally to the escalating scene. The lifeguard reached up into the stand and retrieved a walkie-talkie before jogging to the upset woman and the congregation of nosy observers trailing behind her.

Nick brought the hot dog to his mouth again, his attention back on the water.

Those enjoying themselves in the ocean or on the sandy beach were too far away to have a clue what was occurring, although they would soon enough be well informed by word-of-mouth. By the time that happened, however, the incident would probably be over—at least that was usually the order of events when Lucifer was around.

Nick brought the hot dog up to his face again to get a closer look.

"How can something that looks so unhealthy taste so ridiculously fantastic?" he asked the heavily saturated, inanimate object.

His eyes then returned to the cerulean ocean.

The sound had stopped.

LUCIFER COULD STILL DETECT the faint cry clearly, even as he maneuvered underwater. He could see the small, flailing limbs—a child anxiously fighting to stay above the surface.

He could also see that the child was growing tired.

A sizable distance separated the imperiled kid from the coastline, making it unsurprising that no one had heard his cries from the beach. Lucifer's speed made the gap insignificant. More than simply swimming, he flew through the sea, unconstrained by the water's usual resistance. He would reach the boy in a matter of seconds, not minutes or hours.

He angled his trajectory sharply downward, propelling himself toward deeper, darker depths, and then he changed attitude again, slowing considerably as he rose, closer and closer to the boy's weakly kicking legs...

The child, beginning to sink, started violently when Lucifer touched him, likely mistaking the contact for that of a treacherous sea monster. He seemed about the same size as Lucifer, although that made no difference. Slowly, reassuringly, Lucifer hooked the child's legs around his head and shoulders, raising him slightly and adjusting his position while keeping the boy safely afloat. The child, whether from instinct, or perhaps, in some way, realizing what was occurring, gripped Lucifer's head. Even through the water, the boy could not distinctly see who— or what—he held onto. Lucifer did not bother to surface to grant the child an adequate look.

Slowly at first, Lucifer moved forward, the initial phase of the rescue having been completed in a matter of moments. When confident that the other boy was indeed hanging on, he picked up speed. As the pair moved along the surface, waves formed around them, giving the deceptive appearance that the boy was riding a growing swell—or at the most fanciful, a very large sea animal—back to the coast.

The truth was even more unbelievable.

Lucifer was skimming quickly now, not near the speed at which he rocketed away from the beach, but certainly much faster than any piggyback ride the child had received. They were easily outpacing any waves, a queue of undulations trailing behind them, each shaping up to be more intense than waves that were created naturally. Their ride, however, was smooth, fluid, swift.

"**I**T'S MY CHILD! MY baby is missing, don't you understand?"

Nick pinched a handful of fries from their paper container, careful not to upset the nearly leaking pile of relish, mustard, slaw, chili, onions and other condiments precariously perched on top. He brought the fries to his mouth, making sure to still himself against any sudden movements brought on by the woman's occasional shrieks.

A pair of lifeguards stood amid the crowd of spectators surrounding the woman, and more had already slipped into the ocean. Still, they were stuck searching a wide area, as the woman was uncertain of how far her son could have traveled.

The scene was becoming a circus, better than anything on television, but Nick was only mildly amused. With Lucifer's involvement, the situation was already resolved, one way or the other. It was only a matter of time, really. Perhaps only a matter of seconds now.

Anyway, he was much more interested in the bag of food that sat to one side, and the now-opened copy of The List that Lucifer had brought on the other. He reached for another hot dog—only the second of his designated three—and grasped the bound packet with his other hand, positioning it on his lap again so he wouldn't have to lean over awkwardly to read the names.

THEY WERE GETTING CLOSE.

Lucifer could see the ocean floor inclining rapidly, even through the turbulent waters of the Balboa Peninsula. He was cutting through the shallower depths easily, traveling a direct path to the beach, but he slowed gradually, allowing the trailing waves to draw nearer and propel both him and the rescued child on his shoulders to shore.

As he continued to decelerate, Lucifer slowly loosened the child's grip without the child becoming aware of it, releasing his legs and now mostly pushing the child along with the current. His effort decreased again as he allowed the ocean to supply a greater proportion of the necessary force.

Breaking point.

Lucifer relinquished his grasp on the child completely. He thrust his hands and arms forward and around, his movements creating the wave that carried the child forward with greater magnitude. The energy exhibited was spectacular, the effect unnaturally powerful, teetering on the edge of disastrous but not quite reaching it. The wave surged forcefully toward the beach.

Immediately, Lucifer dived down and away, accelerating rapidly and distancing himself from the beach once more, holding himself just above the seafloor, deeper and deeper, plummeting dramatically, not stopping, not pausing…

Boom!

The muffled rumble of a shockwave reverberated in the depths of the ocean as he sped past. Marine animals in the vicinity stayed clear, the energy of his movement sending pulses all around. He then drove himself steeply upward, still accelerating, ascending at near lightning-quick pace.

Crack!

With a piercing explosion, he broke through the tranquil ocean surface hundreds of miles away from the coastline he had been near just minutes earlier. Lucifer shot high into the bright sky with breakneck velocity, bringing with him a magnificent, cone-like spray of displaced water that shot hundreds of feet into the air, as though erupted from a powerful underwater geyser.

Sunlight danced elegantly through the suspended mist of saltwater, the droplets sparkling in a majestic, awe-inspiring way, dazzling, brilliant prisms of color and shimmering light. It was a stunning, once-in-a-lifetime presentation as the twinkling spray rose and then slowly descended again, a cloud of water, an incredible glimpse into the possibilities and wonders of the natural world, unqualified beauty and absolute radiance.

Lucifer did not notice. He was already soaring back to the coastline, flying through tendrils of air well above the sight of even the sharpest of eyes.

A GRINNING BODYSURFER MOTIONED to his friend a short space away.

"Dude, this is it!" Bryce yelled, gesturing to the incoming wave.

"Dude, this is definitely it!" his friend called back. "Meet you at the bottom!"

Whether he was referring to the sandy floor if they both happened to tumble off in the crashing surf, or to the shoreline if they were fortunate enough to ride the wave to its close, was unclear.

"Not if I beat you to it!" Bryce said.

A moment later, he added, "Here it comes!"

The pair, already in their favored starting positions, began to swim aggressively, making every effort to move with the flow of the tide. For them, the first rule always held that:

The mystifying art of bodysurfing in The Wedge takes a whole lotta skill and a whole lotta luck, but persistence, along with—

They both missed it.

Missed the wave.

Misjudged the speed.

The unbroken swell rolled under them and away, bobbing the surfers only a few unexciting lengths forward and rumbling as if chuckling at their weak attempts.

Another rule of bodysurfing in the Balboa Peninsula stated that:

The Wedge can be, and often is, a fickle mistress. She never loses. One can only hope to draw even. Tempt her if you dare.

"Ha ha, Bryce!" the other bodysurfer called. "You totally missed that!"

"Shut up, dude! You're floatin' right there! You missed it too!"

They both laughed, but only for a moment.

"Dude, check that one out!"

Bryce looked back to the open water and let out an excited whoop.

"Holy ... dude! This is so it!"

He then noticed his friend had already launched himself for shore, leaving him behind.

"Dude!" he yelled in exasperation, beginning his own lead-up.

Initially, he only felt a gentle push, and he immediately thought he had underestimated the speed. As he continued to stroke, disbelief flitted through his mind.

Missed two in a row, man? What is this, amateur hour?

Then, he felt it. The force was much more than he anticipated.

Almost instantly, he lost his balance and began to tumble into the break, quickly losing his orientation. He was completely wiping out: what he and his surf buddies termed "Raggedy Ann-ding"—toppling head over heels, heels over head, continued, uncontrolled,   seemingly lifeless in the center of the crashing wave, surfacing for a brief moment before quickly going under again, foam and water all around.

Another tip from the rulebook read:

If one finds him or herself Raggedy Ann-ding, don't fight it. Stay safe and go along for the ride. Then, thank The Wedge for the privilege of losing to her awesomeness again.

The young surfer continued to tumble, a tangle of limbs in the surf. He bumped into something, though he could not immediately spot what it was through the turbulence of the powerful breaker. There was always that certain danger, although he felt the object give way slightly as he hit against it. That meant it was probably not a rock, or something else that could seriously injure him without knowing the difference. His thoughts immediately jumped to the next options.

Not a shark; too close to the beach, not to mention that it would have tried to bite my head off. Sea lion? Eel? Do we even have eels around here? I don't think I got stung, and it's too hard to be a jelly...

The toppling surfer bumped into the object again, and again it yielded to his contact, although this time, it latched on briefly, maintaining some type of grip … almost like…

He finally caught a glimpse of the mysterious object amid the turmoil of the wave: limbs flailing, hands, feet, head …

It's a kid … it's a kid!

The realization was swift, and Bryce instinctively brought his body around the boy, securing him in his hold while still bracing for further contact.

The wave tossed the pair onto the beach like an afterthought—two Raggedy Ann dolls instead of one, their arms and legs flying in the open air before connecting with the warm Newport Beach sand. The boy landed on top, forcibly expelling the remaining air from Bryce's lungs. The blow made the surfer open his eyes again in surprise.

The rescued boy stared back at him with equal astonishment, breathing heavily.

"Little dude," Bryce gasped when he had enough oxygen to speak.

A new rule for the book:

If one saves another from an unfortunate encounter with The Wedge, consider it a tie, because the Wedge never loses. However, the Wedge will reward your bravery later … if she feels like it.

STILL EATING, NICK LOOKED with interest upon the spirited scene a brief distance from where he lounged. The atmosphere had transformed from increasingly frantic to abruptly joyous. The change in mood had been interspaced with a hesitant, weighty pause that suggested a sudden, unexpected deviation to the predicted course of events; to Nick, it was a pause he was used to, though in a radically different context. It was a pause that carried mystery, anticipation, a hopeful, almost exciting, uncertainty…

And then the sudden cheer of delight for faith maintained and hope preserved.

Wish granted. Merry Christmas. Dreams do come true.

Nick smiled at the thought and took another bite—or at least attempted to, as his mouth chomped down on nothing but ocean air. He gawked at his empty hand, genuinely amazed that he had already eaten the entire hot dog. Returning his gaze to the newest section of The List, he blindly reached to the bag of food for his last hot dog.

His stretching hand encountered another—a hand attempting to grab a morsel at the exact same time.

Not a wise decision by the other hand, he mused.

Nick's eyes quickly broke away from The List to the owner of the offensive hand.

Lucifer sat alongside him in the sand, as if he had never left.

Nick's annoyance evaporated immediately.

"That was fast," he noted, grinning.

The smaller boy reached into the bag again, withdrawing one of the final two Heart-Attack Dogs. As his hand retreated, Nick's hand moved forward again. His fingers delicately clutched at another loaded helping of fries. He brought his fingers up once more—slowly, carefully, cautiously—his concentration honed in, his focus deliberate, only one goal in mind.

Food to mouth, man. Don't drop it. Food to mouth.

He bit into the fries and closed his eyes momentarily—the deliciousness nearly overwhelming. When he opened them, he glanced to Lucifer. Lucifer was looking back at him, his face displaying no emotion at all as he chewed, both of his hands holding the hot dog near his mouth.

Nick grinned at the sight. Lucifer took another bite.

They both turned back to the beach. The onlookers had mostly dispersed, melting away once they realized the impromptu entertainment, however threatening, had reached a satisfying conclusion. Two lifeguards were among the few that remained; one speaking with the mother of the rescued child, while the other examined the boy. Bryce, the young bodysurfer who had spilled onto the beach with the boy, now sat beside him, although his attention was divided unequally among the three distractions—one-third toward the boy alongside him, and very nearly two-thirds focused on the pretty female lifeguard tending to the boy. Whatever little was left was directed to his surfing buddy, who relaxed in front of him, facing away from the ocean.

His friend did not seem troubled, however, as most of his attention was on the pretty lifeguard as well.

Nick glanced at Lucifer again, whose distinctive, penetrating brown-green eyes shifted between his half-eaten portion of hot dog and the scene further down the beach—a scene he had greatly influenced. His eyes settled once more on the hot dog as he took another bite.

Then, he must have felt Nick's gaze on him, as he turned his head in the taller boy's direction. Lucifer raised the hot dog briefly, as though giving his approval for Nick's benefit.

At that, Nick's grin grew considerably wider.

"HE SAID HE WOULD call later in the week with the deets," Eric Johnson finished offhandedly before forking more food into his mouth. He was referring to his friend Sammy's suggestion from a few days before—at the ice-skating rink in Arvada—of a group hangout and possible sleepover.

"*Deet*s?" his mother, Elizabeth, repeated, eyebrows elevated. "What's the deets?"

Before her eldest son could respond, Hank Johnson spoke up from his place at the head of the dining table.

"Deets," he explained in his husky voice, motioning with his fork as though he offered infinite wisdom. "Details. Info. The lowdown. The scoop. The 911."

He rolled his eyes, catching his children's attention and smirking.

"Get with it, woman."

Elizabeth rounded on him, her gaze incredulous.

"Pretty sure you mean the 411, Dad," Eric corrected as he scooped more food from a dish in the center of the table onto his plate.

"Yeah," Hank said, shrugging. "What'd I say?"

"You said 911," replied Sarah, Eric's younger sister by a couple of years, a mirror image of her mother.

"911's for the police," added Riley, the youngest of the clan. "Even I know that."

"Don't forget your broccoli, Riley," Elizabeth observed, nodding at the boy's plate.

"Ugh, I think I'm full."

Riley pouted, grabbing his stomach.

"Aww, that's too bad," Hank said. He rubbed his hands together. "I guess that means more fresh apple pie for the rest of us."

"Apple pie!"

"And, there he goes," Sarah commented as her younger brother shoveled down the remaining vegetables on his plate, his mouth full, his cheeks ready to burst. She crinkled her nose at him in disgust.

"So," Hank directed his gaze to Sarah, "is that sleepover ... whatever ... at Patricia's still going on? Or did her mother come to her senses and call the whole thing off?"

Sarah stuck her tongue out at him.

"Hank, her friend's name is Rebecca," Elizabeth corrected. "Patricia is Rebecca's mother. It's a shame you don't even know the names of your children's school friends."

A wry grin played on her lips.

"Get with it, old man."

Sarah snickered lightly, although the Eric kept a straight face.

"Get it?" his mother asked him, grinning. "He told me to 'get with it' earlier, remember? I just turned it around on him."

Eric arched his eyebrow.

"Oh, so you're a comedy critic now?" his mother asked. "Sarah and I thought it was funny."

"Hilarious," Riley piped up with his mouth full.

Hank chuckled.

"Yep, it sounds like you're ready to take your act on the road, sweetie."

He then nodded at the youngest boy.

"And aren't you going to your buddy's house, Riley?"

"Yeah, and it's gonna be great! Chase said he got this new computer game, and he said it's so awesome! You start off as a zombie, and then, once you eat enough brains, you get to—"

"Okay, okay," Sarah cut in. "Enough with the zombie and brains. Sheesh."

"But I was going to name my first zombie after you," Riley said, his voice syrupy as he looked to his sister.

The annoyance on Sarah's face lessened.

"Well," she relented, "I guess that's not—"

"And then I was going to explode myself!" Riley declared, falling into a fit of laughter.

"Riley Johnson," Elizabeth scolded, "you sure are cutting it close tonight. Apologize to your sister, right now."

"Sorry," Riley said. "I won't explode myself if I name my zombie after you."

"You better not," Sarah muttered.

"It'll be the best zombie ever!" Riley added.

Eric glanced over at his father.

"Dad, you still working on the roof this—?"

Hank's cough interrupted Eric's question.

"Argh, sorry," the large man said, rubbing at his neck. "I think I had something caught in my throat there for a sec."

"Oh, don't even try it, mister," Elizabeth stated as she shook her fork at her husband. "Don't think for one second that I forgot you said you and Bryan would work on the gutters this weekend."

"Forgot?" Hank coughed again. "No, I didn't think that. Not at all. I was just—"

All eyes at the table were directed at him, all appearing unimpressed.

"Ho!" Riley laughed. "You got caught, Dad."

Hank glanced at Riley, and then sent a mild glare in Eric's direction.

"Sorry," Eric shrugged.

"Oh, well. Just for that, I'm not so sure you'll be able to go to Sammy's if he calls."

Eric turned to his mother for help.

"Don't listen to him, Eric," Elizabeth reassured him. "He's deflecting. He just thought he was getting out of the weekend chore he promised his wife and family he would do. Since his judgment is clouded, I'll be the one who decides if you can go to Sammy's."

"Do your chores," Riley declared, pointing his fork at his father, "or no apple pie for you, forever!"

Everyone at the table laughed, except for Hank.

IN BOISE CITY, OKLAHOMA, the single functioning lamp post cast a hazy, sputtering orange hue on the cracked blacktop but reached little else. The rest of the dustbowl playground was only dimly aglow, reflecting the shine of the moon. Case stared up at the flickering light, and then at Beat, who was fiddling with the broken-down carousel. The busted ride tilted into the dirt at an angle, collapsed off its axis.

Beat easily righted the cumbersome object with one hand and peered underneath. Rising once more, she steadied the ride, adjusting and shifting, metal and steel scraping and scratching dissonantly in the otherwise quiet playground. Soon, she let go, and the ride stood on its own.

Beat gave one of the handlebars a slight push, and the carousel twirled, sending a loud screech into the night. Beat halted the ride, extinguishing the sound, and glanced over to Case.

He said nothing, although he returned her gaze, smiling a little.

Beat shifted the contraption again, and then gave the handlebars another gentle shove. The carousel spun once more, this time soundlessly, and Beat turned to her partner again, her grin distinguishable even through the shadowy darkness. Case inclined his head in acknowledgement.

The carousel was brand-new all over again.

In THE ETHEREAL ATMOSPHERE of the country playground at night, Beat and Case strolled through the dirt, dust, and sporadic clumps of grass to the rusted, swirling slide. It was located even further from the orange-tinged lamp, the moonlight painting the corroding metal in soft, off-white tones.

Case reached out to the support railing that led to the top of the slide. It shook, loose and barely attached under his grip. He traced the contours of the ill-maintained structure, moving to the front of the slide as Beat began to climb the ladder, the steps and railings rickety as she ascended but instantly secured and polished as she passed—an enchanting transformation. She reached the top as Case arrived at the front.

Other than their quiet shuffling, the air around them was silent.

At the front, Case looked up to his partner at the slide's summit. Beat paused, her arms outstretched, her fingers peeking out from her oversized shirt to display the V sign.

Case chuckled lightly.

Beat then slid down, feet first, entering the small tunnel and emerging on the other side, twisting, twirling, looping, dipping toward the ground below, and then hopping off nimbly at the bottom, not bothering to hide the grin on her face from such simple pleasure.

THEY RETURNED TO THE rundown blacktop and the light post. Case looked up to the dreary lamp again, then down to the cracked asphalt, and then glanced around to the identical, although unlit, lampposts scattered throughout the playground.

He turned to Beat before inclining his head toward the vacant, single-lane road a short walk away.

"Shall we?" he asked, his voice soft and his grin barely visible, matching the hushed character surrounding the quiet land.

They headed for the road. Behind them and all around, light poles blinked on, shining with an identical, bright orange glow. The working light over the blacktop stopped flickering, now fully alight like all of the others. It illuminated the asphalt clearly, which showed no trace of the cracking and disrepair it had possessed moments before.

The children visiting the dustbowl playground tomorrow would surely be surprised.

TWO PAIRS OF EYES peered over the windowsill into the Phillips' mobile home—one pair a snowy gray, the other a bluish green. Both stealthily took in the scene.

Father and son were seated at a table, huddled over food prepackaged in disposable trays. A television droned from a nearby room. Even through the walls of the trailer, Beat and Case could hear the pair's conversation easily.

"So, whaddaya doin' tomorrow?" Roger Phillips asked, raising his eyes to his green-fauxhawked son as he scooped another bite of food into his mouth.

"Um, playground again," Connor Phillips voiced and shrugged, his words garbled by mashed potato.

"Again?" Roger intoned. "Don't you go there every day?"

Connor shrugged again, looking down at his food to avoid Roger's gaze. His posture was reluctant, guarded. Peeking from behind the window, Beat and Case watched silently.

"I like it," the boy mumbled, still looking down. "It's fun there."

Roger ate another spoonful of the microwaved dinner. Finally, he spoke again.

"I was wonderin', uh…"

He cleared his throat, which caused his son to glance up under hooded eyes.

"Maybe … if you wanted to … uh, maybe riding down to Jump 'n Jack's tomorrow sometime."

The boy looked at him blankly.

"Only…" Roger coughed again. "Only if you want to."

"Really?" Connor asked, his voice still displaying caution. "Jump 'n Jack's?"

Roger struggled with uncertainty, an emotion that, before his divorce, he never felt with respect to his son.

"It's … ahem … it's only if you want. I don't know if you're too old for that, or you, uh, don't like it anymore, or somethin'. It's all right if you don't wanna go. I just, uh, remember that you used to like that place, you know … before."

Roger grimaced and shook his head, as though attempting to will away troublesome thoughts. He passed a hand through his hair before taking another quick bite from his tray.

Connor's face clouded.

"Don't you usually … go out on the weekends?"

Roger's plastic spoon froze midway to his tray. He looked briefly at Connor before glancing to his drink. The cup of water, replacing his usual beer, sat unmoving.

"I'm, uh … I'm tryin' to cut back on that."

He met the boy's gaze again.

"I know you didn't like it, but … I don't know, I did it anyway. I thought it helped. From now on, though, I'm gonna try an' drink what you drink—water and, uh, juice, and stuff like that."

Connor inched his head up slightly higher, a barely-there grin showing on one-half of his mouth—a gesture he had picked up from the man seated opposite him.

"Okay."

Roger looked up at his son again.

"Okay, I wanna go to Jump 'n Jack's," Connor repeated.

"Yeah?" Roger asked, running another hand through his shabby haircut.

"Yeah."

The only difference between Roger Phillips's smile and the one his son exhibited was the faint stubble surrounding the former.

"Okay, then," he said. "Tomorrow. Jump 'n Jack's."

On the other side of the window, Case glanced over at his partner. Beat's grin glowed with the same luminance as Connor's.

"Sweet! Jump 'n Jack's!" the boy declared, his bearing suddenly opposite to what it was just moments before. "Yeah. It's got all the trampolines, and the mazes, and the huge thing with the balls in it, and the pizza, and the—"

"Yeah," Roger intoned, chuckling softly, more relaxed as well. "I remember the place. I was there too, you know."

"But you didn't go in it far," Connor continued. "You've got to go in all the way this time. Inside, the mazes lead to this secret hole of balls only a few kids know about, and when you get to it…"

Outside the trailer, Case looked to Beat again.

"Seen enough?" he asked.

The two sets of eyes peering through the window disappeared as Connor Phillips continued his animated depiction, Roger Phillips watching him with newfound amusement.

As they started for the driveway and the dirt road beyond, Case retrieved his ear monitor. Beat withdrew her handbook from one of the many pockets that lined her frayed pants.

"Imani," Case said quietly.

His monitor instantly found its recipient.

"Yo," Imani's voice replied a few seconds later.

"We just stopped by the Phillips' house in Boise City."

Case looked back at the modest home again as silence filled the line.

"It's all clear here," he finished.

"That's good news," Imani responded.

Beat waved and caught his attention.

"And Beat says hello."

He heard Imani's soft chuckle over the feed in reply. Beat returned her attention to the handbook.

In the night, the deserted dirt road only illuminated by soft moonlight, the small studs that lined Beat's ears glinted softly. On Case's chest, his winged pendant twinkled as well, reflecting the dim light of the peaceful street.

Meanwhile, Case's thoughts turned again to Charlize Brown.

AN ENTIRE STATE AWAY, the rain fell in sheets as a summer thunderstorm swept across the dry Texas prairies. It quickly drenched the landscape, wafting steam languidly into the night air once it passed.

The light posts in front of the biker saloon had unexpectedly dimmed a short time ago, presumably due to the storm, leaving the gravel parking lot bathed in blackness save for the faint glimmer that escaped from the bar. Incidentally, the darkness had coincided with the arrival of two more visitors. Both leaned against a hulking motorcycle and watched the saloon's entrance through the rain. The downpour danced all around, though never touching them; they, and the motorcycle, remained perfectly dry.

Suddenly, the door of the saloon was shoved open from the inside with a loud bang.

The figures in the parking lot, unseen in the darkness, watched as two members of the Rebel Fist Motorcycle Club emerged onto the covered porch at the front of the building. Lightning, and then thunder, revealed themselves across the stormy night skies.

"Yeah?" Cole asked gruffly, his drunkenness evident in his slurred speech.

Dexter Toohey took in the other man a moment before speaking.

"You're done."

It was Cole's turn to stare.

"What?"

"You're done, Cole," Toohey repeated. "You're through here. When the storm lets up, you're gone."

The two unnoticed figures heard Cole snicker softly.

"I'm done? Whaddaya spewin' on 'bout, Dex?"

Toohey stepped closer, his tone even, his words concise.

"I mean what I said. I'm not Snake, or Dom, or Sims, or any of your other pals in there."

He motioned to the saloon door.

"This ain't a game. You're out."

"Whaddaya mean, I'm out?" Cole retorted, his voice gaining an irritated edge. "Outta what? Whaddaya talkin' about?"

"Don't be an idiot," Toohey said. "I'm not goin' through it again. You've had two warnings. Now, you're out."

Cole appeared to sober at the realization of what Toohey was referring to.

"Whaddaya comin' at me for about this?" he answered heatedly. "What's your problem with it? It's not your problem. I'm handlin' it."

Toohey pointed his finger at Cole's chest.

"Your problem"—he gestured to the door again—"is our problem, and that means your problem becomes my problem. In this club, everyone's problem becomes everyone else's problem, Cole. You got tagged before for goin' after these girls before you even came to Rebel Fist, and you're gonna get tagged again.

"Snake told you to knock it off, before any of us even knew about it, but you didn't. Yeah, I heard 'bout that. Once I found out this thing, what you're doin', I told you to knock it off. You didn't. Snake and Dom both came to you and told you to knock it off a few days ago. Yeah, I know that, too. But you still didn't. It's supposed to be two warnings in the Club. You've had freakin' four, Cole.

"This whole thing's gonna blow up right in your face, and you act like you're gonna skate, but I'm tellin' ya—heck, we've all told ya—you're not. You've gone away before for the same thing. I don't know the story about you and your ex, and I don't really care. All I know is she's gone, but instead of dealin' with it directly, you're goin' after, what, random girls who look like her? Are you out of your mind? I know Snake and Dom told you to lay off—they know your deal. I don't care about you; I'm thinkin' about the Club. If you go down again while you're with us, and you will, that's gonna be on all of us, and that's a freakin' problem right now."

Toohey took another step closer.

"And actually, your first chance was to not pull this in the first place. You chose wrong. Four warnings, and each time, you chose wrong. You've been out of warnings. You've been out of chances. You don't wear the Fist anymore, it's that simple. You're through here. We clear?"

As Toohey finished speaking, a teenage boy stuck his head out of the saloon door.

"Hey, Uncle Dex, everything cool out here?" he asked.

In the shadows of the parking lot, the two unseen figures straightened, intrigued by the face they had never seen before.

"Get back inside, Tatum," Toohey said, not tearing his gaze away from the angry rider standing before him.

"It's just that some of the guys were askin' for you, and Cole."

"Cole's not comin' back in."

"Huh?" the boy asked. "Why not?"

Toohey took his eyes off Cole to glance at the boy.

"Didn't I just say get back—"

"Screw this," Cole muttered. He stepped forward, toward Toohey and the saloon entrance.

Toohey, detecting the aggressive move out of the corner of his vision, wheeled quickly and swung hard.

Crack!

The punch connected with Cole's jaw, and he staggered back to the short flight of wooden steps that led down to the parking area.

Toohey advanced and swung again. *Crack!* His fist struck Cole, who continued to reel.

Thunder rumbled in the distance.

"Dex! Dex!"

The teenager tried desperately to hold the bigger, more muscular Toohey back. More bikers swarmed through the door, objects crashing, glass shattering, in their haste to get outside.

"Dex!"

"Dex, Dex, hold up, man!"

"Chill! Chill!"

Cole fell back onto the edge of the short flight of stairs and slipped off, tumbling backwards into space before landing on the wet ground, the rain quickly drenching him. He rolled around for a moment, groggy, holding one of his hands against his jaw.

"Argh!" Toohey snarled, struggling against the bikers who were attempting to bring him under control. "Four warnings! Four! And you can't come up with a better way than this? You step back in here and I swear I'll beat you till you're dead. I don't care who sees it. I don't care who knows! You think I care? You hearin' me? I will kill you!"

"Get 'em inside! Let's get 'em inside!" one of the riders called, and together the horde slowly forced Toohey back into the saloon, the enraged man cursing loudly and repeatedly. The door soon closed shut behind them.

One figure, the teenager, remained on the porch. He looked down at Cole in the parking lot, and began to take a step in his direction.

Immediately, the saloon door opened again, and another Rebel Fist biker appeared. He grabbed the boy before he could take another step.

"Kid, Dex wants you back inside," he said, steering the teen indoors.

The door shut once more.

In the gloom of the parking lot, the two visitors watched Cole gingerly pick himself up off the wet concrete and ease back to the porch steps, out of the rain. Soon, another Rebel Fist rider joined him outside, the word *Snake* stitched into the front of the bandana wrapped around his head.

His BURLY, TATTOO-COVERED ARMS crossed over his thick chest, Lex reached up and tugged at his beard as he thought.

"Right when it was just startin' to get entertaining," he commented in his usual husky tone.

Beside him, Imani remained silent, her own thoughts racing.

"I say we end this now," Lex remarked.

"Duly noted," Imani responded.

She then posed the most pressing question, knowing that Lex was pondering the same, as she continued to watch Cole and Snake converse quietly on the front porch, Cole still nursing his jaw.

"What's the story on the boy?"

Rain continued to fall all around them. Lightning streaked across the night, the deep resonance of thunder obediently following.

Nick WAS SLOUCHED IN the plastic patio chair outside one of the countless burger joints along the boardwalk. Though he appeared asleep, he was not—not really. The umbrella over his table sheltered him from the sunshine beaming down onto Newport Beach. Sunglasses further veiled his attentiveness, and the hood of his multicolored sweatshirt was pulled over his white baseball cap, throwing most of his face into shadow.

Beachgoers walked, jogged, biked, and skated past, until one finally stopped and approached Nick's table, unceremoniously dropping the binder he carried onto the tabletop.

Slap.

Nick startled, his hood slipping off, though his cap remained. A young man with fiery red-orange spiked hair looked on in apparent amusement as Nick gathered himself, straightening his unzipped sweatshirt and adjusting his sunglasses.

He finally looked up.

"Oh, hey! It's Smokey the Bear! You know, only you can start forest fires ... no, wait ..."

Nick presumed Anastasios was rolling his eyes, which were shielded behind heavily tinted sunglasses.

"And that, of course," Anastasios said, "never gets old."

Nick smiled.

"But it describes you so perfectly."

Anastasios pulled out the seat opposite Nick and sat. He gestured to the trussed bundle on the table.

"I brought you a present."

Nick reached for the binder.

"Fantastic, but isn't that my line?"

"So you've taken up catch phrases now?"

Nick looked at Anastasios for a moment, his face expressionless.

"You haven't heard very many Christmas stories, have you?"

"I was being facetious."

"Yeah, sure you were."

Nick started flipping through the pages of the binder.

"How do they always know exactly where you are?" Anastasios asked after a moment, gesturing to the binder Nick now held.

"No clue, man. I used to ask that all the time, and they would never give up a thing. I would even order them to tell me, and they would laugh in my face."

He paused, contemplating.

"I think they like to lord it over me."

"Interesting word choice," Anastasios commented.

Nick smiled again.

"I thought you would like that. You know what I mean, though."

While Nick studied the newest section of The List, Anastasios watched people walk along the boardwalk.

"I haven't seen you in a while, but thanks again for these ear things," Anastasios said. "I hear that you're getting some really nice reviews."

Nick looked up, smirking crookedly.

"Ear things?"

Anastasios's face was blank.

"You know what I'm talking about."

Nick feigned innocence, shrugging, hoping he had concealed the devious curl of his lips.

"Sorry, dude. You mean like a hearing aid or something? That's not really my department, but I'll pass it along."

Anastasios was silent.

Nick's grin only grew wider.

"Dude, 'ear thing' is so insulting," he said, laughing. "Do you have any clue how advanced those monitors are?"

"As they say," Anastasios responded, slightly annoyed, "one can appreciate the hamburger without knowing how it is prepared."

"*They* say that, huh?" Nick joked. "Because I think you just made that up. Hot dogs would have made more sense for that anyway, especially the really good ones, since everyone knows—"

"Okay," Anastasios exhaled, clearly exasperated. "I get the point ... I think."

He reached into his pocket, pulling his earpiece out. It was smaller than a conventional hands-free communication device, and infinitely more sophisticated.

"What will you think of next?" he mumbled, more to himself than the boy sitting across from him.

"'S nothing," Nick stated offhandedly. He looked at Anastasios again. "You like the flames? That's all Sam."

Anastasios nodded, studying the monitor.

"Samantha? Cool touch. My compliments to her. As a matter of fact, she's the one who gave me that."

He gestured to the binder.

"Figures," Nick said. "Probably just an excuse so she could see you again. I think she likes you or something, although I've told her many times that she could do much, much better."

Nick lowered his sunglasses and squinted at the young man seated across from him. Anastasios's smirk in response was mocking.

"If I didn't know her," Anastasios observed, "I would guess she was ten years old. Maybe even younger."

Nick scoffed.

"And I would guess you were in your mid-twenties," he replied, arranging his glasses again and looking at the binder. "But, like you, I would be off by, like, a lot. Anyways, I'm sure she'll be glad to hear that the great Anastasios thinks she is aging well."

He said the last bit in a teasing, girlish tone, and Anastasios chuckled.

"Well, look at that," Nick said, smiling. "Smokey laughs."

"An early Christmas gift to you," Anastasios responded.

"I'll take it. You know that I'm all for giving."

Anastasios shook his head, still smiling.

"So," Nick started, laying the binder back on the table and stretching his arms, "you want to grab a bite before you go? I know you didn't come all this way just to see little ol' me. Where are you headed off to, anyway?"

"Arctic."

"For real? Listen, you have to drop by this place on your way there. It's called Murray Land Shopping Centre, just outside of…Quebec City, I think. Dude, I'm telling you, this place has everything."

Anastasios frowned, waving him off.

"You really need to work on your geography. And here I would think a person in your position would have a significant need to know exactly where places are. Then, you would know that Quebec City is clearly not 'on my way.'"

"Well," Nick replied, shrugging, "maybe there's a Murray Land in the Arctic. Ha! Ever thought of that, smart guy?"

"I guarantee there is no Murray Land in the Arctic."

"Whatever, dude," Nick said. "I was just trying to give you a good food tip."

"Uh-huh."

Anastasios sounded unconvinced.

"Let me ask you this," the red-haired man then remarked. "Do you even know what city you're in right now?"

Nick scoffed again.

"Seriously? I mean, come on … seriously? You're seriously going to ask me that? Seriously? We're in California, dude! California … on the beach…"

Anastasios smirked as Nick tried to sneak a look at nearby signs.

"And…" Nick continued, stalling.

"While you're looking for something that says Newport Beach," Anastasios cut in, "I actually did come for another reason. We could use your talents for something that's probably going to come up in a few days, a week at the most. I was wondering if you would be interested in helping us out."

Across the table, Nick smiled.

"Dude, cool nachos."

Anastasios looked at him, one fiery eyebrow arching over the frames of his shades.

"That means I'm interested," Nick clarified.

Anastasios gave a dramatic, "Ah."

"What do I have to do?" Nick went on. "Do you want me to talk to someone? Do you want me to do a little roughin' up? You know, a little shakedown? Really, just give me a name."

"Wow. No," Anastasios replied. "Since when are your talents beating someone up? It's going to be a couple of phone calls, but we don't know any specifics yet, so I'm not entirely sure who you'll be talking to. I'll tell you more when it becomes more certain, unless, of course, there is a sudden change in her plans."

"Ah, the predictability of free will," Nick observed, nodding. "Okey-dokey, Smokey. You know how to find me. I'll probably be here in Newport News, punching the ol' time card."

He reached behind his head, stretching again.

"You know how it is," he went on. "The daily grind, doing my thang, testin' stuff…"

"There are so many things wrong with what you just said, including that you just named a city on the exact opposite side of the country from where you are sitting right now, but I guess we'll overlook all of that."

Anastasios then gestured to the empty table between them.

"Were you going to order something? Or were you planning to just sit here, loitering?"

"Oh, yeah," Nick said, straightening to attention and catching the eye of a passing server. "You almost made me forget how hungry I am."

He returned his gaze to the fiery-haired, sunglass-wearing figure across from him.

"You going to get something, too? And, before you make up your mind, Anastasia, know that it's on me, so no need to go scrounging for pennies or using the excuse that you're watching your figure."

"Anastasia? That's cute," Anastasios remarked. "It's not funny at all, but it's cute."

IN NORBURY, MASSACHUSETTS, GABRIEL snorted, expressing his amusement as both Raven and Charlie helped pull Jace to his feet.

Again.

"See?" he said through his laughter. "I warned you guys he was pretty terrible at this."

"Dude," Jace retorted, "didn't you just see me trip over that thing?"

"If by *thing* you mean that portion of freshly cut, green grass no different from the rest of the field, then yeah, I saw it."

While the rest of the group on the soccer field chuckled, Jace rolled his eyes. The players— Charlie, Raven, Presley, Jace, Michael and Gabriel—took up only half of one of McCormick Park's soccer fields, and they all stayed relatively close to goal. The weather, although slightly cooler now in the early half of August, was still distinctly summery, ideal for playing outdoors.

"And what makes it so bizarre, man," Michael declared as the laughter diminished, "is that you play football and lacrosse, so it's not like you're allergic to running on grass or anything."

"Oh, wow," Presley expressed. "You play lacrosse? Sweet. I don't know all the rules and stuff, but it looks pretty cool when I see it on TV."

"And not to mention, starting point guard for the varsity basketball team," Gabriel persisted as he took possession of the temporarily discarded soccer ball and tapped it to himself. "Even though that's not on grass, it still takes, you know, a little athletic ability. But you wouldn't guess any of that to watch him play now. It's funny, really, and kind of sad at the same time. It's as if you're trying to play soccer with your hands, but you're, like, doing a handstand at the same time, you know? It's really strange."

Presley laughed as Jace shot Gabriel an irritated glance.

"Okay," Presley said, speechless. "That's just ... wow. Okay."

Gabriel began to dribble away from the rest of the group, showing off with embellished feints and step overs against invisible opponents before Raven came from behind and easily swiped the ball. It took Gabriel a few moments to realize he no longer had possession. Jace returned the teasing he had endured moments before, snickering at Gabriel's delayed realization.

"Forget something?" Jace questioned, still chuckling.

Gabriel sneered in Jace's direction before both boys turned to see Presley and Michael attempting to steal the ball from Raven, with no success.

Michael, looking foolish as he ran small circles in his effort to liberate the ball from Raven, stopped his pursuit, his hands on his hips.

"Could someone remind me exactly why we decided that playing soccer with these two was a smart idea?" he questioned aloud.

"We just wanted to see if they had what it took to hang with the big bad high schoolers, remember?" Gabriel answered, coming alongside Michael. "No one, least of all me, said it was, in any way, a smart idea."

"You guys should probably get used to it," Presley said, having also stopped his pursuit of the ball, leaving Raven to juggle it in the air effortlessly with her feet. "Whoever's been the top athlete at Norbury should watch his back, because he may not hold the title much longer."

Gabriel and Michael turned to look at Jace, and then both fell into hysterics.

"Oops," Presley said, shrugging apologetically. "I'm just sayin'. They're pretty good."

Jace returned the shrug, adding a faint chuckle.

"Exaggerate much, Pres?" Raven's voice was slightly strained with determination as she now tried to keep Charlie away from the ball.

"Exaggerate?" Presley laughed. "Look, you both know I don't pretend to be any kind of athlete—"

Both Charlie and Raven snickered as they continued to battle for the soccer ball.

"Hey," Presley went on, "at least I can admit it. But you two have been the best at pretty much everything you have tried for as long as I've known either of you. If anything, I may not be exaggerating enough."

"He's right," Gabriel agreed, looking to Jace and Michael. "I'm telling you guys, this year, everyone in the state will know exactly who these two are, and they'll know exactly where Norbury High School is, if they don't already."

"Pretty sure people know that Norbury High School is in Norbury," Michael remarked, receiving chuckles from the others.

211

"Dude," Gabriel said, "seriously. It's going to be crazy. You tell 'em, Presley, because they don't want to believe me."

"That sounds silly," Charlie said, "and I agree with Raven. You're both exagger—"

Out of nowhere, Gabriel lunged for the ball. Charlie and Raven niftily moved out of the way, Raven moving the ball between her feet with a neat touch. Gabriel stumbled, his legs slipping from underneath him, his back making sudden impact with the ground, forcing a *whoosh* of air from his lungs.

"—rating," Charlie finished, looking down at the tousle-haired boy.

Once he had sucked in enough air to breathe again, Gabriel exhaled loudly and raised himself into a sitting position, his legs extended in front of him.

"See?" he said by way of explanation. "Who else would have seen that steal attempt coming? I was pretty sneaky."

Michael arched his eyebrow.

"Oh, so that's what that was? I thought that was just you being you."

"I'll tell you one thing. I definitely didn't see it coming," Presley declared, trying hard to stifle his laughter.

Charlie helped to pull Gabriel to his feet.

"Wow, you have soft hands," Gabriel said.

"Ugh. Come on, man," Michael groaned.

Jace just shook his head before looking over at Charlie in apology.

"What?" Gabriel's gaze shifted from a blushing Charlie to his two buddies. "It was just a natural observation!"

As the laughter faded once more, Raven flicked the ball into the air and then dribbled away, with the group promptly resuming chase.

"Hey, when are soccer tryouts, anyway?" Michael asked. "Gabe and Presley here have hyped you two up so much, I might have to come out there and see you going up against, you know, people who are actually good at soccer."

"Speak for yourself," Gabriel said, drawing a look from Michael. "I've got skills."

"It's in a couple of weeks, right?" Raven remarked, glancing to Charlie as she continued to elude the others.

"Yeah," Charlie confirmed. "I need to make sure, but I think freshman team tryouts are the twenty-first."

"Freshman tryouts?" Gabriel repeated, sticking his foot out for the soccer ball and coming up empty. "Why are you going to that?"

"What do you mean?" Charlie asked. "We're freshman. Aren't we supposed to go to freshman tryouts?"

Jace stopped running after the ball, with Gabriel and Charlie pulling up short as well.

"Not necessarily, Charlie," Jace began to explain, turning to her. "You see, freshman tryouts are—"

"Actually, you know, yeah, I think you're right," Gabriel interrupted, his eyes twinkling. "Freshman tryouts are the one you want to go to."

Jace looked at Gabriel with a questioning expression, and then leaned forward when his friend began to mumble something into his ear. Once Gabriel was finished, Jace leaned away again, shaking his head ruefully.

"Whatever," he said. "I think Mike forgot that we're supposed to be at football tryouts, and I'm pretty sure that's the same week as soccer. Since we're already on the team, the coaches like us to come and help out, like student-coaches, kinda."

He then gave Gabriel another look.

"I'm sure you won't be able to keep Gabe here from watching you two try out, though," he added.

"You're not on the football team?" Charlie asked, her eyes shifting to Gabriel.

Gabriel shook his head, grinning.

"Nah. Too violent for me. I'm kind of a softie."

Beside him, Jace scoffed, which drew Charlie's attention back to him.

"What were you saying about freshman tryouts? You never finished your thought."

Before Jace could respond, Gabriel spoke up again.

"Oh, believe me, for your sake, he was finished. He'll bore you to tears talking about the history and intricacies of this and that, and then you'll be pleading to yourself for a way out of the conversation."

Jace threw a stubborn glare in his direction.

"But hey," Gabriel reassured him, clapping him on his shoulders, "I still love you, bro."

He laughed and jogged away, joining the others still battling Raven for the soccer ball.

Jace started to follow, but Charlie's voice stopped him short.

"Hey, um, Jace?"

The older boy turned back to glance at Charlie.

"What's up?"

Charlie looked down briefly.

"I actually just wanted to ask you something about that night at the boardwalk."

Jace waited for her to continue.

"This may sound like a completely ridiculous question, and in fact, I wouldn't be surprised at all if you had no idea what I was talking about."

"Try me," Jace encouraged. "You never know. I may have every idea what you're talking about."

Ice-blond hair. Snow-gray eyes.

Charlie sighed before she spoke again.

"Okay. I know it's been awhile … like, a month now … and we've obviously run into you since then, but there was a boy and girl at the boardwalk that same night Raven and I met you guys. I saw them—for, like, a brief moment, I guess—but, I don't know, I can't seem to get them out of my head, and I was wondering if maybe you saw them or knew who they were. The boy looked a couple of years older than me, probably around your age. He had this whitish-blond hair, kind of spiky, and long enough that it came down across his forehead. The girl was younger, younger than my brothers—you remember them?"

"How could I forget?" Jace asked, grinning.

Charlie chuckled lightly.

"Yeah. Anyway, the girl's hair was really long, probably around Raven's length."

Jace turned briefly to glance at Raven and the others before returning his gaze to Charlie.

"And it was either brown or black," Charlie continued, "I'm not sure which. She was wearing a knit cap like you would wear in the winter.

"It was all so quick, though. It was like, one second they were there, and then, before I could even turn around to get another look at them, they were gone, as if they never existed. Raven thinks I may have been hallucinating because it was just after we saw…"

She stopped herself before she could finish the thought.

Jace looked at her, his eyes questioning.

"Right after you saw what?" he asked.

"Uh, saw you," Charlie managed. "It was just after we saw you … and Gabriel and, um, Michael."

"Why would seeing us make you hallucinate?"

"What? No, um … I was thinking about something else. It's nothing, forget it. But, the boy and girl. Do you, by any chance, remember seeing anyone at the boardwalk who looked like that?"

Jace thought for a moment, his forehead scrunched in concentration. He shook his head.

"I don't think so. I mean, I may have, but if I did, I didn't pay much attention. You think you may have recognized them, though?"

"I don't know, maybe. I just … there was something about them, even though I only saw them for, like, one second in total. It's as if I should know them from somewhere, but … I don't know. It's really strange. I'm probably sounding pretty weird right now."

Both teenagers suddenly flinched as the soccer ball landed very close to their location, rebounding off the grass as it bounced past.

"Heads up!" Gabriel announced far too late, as he ran past them after the ball, with Presley and Michael close behind.

Jace turned back to Charlie.

"Even if it was only fleeting, it sounds as though you got a pretty good look at them, or else your memory is fantastic. Have you given any thought to becoming a TV detective?"

Charlie chuckled, shaking her head.

"That's one of the things that's so weird. It's as if I've seen them before, especially the boy. Like, he's right in front of me, looking at me, but it's so quick, for, like, a split-second. I can even see the color of his eyes."

"Really?" Jace asked, curious. "What color are they?"

"Gray. Like those Christmas cards that show snow falling at night? Like that. A light, snowy gray."

Jace smiled.

"Maybe your mind is trying to work out where you've seen them," he began as he slowly started to back away from Charlie, all set to return to the informal soccer game. "You can always look at it this way, though. Our first three times seeing each other this summer were unplanned and unexpected, after never having even met before. You say you're not sure if you know those two from the boardwalk? Well, with your talent for unscripted encounters, I'm sure you'll bump into them again before you know it."

He winked, and turned to go after the other boys who were, somewhat clumsily, still jockeying for sole control of the ball.

As he left, Raven approached.

"Oooh," she said in a teasing tone. "What was that all about?"

"Oh, be quiet, you," Charlie said. "I was asking him about that boy and girl I saw at Bahia Bay. But he's like you, he doesn't remember."

"The boy and girl?" Raven parroted. "What boy and girl?"

Charlie turned to look at her, her face incredulous.

"Really?" she asked. "The boy and girl I asked you about a few days after we were there, just before that volleyball game on the beach with Presley and the others? Seriously, you don't remember?"

Raven smirked.

"Got ya," she said smugly.

Charlie smiled, although her grin faded as she took in her friend's expression.

"You have no idea what I'm talking about, do you?" she asked.

Raven's grin turned sheepish.

"I remember playing volleyball," she admitted. "I'm sorry. Were they really important for me to remember? Tell me again, and I promise I won't—"

Charlie laughed.

"It's all right. It was nothing, really. For all I know, it may have been my imagination. I mean, you were standing right there beside me when I saw them, and if you don't even remember them, well…"

She shrugged, pushing off against Raven's shoulder lightly before racing for the group of jostling boys.

"So, HERE'S HOPING EVERYTHING turns out okay for little Bridgette. I know I speak for everyone here at News 8 in saying we're all rooting for her. And now, let's turn to Suzie for our weather update. Suzie, another hot one today, eh?"

"That's right, Rodney, but then again, it's summertime in the Southwest, so the high temperatures shouldn't be too surprising, right? The prize for the high of the day—one hundred and one degrees—goes to Rio Rancho, with Albuquerque and Los Padillas both reaching ninety-seven. As you can see when we zoom out a little bit on the map here, it was mid- to high-nineties throughout—"

Emily Hendricks jumped as a knock sounded at her apartment door, her attention turned away from her laptop and the local weather report droning from her television. Duke, sprawled on the carpet in front of the elevated television screen, lifted his head at the knock, his ears pricked. He stared at Emily, as if waiting to see what her response would be.

After lowering the volume on the TV, Emily stood and crossed the living room, entering the short hallway near the door. Duke rose as well, following silently.

Emily looked through the peephole, taking in the two figures on the other side. One was a police officer. The other was Walt Flannery, the security guard from downstairs.

Emily unlocked and opened the door.

"Miss Hendricks."

The officer presented a card affixed with the police department's shield.

"I'm Officer Timothy Gutierrez with the Albuquerque Police Department. I'm not sure if you recognize me."

"In front of my office building when I go out to lunch," Emily said. "Sure."

She then added, in a quieter tone, "Thanks for that, by the way, although I'm still not quite sure it's entirely necessary if it takes away from—"

Officer Gutierrez waved away the words before the Emily could finish.

"It's a part of the job, ma'am."

Walt looked from the officer to Emily.

"Need me for anything?" he asked.

"No," Emily replied, smiling appreciatively. "Thanks, Walt."

Walt nodded, his serious security officer face on display. He hitched up the trousers of his uniform.

"I'm downstairs if you need me."

As Walt moved down the hall to the elevators, Officer Gutierrez turned back to Emily. Getting a closer look at him now, Emily saw that he was indeed young, about her age, if not a year or so younger. He had a handsome, almost boyish face, although his bearing suggested he was certainly capable of enforcing the law.

Emily instantly, and fleetingly, wondered about his name. He appeared to possess hardly a speck of the Latin physical attributes at which his last name hinted.

"Does your security officer walk up all visitors?" Officer Gutierrez asked, smiling. "Or is that just for you?"

"No, he just started that after this ... whatever this is," Emily replied. "I keep telling him he doesn't have to do it, but of course, he won't take that as an answer."

Gutierrez nodded.

"Nothing wrong with being extra vigilant. But anyway, I apologize for disrupting your evening. I—and my Sergeant, whom I think you have talked with, Sergeant Bruce Martin—thought it necessary to speak with you briefly in person. I would also like to show you a set of photographs—a photo lineup—if you don't mind."

"Yes, yes, that's fine."

Emily opened the door wider to allow the officer to enter.

"Come in."

"This will only take a moment," Gutierrez continued, easing past the young woman and stepping into the entryway. He spotted Duke as Emily closed the door behind him. He stared at the dog briefly, and then issued a soft sound of acceptance.

"Nice dog," he commented.

Duke returned the officer's measured gaze in an indifferent manner.

"In my line of work," Gutierrez went on, "an encounter with a German Shepherd usually begins with a bark and a growl."

"Duke's pretty discerning," Emily noted, as she leaned back against the wall of the hallway, facing the police officer. "I think if I had hesitated in letting you in, or if you were here to arrest me, he would be a little more in-your-face."

"Well, fortunately for me, that is not the case," the cop returned. "He looks like he could do some damage."

He turned back to Emily.

"Miss Hendricks, I'm aware that—"

"Emily, please."

The officer nodded.

"All right. I am aware that you told Sergeant Martin you would rather not be kept up to date with the specific details of this investigation. Is that correct?"

"Yes," Emily replied, "but if you feel I need to know something, in terms of who to look out for, then please don't hesitate."

"No, no," Gutierrez replied, shaking his head. "It's nothing like that. I was just confirming before I revealed something you perhaps didn't request. Suffice it to say, we do have a person of interest in our custody, and I have a short lineup of photos I would like you to look at to see if anyone looks familiar."

"I'm not sure how much help I'll be," Emily said. "I've never actually seen anyone following me, and if it weren't for that note, I could just as easily assume it was me being paranoid—stress or something."

The young officer shook his head again.

"No, ma'am. I've talked to quite a few people who are certifiably paranoid, and you're not in that realm, I assure you."

He indicated the three-ring binder he was holding.

"Is it all right if I show you the pictures now?"

Emily ran an uneasy hand through her hair.

"If you think it will help."

Officer Gutierrez nodded, as though understanding her discomfort.

"Okay. Here's how it works," he began, opening the binder and flipping through a few pages. "These are the photographs of six individuals, one of which may, or may not, be involved in this case. I'm not even going to say that the guy we have in custody is in this group of pictures, so there is absolutely no pressure on you to point out any of these photographs in particular. There's also the chance that you don't recognize any of these people, which is perfectly fine. Anyway, just take your time."

He handed the binder over to Emily.

"See if anything … anyone … jumps out."

Emily carefully but quickly examined the six pictures, and then looked through them again, inspecting each photo a little longer, raking through the archive of faces in her memory, making sure of what she had noticed on her initial survey. She then offered the binder back to the officer, shaking her head.

"Sorry. I don't recognize any of them."

"You're sure? Not hanging around any of the restaurants or stores you've been to lately, not around your office building downtown, not anywhere around here?"

She shook her head slowly as she thought again, becoming more confident as her memory turned up blank once more.

"No, not that I can remember. I'm sorry."

Gutierrez offered a supportive smile.

"Nothing to apologize for—you did good. Quite frankly, we're on the trail, and we are chasing down a few leads with concerns to a couple of the other women involved. But this is still in the murky stages. This guy is ... well, I won't get too detailed, but this guy's small time. He's definitely involved, but he's not the only one we're looking for. From what we've gathered, my hunch is we're dealing with a different guy in your case. I would go so far as to say your situation may not even be connected with the other women."

Emily frowned, causing Gutierrez to pause.

"It's a step in the right direction, ma'am," the police officer attempted to reassure her. "It's not a matter of if we find who is responsible for this but when, and odds are, it's going to be pretty soon. But if I may say so, from what I can see, you are handling this entire circumstance very well. You seem to be a very brave, very capable woman, Miss Hendricks."

Emily felt a hot ruddiness spread over her cheeks.

"Please," she uttered in a soft voice, "call me Emily."

"Yes. Of course. Emily."

He studied her for a moment longer before moving for the door.

"Just so you know," he added, "the other women involved in this have received, or are currently receiving, this same visit from other officers. We will be continuing our investigation. And, of course, if you have any questions or anything like that, the card I gave you has all of our contact info—anytime, day or night—along with the cell phone number I can answer if you don't feel comfortable going through Dispatch. If there's an emergency, call 911."

He stepped out of the apartment and into the hallway, with Emily holding the door open.

"So, I guess that means I'm not supposed to call you if there is an emergency?" she asked, allowing herself a hint of humor.

Gutierrez returned Emily's smile with a gentle smirk.

"Ma'am, I am 911. It's just fewer numbers to press. You call either number and I'm on my way."

He gave a casual wave before starting to turn for the elevators. Almost immediately, he spun to face Emily again.

"I'm sorry Miss Hen—Emily, one more thing."

He returned to her door so his voice would not carry.

"The security officer who accompanied me upstairs. Is he the same one who was here when you received the fir—uh, when you received the letter?"

"Actually, yes. Walt…"

Emily paused in the middle of the thought. She looked at the officer curiously.

"Wait … first? You were going to say first letter? There's been more?"

Behind her, still quietly sitting in the apartment's hallway, Duke's ears arched up in attention.

EMILY LET DUKE OUT one of the side doors of her apartment building before following him out. The air, now that the New Mexico sun had set on another Albuquerque summer day, seemed abruptly brisk compared to the stifling temperatures of early afternoon.

Duke, patient and well trained—Emily's occasional teases aside—waited for his owner to emerge from the building before sauntering to the end of the residence, where the grassy lawn awaited. Emily walked more slowly, allowing the dog to take the lead. She and Duke made similar outings to the grass multiple times a day, the routine now almost instinctual.

The sounds of the neighborhood nightlife were muffled along the hushed side street.

"I'm thinking we'll go out to the jogging park sometime tomorrow," Emily announced. "I'll see if Kimberly wants to go, so she can bring Giant."

At her mention of Kimberly's Golden Retriever, or in response to something else completely unrelated, Duke turned to Emily and cocked his head to the side, his pricked ears and the mask-like coloring of his face giving him an inquisitive appearance beneath the glow of the overhead streetlights. He then returned to the grass.

Moments later, Emily's attention was drawn back to Duke when a soft munching sound reached her ears.

"What is that? Is that you?" she questioned, edging closer to the dog while being careful to avoid anything left by owners who had astonishingly forgotten to "Take the Waste."

"Dog biscuits? Where in the world did those come from?"

Duke stopped chewing, coughing up the bits not already swallowed. Sniffing at the remnants, he growled, his hackles raised.

"Duke," Emily voiced in warning.

The dog turned, his growls louder. He moved nearer to Emily, his furry, sinewy body brushing against her legs protectively. Duke's snarls were aimed at shadows along the peripheries of the grassy plot, towards an invisible, elusive threat.

Emily felt the invasive dread of being watched return. She crouched to comfort the provoked dog. Just as she did so, Duke slipped out of her grasp, circling around. Though swift, the dog's movements seemed wobbly and uneven.

He barked; it sounded halfhearted.

Duke lunged just as something was thrust against Emily's face, swathing her mouth and nose and partly obscuring her eyes. Emily struggled, attempting to pull herself away. Duke's snarls grew fainter, less aggressive. Emily's vision began to fade …

…fuzzy around the edges …

...harder to fight, her strength draining away...

Emily leaned against the person who held her, her struggling nearly nonexistent. Still, she tried to push...

She was being dragged, and then felt herself picked up. Her eyes lulling, she glimpsed Duke lying sprawled in the grass.

After that, her world slipped into darkness.

THERE WAS A BEEP, followed instantly by another, before the urgent, undulating emergency tones reverberated across the channels of the police radio.

"Dispatch to Delta, Delta Area Command, reported 10-74 behind 3601 West 52nd Avenue. 10-74 behind 3601 West 52nd Avenue. Units responding, over?"

Officer Timothy Gutierrez was already performing a rapid, improvised U-turn in his patrol cruiser as the police dispatcher announced the address. He cursed under his breath, reaching for his radio.

"Delta 13 to Dispatch, responding to 10-74, over."

Gutierrez flipped his lights and sirens to the ON position in a single, quick motion, speeding up and weaving through the late evening traffic.

"Copy that, Delta 13. 10-74 reported to have occurred in a grassy area just behind the apartment."

Gutierrez gritted his teeth. His hands gripped the steering wheel.

"Delta 13 copies."

A split-second later, he heard: "Delta 14 to Dispatch. Show me responding to 10-74, over."

Boonie, Gutierrez thought.

Delta 14 was his zone partner on patrol, Officer Peter Boondocks, affectionately nicknamed "Boonie."

"Copy that, Delta 14," the police dispatcher noted over the channel. "Address is 3601 West 52nd Avenue. 10-74 was reported by a Walt Flannery, security officer for the apartment building at the address given. He is present at the scene."

Gutierrez slowed as he neared a red light. Pedestrians hurried over the crosswalk, and he shot off again, siren blaring, lights flashing fiercely. Oncoming cars halted to allow him through the intersection in defiance of the red signal light.

"Delta 1 to Dispatch. Show me responding to that 10-74 on West 52nd also, and close any additional response, over."

"Copy response and close additional units, Delta 1."

Delta 1 was Sergeant Bruce Martin, who must have recognized the address as well.

Gutierrez raced through the streets of lower downtown Albuquerque to the scene.

"Emily," he mumbled to himself.

And just when I told her we were making some headway.

"**H**ECK YEAH, DUDE!" ERIC exclaimed into the cordless kitchen telephone he held up to one side of his face. "That would be—"

"Eric Johnson!" his mother called, from her spot at the counter. "If I have to hear you use that kind of language again, I promise—"

Eric turned to face her, covering the mouthpiece with his free hand.

"Sorry," he whispered loudly, excitement still evident in his voice.

Elizabeth gave him an extended stare—Eric's father had long ago termed it her "warning glare"—before returning her attention to the cutting and chopping at the counter.

Eric removed his hand from the mouthpiece.

"Yeah, man, I'm back."

He chanced another glance at his mother, assuring himself her attention was no longer focused on him.

"Yeah, that was her," he mumbled, and then, "Shut up, dude. It's not even that funny."

Without looking up, Elizabeth's lips curled into a smile as she listened to her son's end of the conversation.

"Yeah, yeah," Eric quickly resumed his earlier enthusiasm. "I'll ask her, but I already told her you were planning it, so I'm sure I'll be able to come."

He paused again, listening.

"No, that's not until next Monday, remember? And anyway, Sarah won't be back from her thing until sometime Sunday, and Riley's going to his friend's house, I think."

Eric lowered the phone again and covered the mouthpiece.

"Mom, isn't Riley going to the Buchanan's tomorrow night?"

"Yep, I'm taking him over there around three or three thirty," Elizabeth responded without glancing up from her work.

"Yeah, it's tomorrow," Eric said into the phone. "Yeah, sounds good ... Oh, yeah. Definitely."

He chuckled, and then noticed his mother looking in his direction again. He smiled sheepishly before turning his attention back to the call.

"Wait. So you guys are asking for another beat down? Doesn't it get kind of old losing *all* the time?"

Eric fell quiet, and then laughed. Again, Elizabeth smiled.

"Whatever, man ... Yeah, I'll call you back before then if I need a ride or I can't do it. Otherwise, it's all systems go."

He paused again.

"What? All systems go? ... Yeah, but dude, it's a classic ... See? That's why you're no good in history. No appreciation for the classics."

After he listened to the reply, Eric laughed again.

"Are you even listening to the words coming out of your mouth right now?"

He rolled his eyes.

"No, Sammy, I don't care how many of your 'girls'"—Eric made air quotations with his free hand—"have seen the movies or read the books, it can't be a classic if it's only a few years old. Classics stand the test of time, thus the word 'classic.' Those movies have not had any time that's tested them. Call me back in twenty years and we'll see then … Whatever, dude. Yeah, I'll be there and I'll call you if something comes up.

"Yeah … Okay … Yeah, see ya."

Eric placed the phone back in its cradle and took a deep breath to calm himself. He then whirled around to face his mom, but before he could utter a word, Elizabeth spoke up.

"So," she began, taking on the refined voice of a British dignitary while still effortlessly paring the skins off apples in preparation for another apple pie, "at what time does dear Samuel, the prince of Treeport Avenue, expect you to make your presence known at his doorstep?"

"Afternoon sometime. I guess between three and four," Eric answered, attempting to convey casual indifference. He did not attempt to follow his mother's lead into the Queen's English.

"The plan is for us to go to Buster's around five and stay for a little while, and then go back to Sammy's and play basketball and hang out, and spend the night. His mom and dad are letting everyone come and—"

"Oh, my," Elizabeth interjected, continuing in a British accent. "I'm afraid I'm going to have to interrupt you right there, young man, as I can hardly understand you with that god-awful Golden, Colorado, twang of yours."

Eric gazed at his mother blankly. Elizabeth paused her work and gazed back. This unusual back-and-forth was nothing out of the ordinary. For a moment, it appeared as though neither parent nor child would relent.

Finally, Eric spoke up, paraphrasing his previous response with his own version of Victorian speech. He intentionally tried to butcher words and phrases, hoping his mom would tire of the ruse she had begun.

He should have known it would be no use.

"I shall assume we are speaking of the morrow for these events to take place?"

"Ye, and ye shall be a bountiful occasion of sorts," Eric replied, his grammar quickly becoming nonsensical. He arched an eyebrow at his mother, smirking.

"And who else, pray tell, shall be joining you and Prince Samuel in this affair?" Elizabeth questioned, unflappable.

"Why, it shan't be but Ricky, Brooke, and T.J. Partake ye scrumpets of Sammy shall present proliferously as well, as it were, of course."

His mother appeared to be suppressing a smile, but she soon carried on with a flourish.

"Ah, yes. Dear Ricky, the puckish and precocious royal of Holbrook Court. As I am aware, he is a cherished acquaintance of both you and the aforementioned Prince Samuel of questionable repute, and therefore—"

"Yeah, okay, okay," Eric cut in, dropping his poor accent in the process. "Me, Sammy, Ricky, Brooke, and T.J.—and Sammy's parents, of course. Buster's around five o' clock, then back to Sammy's afterwards. Sammy said Ricky, Brooke, and T.J. all have already said they would be there. So, can I go?"

"Room clean?" Elizabeth slipped back into her regular tone.

Eric breathed a sigh of relief.

"Yep. You saw it this morning, and you said it looked good."

"Bathroom?"

"You could eat out of that tub if you wanted to."

"*Scarlet Letter?*"

"It's, uh … coming along," Eric said, the hesitance clear in his voice.

"I think I'll try that one again," Elizabeth remarked. "*Scarlet Letter?*"

"What was it you told me before about how you climb the highest mountain or walk around the world one step at a time … or after taking your first step, or something like that?"

"Geez, Eric. Not only did you misquote the lesson, but you also tried to use it as an excuse. That could have very well cost you all your fun right there."

Eric sighed.

"You know how these things go, Mom. I promise I will be done by next … in a couple of weeks. Maybe three."

"Stay on it," she commented seriously before continuing with her pre-fun outing interrogation. "*Lord of the Flies?*"

Eric grinned.

"Done."

"Found time to read that one, eh?"

Eric shrugged, though still smiling.

"Gutters?"

Eric's smile vanished, replaced by confusion.

"What?"

"The gutters? You said you were going to clean—no, that was your father. Hank!"

A baritone voice sounded from an adjoining room.

"Yes, sweetie pie?"

"Could you come in here, please?"

Hank Johnson soon appeared at the kitchen entryway. An imposing figure in both height and build, he easily filled the entrance. Eric, all of fourteen years of age, was already well on his way to matching his father's stature.

In height, at least.

None of that mattered to the five-foot-three-and-a-smidge inch matriarch of the Johnson household, however, and both Hank and Eric knew it.

"Yes, sweetie?"

Hank's greeting was overly syrupy, plainly obvious to everyone but him.

"The gutters?" Elizabeth asked, choosing not to look at her husband—another of Hank's signals, the "reverse warning glare."

"Uh…"

Hank hesitated, his eyes darting around the kitchen as his mind worked in overdrive. His gaze soon landed on his son.

"Uh, I thought we said we would let Eric have a go at it this weekend?" he offered at last.

By his tone, it sounded as though Hank was as much trying to convince himself of the spur-of-the-moment notion as he was his wife. Hank shifted his glance to her while his eldest son abruptly turned to him in complete shock.

Elizabeth gave a sly chuckle.

"Maybe we said that in whatever fantasyland you visit when you're dozing off in front of the TV set, but here in the real world, you said you and Bryan would be taking care of the gutters this weekend."

Hank sputtered.

"Uh … wha—uh …"

Still focusing on paring the fruit, Elizabeth directed her next words to her son.

"You can go to Sammy's tomorrow, Eric. I'll drop you off when I take Riley to Chase's."

"Yes!"

Eric pumped his fist in the air. He began to jog over to his mother, holding his arms out wide.

"Hey, watch it, bucko," his mother warned, feigning menace. "I'm holding a knife. Don't try one of those strong, He-Man bear hugs with me like you do with your friends."

Eric froze in his tracks, his arms still outstretched.

"Feel free to give me a kiss, though," Elizabeth added.

Eric walked the rest of the way and pecked her on the cheek.

"You are, as always, the best," Eric said to her.

His mother smiled.

"I don't think your father will be in the mood to agree with that statement in a few moments."

They both turned to Hank, who continued to stand in the entryway.

"Did I mention just how much I love both of you?" Hank's sugary undertones were back. "My beautiful, adoring wife, and my handsome, upstanding, responsible—"

Elizabeth scoffed.

"I'm not buying that," Eric said. "You just tried to hang me out to dry. Me! Your own flesh and blood!"

He made his way to the doorway his father was blocking. Hank backed away in a subtle attempt to slow his son's departure.

"Oh, you thought I was serious?" he asked as Eric approached. "I was just kidding. Ha ha! Hey, um, before you go, do you think you could help me out here? You know how your mother gets."

"Not a chance," Eric replied, edging past his father's large frame. "I guess that makes us even."

Hank forced out another laugh.

"Ha ha! Okay, then! I'll catch you later, bud. Maybe I'll drop you off at Sammy's tomorrow, huh? How about that?"

"I don't think you'll have the time," Elizabeth brought her husband's attention back to the kitchen. "I believe you have a date tomorrow, if I'm not mistaken."

"Hmm? Oh!"

He smirked.

"You got us those reservations at Ferdinand's since all the kids will be away?"

"No, not a date with me, silly," his wife clarified. "I believe you…"

She tapped her chin with her free hand as though she were thinking.

"Oh yes, you and Bryan, have a date with the gutters tomorrow? I'm sure you will want to spend some quality time together, so I wouldn't want to disturb it by sending you to drop the kids off."

Hank Johnson looked at his wife without speaking, his face disbelieving.

"You know what? I think you're just evil," he finally said in a low voice. "You like to torture me."

Elizabeth Johnson turned to her beloved husband and smiled adorably.

"**D**RINK UP, EMILY. YOU really need to drink it. It'll help you wake up."

Sobbing.

"Please ... please, just let me go."

No response.

THE TWO ADOLESCENT LABRADORS sprinted after the tennis balls, their tongues waving, ears flapping. The Johnson's front yard was expansive and, due to Hank Johnson's continued efforts, always a perfect shade of green. Eric stood and watched as the two chocolate-brown puppies bounded after the same ball, and when one finally clutched the toy in its jaws, the other raced to the other ball only a short distance away. Both puppies hurried back to Eric with their prized possessions, each losing their still-youthful grip on the ball only once during the return trips.

The heat of the day lingered, although milder than it had been a few days prior. Eric wore what had become his summer fashion staple: shorts, and, in a curious rebellion against the weather, a long-sleeved shirt illustrating his support for the Colorado Avalanche hockey team, though he did roll the sleeves up to his elbows. The shirt was well-worn and slightly faded, but he never minded showing his fondness for both the sport and the team.

Eric reached for the tennis balls and a short tug-of-war ensued, each dog soon losing its grip. Their defeat was short-lived and quickly forgotten when both tennis balls were tossed through the air once more. With an energetic, "Go get 'em!" from Eric, the race to capture their playthings was on again.

Agro and Terri—short for Aggressive and Terrifying—soon came bounding back, each clutching a slobbery tennis ball. The soggy state of the toys after a few throw-and-retrieve cycles had quickly turned twelve-year-old Sarah Johnson off the game, leaving only Eric, Riley, and occasionally Hank to participate in the puppies' favorite sport.

"Seriously, you guys should just stop fighting it. I'm way too strong for you," Eric bragged as he grasped the tennis balls again. His arm began to cock back to launch the first ball when he saw an unexpected movement. He shifted his gaze to look closer, his arm still raised in hesitation.

A young boy—dark hair, olive-tanned skin—stood far enough away that Eric could not make out his face or identity, although he was pretty sure he had never seen the kid before. The boy was weaving his way, almost dreamily, along the edge between the Johnson's deeply green lawn and the currently empty street. Eric assumed the boy was lost in thought, completely unaware of his surroundings.

On a whim, Eric shot his arm forward.

"Hey, kid!" he called loudly, sending first one tennis ball and then the other soaring into the wandering boy's vicinity.

Agro and Terri took off.

Even from his location, a sprawling yard's length away, Eric saw the child wince as he brought his hands up to his ears, only to just as quickly bring them down again. The boy then stared around frantically for a moment before his gaze settled on the puppies heading directly for him.

The tennis balls plopped down short of the boy. The puppies, anticipating where the balls would land even as they left Eric's hand, did not hesitate. Agro immediately sought one of the toys, while his sister completely ignored them both, continuing a straight dash toward the boy at the edge of the yard. She stopped and stared up at the child, her head tilted sideways. The boy stared back, not moving.

"Terri! Get the ball!" Eric called.

"Arf!" Terri barked at the younger boy, who jumped back in surprise. The dog abruptly did an about-face and raced back to Eric, completely ignoring the ball she was meant to retrieve.

"You forgot the ball, Terri!" Eric declared as the dog ran across the manicured lawn.

Along the street, the young boy looked after the departing Labrador puppy a moment before looking down at the abandoned tennis ball. He knelt and reached for it.

"Hey, kid! You don't have to do—" Eric attempted to warn him off.

The boy stood back up, the saliva-covered ball in his hand.

"—that," Eric finished, his tone significantly lower.

Dog spit strikes again, he thought.

He began to jog out to the boy, the dogs running at his side, slowing his jog as he approached and then stopping in front of the quiet boy. Agro and Terri mirrored his actions, looking up to Eric to see what to do next.

"Sorry about that."

Eric motioned to the ball in the boy's hand.

The boy looked from Eric to the damp tennis ball again, squeezing it. Moisture oozed from the object's fuzzy felt skin.

"Wow. You have to be pretty strong to be able to do that," Eric commented.

The boy looked up at him, his black hair fringing his eyes.

Eric waved at the ball again.

"That's dog slobber, you know."

The boy squeezed the toy again, producing more gooey spit.

Eric chuckled.

"You're weird, like my brother," he said, grinning. "Most people don't want to get dog slobber on their hands."

The silent boy held the tennis ball closer to his face, giving it a more critical look. He squeezed it again. Eric watched him, amused.

"What's your name, kid?"

The boy did not respond, instead studying the ball he held to his face with both hands, twisting, turning, and squeezing. Before Eric could repeat his inquiry, a familiar voice called out from behind him.

"Hey, Eric! Mom said to get your crazy butt in here! Food's ready!"

At once, Agro and Terri turned and ran to the house. Eric looked back to see Riley on the front porch, gesturing dramatically. A muffled voice—almost certainly his mother's—floated out from inside, but he could not make out the words.

Riley's over-the-top waving lessened.

"And Mom says bring your craz—bring your friend, too! Dad cooked, so we've got plenty of food to go around!"

Another mumble came from inside, and Riley darted into the house after the puppies entered.

Eric turned back to the younger boy.

"Are you new around here? You think it would be okay with your mom and dad if you ate with us? My dad cooked tonight, which means he made way too much."

The boy lowered the tennis ball. Eric raised his eyebrows in question. A moment passed, and then the boy gave his reply by bursting into a mad dash across the lawn to the Johnson's large, rustic house. Eric grunted, chuckling again, as he spun to give chase.

"WHY AM I HERE? Who are you? Why did you take me? Let me go. Let me go!"

"Stop yellin', Emily."

"I said let me go! Let me go!"

ELIANNA INSERTED THE MONITOR into her ear as she stole a glance at Elias, who flew alongside her dozens of miles above the Earth's surface and a thousand miles north of Golden, Colorado, near Edmonton, Alberta. Cloudy Canadian skies streamed by beneath them.

"Hello?" Elianna addressed once the monitor was in place.

"Hi," a woman's voice came through clearly. "My name is Elizabeth Johnson. I'm sorry to bother you, but I have your son here, and I was wondering if it would be okay if he stayed for dinner—that is, with my husband, my children, and myself. It would be absolutely no imposition at all. We have more than enough food, thanks to my husband's heavy hand, but I wanted to make sure that you knew where he was and that he wasn't in any danger. He says you all live up the street?"

"Oh, yes, Mrs. Johnson. I'm Elianna," Elianna replied in her usual melodious timbre. "Yes, we actually just moved into the Erickson's place a few days ago. We're still getting the lay of the land, as they say, and Lucas wanted to do a little exploring of his own."

LUCAS.

"Well, welcome to neighborhood, if I can call it that," Elizabeth said over the phone. "I guess it completely slipped past me that someone had moved in up there already, or I would have made the trek to formally introduce myself."

She looked to the young boy who, seated at the dining table, appeared to be listening intently to whatever her youngest son Riley was animatedly explaining.

"Lucas, you say?" she continued. "That's a beautiful name."

Elizabeth noticed the boy's gaze shift to her at the mention of his name. Then, just as quickly, his attention returned to Riley.

ELIANNA LAUGHED LIGHTLY, TENS of thousands of feet in the air.

"Yes, Lucas. I hope I am safe in assuming, Mrs. Johnson, that you have noticed something … different … about him?"

"Call me Elizabeth, please."

There was a pause, followed by a soft chuckle.

"He wouldn't even ... I mean, I know it is probably none of my business, but ... is he ... I mean, is there anything ..."

Elianna laughed again.

"Elizabeth, I assure you it's nothing to be concerned about. I don't want to keep you from your dinner, but suffice it to say that we all have our quirks. I'd like to think it's what makes each of us special. Lucas's quirks are, I guess, more apparent than most, but he is just as capable as you or I were when at his age, if not more so. He will understand whatever you ask of him, and he is respectful—at least, he better be."

Both women chuckled at that.

"He probably just won't give a verbal reply," Elianna went on. "But believe me, he's good at finding other ways to get his point across if he needs to."

"Yes, of course," came the response through her earpiece. "I've already noticed his beautiful handwriting, which is how he gave us your number. I mean, I just feel foolish for even asking. It's just..."

"It's absolutely okay, Elizabeth. Completely understandable, and I'm actually glad you asked; many people don't. But, I don't want to keep you from your family. If you're sure that it's all right, he can stay, and I can walk down to your house in about an hour to pick him up, or if you would prefer to call us..."

"Oh, no, don't be silly. I'm sure one of my boys, Eric or Riley, or both, would be more than happy to walk him up. Is there a certain time you expect him back?"

"Whenever you all get tired of him, I guess. I wouldn't want to take him away if he is having a good time with you all."

Hearing Elizabeth Johnson chuckle, Elianna added, "But seriously, please feel free to call if you would like us to come pick him up."

"It's not a problem at all. Like I said, I'm sure we'll see each other in person before too long. And again, welcome to Golden."

The two exchanged their goodbyes, and as the connection ended, Elianna noticed her partner looking at her.

"What is it?"

Elias smirked, but said nothing. Then, without warning, he shot ahead, a sonic boom reverberating across the sky as he accelerated through the sound barrier.

Elianna smiled and went after him, another echoing crack rumbling through the air.

LUCIFER POINTED TO THE serving plate heaped with broccoli in response to Elizabeth Johnson's question.

"I think he and Sarah have the same dietician," Hank commented slyly as Eric passed the platter over.

Lucifer and the Johnson family—minus Sarah, who was at her sleepover—were seated around the wooden dining table in an alcove off the kitchen. Serving dishes were piled high with mouth-watering home-cooked food fit for a holiday feast. For the Johnsons, the spread was the predictable result of Hank Johnson's work in the kitchen. Leftovers were certain.

"All ready to hang with your homies tomorrow?" Hank ventured before taking another bite out of his baked chicken.

"Yeah."

"Yep!"

Both Johnson boys responded at the same moment, Riley's adolescent cheerfulness matched by his older brother's feigned coolness. Hank's chewing hardly covered his low chuckle.

"See, honey?" he asked, still chewing. "Everyone's getting to hang with their homies tomorrow, except for me."

Elizabeth's fork pierced a piece of chicken.

"Oh, please. You and your 'cool homie' Bryan have your own little play-date scheduled on our roof tomorrow, but you can invite all the friends you want to help you out, although I would think two overgrown men would be more than enough to get the job done."

Hank chewed contemplatively.

"Hmm. Actually, I think I know just the crew to handle this," he replied. "I'll get Phillips and Morrisett, and Bryan can get a hold of Pendleton."

"Phillips and Morrisett?" Elizabeth interrupted. "Who are they? A couple of guys from work?"

Hank tried to hold in his laugh, but it was a lost cause. His guffaw obviously startled Lucifer, seated at the other end of the table.

Eric shook his head.

"He's talking about a Phillips screwdriver, a Morrisett ladder, and the Pendleton pressure-washer Mr. Sparrow owns," Eric explained. "I think he got that joke off of that hardware show he watches."

Hank was still laughing heartily, although he tried to control his amusement when Elizabeth's glare threatened to bore holes into the side of his head. Riley, seated adjacent to Lucifer, attempted to sneakily transfer some of his vegetables onto Lucifer's now-empty plate while his parents' attention was diverted.

"I saw that, Riley Johnson."

Elizabeth's gaze shifted to her youngest child.

"But I thought Lucas wanted more," Riley whined. "And we don't want to let our friends go hungry. You said that."

Hank's guffaws resumed with greater force, joined by Eric's snickering at his brother's pathetic excuse.

"Oh, that's so nice of you, Riley," Elizabeth said with obviously feigned sincerity. "And you're right. Since we don't want anyone to go hungry, including you, can I offer you some more vegetables to replace the ones you so selflessly gave to Lucas?"

"I'm, um ... I'm not hungry anymore."

Hank tried mightily to hold in his laughter during the pause that followed, but a few stray snickers escaped anyway. Eric concealed his grin, hastily shoving another forkful of food into his mouth. Lucifer looked on, inexpressive, his gaze shifting between Riley and his mother.

"I'm not sure you heard me, Riley Johnson. I asked if I could offer you more vegetables to replace those that you gave Lucas," Elizabeth repeated.

"I don't think so?"

Riley's hesitance had the effect of transforming his statement into a question. His eyes were wide and his bottom lip quivered slightly, as though he were on the verge of tearing up.

Hank felt on the verge of crying for a different reason.

"This ... is ... so ... painful," he choked out, his eyes watering as he tried not to let his muffled laughter become full-fledged hysterics at his son's misfortune. "Just ... just take a little ... a little more, Riley."

The large man clenched his teeth together in an effort to control himself.

Riley's face had a sad puppy expression, but Elizabeth's arched eyebrows suggested she would not be so easily swayed. Finally, Riley reached for a nearby bowl and scooped out a small serving of carrots. He looked to his mom again with the same sorrowful expression, and was met with the same no-nonsense glare.

He scooped out another small spoonful.

"EMILY, EAT THE FOOD."

Silence.

"Eat the food."

Silence.

"Eat the food, Emily! I need to see you eat the food! Eat the food!"

Silence, and then the *clank* of glass falling softly against wood but not breaking.

A curse.

"Eat the food, Emily."

N<small>EWPORT</small> B<small>EACH IN THE</small> evening hours was just as packed with activity as it was at midday. Various lights and beacons illuminated the seaboard and its assorted attractions in dazzling display, sending a mixture of colors out and about, illustrating and beckoning in tones of excitement and celebration.

Nick shrugged on his hooded sweatshirt as he rose from the outdoor table. A young server, watching from nearby, was ready to swoop in.

"Will that be all for you tonight?" she asked with an appealing grin.

"It should hold me," Nick responded, smirking. "For a few hours, at least."

"I've seen you here before," the waitress remarked, flipping her hair out of her face. "How do you eat so much and stay so in shape?"

She then boldly prodded the exposed upper portion of Nick's bare chest, forcing him to suspend the action of zipping the hoodie.

"You must work out a lot," she went on, grinning.

Nick shrugged.

"Fast metabolism, I guess," he offered.

The server gathered the plastic basket that had contained Nick's food.

"You should lend me some of your fast metabolism," she returned playfully.

Feeling a pulse emanating from his pocket, Nick studied her briefly as he retrieved his earpiece, the night scene along the boardwalk playing out all around them.

"Heh, I don't think so," he said, grinning again as he slipped the ear monitor in place. "Seems as though you're doing just fine without it."

His attention then turned to the voice in his ear.

"You done?" Nick heard.

"Done?" Nick asked, confused. "Done with what?"

"Done flirting with whoever that is you're flirting with."

"What?" he asked again before realizing that someone had sabotaged his new earpiece. He shook his head in disappointment at the trick.

"The North Office," he mumbled, and then, more loudly, "To whoever is listening in, Christmas is cancelled. And yeah, I can do that."

"Wow," the waitress said, "is that a phone? It's so small."

"That's not the only thing," Nick heard Anastasios mutter, chuckling.

"Seriously?" Nick questioned. "You heard that too? This is ridiculous. How sensitive is this thing?"

He looked to the young girl.

"It's actually a super-secret spy phone," he whispered, covering his mouth with his hand as if conveying something confidential. "It'll probably be released to the general public eventually, but not for another five or ten years. You didn't hear any of this from me, though."

The teenager giggled and winked, pretending to lock her lips closed with a key. She departed into the restaurant with Nick's empty container.

"Living a little dangerously, aren't we?" he heard Anastasios comment over the connection.

Nick strolled out of the open-air restaurant onto the populated seaside boardwalk once more. Happy, excited people passed by, paying him no mind.

"It would only be dangerous," Nick replied, "if she were going to remember the conversation."

"Excuse me! Excuse me, sir?"

Nick stopped and turned.

The waitress from the restaurant caught up to him, weaving past other pedestrians. She clutched a tidy stack of bound papers.

"I'm sorry," she explained, handing Nick the neatly bound packet. "You're Nick, right? This binder came for you while you were eating, and my idiot manager just told me about it."

She rolled her eyes in annoyance.

"I hope I'm not getting it to you too late. It looks kind of important."

Nick heard Anastasios chuckle again over the linkup.

"Dude, I can so hear you laughing right now," he grumbled, turning his head so the girl would know he was not speaking to her.

She caught a glimpse of something in his ear.

"Wow," she said, "is that a phone? It's so small."

A louder laugh sounded through the earpiece. Nick ignored it, returning to the waitress.

"Thanks for this," he remarked, holding up the binder. "You were right on time."

The girl smiled and gave a small, quick wave as she turned back in the direction of the restaurant. Nick turned as well, continuing along the boardwalk, past the silhouetted ocean, the newest portion of The List now tucked under his arm.

"Okay, Annie," Nick declared. "Did you call me just to laugh in my ear?"

The briefest moment of silence fell over the connection before Anastasios replied, "First off, again, that's not funny. Second, no, I didn't call you just to laugh. Remember that thing we talked about?"

"Um ... you mean the thing, or the *thing*?"

Another pause.

"The phone calls. I'm talking about the phone calls you said you would help us with."

"Ahh, the phone calls," Nick replied. "See, when you said *thing*, I didn't know if you were talking about that other thing, or if it was this thing."

"Okay, okay," Anastasios breathed. "Point taken."

"So, what about the phone calls thing?"

"It's going down now, so whenever you're ready."

"Oh, that's happening today? Cool."

Nick noticed a small kid staring at him as he approached. The boy's name flashed through his mind instantly.

Jeremy Thompson.

He gave the kid a thumbs-up, causing the child to smile brightly.

"I don't think cool is quite the sentiment for it," came Anastasios's reply.

"Well, I think I may just hang out for a bit," Nick said. "They've got this night-surfing contest that's supposed to start in a few hours, and I'm thinking I might—"

"Okay. So when I say 'it's going down now; whenever you're ready,' it means make the call now."

"But," Nick countered mischievously, "you know that's not really what 'whenever you're ready' means, right? Because, really, if it's 'whenever you're ready,' which means 'whenever *I'm* ready,' then—"

"Didn't think it was going to be this difficult talking to you today. Just make the call, Nicholas."

"Okay, okay," Nick said, chuckling. "I'm on it."

He stopped at a less-crowded portion of boardwalk and leaned against the low wall that separated pedestrians, skateboarders, and bikers from the sand. Out on the darkened waters, a surfer skillfully rode a large wave, carving his way up and down the cresting break, throwing up a mist that hung suspended in silhouette against the orange, red, and purple vestiges of sunset behind him. He reached the top of the wave, and then plummeted down again.

Within moments of Anastasios's disconnection, Nick's monitor activated again.

"This is Gutierrez."

Nick smiled.

"Guti, it's Martin," Nick replied, altering his voice to perfectly replicate that of Gutierrez's sergeant in the Albuquerque Police Department. "Got somethin' on that Hendricks abduction."

"Yes, sir. What's going on?"

Nick could hear the rising eagerness in the young officer's voice.

"Look, we're gonna be walkin' a tightrope here. There's a lot of unconfirmed information coming in fast, some of which is that whoever has her is monitoring our channels, which is why I'm calling you on your cell. That guy we picked up the other night suddenly decided to spill his guts, and we've got a possible—hold on a minute."

He paused, giving the impression of juggling multiple tasks at once.

"Okay," he went on, "so he gave us a possible location and I need you there ASAP on quiet Code 1. It's somewhere out past La Cueva, around Route 126, but that's as specific as I've got so far."

"Did you say La Cueva, sir?" Gutierrez interjected. "You're talking about the Jemez Mountain Trail? That's an hour and a half away! Have you already talked to the PD up there?"

"No PD. It's out in the badlands—hikers and campers and all that. Not a lot of people. County and state typically handle those areas, but ... hang on, again ... Guti, we're playin' this thing with too many balls in the air, but we need to jump on it now if it turns out to be the real deal. Like I said, we don't have an exact address yet, nor is it confirmed that the guy we're looking for is out there, or that he has the Hendricks girl, which is why I need you movin' on the off-chance that what this slimeball's saying is all true."

"I'm putting it in my GPS now," Gutierrez stated. "Can I get Boonie to back me up on this, or am I solo?"

"I'm callin' him right after I get off with you," Nick said in the sergeant's voice. "Radio silence on this, Guti. Stick to your cell. I don't want this guy knowin' we're clued in if he's listening. Radio silence from you and Pete unless you go hot or you've got eyes on the Hendricks girl. Silent Code 1. Put it out as a 10-88 on the radio as soon as Boonie calls you and you're both headed north. Copy all that?"

"Radio silence and Silent Code 1. 10-88."

"Good. Let me get to Pete. Eyes open up there, Guti."

"10-4, sir. I'm out," Gutierrez concluded, ending the call.

Nick waited only seconds before his newly revamped earpiece contacted Officer Peter Boondocks. He breezed through the exchange concerning the possible location of Emily Hendricks a second time, sending Officer Boondocks speeding to catch up to Gutierrez on the way to La Cueva and the rough country beyond. His tasks completed, Nick barely had time to recognize the Albuquerque officer had severed the connection before the monitor switched yet again.

"Yeah," came Anastasios's quick greeting.

"Do I get my reward now?" Nick asked, grinning at a girl who passed him on the boardwalk, surfboard in tow. The girl grinned back at him.

"Good job."

"Meh," Nick shrugged. "That's not really the kind of reward I had in mind, but I guess it'll do."

"Whatever," Anastasios replied, chuckling. "Hot dog on me the next time I see you."

"Now you're speaking my language," Nick said. "By the way, you'll hear the officers' callout when they start for you. It's a 10-88."

"10-88?" Anastasios questioned. "What's that mean?"

"No idea," Nick replied. "I just made something up."

He flipped open the binder that enclosed the latest section of The List. The nighttime lighting along the boardwalk was more than adequate for reading.

"And hey," he went on, "I'm testing another version of these ear monitors. You guys are going to love them."

"**D**ELTA 13 TO DISPATCH. Show me and Delta 14 10-88."

"Delta, copy 10-88, 13 and 14."

Those needing to listen in heard the brief exchange over their ear monitors, and Nick's imitation of the police dispatcher's voice was pitch-perfect.

A SOFT QUESTION. "WHO are you?"

Silence.

"You can't even tell me your name?"

A loud clink, metal against metal.

"Why am I in this? Why am I here? Hey! Where are you going? Who are you? Let me go!"

"Stop yelling, Emily, and stop askin' all the fu—"

"Let me go! Let me go! Let me go!"

ERIC.

Agro and Terri.

Eric.

Agro and Terri.

Eric.

Agro and Terri.

Eric had noticed the pattern after the first few cycles. It was deliberate, and almost blatantly mechanical, as though Lucas were putting intentional effort into continuing it. Agro and Terri seemed to detect the back-and-forth as well, as they sat waiting patiently before springing into action for their turn.

The boy tossed the tennis ball to Eric again, his motion smooth and fluid, effortless. The ball landed softly in Eric's hands, the teenager hardly having to expend any energy to catch it. Eric grinned.

"Yeah, I think you would be a good baseball player," he commented, winding his arm back to return the ball to Lucas. "You've got a strong arm, and you're accurate. And, you're fast."

Lucas said nothing as he positioned his hands to catch the toss. Then he turned and threw it out into the yard, the glow of the drooping sun casting deep orange highlights across the grass. The chocolate labs instantly ran in pursuit of the ball, barking and yelping excitedly.

Eric continued talking, knowing not to bother awaiting a verbal response from Lucas.

"I don't think I would be that good at baseball. It's too slow. A bunch of standing and sitting and waiting and stuff like that. Then it's thirty seconds of fun, and then you're back to standing and waiting again."

The boys watched as the dogs reached the ball, each dog jostling for a firm grip on the toy before its sibling knocked it away.

"I'm more into hockey," Eric went on. He pointed to his Colorado Avalanche shirt. "And soccer's cool, too. They're both pretty much nonstop, and everyone's always moving, you know? Not a lot of waiting around."

Terri had somehow wrestled the tennis ball away from her brother and was now trotting triumphantly back with the prize clutched securely in her mouth. Agro hopped and skipped around her, as though trying to distract her into dropping the toy.

"My friends Sammy and Brooke play baseball," Eric said as the puppies returned. "They're pretty good, although I'm sure I'm not that good a judge of baseball talent."

He watched Lucas neatly pluck the ball out of Terri's jaws. The pup didn't even bother wrestling for possession like she usually did, giving the ball up willingly.

"I've known them since, like, second grade or something. I'm actually going over to Sammy's tomorrow—that's what my dad was talking about at dinner. We're just supposed to hang out and stuff."

He caught the boy's now-familiar deadeye toss of the tennis ball without a thought.

"I'll be sure to mention you to them. They'll probably be over here trying to get you to play baseball before you know it."

Eric paused his windup and gave Lucas a smirk.

"Watch out, though," he said, grinning. "I know you don't like to talk too much, but Sammy'll yack your head off, especially when he also sees that you don't like to talk too much."

Eric completed his throw, sending the ball sailing into the yard, Agro and Terri already racing to where they predicted it was going to land.

"Sammy's just crazy like that," Eric finished almost as an afterthought, keeping an eye on the tennis ball as it began to plummet out of the sky.

He soon noticed that the dogs had guessed wrong; they would have to make a sharp adjustment in their course once they saw the ball bounce.

Then he noticed that the two chocolate Labradors had another objective altogether.

"Who's that?" Eric asked aloud, spotting the two figures Agro and Terri were dashing toward. He glanced over to Lucas and saw that the smaller boy was staring out into the street as well.

A man and woman, dressed casually and comfortably for the Colorado summertime, traveled the roadway bordering the Johnson's front lawn. The woman, her golden-tanned skin not dissimilar to Lucas's olive complexion, was ahead of the man and walking backwards in the midst of what seemed an animated and comical discussion, evidenced by the man's laughter.

Soon, the puppies were near enough to make their presence known. The woman startled visibly—not unlike Lucifer had done earlier, with the exception of a small shriek, to which the man laughed playfully. The woman hit her companion in jest before they both bent down to pet the dogs, which basked in the attention. The man glanced up, waving to Eric and Lucas across the yard. When the woman saw them, she waved as well.

"Your mom and dad?" Eric asked, looking to Lucas as he waved back to the approaching couple. "Sweet."

The boy did not respond, instead taking off at a sprint after the forgotten tennis ball. The couple had resumed their walking, heading toward the Johnson's driveway, Agro and Terri encouraging them along.

Eric watched Lucas reach the ball and bend down to grab it. Agro and Terri must have finally noticed him as well. They turned away from the couple and raced toward the boy, yelping eagerly.

Lucas picked up the ball and threw it to Eric in a deft action, his ease belying the distance the ball had to cover. He then ran, moving in a zigzag course across the lawn. Agro Terri pursued him, enthused by this modification to their game. The boy kept just ahead of them, allowing the dogs to stay close behind.

Eric barely had to hold his hand away from his body; the tennis ball dropped smoothly into his palm.

By then, the couple had reached the gravel walking path that connected the driveway to the set of wooden steps leading to the Johnson's front porch. Eric, still gripping the ball he had just caught, turned to them as they came closer.

"Are you Lucas's parents?"

He gestured to the boy still being energetically pursued by Terri and Agro around the yard.

"He's got an amazing arm," Eric commented. "I was just telling him he would be a natural at baseball."

The man laughed.

"I think I tell my wife that every day. No joke, Lucas can definitely throw some fire. But if you want to see something that would knock your socks off, just—"

His reply was cut off suddenly as the woman's elbow jabbed into his stomach.

"Don't encourage him," she said, winking at Eric while the man rubbed his abdomen, feigning pain. "If this one had his way, our little Lucas would be playing one sport or another twenty-four hours a day with no time to rest in between."

Her companion shrugged, and the woman held out her hand.

"I'm Elianna, and this is Eli," she said, her amused grin transforming to an elegant, beautiful smile. "I believe I spoke to your mother earlier, Elizabeth Johnson? I guess that would make you either Eric or Riley."

Eric was transfixed by Elianna's lyrical voice and captivating smile, but he recovered after a moment.

"Yeah, uh, that's me, um, Eric. My mom didn't say what time I was supposed to walk him back, so I hope I didn't—"

Elianna waved him off graciously.

"No problem. We just thought it would be a good chance for us to come down and finally meet some of the neighbors. We've been so busy with work and moving in and all."

She then looked up at the house, which seemed to glimmer in the setting sun.

"This is truly a beautiful home. I thought the Erickson's house was the nicest property I had ever seen, but then I saw yours and I knew I would have to be satisfied living in the second-loveliest house in the world."

Eric grinned.

"Whatever you do, don't let my dad hear you talking like that, or else he'll be like Mr. Eli here and—"

"Did I just hear someone complimenting the expert craftsmanship of my humble abode?" came the low baritone of Hank Johnson as he stepped out onto the porch.

"Now you've done it," Eric told Elianna and Elias, rolling his eyes in mock annoyance.

The couple smiled at the display as they turned from Eric to Hank.

As the introductions began, Eric felt something press against his leg. He glanced down to find Terri and Agro rolling around in simulated battle. He was surprised he hadn't heard their approach, nor that of Lucas, who was now standing quietly beside him.

"Dude, where did you come from?" Eric inquired, low enough that the adults wouldn't overhear.

Lucas looked up at him momentarily and then turned, pointing into the yard.

Eric rolled his eyes once more, thinking the younger boy was being sarcastic.

"No," he said, trying again. "I meant—"

His attention was diverted by his father's low drawl.

"So, back to the house. When my wife and I bought this place, imagine my surprise when we learned the house was built in 1857 by a just-settled Colorado family who worked—"

"Hank Johnson," his wife interrupted, stepping onto the porch as well. "I know you're not standing out here talking about this old house to the new neighbors without inviting them inside."

Hank turned.

"Well, honey, what I was actually doing was—"

"That's exactly what he was doing, Mom," Eric called out, giving his father a mischievous smirk.

Elizabeth smiled warmly.

"Thank you, Eric."

Hank shrugged. Elias, Elianna and Eric chuckled.

"Yeah," Elizabeth voiced, unconvinced. She motioned for the new neighbors to enter. "Please, come in. I have cold drinks, or I can whip up some coffee if you like? Or maybe a glass of wine?"

As Elianna and Elias passed Lucas on their way up the porch steps, Elianna bent down to kiss the boy gently on a part of his forehead not presently hidden beneath his long, black hair. Elias then ruffled his hair affectionately. Elizabeth led the way, with Hank, bowing as the young couple passed, bringing up the rear.

Once the adults were inside, Eric and Lucifer took up their previous positions in the yard: Eric tossing the tennis ball to Lucas as he ran. The boy caught the ball easily with one hand and Agro and Terri followed him, joining in once more.

In the distance, the sun's flaming orb slowly edged its way below the horizon, the sky reflecting the orange, red, pink, and violet hues of twilight.

As Lucifer tossed the ball into space for the puppies to fetch, Eric finally broke the tranquil silence.

"Hey, so what was that fire your dad was talking about before? Something about 'knocking my socks off?' Can I see it?"

Lucifer simply glanced at him, his face inscrutable in the slowly fading light.

IN SOME UNCERTAIN PLACE within the Jemez Mountains in northern New Mexico, a forest inferno raged, setting the rugged nighttime scenery aglow. Anastasios moved slowly, meticulously, persistently, the sweltering fire surrounding him on three sides, stalking his every footstep. The flames engulfed everything, save for the landscape before him, and stretched as far as the eye could see, scorching fingers of flame reaching into the evening sky.

Anastasios's trek through the forest should have been challenging, if not altogether treacherous, with low-hanging branches overhead and all around; fallen tree limbs; stubborn, prickly undergrowth; twisting, snaking roots emerging from the woodland floor; uneven, haggard, unmarked terrain. Yet he moved with an assured, relaxed ease. If anything, nature's obstacles seemed to drift out of his way as he approached, clearing a path.

And the inferno continued to burn. A firestorm.

Anastasios felt none of its effects. He was dressed normally, complete to his well-worn boots. His hair, which mimicked the hues of a fire anyway, now suitably fit with his sweltering backdrop. His eyes glowed a blistering red-orange as well, emitting their own singeing radiance, distinct amidst the immense conflagration.

As he moved forward, the blaze progressed alongside, tantalizingly licking at his advancing figure. Mostly, he kept his head down, listening as much as watching for the unexpected. When his gaze did shift up, his eyes danced between potential pathways of escape, looking, searching, analyzing. A glance to the side halted the flames that escorted him, freeing his view even further. If he stopped moving, a similar effect resulted, with the fire stopping as well. Only rarely did he have the inclination to look back. Behind him, the view was predictable.

A firestorm. Devastation.

His pace was slow enough that the blaze raced to the treetops before he ventured too far. Embers and burning sparks jumped and floated from tree to shrub to tree again, sending angry cackles forth from the forestry as it burned. Thick smoke bellowed out of the canopy in vast, cumulous puffs, barely distinguishable from the dark sky, but blotting out the twinkling stars. However, the glow of the fire fiercely lit the burning forest.

The ocean of flame separated and shifted according to the course Anastasios moved in, or the direction of his gaze, whether forward or back. Occasionally, he stopped and turned, heading directly into the heart of the inferno. The flames welcomed him in, the unaffected forest ahead shielded behind a towering wall of fire.

As he moved into the fire, the flames immediately encircling him would retreat slightly, giving him a distinct circle of space and sparing him from direct contact; it was a courteous gesture, but unnecessary. Soon enough, after the reason for his turnaround was satisfied, he would turn forward again, the ocean of fire parting once more until he reached its boundary. His travel would then resume, and the blaze, seemingly powerless to proceed without its creator, would roar and carry on anew.

Anastasios's burning gaze flickered left and then right before returning to the forest floor.

His presence in this section of the New Mexico wilderness was no mistake, nor was it entirely unforeseen. Like a naturally occurring forest fire, his attendance could drastically alter the landscape, so the absence of wildlife was predictable. The animals and birds who claimed these mountainous woods as home had already followed their primal instincts, sensing, and thus avoiding, Anastasios's company. Anastasios had long since become used to the phenomenon, but he remained vigilant. Centuries of experience told him that forest animals need not be the only thing to watch for.

Only a few others could perform the distinct functions he was assigned. They were scattered around the globe within their own territories, perhaps all doing as he did—or a geographically specific variation—at that very same moment. Their contingent was entrusted with special responsibilities, and they remained, as always, extraordinarily proficient at executing them.

He was resurrection, transformation, the natural, ever-continuing cycle of destruction and restoration—personified. In due time, after his task was complete, resources would be plentiful and the beautiful New Mexico forest would thrive once again.

But now, as he reached an open space among the hilly, wooded terrain, the blistering flames around him consumed everything they touched. For miles in every direction, the fire he brought with him burned on, long after a natural fire would have exhausted itself. Conceivably, it was a fire that could burn forever.

However, the wildfire was not the only explanation for his presence.

He soon spotted the others, already waiting. He stepped into the clearing, and the blaze did not follow; instead, it began to circle around the tree line, keeping even with his pace.

Anastasios's faint grin fell on Beat and Case. Imani was also present, standing close by.

"So, I hear our little secret may be about to get out," Anastasios said.

"Are you worried?" Case asked quietly, looking at him.

Anastasios's smile widened as he gazed at the younger boy, whose silvery hair glimmered in the firelight. Beside Case, Beat watched as the inferno continued around the edge of the clearing, even after Anastasios had stopped walking. The flames finally joined on the other side, hemming the group in among a wall of flame.

"Of course not," Anastasios soon replied. "Beat and Case are on it. I have faith in you."

EMILY GENTLY TOUCHED THE reddened band the handcuff had left around her wrist before letting the shackle slide back into its normal position. Once more, she glanced about the room.

Save for her closely monitored, blindfolded bathroom breaks, she had been confined to the same small space for nearly twenty-four hours. Still, the room remained just as unfamiliar—barren, grimy, gray. The stale, unmoving air seemed thick, so heavy she could almost touch it. In the weak lighting from a lone lamp, the air was practically visible, its dreariness feeding the room's miserable appearance. During the day, a single small, smudged window on the far side of the room let in just enough dulled sunshine to dimly illuminate the space and little else. Now, it appeared pitch-black, illustrating the emptiness of the night outside.

The walls were smudged and peeling, the floor soiled with dust and filth. The mattress on which she sat was just as dirty, although considerably more comfortable than the hard floor. The lamp sat on the floor just to the side of the mattress, casting silent, eerie shadows, with a glass of lukewarm water placed close by.

Emily's gaze came to rest on her wrist again. She was handcuffed to a rusting metal pipe that emerged from, and then quickly disappeared back into, the bare floor. As though by impulse, the young woman tugged at the chain again, watching, feeling, as the metal ring bit into her sore wrist with increased severity. Soon, she heard footsteps.

"Let me go!" she yelled at once. "Do you hear me? Let me go!"

"Stop yellin', Emily," a gruff voice commanded from the other side of the door.

"Why are you keeping me here? Why are you doing this? Let me go! Let me go!"

"Fine," the low voice replied. "Yell all you want. See if I care."

"Let me go!"

Emily heard her abductor's heavy footfalls withdraw back down the hall. Shortly, the stale, suffocating silence of the room again reigned.

And again, her eyes drifted from the shackle to the metal pipe, and back once more.

"**A**ND YOU SAID THREE-THIRTY tomorrow, right?" Eric asked again as he walked beside his mother down the hall.

"Yes, for about the sixth time, sometime around three-thirty," Elizabeth Johnson replied, giving her oldest son a particular look, but seeming to understand he was simply excited about his impending outing with his friends. "I'm taking you and Riley at the same time. Are you going to bust my chops if I get you there at 3:32?"

"Nah, but I think we can both agree that 3:33 would be pushing it."

The pair reached the threshold of Elizabeth and Hank's bedroom. Elizabeth turned to look at her son.

"Oh," she said in a mocking tone, "so I guess we shouldn't even speak about 3:34, then?"

"That would be blasphemous," Eric agreed, grinning.

Elizabeth rolled her eyes, though Eric noticed she smiled faintly.

"Good night, Eric."

"'Night, Mom."

Eric made to walk back down the hall.

"Eric?"

The teenager turned back. Elizabeth beckoned with her finger, and Eric leaned in closer and bent his head down. His mother clutched at it with both hands. Once he was down far enough, she planted a kiss on his head. She then let him straighten back enough that she could see his eyes, although she still held onto his head.

"Good night, Eric," she repeated.

"Good night, Mother," he replied, smiling.

She released his head and gave him a soft push away from her.

"Now, go get some sleep, because I know you boys will probably stay up all night tomorrow."

"You got it, Mom."

He stepped away as she entered the bedroom, retracing his steps down the hall, stopping in front of the door that led to the basement and his bedroom. Hesitating for only a moment, he resumed his travel down the hallway, halting where it widened at the living room.

In the time it had taken for him and his mother to walk down the hall, and for Eric to return, Hank Johnson had dozed off again, even as the television he was facing produced crackling gunfire interspersed with shouted curses. Although Eric could not see the television screen directly, dynamic flashes throughout the darkened room and across Hank's snoozing body told enough.

After watching his father for a moment, Eric began to turn away.

"What, too good to say goodnight to me?"

Eric looked again to see his dad gazing at him, as though he had been awake the entire time.

"You were asleep," Eric declared.

Hank lowered the volume on the television.

"That's just what I wanted you to think."

"Yeah, whatever."

Eric knew it was a lost cause to get his dad to admit to dozing off.

"I'm headed down. See ya on the flipside."

He began to turn away, but was again halted by his father's voice.

"So, uh…"

Hank cleared his throat dramatically, his tone conveying seriousness.

"So I was thinking, about tomorrow, you know. If, maybe, instead of hanging out and having a great time with your, uh, 'friends'"—Hank put air quotations around the word—"maybe you wanted to spend some good ol' fashioned quality time out on the roof with your old man, slaving away in the heat, working up a good sweat."

"'You never give it up, do you?" Eric said, grinning and shaking his head. He began to turn away. "'Night, Dad."

"See ya," Hank chuckled in his rumbling tenor. He leaned back in his favorite recliner and closed his eyes, turning the volume back up on the television.

Two Albuquerque Police Department patrol cruisers raced across the road, the vehicle traffic decreasing as they zipped through ramshackle towns and unused land, distancing themselves from the populace. Their flashing lights pierced through the night, but their sirens remained turned off unless absolutely called for, and then only for a second or two. The hum of their engines was the only sound forewarning their presence.

Silent Code 1.

Other motorists, spotting the flashing lights in their mirrors, knew to ease out of the way, giving the cruisers ample room to overtake them, where they dashed ahead and quickly out of sight into the distant nightfall.

Emily grimaced, noticing the dirt and grime from the filthy mattress outlining the edge of her hand. Her clothing was in a similarly foul state, crumpled and soiled from her having not changed or showered. Her eyes traced the ridges of the handcuff on her wrist, the shine from the lone, faint lamp throwing the restraints into contrast.

She pulled at them again, keeping her efforts hushed, not allowing the chain to jerk noisily against the pipe. Even as hard as she tugged, the struggle had no effect except for a deepening sting as the cuff tore into the tender skin of her wrist. She was soon forced to stop, the ache too intense and neither the handcuff nor the pipe willing to yield an inch.

Her breathing grew shallow as she listened again.

All was quiet.

Emily rolled off the mattress and lowered herself closer to the metal pipe. She edged the chain along the length of the tube, pulling occasionally and examining the piping for any sort of split or failing.

Nothing.

Her gaze darted around the room again, searching for anything she could use, only to again observe the absolute bleakness of the space in which she was held. A quick glance at the door proved of no assistance. She attempted to look under the mattress, but its weight and the limited mobility of her shackled arm made it a waste of exertion.

Her movements were quiet, her breathing measured.

No sound came from the other side of the door.

She then turned, her body aligned against the piping and the bare wall. Pushing her feet against the bottom of the wall, she grabbed the links of the handcuff with her constrained hand and clutched the metal ring encircling her wrist with the other. She heaved with all her strength, pulling on the ring, too, to limit pressure on her raw skin. She gritted and strained, the metal clawing into her flesh anyway.

Errrr . . . the rusted metal groaned as it caved inward slightly.

Emily pulled harder.

Errrr—errckkkk.

A crack. And then . . .

SPRISSSSHHH!

The corroded metal split, sending a gush of heated gas spewing from the breach. Emily fell backwards, bumping into the lamp and water glass, her handcuff now loosened from the pipe. The lamp toppled over, flickering off as its cord ripped away from the wall.

A spark, and then an intense, bright flash.

FLOOOMM!

The room erupted.

Flames hurried up the tattered wall, ascending to the ceiling, while more flowed down to the pipe. The heat was immediate and intense, and Emily scampered back, covering her eyes against the explosion. The blaze swiftly took over the wall above the ruptured pipe, the ejecting gas instantly bursting into flames.

Emily continued blindly in reverse, backing into the wall on the other side, fire crawling overhead and spreading in feverish tendrils. Shattering crackles sounded as the room combusted repeatedly, incessantly.

The door to the room flew open, and the man wearing the leather bandana was immediately halted as the blaze leapt toward him like a flaming arm, staggering him back into the hallway. Just as rapidly, the fire retreated again, swarming up to the ceiling and, from there, around the room. Emily, close to the floor but barely able to distinguish anything amid the sputtering darkness and mushrooming smoke, scrambled for the exit.

"Wh—Emily!"

The man coughed harshly, struggling for breath through the streaming smoke. Enveloped by the smolder, Emily shoved past him, both of them stumbling to the ground, Emily still scampering, able to scurry away from her abductor. He grabbed for her blindly, an instant too late, and she kicked out, her foot finding the man's face in her hurry to escape.

"Argh! Em—"

The man coughed, expelling more smoke from his lungs.

"Emily! Get back here!"

Emily stumbled out of his reach, lurching into the wall of the darkened hallway as she struggled to get to her feet.

BOOOSSSHH!

Another explosion.

Emily flinched, instinctively covering her head. She was hardly able to make out anything in the obscurity of the corridor, but she scrambled forward, feeling her way along the wall. Smoke wafted overhead, and she coughed, her eyes watering.

"Em—"

Without warning, she felt the man grab at her arm again. Emily twisted quickly, crying out as she attempted to jerk herself away while simultaneously swinging for her captor's face. Her punch just missed, but the dangling handcuff, trailing a split-second behind, belted him squarely along his stubbled jaw.

His head recoiled, but he continued to stumble forward, briefly losing orientation and colliding with the doorframe to the bathroom head-on, his face violently smashing into the wooden edging.

Her punch, coupled with her abductor's momentary grasp of her arm, hurled Emily off-balance, turning her in the opposite direction, toward the wall opposite the bathroom ...

...only to find that there was no wall.

She let out another shriek as she plunged backwards, the floor beneath her unexpectedly dropping away. Her foot grazed the next step on the descending staircase. She crashed hard onto her back, her head slamming against the stairs. She continued to tumble backwards, losing consciousness before she reached bottom.

EMILY'S EYES FLUTTERED OPEN. The world around her flashed for a second, and then immediately darkened.

She winced, groaning, stabs and twinges of pain radiating from various parts of her body all at once in hot, pounding waves. The worst was the overwhelming pulsating sensation coming from one side of her head.

Slowly rolling on to her front, she then attempted to stand. A flare of intense pain spiraled from her bruised wrist and crumpled her to the floor again.

Torturously slowly, she tried again, soon righting herself and rising to an awkward sit. The space she found herself in was colder; the floor, unforgiving concrete. She glanced around through watery eyes, not detecting much. A faint glow from the staircase she had toppled down revealed evidence of the fire on the floor above. Wisps of smoke wafted languidly down the flight of steps, beginning to swirl overhead—a dark cloud creeping into an already dark room. Her gaze finally fell upon the outline of a door along the far wall.

"Emily."

She stilled at the breathless call of her name. She slowly turned her head to the staircase again.

"Emily?"

Straining to pull herself away, and streaking a trail of scarlet across the cold concrete as she moved, Emily at last rose and staggered the rest of the way to the door. Panic and adrenaline streamed through her body, thinly dulling the pain. Her abductor's footsteps began to thud down the stairs as she reached for the door.

"Emily? Emily!"

Emily wrestled the door open, nearly falling again as a lightning twinge streaked up and down her side. Outside, the moonlit night stared back at her, a distant orange halo above the treetops the only discrepancy in the dark. Without thinking, she hurried out and in the direction of the glow, bursting into a hobbled run, her lower leg aching sharply with every step. She crossed the small yard and crashed the wooded terrain, stumbling, but not falling.

Another explosion sounded behind her.

Then, the man's voice.

"Emily! Stop!"

She kept moving, ignoring the shouts, plowing through shrubbery, twisting around towering tree trunks, propelled by absolute fear that pushed all pain from her immediate awareness. Still, blood oozed from the wound on the side of her head, spilling down the contours of her face. She pushed forward, more staggered running, dodging, ducking, skirting, her passage through the woodland both frantic and frightening.

Finally, after covering some distance, she paused behind a large tree, catching her breath. The bark scratched her skin. The glow ahead shone dimly brighter through the trees.

She glanced around the shadowy forest, every direction appearing dangerous and untried.

She had no idea where she was.

Or which way she should be going.

WHITE.

Empty.

Space.

All around and as far as the eye could see.

Eric looked at Lucas. The smaller boy had changed his clothing from earlier, as he was now...

Wait.

Eric glanced around the blank expanse once more, only then realizing where he was.

Or, more accurately, where he was not.

"Yep," he said aloud, the casualness of his voice contradicting his surprise. "I'm definitely dreaming."

He looked at Lucas again.

The younger boy began to make precise movements with his hands.

This is not a dream, Eric.

Eric felt his eyes widen as he glanced from the boy's hands to his face, to his hands, and back to his face again.

"Okay," he said, slightly puzzled. "What's going on? Was that sign language? I don't know sign language. Do I know sign language?"

Lucas moved his hands again, his face devoid of expression.

You may not know sign language, but for right now, you know my language.

Eric studied the boy intently for a moment.

"What is this?"

He glanced around the empty space once more before turning back to Lucas.

"Seriously. If this isn't a dream, what am I doing here?"

Lucas did not respond immediately, instead mirroring Eric's attentive gaze.

Hold on. Can you understand what I'm saying right now?

Eric did not speak the words aloud, testing just how surreal this dreamscape was.

Lucas tilted his head slightly.

Yes.

Eric's eyes widened as a child's voice echoed through his mind. He backed away a little.

Lucas moved his hands again.

Would it be better if I just used my hands?

"Yeah, yeah," Eric replied, nodding. "Just do that. The other way is, really, like ..."

He shuddered. Then, his attention turning to the white space surrounding them yet again, Eric patted his body with his hands, and then moved up to his face—feeling, tugging, pinching.

"This is way too weird," he said. "I still feel the same. I feel normal, like I'm awake."

You are the same, came Lucas's signed response.

"What is this place?"

Eric moved his arms and hands about, feeling for an invisible boundary and soon realizing there was none. He looked down, crouched slightly, and jumped. He landed in the same place, the leap revealing nothing extraordinary.

Lucas watched the teenager's antics in silence.

Eric turned away and started to run as fast as his legs could pump, staring ahead into the blankness that revealed absolutely nothing about how fast he was moving or how far he traveled. It was all so bizarre. The sensation disconcerting, almost dizzying.

Nothing but white in every direction.

He glanced over his shoulder as he ran, expecting to see the smaller boy somewhere in the distance.

Eric stopped abruptly.

Lucas was directly behind him, gazing at him with the same cool, composed expression. His casual posture indicated that he had not moved at all since Eric had started running.

"Seriously?" Eric asked, a frown illustrating his confusion. "Not a dream, huh?"

Take your time, the smaller boy motioned fluidly.

"This is completely insane," Eric insisted with excited disbelief.

He started walking backwards, keeping his eyes on Lucas, the distance slowly increasing between them. Eric felt his lips curl into a triumphant grin.

After a considerable distance, he stopped quickly, his eyes focused on Lucas's stationary figure, yards away. Eric's smile vanished as a peculiar feeling washed over him. He turned slowly, guessing he was about to see the impossible ...

Standing right behind him again was Lucas, his expression the same, his stance identical to what it had been moments before, except opposite, as Eric now stood on his other side. It was as though Eric had not moved away from the boy at all, but simply around him.

Eric glanced back to where he had presumably stood a few moments before, now seeing nothing. Completely confused, he could not be certain what ... or where ... or how...

Nothing but white.

White.

Empty.

Space.

EMILY WAS COUNTING ON the modest shine filtering through the trees ahead as her most likely course of escape.

But it was impossible to know for sure.

"Emily!"

Her pursuer's rough voice sounded angry, eerie, menacing. Incited into action once more, she willed her aching body to move and pushed off from the tree she had been leaning against, faltering slightly.

Cuts and scrapes across her body created rivulets of blood that stained her skin and dirty clothing with trickling crimson. The wound along the side of her head throbbed with her continued exertion. She headed for the glow, scarcely able to see a few feet in front of her as she dodged exposed rocks and sharp, suspended branches.

She could hear the man's commotion as he chased her.

Her head was pounding unmercifully. As she desperately hurried for the glimmering light, each dire, darkened section of woodland looked exactly the same, giving no indication of her nearness to the edge of the forest, nor any evidence of a trail or road that might lead her out. For all she knew, she was venturing deeper into the woodland, further away from help.

She slipped over something hard on the forest floor and almost fell, barely grasping another tree trunk, the rough bark tearing into her skin. With all of her other injuries, she barely noticed. Once she gained her balance, she shoved off again.

Keep moving.

Her nostrils pinched at the scent of smoke.

From the explosion in the house, she thought, until she realized it was the smoldering of the glow ahead.

"Emily, stop! You're miles away from anyone out here!"

She dared not turn around, afraid of realizing just how close her pursuer was. She could hear his thrashing clearly now, and he could almost certainly hear hers. If she stopped to turn, he would only get closer.

She kept going, kept hobbling, kept staggering from tree to tree. Reaching branches seemed to grab at her roughly, tearing at her skin and her soiled clothing as if to hold her back or at least obstruct her advance. Fallen trees, boughs, and thick, exposed roots thwarted every stumbling, scrambling footfall. They seemed to rise from the ground as though she were living out a demented nightmare—possessed, haunted stems grasping, clutching, forever reaching through the darkness.

The glow of flames and the acrid scent of smoke ahead intensified.

Behind her were the sounds of the man's pursuit through the shrubbery. He was not gaining ground, but not losing it either.

Everything else lay hidden in sinister shadow.

Her back against another sturdy tree, she fought her instincts in an attempt to catch her breath, forcing her eyes shut and then instantly snapping them open again. She could feel her heartbeat hammering against the bruised ribs in her chest. The same thumping from her heart resonated in her head, her brain throbbing mightily against her skull. The abrasion on her temple seemed to open with each pulse, fresh blood seeping into her hair, some trickling down into her face.

She glanced around once more.

Only the dark, desolate forest. Only the glow that potentially led to nowhere.

Emily remained still. She halted her breathing, not daring to move.

Waiting.

She heard nothing.

The man had stopped.

Quiet.

The smell of burning forest hovered, suspended in the air.

A twig snapped. He was moving again, slowly. However, something had changed. His footfalls seemed to be moving away.

"There's no way you gonna make it outta here, Emily. You hear me? There's no way."

Silence again.

Emily exhaled softly—

Crack!

IN THE ABYSS, LUCIFER waited for Eric's attention to return to him. Both boys looked at each other, silently. The seconds, if any existed in this infinite, bizarre place, ticked by.

"I'm not dead, am I?"

Eric's voice was soft, hushed.

Lucifer studied the teenager for a moment.

No, he gestured.

"But I'm going to die?"

Everyone dies.

"I'm going to die ... soon?"

The teenager's voice wavered slightly.

Lucifer gazed at him again before he responded, allowing his eyes, his face, his entire being to shift slightly.

It was a change, from impassiveness to … empathy. From emotionless to emotive.

He noticed Eric's fear instantly ease somewhat, though it did not—could not—completely dissipate.

Are you afraid?

Eric only nodded in response to Lucifer's question, as if not trusting himself to speak, the movement of his head so slight as to be barely noticeable.

Don't be, Lucifer gestured, his smooth movements comforting in their own way. *This is why I came to you.*

CRACK!

The sharp strike echoed close to Emily's hiding place as a rock slammed into a neighboring tree trunk. She startled, stumbling, turning away from the noise, and barely holding back the shriek that caught in her throat.

The crunching under her feet as she tripped, however, gave her away.

"Emily!"

She started running again. She tore through the undergrowth, lingering branches scratching and snatching at her. Breaking, crunching, ruffling, and snapping resonated on all sides, the chase even more urgent than before. The glow ahead became increasingly brilliant, more vivid, although it still appeared a fair distance away, serving to make the rest of the dark forest even more daunting.

Yet the invading fear of what her abductor would do if he caught her again kept her moving.

"Emily!"

She slipped again, this time falling completely, not able to catch herself, an *"umph"* forced from her sore lungs. The impact caused her to bite her tongue, and blood slowly seeped into her mouth. She scrambled forward, recovering hurriedly, but soon fell again, her foot ensnared by a tangle of roots. Her handcuffed wrist twisted awkwardly beneath her, drawing a sharp cry from her lips.

"Emily, stop! Stop runnin' from me!"

Stinging pain corkscrewed from her wrist to her elbow. She rested her weight on her other wrist to push herself off the ground again, cringing from the strain. She staggered, and then continued on, her hobble now even more pronounced. A red-hot stab shot through her leg with every step. She grasped at another tree, just barely making it as she tottered once more.

CLOSE YOUR EYES, LUCAS gestured fluidly.

Eric's eyelids lowered, though his body trembled a little, reporting his unease.

"It's okay."

Eric recognized the soft, youthful voice as the one he had heard in his head earlier. Something touched his hand, and he jerked at the contact. He realized he had been clenching his fist, and now Lucas was lightly grasping his hand. He felt his tension ebb, easing out of his body in a slow, steady wave. The feeling that remained was serene, complete calm.

"Are you ready?"

"Y-yes," Eric stuttered, his voice raspy.

"Don't be afraid. Open your eyes."

Eric cracked one eye open, but the familiar scene before him made him open both eyelids fully in surprise. He glanced around his basement bedroom, its appearance just as he remembered it from when he had come down to bed earlier that night. Dull lighting from outside shone through the lone, high window to pinpoint a slumbering form on his bed beneath the covers.

Lucas was standing at the bedside, watching as Eric took in the sight.

"What's going on?" Eric asked, trying to keep his voice low.

He pointed to the form under the bedsheets.

"Is that me? Am I..."

He faltered, but Lucas's motion interrupted him before he could finish the question.

You're asleep.

The simple statement was reassuring. Eric examined the room again before returning to Lucas and gesturing to the bed once more.

"Can I, um..."

Lucas stepped away from the bed, and Eric crept closer, his steps wary, his glance flitting between Lucas and the bed.

It's okay, Lucas signaled.

Eric reached the bed frame and pulled back a section of the comforter, taking a glimpse at his own sleeping form before replacing the blankets.

"That is way too weird," he commented, softly.

Would you like to go upstairs?

Eric glanced at the steps that led to the first floor, and then back to the surreal image of his own slumbering figure.

"Yeah," he answered after a moment. "I think ... yeah."

He began walking to the steps, Lucas trailing him. The staircase was wide enough for them both, and Eric slowed to allow the smaller boy to draw even with him so they could ascend together.

"So this is for real, then?" Eric questioned. "I mean, like, this is happening? It really isn't some weird dream?"

Lucas shook his head.

"I remember lying in bed, and I guess I fell asleep, but ... and this is all the same night, like right now?"

Lucas nodded.

"This is so—"

The pair had reached the landing at the top of the staircase, and the teenager turned to Lucifer abruptly.

"Are you some type of ghost or something? Or an angel?"

Lucas's hands moved.

What's an angel?

Recognizing the motion as sincere, Eric blinked and studied the small boy for a moment. Lucas's expression remained placid. Eric turned back and opened the basement door.

SHE HAD TO KEEP moving. The man sounded as if he were closing the distance between them. The fire, however, seemed too far away, and there remained the chance that it offered no escape at all.

Doubt began to creep into Emily's mind.

"It's no use, Emily," her attacker called. "Just stop now. Stop runnin'!"

Judging by his voice, he seemed only a short stretch behind. Even as she continued to force herself forward, Emily felt slower, her body uncooperative, every stride, every movement, becoming torture. Every agonized, staggered, aching footstep becoming...

It was a wonder he had not grabbed her yet.

The raging shapes and outlines of the forest fire were becoming clearer; the smoldering stench unmistakable. Emily lost her footing yet again, falling to her hands and knees, a fresh and almost nauseating amount of trauma radiating from her shackled wrist. She winced, clenching her teeth to force back any sound. Tears threatened to spill from her eyes as she pulled herself around to the far side of another tree.

Dizzying, sickening pain throughout every part of her body.

Intense fear.

She could not go on.

She knew she was not going to make it out.

The commotion caused by her tormentor's chase drew nearer, then slowed, and then stopped. Emily could hear his labored breathing, even through the thick shrubbery. She tried to keep her own breathing as hushed as she could manage.

He was close—alarmingly close. It was only a matter of time now, only a matter of moments before he found her.

She shut her eyes in desperation. Her heart pounded—persistent, hurried cracks of thunder. Her head, her entire body, throbbed.

Any second...

Ever so slightly, she cracked one eyelid, peeking. Then her eyes snapped open, wide, shocked. Sudden astonishment surged throughout her stricken body.

THE MAIN LEVEL OF the Johnson house was as still and quiet as the basement below. Eric moved cautiously, making an effort to muffle any noise, not noticing that his movements were already soundless. Lucas followed dutifully, stopping when Eric paused at an open door on the left-hand side.

Eric peeked in, not venturing any further. He looked back to the boy.

Lucas gave a small nod, and Eric stepped into the room. He crept to the large bed, his movements just as deliberate and careful as they had been in the hall. Dim light filtered through the bedroom window in fat slits through the partly drawn shades.

Eric noticed, and not for the first time, that his father's side of the bed was in considerably more disarray than his mother's, even while they were both sleeping in it. Hank Johnson's portion of the bedspread was pulled halfway down his body, rumpled and twisted, revealing the old white T-shirt he slept in. He lay on his back, one arm raised above the pillows under his head, his body noticeably askew. His snores were light, but persistent.

Eric leaned in closer, watching his father for a moment before leaning closer still to rest his forehead atop Hank's in a familial, intimate gesture. He knew it to be an action his father had performed numerous times when Eric was younger, and one he still made from time to time when he thought his eldest son was asleep. Sometimes, it was carried out in a playful, teasing manner, denoting Eric's need to concentrate during sporting events or during exams in school. Now, Eric assumed the fatherly gesture as his own, although his father would never know; still, the action brought them closer. With Hank asleep and consciously unaware, the contact was made that much more personal.

Eric rose, moving to his mother's side of the bed. While her husband's half was disordered, Elizabeth Johnson's was noticeably tidier, giving hers a tucked-in angelic beauty in contrast to his chaotic disaster. Her hair was laid out delicately on her pillow, her expression peaceful.

Eric kneeled, his elbows resting in the small space left available by his mother's sleeping form, his head only a few inches away from her face, a portion of which was snuggled under the sheets. He watched her soft breathing, taking in every inch of her face without disrupting her.

Although he was trying to hold it back, his eyes began to water anyway. He desperately did not want to cry, not right now. He felt he did not have the time, and once he started, he would never be able to stop.

Eric pulled his shoulders back, sensing Lucas's movement behind him. The boy's presence was soothing, even more so when he kneeled down beside him, mirroring Eric's prayer-like position.

"Why is this happening to me?" Eric whispered, his voice trembling. "Why now? Why does this have to happen now?"

He could not pull his gaze away from his mother's face. When Lucas failed to reply, Eric finally looked at the smaller boy.

Lucas returned the stare, silent, his captivating hazel eyes glowing in the light coming from the windows.

Eric severed his gaze and looked down, his head bowed, before returning his eyes to his mother. He lifted his hand, noticing it tremble slightly, and moved it to her head, smoothing a few strands of hair that lay across her face. Then he cupped her cheek tenderly. He felt a sad smile forming as he made contact with her skin.

"She always tries to act so tough around us, but I don't—"

The words caught in his throat.

Lucas edged a little closer.

Eric reached up to stroke his mother's head again, leaning in closer still so he could kiss her cheek with the same delicate innocence she had shown him earlier that night. As Eric drew back, he saw that her lips had formed a small smile. His gaze darted to Lucas.

The smaller boy nodded, and Eric, his hand still resting on his mother's hair, said, "I never liked saying goodbye," his tone so soft as to be nearly indistinguishable from the hush of the room. The entire house seemed muted; Eric had never before noticed how quiet it was with everyone asleep.

He turned to Lucas again.

"Can I see Riley and Sarah, too? I know they will be asleep, but—"

Even as he looked at Lucas, he noticed the scene shift instantaneously. Suddenly, he was kneeling on the carpeted floor of Riley's room across the hall, his lanky teenage body leaning over his younger brother's bed.

Riley Johnson's slumbering outline was nearly identical to his father's. His mouth was open, though he emitted only an airy breathing sound instead of snores. Eric gazed at his brother for a moment before brushing his knuckles across the boy's cropped hair—a half noogie, half caressing, brotherly gesture.

"See you on the flipside, dude," he whispered.

Pausing for a moment, he then added, looking to Lucas, "Is … whatever this is … is it inherited? Does my dad have it? Will it happen to Riley?"

It can be, the smaller boy responded.

Eric's felt his eyes widen.

Your family will be fine, though, Lucas added. *You are the only one.*

Eric was somewhat surprised that the statement relieved him, and he rose from the ground after giving his brother a final, parting glance.

The room immediately transformed again, becoming an area Eric did not recognize. He and Lucas stood just inside an entryway where a maze of sleeping bags was laid out on the ground, each occupied by a huddled bundle. A flat-screen television was turned on, although the unremittingly blue display was on standby, a DVD icon drifting idly around the screen.

Sarah's sleepover party.

Eric spotted his sister's burgundy and steel blue sleeping bag—Colorado Avalanche colors; Eric owned a larger one just like it. He carefully stepped over and around the other sleepers as he crept to Sarah's position, Lucas behind him. A small, nearly empty bowl of popcorn sat nearby.

Eric crouched down nimbly as he studied his sister up close. There seemed hardly enough room to lie down beside her.

But there was enough.

He glanced to Lucas before sinking lower, stretching his body out horizontally on his back, his hands folded loosely over his chest, his fingers comfortably intertwined. He stared up at the ceiling before turning his head slightly, his face only inches away from Sarah's. After a minute, he turned to the ceiling again, the glow from the idle television casting azure shadows overhead.

"What happens to them after … you know, after I'm gone?"

Eric's quiet question drifted up to the ceiling, although it was directed to Lucas.

"Where are you going?" said the same calm, youthful voice from earlier.

Eric sat up, looking around for Lucas briefly before noticing the smaller boy lying down on the other side of Sarah's sleeping body. "You said I was going to … to die, right?"

Lucifer sat up also, gesturing.

So? Where are you going?

Eric frowned, feeling his brow gather.

"But, I thought when someone dies, they—"

Would you like to leave?

Eric glanced at his sister. He shook his head after a moment.

"I don't want to leave my family," he acknowledged, "or my friends. I'm supposed to go to Sammy's tomorrow…"

He clenched his jaw determinedly.

"I don't want to die," he said, finally.

Lucas's hands remained still. Eric met the boy's solemn gaze for a few moments, and then exhaled silently, his eyes back on his younger sister. He bowed his head to give her a final kiss, closing his eyes during the act. When he opened them again, he was standing once more in the white, blank nothingness, with Lucas directly in front of him. Shaking his head in resignation, Eric looked down to his feet.

A CHILD.

A girl, staring back at her.

The girl was young. Dark bangs emerged from under her knit cap and nearly concealed her eyes as she stared at Emily, a smile upon her lips. Emily had neither seen nor heard signs of the girl's approach, yet here she was, crouched directly in front of her.

The girl brought a finger to her mouth, a clear request for silence. Emily, though still thoroughly unnerved, gave a jerky nod. The girl raised her hand to the throbbing wound on Emily's forehead. Emily felt an abrupt, numbing sensation, the aching pain that coursed throughout her body vanishing rapidly. Despite the welcoming sensation, the effect was so swift that it was almost terrifying.

The girl drew her hand away from the wound and to Emily's shackled and likely broken wrist. Emily noticed the little girl's fingers were coated in fresh blood, even though it had felt as if the girl had barely grazed her skin. Crimson dripped from her slender fingers like rainwater as she deftly removed the handcuff. Then, grasping Emily's hand in both of her own, she moved Emily's wrist forward and back.

Emily felt none of the crippling pain of moments before. In front of her, the girl continued to grin, as though she had heard Emily's thoughts.

Chikt.

A twig snapped nearby.

Emily felt her body instantly set rigid with terror.

"Emily."

She heard the man whisper loudly, although he again seemed to be moving away from her hiding place. A fresh wave of panic washed over her, even as she stared at the mysterious girl.

The child raised two fingers and gestured between herself and Emily.

Keep your eyes on me, the gesture seemed to say.

Then she nodded her head, her lips curling upward in reassurance.

You're doing fine.

Another sound swept through the forest: wood splintering, followed by an even louder commotion, as though someone were attempting to make a break through the dense brush.

"Emily, wait! Stop!"

Emily heard her kidnapper chase after the retreating sound. She shook, alarm still flowing through her, but she did not break the girl's steady gaze, not even risking a quick glance in her abductor's direction as he continued moving away.

Precious moments passed before the girl pointed to the glowing fire ahead. Her accompanying command was soft, but direct.

"Run now."

Emily's muscles tensed in anticipation, but she stayed rooted to her spot on the forest floor, gazing at the much younger girl. Her voice was a hoarse whisper.

"I think there may be someone else—"

"It's my brother. He won't catch him."

The girl pointed again.

"Go."

Emily hesitated, but only briefly. She pushed herself up, the action infinitely easier and less painful than it would have been minutes before. She glanced over again.

The girl had vanished.

Emily gave it only brief thought before she began to hurry through the tangled shrubbery, heading directly for the blaze. She was able to move much more fluently now, her natural athleticism and regular exercise regimen apparent, dodging the obstacles that would surely have tripped her earlier, her mind and vision not nearly as hazy since the little girl had so gently touched her head. As she dashed through the woods, her fear dissipated, replaced by something else, something very much absent through much of her ordeal.

Hope.

Ducking, darting, moving, cutting, she neared the wildfire, the brilliant, nearly blinding flames enveloping the woodland. Emily started to slow. The heat was becoming intense, and the smell of smoke was staggering, as if warning her of the danger of venturing too close.

The little girl suddenly appeared again, standing just before the fire and urging Emily forward; how she made it there so swiftly, Emily did not know. The flames behind the girl formed a sizzling curtain of light, her form thrown into radiant profile. The girl continued to beckon, and Emily continued to come closer, stopping at the edge, just in front of the girl and the towering inferno.

The child reached for Emily's hand again. Slowly, she drew it toward the lapping flames. Emily's hesitance grew as the heat intensified further.

"It's all right," the girl said, her soft voice clear even over the hiss and roar of the fire. "Close your eyes."

Emily gazed at the girl a moment before she took a calming breath, closing her eyes. She felt the girl gently pull her forward.

The warmth around her rose, and then almost instantly dropped again.

"Keep going."

Emily opened her eyes.

The firestorm surrounded her. Fire consumed every available space—limbs, branches, shrubbery, entire trees blazing fiercely, red, orange, yellow everywhere, overwhelming.

Emily shrank back but quickly realized she could not feel any of the fire's heat. It was as though the flames were not present at all.

"Run, Emily."

She heard the girl's voice again, but a glance around her found nothing but fire. She took a step forward.

The flames encircling her retreated slightly, providing her space.

Another step.

Again, the fire held back.

Emily ran. Straight ahead, quickly, as though her abductor were still close behind. She had no idea where he was, and she did not care to guess; the possibility of escaping him and the forest was her highest driving force.

Through the blaze she sprinted, the flames neatly avoiding her as she moved. Overhangs from the towering trees seemed to avoid her now; their spindly limbs held clear as she progressed. Roots that would have caused her to trip before crumbled like torched wood under her pounding feet. Emily did not even consider her injuries—her limp, the wound on her head, her wrist—all pain was forgotten as she rushed on, hardly aware of anything else.

Except for her rescuer.

Through the flames, the mysterious girl kept appearing, kept beckoning, kept motioning, kept encouraging. And through the flames, Emily kept hurrying, kept approaching, kept progressing, kept escaping.

"I STILL DON'T UNDERSTAND why this is happening," Eric muttered, his head tilted downward. "What did I do wrong?"

The teenager looked up to find Lucas studying him contemplatively. Then, the boy's hands began to move.

What did you do wrong? You, Eric Johnson, proud son of Hank and Elizabeth, caring, dutiful, protective brother of Sarah and Riley? What did you do wrong?

You should know that you are not the first to go through this, nor will you be the last. Exactly 7,074,736 others from every corner of the world will face this same circumstance in the next year—that is nearly two million more people than the number that live in your state of Colorado. Over 7 million people will experience what you will.

Over 42,000 of them will be children under the age of eighteen. Some of these children will be older than you. Many will be younger. There are exactly 2,122,420,994 kids, including you, alive in the world at this moment, and in the next 365 days, 42,448 of them will perish from the same thing you soon will.

That's 16,979 by the end of this year.

7,980 by the end of this month.

Exactly 877 children around the world before this weekend is through.

You are one of those 877, Eric.

What did you do wrong? Some children do not live nearly as long as you have, or under such pleasant conditions. Some do not live to Riley's age. Some do not live to their first birthday. Some live under the most depressing, the most miserable, of circumstances, the likes of which you cannot begin to imagine. What did you do wrong, you ask?

What did they do wrong?

Already, 25,468 children this year have died from the same thing you will, with no one—doctors, parents, family—having any idea what, or why, it happened. These children collapsed at their school, at their home, at the playground, at a friend's house, doing homework, playing sports, mowing the lawn, sitting in church. Some were sleeping and did not wake up. It was shocking, and it was unexpected.

But it was no one's fault. No one did anything wrong.

Of the 25,468 children, and the 3,938,081 adults who have died so far this year from the exact thing you will experience, not one was alone when it happened. None of them. Not one. Of the many that have gone through it, not one of them was alone, and of the many that will go through it, not one of them will be alone.

And you will not be alone. I promise.

That is why I am here.

Lucas's hands stopped as Eric broke eye contact, again looking down to his shoes.

"Look at me."

Eric looked up again.

I, and others, will watch over Sarah. We will watch Riley. We will watch your mom and dad, your friends, your family, those that live close by and far away. We will watch everyone—we always have. They will never know it, but that does not stop us from doing it.

But, more importantly, you will be there to watch over them, too. They may not see you like they are used to seeing you the last fourteen years, and they may not hear you as though you were standing right beside them, but that will not mean that you are not there with them.

Do you think you will not be there with Riley as he grows, as he gains new friends and joins new sports teams and tries to live up to the standards that he—and you—have set? Do you think you will not be there with Sarah as she matures, learns, experiences, falters, fails, and picks herself up again? Do you think you will not be there for that?

Do you think you will ever leave your mother and father? Are you afraid they will forget you? Do you think they would ever want to? Do you think it would ever be possible for them to leave you behind, or for you to leave them?

You asked what you did wrong.

I am here to tell you all that you did right.

Eric could not help but look down again, a gentle smile lighting his face at Lucas's message.

"Yeah, you're an angel," he commented quietly. "I think all of that just gave it away."

He then looked up and spotted the object now clutched in Lucas's hand.

"Hey, that's Agro and Terri's ball!" he said, his tone one of adolescent surprise.

Lucas examined the tennis ball, twisting and turning it as he had done before, squeezing it as though to assess its firmness and bringing it close to his face again. Finally, his attention shifted to Eric.

You're ready now, he motioned, the ball still clutched in his hand.

Eric exhaled, and then nodded.

"And you're going to be there?" he asked, his voice soft.

Always, Lucas motioned.

THE FIRE HALTED. EMILY did not. She broke through the perimeter of the blaze, continuing without pause.

And then, moments later, finally.

A road.

It was a two-lane street, obviously newly paved, although dark in the night without streetlamps, and deserted.

Suddenly exhausted, though thoroughly relieved, Emily dropped to her hands and knees along the edge of the asphalt, her strength sapped and her breath coming with great effort.

From the building in the forest to the road, she had run, seemingly, for miles, her face, body, and hair illustrating her exertion, all damp with sweat. A trickle of it ran down her face and dripped from the bridge of her nose to wet the loose gravel she had collapsed upon. Each drip kept time with her labored breathing, which kept time with the accelerated thumping of her heart.

Sensing someone nearby, she glanced sideways.

It was the little girl.

Her rescuer, her savior.

The girl crouched down beside Emily with a contented, almost pleased expression.

"You run fast," she commented, grinning.

Emily, still panting, could not stop her lips from turning up as she looked at the girl's face.

"Who are you?" she asked, her voice raspy. "How did you ... find me?"

The girl's grin grew slightly wider, and she shrugged.

"But—"

Emily stopped herself.

"Was someone else back there? Your brother! That man, with the bandana. He's chasing him!"

The girl dismissed it casually.

"He's fine. No need to worry about him."

"But the man ..." Emily pleaded. "What if he catches him? He abducted me. What if your brother can't get away? We have to find help."

"You just ran through a forest fire without getting touched," the girl said, lightly. "Do you really think when I say my brother won't get caught that there's even the slightest chance that he will?"

"But how—"

"You did great, Emily. Just make sure to get yourself to a hospital, first thing. You're still hurt; you just don't feel it right now."

The girl giggled.

"But you'll probably have to take a break from all that exercise you do with your dog for a little while. And, before you ask, he's fine, too."

"Wait."

Emily stared at the girl, astonished.

"Really, who are you? What are you? How do you know my name? How did you find me? How did you know I was in there?"

The mystifying girl's smile grew wider, her eyes, along with her earrings, seeming to twinkle even in the dim light.

"Feel better, okay?" she murmured with sincerity.

The small girl in the knit cap then looked behind the woman, down the road.

"I think your ride's coming," she said. "Ooh, flashy lights."

AT THAT VERY SAME moment, Eric Johnson woke abruptly, his eyes snapping open as though he'd heard something. He lay still, letting his vision adjust to the sparse lighting in his basement bedroom. He recognized the slow, familiar ticking of the intricate cuckoo clock on his wall—a gift from one of his father's business travels in Germany—and he listened for a moment.

Fourteen ... fifteen ... sixteen seconds, he counted.

His throat was dry, and he remembered he had forgotten to bring a drink of water down with him last night.

Then he noticed the other figure in his room: a small boy, at least as small and as young as Riley, with slightly curled hair all but covering...

Recognition dawned.

Lucas, Eric thought, *the quiet boy from earlier.*

The boy continued to stand there, in the same position, silent, watching him. Eric pulled back his bedsheets and slowly righted himself, rubbing sleep out of his eyes. He felt his brow furrow slightly in question as he glanced at the boy.

Still groggy, he pushed himself out of bed, shivering at the slightly cooler temperature of the room. When his bare feet touched the carpet, he took a moment to rub at his face again, yawning. Then he stood up fully.

Lucifer's steady, unaffected eyes never left Eric's.

Eric stared at the boy briefly. He took a step forward, and then another, intending to pass by the silent boy on the way to the staircase. He motioned to the flight of steps, mumbling faintly.

"I'm gonna get some…"

His third step faltered, and he felt a sudden heated sensation pulse from his chest through the rest of his body, followed immediately by a chilling coolness. He glanced at Lucas again.

The quiet boy stared back.

Eric's third step swayed, and he was unable to steady himself, his legs loosely buckling beneath him, bringing him first to one knee, and then to the other, fleetingly… his hands coming up instinctively, bracing to catch his fall, but somehow not strong enough, folding, crumbling beneath him, the heated and then chilled wave traveling through his body again, quickly, and then another, increasing in frequency…

Falling still, Eric could clearly see Lucas's tranquil expression in his mind. Even while his unfocused gaze was on the ground, he still sensed the mysterious boy's reassuring, entrancing eyes … flashes … losing control … numbness all over … falling … falling … falling…

Lucifer remained.

EMILY TURNED HER HEAD, following the girl's gaze. The road remained blanketed by night, but over the untouched treetops that bordered the street, she could easily spot the glow of the wildfire, seemingly covering hundreds of miles. Otherwise, her surroundings were quiet and still, as though nothing moved.

She turned back to the girl.

"What—"

The child had vanished again. Emily glanced about, but a reverberation brought her attention back to the road.

A police car, followed closely and swiftly by another, skidded around a bend in the road, lights flashing manically. She heard the engines accelerating as they came into the clear straightaway, the rumbling growing louder as the vehicles rapidly approached. The officer in the leading car must have spotted her, as the powerful engine suddenly revved louder, racing for her position. Soon, the first car crossed the median line and came to a quick stop, its tires squealing. A uniformed officer bounded out of the driver's side.

"Miss Hendricks?"

Emily let go a heavy sigh of relief. Tears began to well in her eyes once more, the storm of emotions from the entire awful episode beginning to build.

Officer Timothy Gutierrez raced to her kneeling form, while his senior, more-experienced partner followed, one hand on his holstered weapon, his eyes searching the area.

Gutierrez crouched in front of Emily, reaching out to cradle her face in his hands.

"Miss Hendricks, I'm Officer Gutierrez. Are you all right? Is anything—"

His words were cut short by Emily embracing him, her arms surrounding him tightly. He hesitated, but soon returned the hug, pulling Emily close.

"I am so sorry, Miss Hendricks," he whispered. "You're safe now."

"Emily," she murmured back. "Please … Emily."

Glancing back to the pair on the ground, Officer Peter Boondocks cleared his throat.

"Hold tight," he said. "I'll grab the medic bag."

As Boondocks reached into the trunk of his patrol cruiser, his cell phone rang. He answered it.

"We were about to get a hold of you, Sarge."

And then, "What?"

The senior officer paused briefly, listening, the medical kit still in his grasp.

"We're out here off 126, like you said," he explained over the line. "We've got the Hendricks girl. She was—"

Listening to Sergeant Bruce Martin on the other end of the call, Boondocks returned to his partner, handing over the kit so Gutierrez could tend to Emily. Boondock's face took on an air of disbelief.

"Are you kiddin' me, Sarge? Me and Gutierrez, who else? You sent us up here as a possible 10-18 for the stalker."

Boondocks fell silent, listening again. Gutierrez, who had been treating Emily's visible injuries, glanced to his partner.

"What's going on?" he asked.

"He's saying he never sent us out here," Boondocks mumbled, clearly puzzled.

His gaze flicked from Gutierrez to the woman they had been sent to find.

"Any idea where the guy is who did this?" Boondocks asked her softly, while still partly listening in on his phone.

Emily shook her head.

"I don't know. I think … he must have lost … after the fire, I don't think he was chasing me anymore."

"He's probably still stuck out there," Gutierrez observed, nodding to the forest. "These wildfires move quick. One minute, you think you've found a way out, and the next…"

Boondocks returned his attention to his cell.

"Sir, the suspect is missing in the woods up here. I called you about a possible 10-37-9 on the drive up about ten, fifteen minutes ago, and the Hendricks girl just confirmed it. We're lookin' at a pretty bright glow here, and it's extensive. You said you'd radio it in, but since you don't even remember sending us up here, you probably—"

He turned suddenly, along with Gutierrez and Emily, to the road they had just come from.

"He must have gotten that message after all," Gutierrez said, as the approaching sirens grew louder. Gutierrez looked back to Boondocks, whose face held a bewildered expression.

"Sarge, how in the world did you remember that call but—"

Officer Peter Boondocks stopped again to listen.

An ambulance sped around the bend, followed by the first fire truck.

The senior officer returned his gaze to Gutierrez.

"Can you believe this guy? He's saying he didn't call anyone about a forest fire, and he never got any call from us. He thought we were still working that car crash downtown. He has no idea what I'm talking—"

Boondocks returned his attention to the phone conversation.

"Okay, Sarge," he said. "Yeah, we've got EMS and FD in our sights right now."

He paused.

"Sounds fishy, you say? Well, that ain't even the half of it, sir. From where me and Guti are standing right now, we've got a bit of a mystery on our hands. We've got someone walkin' around APD who apparently sounds exactly like you but is not you, who has access to your cell phone and who knows to call me and Guti's numbers. This mystery person is familiar with all our radio codes, not to mention knowing what a 10-88 is, and directed us out to the Jemez Mountain Trail—on the edge of nowhere, mind you—where we just so happened to find the girl who was abducted from right under our noses barely twenty-four hours ago. Seriously, if all that wasn't you, Sarge, then that's one heck of a string of coincidences."

He listened again, briefly.

"That's what I'm sayin'. If it wasn't you, sir, then who in the world was it that sent us up here?"

Gutierrez turned back to Emily as the ambulance and fire truck pulled to a stop beside the two patrol cruisers. He smiled as she met his glance.

"I have no idea what's going on," he said softly, dabbing at a cut on her head with a swab, "but whatever it is, it sounds like someone, somewhere, was watching out for you, Miss Emily Hendricks. I guess our guardian angels are always there for us when we need them most."

COLE CONTINUED HIS PURSUIT, aggressively tearing through the foliage, hot on Emily's trail and gaining. He was close, he knew, but the continued movements and sounds of her evasion ahead told him she remained barely out of reach.

"Emily, just stop runnin'! I know you're hurt!" he called to her. "You wanna die out here? Just stop! You hear me? Answer me! Stop runnin' so you don't hurt yourself any more than you already are. Otherwise, it ain't gonna be pretty. Emily!"

He stumbled as he suddenly burst forth out of the tree line into an open field, only to stop himself short. His eyes widened at the sight that greeted him.

A single figure stood in the open space, the moon's reflected luminance illustrating her in an eerie way, like a ghost, or demon, of the night. She stood facing him, her dark skin shadowy in the distant obscurity. Her midnight-black clothing was easily distinguished, however, and her tinted sunglasses completely shielded her eyes. The manner in which she was poised—calm, silent, and alone in the dark clearing—was sharp and intense, a compelling scene. It was as though she expected him.

Cole was immediately uneasy.

"Is it all how you imagined it would be?"

The unexpected voice came from very close, and Cole jerked his head around to look.

Another man appeared, about fifteen years his junior, Cole guessed, approaching leisurely. He gave off the same strange, gripping, otherworldly aura as the woman in the field. His face, like hers, was striking, seemingly perfect, even in the darkness, and his vivid, red-orange hair seemed to glow on its own, as though close to bursting into flames at any moment.

Cole could see that the mysterious man's eyes had a similar fiery coloring, making his gaze piercing without any effort.

"Who ... who are you?"

His voice sounded hoarse, even to himself. He glanced nervously at the woman in the clearing again before returning to the young man.

"Who are you?" he questioned again, his tone slightly more assured, attempting to convey that he was not afraid.

The mysterious man's lips curved upward a little.

"Who am I?" the man repeated. "Who am I? Who are you? Who are you to find yourself here, in this place? Who are you to do what you've done?"

The man's slow walk finally stopped, and he leaned in closer to Cole. His tone turned quiet, sinister.

"Who are you to even ask me that question? As though my answer would make a difference in how this is going to play out."

Cole again attempted to suppress the terrifying emotions that stirred, crashing, within.

"What ... do you want with me?" he asked, his eyes flickering between the man and the woman out in the field.

The red-haired man studied him for a moment, not speaking, as if taking note of the injuries and smudges Cole had sustained from his earlier struggles with Emily, and from the fire in the house where Cole had held her, confined. The man's brilliant gaze loitered on Cole's scraggly mane of hair, loosely secured by a leather bandana; his scruffy beard; his burly, rough-edged appearance. Then, he returned to Cole's eyes.

"So, you believe you deserve an explanation from me?" the stranger asked, his burning gaze less than a foot away.

Cole, silenced, did not reply.

"Answer me."

The man's tone was quiet but commanding.

Cole stared back, though his gaze was shifty compared to the steadfast, incisive stare of the other man, which seemed to cut right through him.

The man stalked closer still, bringing his face to within a few inches of actually touching Cole's nose.

"Answer. My. Question."

Just as Cole parted his lips to speak, he felt a tremendous shift in the atmosphere around him. His senses were assaulted, a searing burst of heat and power crashing into him, nearly knocking him to his knees like a mighty punch to the midsection and forcing him to close his eyes briefly. The heightened, inexplicable tension he had felt since he first entered the clearing exploded, the sensation either of awe-inspiring magnificence or apocalyptic disaster; he could not tell which.

Suddenly, the entire world seemed to be on fire.

Cole's eyes snapped open, and he was met with the man's intense, blistering gaze. The irises focused on him actually appeared to be ablaze, flames reaching out to singe Cole's eyelashes. Yet there was a passion, a burning intensity also present, one entirely separate from the actual fire that enveloped the mysterious man's pupils.

The man stepped back slightly.

Cole's stunned gaze leaped to the blazing wings that framed the man's body, the burning, outstretched appendages glowing with white-hot intensity, nearly too bright to look at directly. Even the man's clothing seemed to emit radiance, highlighting the unwrinkled, untainted nature of both the outfit and its owner.

The lapping flames of the encompassing forest fire pulled Cole's attention away. An enormous, fiery barricade circled the clearing, burning forest shrubbery outlined in the background. The inferno completely blanketed the trees from floor to canopy, but did not venture into the short grass of the clearing, as if an invisible wall prevented it from racing across the open space and shrouding them all.

Cole's eyes were drawn to the pair of absolute, soul-sucking black wings that framed the woman in the field, a black as dark as the most harrowing of nights. The woman remained stoic, at ease despite the thoroughly unsettling scene.

The effect was spine-chilling.

The blaze from the fire lit up the night. Cole took in the terrifyingly wondrous picture, his eyes darting between the flames, the calmly powerful beings with their imposing wings, and back to the fire again. He stared, his mouth hanging open slightly, his eyes unblinking.

"What ... what is ..."

Cole faltered, still awestruck.

"You asked for an explanation?" the man spoke again. "Quite frankly, I'm not the one you need to talk to about that. But..."

He left the sentence unfinished, turning.

Cole followed his gaze to the advancing female figure, her black wings outstretched ominously. As he watched, Cole recalled where he had seen her before:

Joe's Roadhouse Tavern.

The night at the bar instantly replayed in his mind.

Cole stood petrified, unable to move. His heart felt as though it had stopped beating.

The man with the burning wings glanced back at him.

"See you around," he muttered, before adding, "Maybe. If you pray hard enough."

He stepped away, a slight smirk apparent on his face. Giving the woman a soft nod, he shot silently, swiftly, straight up into the night sky, the inferno continuing to blaze all around the clearing.

Cole's eyes, however, never left the woman. For him, the surrounding air had taken on an unnatural, ill-omened feel.

Foreboding.

Threatening.

Utterly dark, bordering on pure evil.

Complete silence; even the inferno around them blazed without noise.

"You remember me."

It was a statement, not a question. The woman's voice was dark, looming, as though suspended in the night air, ice-cold compared to the fire that encircled them.

Cole could not will himself to utter a sound in response. He only watched, transfixed.

"I told you if we saw each other again," the woman declared, continuing her advance, "it would not be a pleasant experience."

She now stood an arm's length away. Cole's gaze never left the lens of her mirrored shades. A terrified man stared back at him, with scorching flames just behind, seemingly licking their chops, waiting with anticipation.

"Consider this your unpleasant experience," she said. "Welcome to hell."

The smile that followed was arresting—beautiful yet absolutely frightening at the same time.

She was easily the most terrifying being Cole had ever laid eyes upon.

Imani moved faster than he could blink.

Sound suddenly returned—loudly. The blaze roared, sending fiery sparks into the sky.

FLASHES.

Glimpses.

Brief scenes played through Elizabeth's daydream like an old-fashioned, homemade movie.

Eric as an infant, with a doting Hank and Elizabeth holding him lovingly in their arms.

Eric, still a young child, playing with an even younger Sarah, and then Riley, his actions charming, sometimes bothersome and annoying, but always brotherly.

Eric growing: his first day of school, kiddie birthday parties, gatherings with friends and extended family.

Homework. Eating. Playing sports.

Laughing. Angry. Frustrated. Saddened. Scared. Joyous. Content.

With and without friends. With and without her and Hank, Riley, and Sarah. With and without people Elizabeth was and was not familiar with—dear friends or complete strangers. In either case, Eric seemed to know them.

Then, Eric growing older, maturing into a young man.

Experiences. Adventures. Loves. Heartbreaks.

Older still. Marriage. A wife and children of his own. His face and body all grown up, matured, capable. Nevertheless, he remained distinctly, absolutely, entirely Eric.

Still, always, her Eric.

Elizabeth broke out of the reverie, smiling. As she leaned against the railing that ran along the length of the front porch, she felt a presence beside her. She turned her head.

From his position, perched on the top steps, her oldest son gazed back at her, smirking, with that cool, clever expression teenage boys somehow acquired naturally.

"You're weird," he commented. "I've been standing here for five minutes and you didn't even know it."

"You have not been standing there for five minutes," Elizabeth retorted.

"Okay, then. Four and a half."

"I don't believe that, either."

"Okay, like, thirty seconds only," Eric declared. "But that's as low as I'm going."

The teenager climbed the rest of the steps, circling behind his mother to join her as she rested against the porch railing, her gaze now on the wide, green front yard.

It was a radiant day, sunlight shimmering down on the Colorado landscape, giving the vista an alluring, dreamlike quality. In the yard, the two youngest Johnson kids were present: Riley playing fetch with the puppies while Sarah practiced one of her gymnastic routines.

Hank, Elizabeth could only assume, was busy in the backyard, or else running errands with his best friend and neighbor, Bryan; otherwise, he would have been out in the yard in the midst of his children's antics.

Elizabeth watched her daughter complete a series of moves, ending with a nimble back flip.

Her exploits caught Agro and Terri's attention, the puppies suddenly unable to decide between chasing tennis balls and chasing Sarah. Amongst themselves, they must have decided to do both, as Agro jumped to run after Sarah, while Terri split away to track one of the thrown tennis balls.

Sarah let out a yelp of surprise as Agro tackled her legs when she landed. Elizabeth and Eric laughed from their elevated viewpoint, and out in the yard, Riley howled with amusement.

Hearing Eric's chuckle, Elizabeth glanced at him.

"And why aren't you down there protecting your sister from that vicious dog?" she questioned, nudging him while continuing to chuckle quietly.

"Because I'm up here with you, laughing about it."

"Smarty pants," his mother replied.

She continued to watch him for a moment, as he focused on the games out in the yard. She took in the details of his profile— the varying brown and blondish tones of his hair, as though random strands had been highlighted and lightened by the bright rays of the summer sun; the particular and characteristic lines, angles, and curves of his features; the remnants of his smile at Agro's play in the grass; the hue of his skin, the relaxed tendons of his neck.

He turned, catching her stare, and grinned.

"Now what are you thinking about?" he asked.

"You," she answered simply, smiling back.

"What about me?"

He glanced to the yard again, the sunlight seeming to sparkle on everything, including him.

"About how fortunate I am to have you—all of you," she replied, gesturing out into the front yard.

The teenager pointed a finger into his mouth and made gagging sounds, and Elizabeth shoved him lightly in admonishment.

"Stop that. I'm being serious."

"And what were you thinking about before, when I was standing on the steps?"

"The same thing," Elizabeth replied. "And seeing you grow and mature, and of how proud I am to have such a wonderful son and such a special family."

"Eww."

Eric wrinkled his nose.

"You asked," she chided.

"But still, it's a little gross when you say it out loud like that."

Elizabeth continued to look at him.

"Mom," Eric said, keeping his gaze directed to the yard, "you're doing it again."

"You're a boy-prince, you know that?" Elizabeth remarked. "You may not like to hear it, but it's true."

"I guess that makes you the queen, then?" Eric returned, smiling, as though the grin itself was answer enough.

His smile struck Elizabeth as oddly telling. It was a rarity, exhibiting her son's love without a trace of his usual teenage indifference.

On the grass below, Sarah had resumed her flips and somersaults, Agro continuing to trail after her with playful abandon. Meanwhile, Riley was busy attempting to fake his tennis ball throws, but Terri seemed to be having none of it, waiting patiently until he actually released the toy, which he finally did.

"What do you think about?" Elizabeth inquired, looking again to the teenager alongside of her.

For a moment, Eric did not respond, instead maintaining his stare out into the bright green expanse where his brother and sister and the two puppies romped. At last, he broke his silence.

"I think ... I think you're going to be just fine," he said, his voice softer and more reflective.

"Huh?" she mused, her voice conveying her surprise. "Getting a little cryptic, aren't we?"

Eric glanced toward his mother quickly, a smile ghosting across his face, before returning his gaze to the front lawn.

"Not really. I mean it. I think you're going to be all right. You all are. We all are."

"What does that mean?"

Her eldest child turned to her once more, his eyes seeming to flicker with something extra, something more.

Something only a mother would notice.

He grinned and shrugged, before shifting his gaze back to the brilliantly lit scenery...

Brilliantly lit.

Elizabeth Johnson's eyes opened.

Focused rays of morning sunlight streaked through the bedroom windows, spotlighting the dust motes that floated lazily in the air. The room, and the Johnson household, was silent and still, save for Hank's light snoring beside her.

Still.

Silent.

Brilliantly lit.

Elizabeth's mind returned to her dream as she noted the morning glow streaming through the window shades.

Brilliantly lit.

She recalled, particularly, what her eldest son had said. She then slowly sat upright and swung her feet off the bed, onto the carpeted bedroom floor.

MANY HOURS LATER, HANK Johnson lifted his youngest child gently off the cushion in front of him so he could get up to answer the door. Hank's rise and gait was slow and weary—he felt as though cloaked in a thick haze. The silence of the living room, only delicately broken by an occasional sniffle, added to the strange, dream-like state of it all, as if the entire world had stopped its usual slow rotation—if only for a moment.

The lights in the room were off, but sunlight spilled in, throwing shimmers and shadows across the interior. Elizabeth and Sarah sat curled into each other on the couch, Sarah resting lengthwise along Elizabeth's lap, her head on her mother's shoulder. The glow arriving through the windows shined on both of them, highlighting the lighter tendrils of their hair and dancing nimbly over the rest. Elizabeth rocked them both lightly, their eyes closed, a natural, comforting interaction between mother and daughter, even if Sarah was past the age of willfully sitting in her mother's lap.

Upon leaving the large, comfy armchair he had occupied with his dad, Riley Johnson kneeled down in front of it. He placed the framed photograph he clutched into a sharp beam of light that stretched over the carpeted floor. He stooped further, drawing closer to the picture to study it.

The photo had been taken from its usual place atop the mantelpiece. Eric Johnson's exuberant expression grinned back, his face devoid of hurt or worry, his eyes sparkling with mirth and a touch of mischief. It was an innocent, but definitive, portrait, capturing every conceivable feature of the eldest Johnson child except those qualities that were impossible to depict in a still image.

Like his voice.

Now, there was only silence.

Even Agro and Terri seemed to perceive the subdued atmosphere of the household. Out of the way, they each lay stomach down on the carpet, their heads resting between their paws, their eyes taking in the scene, but their bodies stationary.

Hank finally reached the front door, unlocking it and pulling it open with the same exhausted slowness. More daylight streamed in, the visitors at the door standing in near silhouette. The twinkling light shined around them and radiated off their spotless white clothes, appearing to give them a halo.

Hank blinked before he recognized them.

"Eli … Elianna … Lucas," he murmured, with a touch of surprise.

The puppies' eyes flickered to the visitors.

"If you would rather be left alone right now," Elias said, "we would understand."

Hank, still in a daze, took a moment to respond.

"Yeah. I mean, no, no. Please, come in."

He stepped aside.

Elias let Elianna and Lucifer go before him. He then paused in front of Hank, looking toward him patiently, waiting.

"Uh…"

Hank cleared his throat, rubbing his eyes and then opening them wide again, attempting to hold back tears.

"It's all right, Hank," Elias said softly.

"It's, uh … it's Eric. He's … ahem … he's … gone. He got out of bed sometime during the night and just … collapsed. I don't…"

Hank looked away, toward the floor, struggling to regain his composure.

Elias took a step closer.

"Hank."

Hank met the other man's gaze, his eyes wet but not spilling over. Elias reached out and patted Hank's shoulder, leaving his hand there in support.

Hank sniffled and exhaled loudly, shaking his head.

"It's … it's…"

Elias stepped closer still, wrapping his arms around the distraught father. Hank returned the embrace, a tear escaping down his face as he shut his eyes.

On the sofa, Elianna consoled Elizabeth and Sarah in a similar manner, her arms wrapped around them both, following Elizabeth's rocking movements. The embrace held a power of its own, soothing their inner turmoil appreciably. Elizabeth's sobs were quiet, faint but present. Sarah remained hushed, her eyes shut tightly, as if attempting to will the entire dreadful circumstance away.

As if shutting out the world could somehow shield her from the unfortunate reality.

Riley and Lucifer—the former bowed on his forearms and knees, the latter lying flat on his stomach—studied the framed image of Eric, which seemed to glow in the shaft of sunlight. A few strands of Lucifer's hair had fallen forward on his face, and his eyes shifted furtively between the portrait and the youngest Johnson child. Riley sat unmoving, even as Elias and Hank passed behind him, his eyes roving over every aspect of the photograph, and then examining every aspect anew.

Elias assisted Hank back to the recliner.

"We won't stay long," he said quietly, catching Elianna's eye before returning to Hank. "We don't want to impose."

"It's ... all right."

Hank unfocused eyes were directed toward nothing in particular.

"You all just moved here, though. I don't know ... it's ... I wish ... argh."

He sniffled, and, blinking, brushed at his eyes.

"I am so, so sorry," Elianna spoke up from the couch, looking between Elizabeth and Hank. "I can't begin to understand how you must feel. I can't imagine how hard this must be."

"It's just..."

Elizabeth struggled to find the words.

"He's ... he's so young. My baby. Is it something ...I mean, could we have..."

"What you must know," Elias said in a soft voice, "what must be absolutely clear, is that this was not your fault. It wasn't anyone's fault. You did everything exactly right, and I'm sure Eric could not have asked for a better family. This ... what happened ... this is what makes us human. It's what makes us who we are."

Red and bleary-eyed, Elizabeth looked to Elias.

"You sound as though you've been in this position before."

After a pause, Elianna answered quietly, "We have."

The room was still.

"You've..."

Elizabeth's voice caught in her throat.

"You've ... lost ... a child?"

Elianna looked at the grieving mother a moment.

"You haven't lost him."

Four sets of eyes—Hank's, Elizabeth's, Sarah's, Riley's—turned to the strikingly beautiful woman. Elianna's eyes remained on Elizabeth.

"But..." Elizabeth started. "He's..."

"He's exactly where he has to be, where you need him to be," Elianna finished. "The same place he has always been."

She met the eyes of each of Eric's family in turn.

"In your dreams, for instance."

Elizabeth startled, and Sarah lifted her head, still gazing at Elianna. In the armchair, Hank straightened, crinkling his brow as he looked up to Elias, and then back to Elianna and Elizabeth on the sofa.

"Dreams?"

Riley's voice broke the silence. He raised himself up from the carpet to meet Elianna's glance.

"I had a dream last night," he offered, "and Eric was in it. It was a good dream. He was funny."

Elianna smiled, nodding.

"Me too," Sarah added. "He came to Rebecca's house while we were all sleeping, but I woke up for some reason, and he was lying there beside me, and we just talked. No one else could hear us."

Fresh tears brimmed in Elizabeth's eyes.

"Oh, sweetie," she cooed, hugging her daughter closer.

On the floor, Agro and Terri's eyes followed each speaker as if they understood. Hank, meanwhile, appeared deep in thought.

"We were throwing a baseball back and forth in some field," he began slowly. "I don't even know where we were. It was weird, since he doesn't really like to play baseball that much, you know?"

He smiled to himself, remembering.

"But I guess he was just humoring his ol' man. It was an ordinary, laid-back conversation, no rush, no worries. Same one we've had bunches of times. We talked about everything, and nothing, and it seemed to go on for hours, but it was all so ... easy, so relaxed. It was as though it was the only place we had to be."

He rubbed his hand over his face as he finished speaking, stroking against the fine stubble on his jaw. Beside him, Elias reassuringly gripped his shoulder. Hank nodded in absent-minded acknowledgement.

Elizabeth, meanwhile, held her hand over her mouth, as though trying to stifle her cries.

"It's completely understandable to feel you've lost someone in a circumstance like this," Elianna remarked in her peaceful, melodious way. "It's almost instinctual. But it's not true when you think about it, not really. Sure, there is a physical absence, but I don't think Eric's just being here was all that made him who he was and is to you. There is so much more, so much more that made him a son, a brother, a bright and captivating human being, than his physical presence alone. Do you think your dreams, your thoughts, your love—do you think these things are simply a product of Eric living in the same house as you? Do you think that, because you can't touch him anymore, his existence is completely erased, never to be seen or heard from again? Or, do you think there is something more?

"We—Eli, Lucas, and I—only knew Eric for a fraction of the time you all did, but even that brief moment was enough to affect us tremendously. We will always remember him, and through us, he will live forever. As his mother, as his father, as his sister and brother, it is precisely because of you that we were fortunate enough to have met him, and it is because of you that he will never be gone. You haven't lost him. You all gave him life, and you will continue to."

The living room was silent once more.

On the floor, Lucifer lifted himself into a kneeling position, mirroring Riley's. The attention of the others in the room shifted to him as he gently reached for Riley's hands, opening and extending them. As the boys faced each other, Lucifer reached into the pockets of his cargo pants, pulling out two brand-new tennis balls. The furry exterior of the yellow balls glowed in the golden-tinged sunlight streaming in through the window. Remaining silent, he placed them delicately in Riley's hands.

Riley's face was a mixture of surprise and puzzlement. Both puppies, seeing the balls from their positions on the floor, thumped their tails lightly against the carpet, expressing their approval.

After a moment, Lucifer's striking hazel eyes shifted from the tennis balls to Riley, as he motioned for the boy to turn them over.

Small, elegant stitching on both balls presented a simple message.

I am always with you.
Love,
Eric

Riley's widened, astonished eyes glanced around to the others in the room before returning to the boy in front of him. Lucifer leaned forward, patting Riley on the head. He then sat back again, his expression unreadable, his eyes seeming to swirl with mystique and wonder.

"OKAY, YOU TWO, GOOD luck," Rosalind Dos Anjos said to Charlie and Raven as the teenagers gathered their soccer gear from the car.

"It shouldn't be too bad," Raven assured her mother. "I'm just hoping we don't have to run too many laps."

"Well, I'm going to run a few errands, and then I'll be back. I shouldn't be more than thirty minutes."

The girls slid out of the back seat.

"You're going to sit here that long?" Raven asked, turning back to talk through the open passenger-side window. "You do know that these tryouts can take over an hour, and maybe longer, right?"

"That's why I brought this."

Mrs. Dos Anjos held up an audiobook case.

Charlie glanced in.

"You'll probably finish it by the time we're through, Mrs. Dos Anjos," she said, laughing.

"Oh, really, Miss Brown?"

Mrs. Dos Anjos turned to the audiobook's back cover.

"So, you're expecting this tryout to last, let's see … ten hours and twelve minutes?"

She grinned at both teens.

"Sorry, girls. If your tryout lasts that long, I think you're going to be running a whole bunch of laps."

"Okay, maybe you'll get a tenth of the way through by the time we're finished," Charlie responded, laughing again.

"Yeah, you have fun with that, Mom," Raven said as she tugged at the athletic bag on Charlie's shoulders. "Come on, Charlie. If we're late, I'm sure we'll have to run as punishment. Bye, Mom."

"Bye, Mrs. Dos Anjos."

"See you later, girls. I'll be here when you're done."

The teens turned away from the car.

August brought the same temperate weather to Cape Cod that June and July did, always moderated by the seafaring coolness that made the region such an attraction. Charlie looked at Raven as they began toward the field where other players congregated.

"I knew that was why you always played goalie," Charlie remarked. "You're just a lazy bum who doesn't like to run."

"Ugh, whatever! Are you forgetting who you play basketball with? I just hate that slow, stupid jogging laps stuff. It's so boring. I'd rather just sprint around randomly."

"Oh, so ... like a crazy bum, then?"

"Exactly."

The pair laughed, and then nearly screeched in surprise, as Gabriel suddenly appeared beside them.

"Hey," he said, grinning.

He wore a casual polo shirt and athletic shorts with colorful sneakers. A baseball cap, turned backwards, mostly covered his wild, honey-streaked curls, although some extended from under the edges.

"Gabriel!" Charlie yelped as Raven tried to calm herself. "Where did you come from? What are you doing here?"

"I wanted to see you guys ... uh, girls ... ladies ... whatever!"

Charlie and Raven smirked at each other.

"I wanted to see you try out, remember? Is that all right? I couldn't wait for the first game to see Norbury's two newest phenoms."

"You understand that this is only tryouts, right?" Raven said. "We haven't even made it onto the team yet."

"Oh, yeah," Gabriel chuckled. "This is gonna be great."

His eyes shifted to the soccer bags Charlie and Raven had brought along.

"Hey, you want me to carry those?"

The girls looked at each other and shrugged again. Just as they finished handing the gear to Gabriel, they noticed another girl approach. She was holding a clipboard and she looked a little older, perhaps an upperclassman if she was a student at Norbury High.

A slightly panicked look clouded Raven's face. Upon seeing it, the older girl laughed.

"It's okay, calm down. You're not late. I just have to collect your physical release forms and get you to sign in."

She handed over the clipboard.

Charlie took it, and the pen the girl offered, while Raven, issuing a sigh of relief, reached into the bags Gabriel had slung onto his shoulders and retrieved the forms.

"So, you're planning on going out for the Freshman Girl's team, too, Gabe?" the girl inquired, her eyebrow arching at Gabriel.

"Nah," Gabriel replied, shaking his head as he gave her a crooked grin. "I just thought I'd come check out the talent on the team this year."

"Uh-huh."

The girl seemed unconvinced.

"You know Coach Parks is here."

Gabriel grinned in response, and the older girl laughed and shook her head. She took the completed forms and clipboard back from Charlie and Raven.

"Word of advice: you two should watch out for this guy."

She nodded vaguely at Gabriel as she looked over the paperwork.

"He may be cute, but ..."

She stopped speaking as she read, and then reread, the papers. Soon after, she eyed the two girls, suddenly curious.

Charlie peeked at the clipboard again.

"Did we fill in something wrong?"

"Charlize Brown and Raven Summerset? Did you two play soccer at Walker Middle?"

Charlie and Raven looked at each other quizzically, not noticing Gabriel's mischievous smirk beside them. The older girl, however, did notice, and she looked at him for a moment before returning to the younger girls.

"I knew it. I knew I recognized those names. Why on earth are you out here for freshman tryouts?" she asked.

Charlie, confused, looked from the girl to Raven, who looked similarly puzzled, to a grinning Gabriel, and then back to the girl.

"Umm, because we're going to be freshmen when school starts and we're trying out for the team? Isn't this where we're supposed to be?"

"You're not going out for Varsity?" the older girl asked, her brow crinkled as she looked at the two players.

"Varsity?" Charlie parroted, surprised. "Don't you have to be more experienced to try out for Varsity?"

The girl stared at Charlie and Raven, clearly befuddled.

"You are Charlize Brown and Raven Summerset, right? I mean, those are your real names?"

Both girls nodded.

"And you played soccer at Walker?"

More nods.

"And you go by Charlie, right?" the girl asked.

Charlie nodded again.

The girl stared for a few moments more, as if waiting. She then turned to Gabriel.

"Okay, this has your fingerprints all over it, Gabriel," she accused. "This is some sort of joke, right?"

Before Gabriel could reply, brisk, heavy footfalls alerted the teenagers to someone's approach.

"Stevens! What's the—oh, no."

Coach Parks, an athletic-looking middle-aged man with a glistening, bald dome but ample hair around the sides, focused in on a grinning Gabriel. The thick mustache under Coach Park's nose twitched.

"I shoulda known," he growled. "Always causin' some sort of distraction, aren't you, Adams? All right, out with it. What's goin' on?"

"Sorry, Coach," the girl Coach Parks called Stevens spoke up. "Everything checks out. It's just that these two may not be what you're looking for on the Freshman squad."

The coach kept a suspicious eye on Gabriel for a moment longer before addressing the girl.

"I think I'll be the judge of that, Stevens," he huffed.

He shifted his gaze to Charlie and Raven.

"Okay. I'm Coach Parks. You can call me Coach Parks. For the next couple of hours, I'm your worst nightmare."

Stevens rolled her eyes, shaking her head almost imperceptibly. Gabriel snickered. Coach Parks cut his gaze again toward the boy briefly, his eyes alighting on the soccer bags Gabriel shouldered.

"Whose bags are those?"

"They're ours, Coach Parks," Raven answered. "Gabriel offered to carry them for us."

She made to reach for the bags.

"No, no, that's all right. That's good. That's good," Parks said, stopping her. "That's good thinkin', girls. Gives Adams something constructive to do for a change."

The coach's glare leveled on Gabriel.

"Because we all know what they say about idle hands," he growled lowly, causing Gabriel to laugh again.

"You mockin' me, boy?" Coach Parks questioned loudly.

Still snickering, Gabriel shook his head. The coach returned to Charlie and Raven.

"You two can join the others out there," he said, gesturing to the practice field. "Just stretch and, you know, warm up your muscles and whatnot. I'll be up in a sec."

After receiving a covert, reassuring nod from the older girl, Charlie and Raven started to jog over to where the other incoming freshman players were already warming up.

Coach Parks turned back to Gabriel.

"And you don't set foot on my field unless I say so, got it, Adams?"

Gabriel nodded, a lighthearted grin stretching across his face, his eyes twinkling.

"You eyeballin' me now, Adams?" Parks exclaimed.

"No ... sir ... Coach," Gabriel managed, struggling to hold back his laughter.

"Well then, what are you waitin' for? Get outta here! And stop lookin' at me like that!"

Gabriel strode off toward the field, still snickering, Charlie and Raven's soccer bags still slung over his shoulders.

"Now, what did you mean by 'not what I'm looking for on the freshman team,' Stevens?" he asked the girl at his side, gruffly.

"I meant exactly that," she declared. "No offense to the other girls out here, but those two are locks for Varsity."

Coach Parks huffed into his bushy mustache.

"You know them?" he questioned as he began walking briskly back to the field, prompting Stevens to break into a near jog to keep up.

"I know of them," she corrected. "And, if what I heard is right, two of the best soccer players in the entire conference—heck, the entire region—are about to try out for the Freshman team. You'll see."

Coach Parks looked toward her and huffed again.

"Yeah, I'll see."

LESS THAN FIFTEEN MINUTES later, Coach Parks did indeed see.

He popped his whistle into his mouth and blew shrilly, causing the upperclassman, Stevens, to flinch noticeably beside him.

"What the—" he spoke abruptly, talking around the whistle before letting it fall.

Further down the sideline, Gabriel could be heard laughing hysterically.

"Knock it off, Adams! Brown, Summerset, get over here! The rest of you, keep going! I want clean, crisp passing! For cryin' out loud, keep it under control out there, ladies!"

Charlie and Raven trotted to the edge of the field, their blond and black ponytails respectively swaying behind them as they ran. Neither had yet managed to work up a sweat.

"That's the way to go, Gibson! Pass and move!"

Coach Parks turned to look at the two girls.

"Is this some type of joke?"

He shifted focus to Stevens.

"Is this a joke?"

And then back to Charlie and Raven.

"This is some type of joke, right?"

"I tried to tell you," Stevens said in a singsong, satisfied tone.

Coach Parks abruptly whirled, looking down the sideline toward Gabriel.

"Adams, get over here!"

As Gabriel jogged over to the group, Coach Parks glanced at Stevens again.

"Why didn't you say anything?" he asked, as though he had not heard her previous warnings. His attention shifted again, this time to the field.

"Control over power, Bernard! You're wastin' it if you can't control it!"

His eyes swung to Gabriel.

"The jig's up, Adams!" Coach Parks declared, spittle flying from of his mouth as he spoke. "It took me a few minutes, but I caught ya! It's all over!"

The coach turned to Raven and Charlie.

"Okay, I'm not sure how he put you up to this, but you two are pretty much done here. You can stick around if you want—if your ride's not here, or if you want to help out and whatnot—but I've seen more than enough. First Varsity practice is scheduled for Thursday. I'll make sure Coach Franks is expectin' you."

Just as abruptly, he turned and jogged out onto the field toward the other girls.

"Watch the high kicking, Collins! This ain't a stinkin' ballet class I'm runnin' out here!"

Charlie and Raven watched the coach's departing figure, and then turned to one another, speechless. They both then looked to Gabriel and Stevens, both of whom were grinning brightly.

"Sorry, I didn't introduce myself properly before," Stevens started. "I'm Miranda Stevens. Sounds like we're going to be teammates. I can't wait to see what you two can really do out on the field once practice starts. This is definitely going to be a fun year."

"That was classic," Gabe acknowledged, laughing. "I knew when you said you were going out for the Freshman team this would happen. And with Coach Parks, no less! That's just icing on the cake."

He looked around at the three girls, smiling.

"And, I hope I'm not out of line by saying this, but—"

"Stevens! Grab my dry erase board, would you?" Coach Parks called from the field.

"I'm on it, Coach!"

Miranda gave Charlie and Raven a parting smile and left to retrieve the coach's board.

"Varsity?" Charlie murmured, looking at Raven.

"I know," Raven said. "I still kind of ... like ... I don't know ... you know?"

Both girls turned to Gabriel, who grinned, wiggling his eyebrows mischievously.

DEXTER TOOHEY WAITED IN line in front of the cash register. Behind him, close to the diner's entrance, Imani sat in a straight-backed chair, her attention never leaving the Rebel Fist rider.

"Order up!"

The authoritative broadcast coming from one of the busy, short order cooks managing the kitchen rose above the general din of the eatery.

"That's mine," replied one of the waiters.

As the customer completed his transaction at the register, the others in line, including Toohey, advanced a bit closer. The tinkling bell over the diner's exit soon signaled the customer's departure.

A few stools aligned in front of the long, laminate countertop were available. However, Imani remained in her position near the door. Her sunglasses were absent, allowing her unwavering gaze to continue unhidden. The rest of her usual attire was in evidence, however, and her appearance, along with her calculated, emotionless demeanor, was more than enough to keep the curious at bay.

"I've got one," another server called out, standing just outside the cooking area that lined the back of the diner.

"Go ahead with it," one of the cooks acknowledged.

"Okay, give me a triple pancake platter with four eggs scrambled hard instead of three, two single pancake platters…"

Imani watched as Toohey's gaze swept briefly over the others in line, and then to her and the few customers sitting near the entrance before returning to the front again. As he was dressed casually in worn jeans and a T-shirt, by appearance alone, Toohey gave off no sinister air. Looking at him, no one present would recognize him as the shadowy, unassuming head of a notorious outlaw motorcycle gang—the mastermind of an emerging criminal syndicate.

Toohey turned again. His eyes halted when he caught sight of Imani gazing impassively back at him. Toohey returned the same, fixed stare.

The bell atop the diner's door jingled again, interrupting Toohey's gaze, which flicked toward the entrance.

"Uncle Dex, you ready? The other guys are all set to head back to the 'house.'"

Imani's stare shifted to the door as soon as she heard the voice.

"Does it look like I'm ready?"

Toohey gestured to the line, which inched forward again.

"I'm still in line, ain't I? If the others want to go, let 'em go."

"Okay, okay. Geez," the boy muttered. "Thought they said you weren't as cranky after…"

The boy's words faded as he turned to go back outside, the door closing behind him.

Toohey turned his attention back to the counter. The register was now only a single customer away.

Imani twisted in her chair to watch the departing boy through the diner's front windows. The kid soon rejoined a small collection of Rebel Fist bikers, each wearing the distinctive colors and patches of the club, although neither Toohey nor the boy wore any noticeable sign of their affiliation. Imani shifted her watch back to the line in front of the register.

Moments later, Toohey turned from the counter, pocketing his receipt, his eyes directed downward as he headed for the exit. As he neared the door, he glanced up again, his eyes stopping on Imani's once more. He slowed his advance.

"You got a problem?" he asked, his voice quiet and gruff, though, for the most part, non-threatening.

Imani held his cold, blue stare for a moment.

"No problem."

Neither blinked. Toohey's jaw tensed. Beside them, the door chimed again.

"Come on, Uncle D! Man, you're slow as dirt!"

Both Toohey and Imani turned to the teenager in the doorway before locking eyes once again. Imani lifted one eyebrow, infinitesimally.

"All right," Toohey relented, reaching into his pocket, his stare lingering on the woman in black before finally swinging to the boy. "Show me how to start it up."

He tossed the bike keys to the spiky-haired teen, who, distracted and looking toward Imani as well, bobbled the catch, nearing dropping them. His eyes brightened once he recognized what he was holding.

"Cool! So I get to—"

"No. I said start it."

"But I've got the keys, though," the boy said, smirking and twirling the key ring on his finger.

"So?" Toohey challenged. Leveling a final, measured glance toward Imani, he brushed past the teenager and exited the diner.

The boy looked after him, and then his eyes met Imani's briefly before he too turned away, the bell tinkling lightly as he exited.

Imani rose and made her way to one of the empty stools along the counter. The large man she sat beside looked over—his grin nearly masked by his thick beard—as he cut into his syrupy pancakes.

"Always tryin' to start something up, ain't ya?" Lex questioned, before forking a pile of pancakes into his mouth. "You're worse than I am."

"Just water for now, please," Imani instructed the waitress. She then looked to Lex.

"I didn't do anything," she replied.

"*I didn't do anything?*" he repeated. "Now, why does that phrase sound so familiar?"

Imani sipped her water, which had almost immediately appeared in front of her. Lex, meanwhile, gulped noisily from his coffee mug. Imani looked at him.

"It's good joe," he stated simply, continuing to cut out another large portion of pancake. "So, you still wonderin' about that Toohey guy? I thought that would've gone away after that little discussion you had in the woods with that other dude. When was that, close to a week ago now?"

"Toohey didn't have anything to do with that," she replied after a moment's contemplation. "In a way, he tried to prevent it from getting that far, and he almost did."

"The kid, then?" Lex asked, shoving the food into his gullet.

"Something's still not right. I'm still wondering why Toohey was in the handbook in the first place," Imani returned. "He didn't get involved at the tavern. And then, the boy comes out of nowhere. He wasn't at the tavern or when I saw them at the gas station, and he's not in the handbook at all."

She glanced over to Lex, who was looking back at her as he chewed. He scoffed.

"The handbook's never off," he insisted once more, his mouth full.

Imani turned to look out the diner's windows again, her gaze flitting across the empty spaces where the Rebel Fist riders had been parked.

"Well, if the handbook's never off, then that means I'm still wonderin' about that Toohey guy," she stated in a low tone, repeating her partner's phrasing as she continued to gaze outside. "And the kid."

CASE AND BEAT SPED swiftly through the black sky. A vast, slow kaleidoscope of stars glimmered above them and all around.

An instant later, they accelerated, moving even faster and eclipsing unfathomable velocities.

They headed east.

EXCEPT FOR THE DIM moonlight that flitted in through the window, Charlize Brown's upstairs bedroom was dark. The sleeping teenager twisted restlessly in her bed again, the sheets crumpled awkwardly around her body and strewn across the mattress.

"CRAP," TONY BROWN, CHARLIE'S father, muttered from the front passenger seat. "I guess I spoke too soon. Here it comes again."

The rain fell with force once more. He attempted to peer through the front windshield, but could distinguish very little through the heavy shower. With the sun having long since set, and the periodically heavy rain, road conditions were poor. He looked over to the driver's side.

"How you doing?" he inquired.

"I'm fine," Sherry Brown said. "But what have I said about using that kind of language when the kids can hear you?"

Tony twisted his body so he could glance into the back seat.

Charlie sat in the middle—dubbed the "toilet seat" by her two younger brothers—with her head resting just above Colby's, whose head lay on Charlie's shoulder. Colby was sound asleep in the opposite direction, his head tilted back, snug in a tiny corner between the seat cushion and the windowsill. His mouth hung open limply, his breathing hushed against the cadenced pattering of the rain outside.

"They're out of commission," Tony responded, turning away from the kids.

Sherry, her eyes glued to the diminished areas of road she could make out through the rain hurled at the windshield, retorted, "You didn't know that when you said it."

"Sure, I did."

"Oh? And how is that exactly?"

"Because I know my kids, babe. The gentle swaying of an evening drive after a night out on the town, the warm, welcoming blanket of heat gently vented from the air-conditioning, the soft pitter-patter of raindrops emanating from the heavens—"

"Um, excuse me," Sherry interrupted. "Gentle swaying? Soft pitter-patter? Honestly, babe"—she emphasized the word mockingly—"you may think you know something about our kids, but we both know you don't have a clue in the world when it comes to the weather. So, why don't you just do us both a favor and keep those pretty little lips of yours shut, hmm?"

"Sure thing, sweetcheeks," Tony grinned. He added in a loud whisper, "But, babe, I really think you need to watch your tone. You know, with the kids in the backseat and all."

"I didn't say anything wrong," Sherry replied. "And anyway, I'm not worried."

She performed an exaggerated imitation of Tony's voice.

"They're out of commission."

"Oh, touché, you ol' so-and-so," Tony said, chuckling.

Outside the car, the rain continued to pour.

Cʜᴀʀʟɪᴇ ᴛᴏssᴇᴅ ᴀɴᴅ ᴛᴜʀɴᴇᴅ in her bed. The dream, although veiled in an air she could not quite identify, was very lucid—very real—placing her directly in the car again. The moods, the forms, the sounds, the sensations, were exactly as she remembered, fully ensnaring her, unwilling to relinquish their hold. She whimpered softly in her sleep, though the distress was not nearly enough to rouse her.

It was all too familiar.

Tʜᴇ ᴡᴏʀsᴛ ᴏғ ᴛʜᴇ downpour had apparently moved on, but a steady rain continued to linger, peppering the moving car, the road, and the ground, making the feat of driving decidedly less favorable. Tony, his fingers drumming on the windowsill, turned toward his wife.

"What do you think they dream about?"

"Who?" Sherry asked.

She glanced over to Tony, who motioned to the children in the back.

"The kids," he clarified. "Sometimes, when I watch them sleeping, I wonder what it is they dream about."

"Oh my God, you are such a sap," Sherry chuckled, which caused Tony to grin.

"No, I'm serious," he continued, although his smile remained. "I mean, you don't have many problems to face at their age—at least, not the same type of problems adults face. They're free from all that stuff, you know? Free to be ... themselves. Free to live, free to enjoy, free to discover, free to explore. No qualifications, no made-up barriers too tall to climb, no conditions, no hang-ups, no ceilings. I just wonder sometimes if they are really as free in their dreams as they seem to be when I watch them play. I hope they are. I mean, I hope they dream of doing things that we would think to be impossible, things you and I never imagined even attempting, much less accomplishing."

Tony paused. When his wife failed to comment, he grinned and went on.

"I believe it was a very wise man who once said something to the effect of, 'They see things as they are and ask "why?" I dream of things that never

were and ask "why not?'" I hope nothing stops them from dreaming, or living, like that."

He stopped, glancing at Sherry again, seeking some form of reassurance.

Sherry remained quiet for a time, her gaze shifting to Tony before returning to the road and the dreadful weather.

Finally, she said, "For someone who spends half of his time spewing nonsense, you really can be very sweet when you put your mind to it."

"Oh, shut up," Tony responded, not bothering to hide his grin.

CHARLIE'S BREATHING QUICKENED. HER mind and body, both fully engrossed in the dream, were both waiting for an event neither was prepared to avoid. She tossed restlessly yet again, her blond hair shrouding her face.

OUTSIDE, THE HEAVY RAIN had returned. Though she continued to flutter in and out of consciousness, Charlie was able to grasp bits and pieces of her parents' conversation up front.

"You're crazy," Sherry said as she laughed lightly at her husband's remark.

"My psychiatrist told me you would say that," Tony replied. "Oh yeah, to you it sounds funny, but believe me, old lady gangs can get vicious if you don't show them the proper respect. All I'm saying, though, is that the entire custom is antiquated. Like, really, of all the advancements throughout the history of humankind, as far as we as a society have gotten, women are still too frail to do this kind of stuff? As my dad used to say, "Huh. That dog don't hunt."

Sherry Brown glanced at her husband, shaking her head in resignation before returning her focus to the road ahead. The windshield wipers worked mightily to provide an adequate view.

"You remember what I was saying earlier about you being so sweet sometimes?" she asked. "Well, you can forget that now, bucko."

"Aw, sweetie," Tony purred lightheartedly. "Don't be like that."

He made kissing sounds, and then turned around to check on Charlie, Colby, and Caleb in the backseat.
Then...
"Oh, no," Sherry moaned, her voice low, but still distinct.

THE SLEEPING TEEN HAD begun to sweat, her breathing erratic and rushed, her heart pounding against her chest as though she raced in an all-out sprint. It felt trance-like, as though the entire, vivid scene held her prisoner. The dream—the nightmare—was an old acquaintance of Charlie's, though it had been years since its last visit. She knew from experience that she would not be able to escape its company until the worst possible moment—the moment she dreaded most, the moment she had been forced to relive over and over. Inside, her body tensed with heightened turmoil.

And outside, in her room, all was still.

TONY BROWN JERKED HIS head toward the front again.
"What is it?" he asked, alarm interlaced in his tone. "What happened?"
"Wipers," Sherry grumbled. She flicked the handle up and then down again with no effect. "Something must have gotten stuck."
She took her foot off the gas, shifting toward the brake.
"Just pull over right here," Tony said, gesturing to the side of the road, barely visible in the rain. "I'll jump out and—what the hell?"
At her father's abrupt change in tone, Charlie startled awake in the backseat. Her eyelids blinked open drowsily.
Gray eyes materialized in front of her, the color of dozing winter nights.
And then, suddenly...
BOOOM!
A shattering, ear-piercing, explosion of noise—

CHARLIE FLINCHED IN HER bed, her brow furrowed. The thunderous crash was a usual feature of the dream. The gray eyes, however, were entirely new.

JAGGED STEEL AND RIPPED aluminum immediately crunching, contorting, and combining together, the hoods of the two vehicles collapsing into one another like the flexible and layered bellows of an accordion, shards and slices of glass and metal flying everywhere, millions of large and tiny particles suddenly airborne, the sounds harsh and deafening …

And just as suddenly, Charlie was weightless.
Flying hurriedly through the air.
Something soft, yet completely solid, was holding onto her.
An abrupt, controlled stop.
Cool, gray eyes again. Icy-blond hair.
His face.
The boy.

THE ADDITION OF THE boy to her dream was startling, nearly overwhelming. In her sleep, Charlie's breath caught in her throat.

THE BOY.
Charlie noticed the large, brilliantly white wings framing the boy's back before her pale blue eyes met his gray ones again.
"You guys think you could help me up?" he asked innocently, gazing at Charlie, and then to Colby beside her, before returning to Charlie. His voice was serene, unruffled, completely relaxed and at ease.
For Charlie, it all seemed immediately impossible. But … a horrific car crash …
Weightless.

Wings.

The boy smiled softly at her. Nearby, her other brother, Caleb, was already helping a young girl to her feet. Similarly breathtaking wings spread behind the girl's back and shoulders, her hair dark and long...

CHARLIE'S EYES SNAPPED OPEN.

Her vision quickly adjusted to the darkness of her room, the ceiling above coming into view. Even with the bedroom windows partway open, she felt coated in a thin sheen of perspiration. Her breath came heavily, as though she had been running nonstop for miles, and her heart drummed mightily against her ribcage, sending strong, consistent pulses throughout the length of her body. Her bed sheets were haphazardly thrown about from her tossing and turning.

She attempted to calm herself, a practice she was often able to do when playing soccer or other sports. Her mind, however, was much harder to restrain. It raced out of control, a continuous, unrelenting torrent of thought.

Wiping at her forehead, Charlie slowly raised herself to her elbows ... and then she froze, gasping in surprise.

She was not alone in her room.

In the darkness, faintly visible, two figures gazed back at her.

The boy.

Even in the dark, she recognized him instantly, her eyes widening even more. The faded light from outside drifted across his hair.

Pale, icy-blond.

Charlie's gaze moved between the boy and the small, dark-haired girl accompanying him. Reflexively, she drew back, sliding away from her unexpected visitors and closer to the top of her bed.

She could see the boy's head tilt to the side at her movement, the faintest grin evident on his face.

Charlie's distress immediately diminished.

For seconds, the room remained quiet. No one moved, each party studying the other. The boy and girl watched Charlie in her bed, and Charlie returned their gaze, taking in the mysterious pair.

At last, the boy's voice calmly resonated throughout the room.

"Hello, Charlie. My name is Case, and this is Beat."

He motioned to the smaller girl beside him, whose smile grew wider. Even in the darkness of the room, it was adorable, charming.

"We are..."

He paused, thinking.

"We are ... Intermediaries."

Epilogue

"AAAH!"

Nick fell from mid-air to the powdery surface, landing on his back as though plummeting onto a feathery pillow. Swirls of snow billowed up around him. From the ground, he looked up into the gray sky. Snowflakes descended, silently teasing his face. Nick's eyes came to rest on the boy who looked down on him with smile.

"Watch out for that fall there," Zylan commented, chuckling.

The boy was young, seemingly only seven or eight years old, and had a flawless, childish face. He wore clothing reminiscent of an impoverished youth from Victorian-era England, with patches and hand-woven threading covering heavy, worn fabrics. A floppy cap, similarly styled with a fluffy brown ball hanging off the tip, completed the look.

Nick, clothed in a stylish snowboarder's jacket, looked up at the boy and explained, "You don't know it, Zy, but I actually meant to do that."

"Oh," Zylan said. "Does that mean you intended to scream like a little girl also?"

Nick frowned.

"Actually, it would be great if we could just keep that piece of information between you and me."

The boy shrugged and helped Nick to his feet. Then, Zylan reached into his waistcoat pocket and retrieved a small, high-tech remote control that fit easily into the palm of his small hand. As

Nick brushed some of the white powder off his clothes, Zylan spoke again.

"Sam, we're coming in."

He pressed one of the buttons on the remote. Instantly, the two materialized in a spacious, darkened room. The living quarters was decorated like the interior of a cabin or ski lodge, with an expansive bed that drew the eye, and big, comfortable-looking chairs facing a roaring fireplace. The glow from the flames danced warmly around the cavernous room. Nick took off his jacket and tossed it onto the bed before he and Zylan exited the room into a large, long, quiet hallway.

Zylan's youthful voice broke the silence.

"Among the usual, there is a learning computer tablet for Marena and a pair of nice-looking roller skates for Miss Meredith Anthony, both specially designed per your request and awaiting your approval in the rundown."

"Aha!" Nick exclaimed, causing Zylan to look at him curiously. "It's Meredith Joyner, now, Zy, not Meredith Anthony. Aren't you supposed to keep up with those types of things?"

"Of course," Zylan nodded before adding, "She's from Fremont, by the way."

"Ahh, so I was close. See, I knew I was getting better with addresses."

"Fremont, California, is actually 384 miles from the city you referred to," Zylan corrected, "which, I should say, is called Garden Grove, not Grove Gardens."

"But it's the same state, right?"

"If they were driving, it would take them six hours to get from one city to the other without stopping."

"Still, it's in the same state. See, I knew I was getting better with addresses."

Zylan arched an eyebrow but remained quiet. The pair soon turned a corner, the sounds of work and play rising in volume as they neared one of the main manufacturing areas. Strains of music also became more audible as the moved down the hall. Nick was not at all surprised to hear that it was not a holiday tune; in fact, it was Top 40.

Contrary to what others would believe, the North Office was not afraid to switch up the musical selection on occasion.

"Those improvements to the ear monitors worked brilliantly," Nick offered. "I think someone may have sabotaged mine, though."

He stared pointedly at Zylan.

Zylan grinned.

"That's an easy fix."

"Oh, I know it's an easy fix," Nick responded. "I guess it was also an easy trick."

"Hey, don't look at me!"

"And yet I am, Zy. I'm looking right … at … you."

Another child, with a delicate, pretty face, waited for Nick and Zylan before the wide entrance into the production hall.

"Welcome back, Santa," Samantha greeted, smiling warmly. "Ready for your rundown, or should I give you a few moments to collect yourself? It must have been terrifying for you to fall five feet into soft snow to cause you to scream like such a little girl."

Standing beside him, Zylan looked to Nick fleetingly before he turned away, snickering.

To be continued…

Acknowledgements

Again, thanks to my family and friends, and their respective families and friends. You know who I am, so you know who you are.

Thanks to Karin Cox for her extreme patience and her editorial superpowers. And yes, for the last time, I do understand the virtues of the three-act structure, but let's not have this argument while everyone else is listening, okay? Stubborn writers...

Thanks to Najla Qamber and Najla Qamber Designs for the fantastic and seemingly effortless cover design, and thanks to Ravven Kitsune and Matthew Dawson for steering me in the right direction starting out. I would not hesitate in coming to any of you in the future.

Thanks to Glendon Haddix and Streetlight Graphics for the map design and flourish. The high quality I predicted; I'm just surprised you were able to squeeze me into your schedule.

Thanks to the writing and publishing blogs. Too many to list, though without them, I would not have known the steps to take after finishing the story.

Thanks to every story I have ever read, heard, or seen, from every person that wrote, told, or acted them out for me.

And, finally, thanks again to YOU for reading this. I hope Beat, Case, and the others have provided you with at least a little bit of entertainment. They say hello, by the way.

About the Author

The Intermediaries: Beat & Case is Taylor Dye's debut novel and the first in the Intermediaries series.

You can find Taylor on our website at
Samanedna.com

Want the latest news and upcoming release info from Taylor Dye and Samanedna Publishers?
Sign up for our newsletter at
Samanedna.com